GULLIVER'S TRAVELS

GULLIVER'S TRAVELS

by

JONATHAN SWIFT

PRINTED IN   GREAT BRITAIN
DEAN &   SON Ltd.
41/43 Ludgate Hill   LONDON E.C.4

MADE AND PRINTED IN GREAT BRITAIN BY PURNELL AND SONS, LTD
PAULTON (SOMERSET) AND LONDON

SBN 603 03029 7

A LETTER FROM CAPTAIN GULLIVER
TO HIS COUSIN SYMPSON

Written in the Year 1727

April 2, 1727.

I HOPE you will be ready to own publicly, whenever you shall be called to it, that by your great and frequent urgency you prevailed on me to publish a very loose and uncorrect account of my travels, with direction to hire some young gentlemen of either university to put them in order, and correct the style, as my cousin Dampier did, by my advice, in his book called *A Voyage Round the World*. But I do not remember that I gave you power to consent that anything should be omitted, and much less that anything should be inserted: therefore, as to the latter, I do here renounce everything of that kind; particularly a paragraph about her Majesty Queen Anne, of most pious and glorious memory; although I did reverence and esteem her more than any of the human species. But you, or your interpolator, ought to have considered that, as it was not my inclination, so was it not decent, to praise any animal of our composition before my master Houyhnhnm: and besides, the fact was altogether false; for to my knowledge, being in England during some part of her Majesty's reign, she did govern by a chief minister; nay, even by two successively, the first whereof was the Lord of Godolphin, and the second the Lord of Oxford; so that you have made me say the thing that was not. Likewise, in the account of the academy of projectors, and several passages of my discourse to my master Houyhnhnm, you have either omitted some material circumstances, or minced or changed them in such a manner, that I do hardly know my own work. When I formerly hinted to you something of this in a letter, you were pleased to answer that you were afraid of giving offence; that people in power were very watchful over the press, and apt not only to interpret but to punish everything which looked like an innuendo (as I think you call it). But, pray, how could that which I spoke so many years ago, and at above five thousand leagues' distance, in another reign, be applied to any of the Yahoos who now are said to govern the herd, especially at a time when I little thought on, or feared, the unhappiness of living under them? Have not I the most reason to complain, when I see these very Yahoos carried by Houyhnhnms in a vehicle, as if these were brutes and those are rational creatures? And, indeed, to avoid so monstrous and detestable a sight was one principal motive of my retirement hither.

Thus much I thought proper to tell you in relation to yourself, and to the trust I reposed in you.

I do in the next place complain of my own great want of judgment, in being prevailed upon, by the entreaties and false reasonings of you and some others, very much against my own opinion, to suffer my travels to be published. Pray bring to your mind how often I desired you to consider, when you insisted on the motive of public good, that the Yahoos were a species of animals utterly incapable of amendment by precepts or example; and so it has proved: for, instead of seeing a full stop put to all abuses and corruptions, at least in this little island, as I had reason to expect; behold, after about six months' warning, I cannot learn that my book has produced one single effect according to mine intentions. I desired you would let me know, by a letter, when party and faction were extinguished; judges learned and upright; pleaders honest and modest, with some tincture of common sense, and Smithfield blazing with pyramids of law-books; the young nobility's education entirely changed; the physicians banished; the female Yahoos abounding in virtue, honour, truth, and good sense; courts and levees of great ministers thoroughly weeded and swept; wit, merit, and learning rewarded; all disgracers of the press in prose and verse condemned to eat nothing but their own cotton, and quench their thirst with their own ink. These and a thousand other reformations I firmly counted upon by your encouragement; as indeed they were plainly deducible from the precepts delivered in my book. And it must be owned that several months were a sufficient time to correct every vice and folly to which Yahoos are subject, if their natures had been capable of the least disposition to virtue or wisdom. Yet so far have you been from answering my expectation in any of your letters, that, on the contrary, you are loading our carrier every week with libels, and keys, and reflections, and memoirs, and second parts; wherein I see myself accused of reflecting upon great statesfolk, of degrading human nature (for so they have still the confidence to style it), and of abusing the female sex. I find, likewise, that the writers of those bundles are not agreed among themselves; for some of them will not allow me to be the author of mine own travels, and others make me author of books to which I am wholly a stranger.

I find, likewise, that your printer has been so careless as to confound the times, and mistake the dates, of my several voyages and returns; neither assigning the true year, nor the true month, nor day of the month: and I hear the original manuscript is all destroyed since the publication of my book; neither have I any copy left; however, I have sent you some corrections, which you may insert, if ever there should be a second edition; and yet I cannot stand to them, but shall leave that matter to my judicious and candid readers, to adjust it as they please.

I hear some of our sea-Yahoos find fault with my sea-language, as not proper in many parts, nor now in use. I cannot help it. In my first voyages, while I was young, I was instructed by the oldest mariners, and learned to speak as they did. But I have since found that the sea-Yahoos are apt, like the land ones, to become newfangled in their words, which the latter change every year, insomuch as I remember, upon each return to mine own country, their old dialect was so altered that I could hardly understand the new. And I observe, when any Yahoo comes from London, out of curiosity, to visit at my house, we neither of us are able to deliver our conceptions in a manner intelligible to the other.

If the censure of the Yahoos could any way affect me, I should have great reason to complain, that some of them are so bold as to think my book of travels a mere fiction out of mine own brain; and have gone so far as to drop hints, that the Houyhnhnms and Yahoos have no more existence than the inhabitants of Utopia.

Indeed I must confess that, as to the people of Lilliput, Brobdingrag (for so the word should have been spelt, and not erroneously Brobdingnag), and Laputa, I have never yet heard of any

Yahoos so presumptuous as to dispute their being, or the facts I have related concerning them; because the truth immediately strikes every reader with conviction. And is there less probability in my account of the Houyhnhnms or Yahoos, when it is manifest, as to the latter, there are so many thousands, even in this country, who only differ from their brother brutes in Houyhnhnm-land because they use a sort of jabber, and do not go naked? I wrote for their amendment, and not their approbation. The united praise of the whole race would be of less consequence to me than the neighing of those two degenerate Houyhnhnms I keep in my stable; because from these, degenerate as they are, I still improve in some virtues, without any mixture of vice.

Do these miserable animals presume to think that I am so degenerated as to defend my veracity? Yahoo as I am, it is well known through all Houyhnhnm-land that, by the instruction and example of my illustrious master, I was able, in the compass of two years (although, I confess, with the utmost difficulty), to remove that infernal habit of lying, shuffling, deceiving, and equivocating, so deeply rooted in the very souls of all my species, especially the Europeans.

I have other complaints to make upon this vexatious occasion; but I forbear troubling myself or you any farther. I must freely confess that since my last return some corruptions of my Yahoo nature have revived in me, by conversing with a few of your species, and particularly those of my own family, by an unavoidable necessity; else I should never have attempted so absurd a project as that of reforming the Yahoo race in this kingdom: but I have now done with all such visionary schemes for ever.

CONTENTS

PART I

A VOYAGE TO LILLIPUT

CHAPTER I

CHAPTER II

CHAPTER III

CHAPTER IV

CHAPTER V

CHAPTER VI

PART II

A VOYAGE TO BROBDINGNAG

CHAPTER VII

CHAPTER VIII

PART III

A VOYAGE TO LAPUTA, BALNIBARBI, LUGGNAGG, GLUBBDUBDRIB, AND JAPAN

CHAPTER I

CHAPTER II

CHAPTER III

CHAPTER IV

CHAPTER V

PART IV

A VOYAGE TO THE COUNTRY OF THE HOUYHNHNMS

CHAPTER III

CHAPTER IV

CHAPTER V

CHAPTER VI

CHAPTER VII

CHAPTER VIII

CHAPTER IX

CHAPTER X

CHAPTER XI

CHAPTER XII

INTRODUCTION

AN EMBITTERED, middle-aged man sat down to write a book that would scourge the vices and follies of mankind. That book, with its sting mellowed during the passage of over two hundred years, has become—of all things—a children's classic. *Gulliver's Travels* was the splenetic outburst of a passionate mind, whose genius gave immortality to so transient a thing as satire; but that immortality had a permanent basis—a child-like delight in marvels, a freshness of invention, a limpid style and a selective perception that created images of giants, dwarfs and fabled races with a vivid, pulsating life of their own. The names of its characters have been added to our everyday speech and Gulliver is now an integral part of our national folk-lore.

The author, Jonathan Swift, was born in Dublin, in 1667, and after a wild and turbulent youth he became secretary to Sir William Temple, whose wife, Dorothy Osborne, has left us some of the most charming letters ever published. Swift studied to enter the church and in 1694 he was ordained. He returned to Sir William Temple's household, however, and remained with him until his death five years later.

It was during these years that he met the girl he was to make famous—"Stella," as he called her, little Esther Johnson.

To Stella he wrote his famous "Journal" in which he revealed all the tenderness and gentleness that lay concealed behind his usual mask of ferocity. For Swift suffered from frustrated ambition, and this, combined with his natural sensitive nature, was to cause him unspeakable torment all his life and make him adopt a defensive armour of quarrelsomeness and lack of manners. In addition, he was passionate in his hatred of oppression and infamy, and his contacts with the corrupt politics of his time did not sweeten his nature.

In 1699 Sir William Temple died and Swift returned to Ireland, where he was given the prebend of St. Patrick's, Dublin, and the living of Laracor. The political and religious stream of pamphlets, satires, epistles and lampoons had already begun to flow ("The Tale of a Tub" and "The Battle of the Books" appeared in 1704), and during his many visits to London he was acclaimed by the whole galaxy of famous names that graced the literature of that period. Steele, Congreve, Pope, Arbuthnot and Gay were among his acquaintances and with whom he founded the famous Scriblerus Club. Addison was his friend and evidently penetrated to the real man since we find him saying: "Swift was the most agreeable company, the truest friend and the greatest genius of his age."

"The Journal to Stella" began in 1710 and continued for more than three years. In it he described his daily life in England, the people he met, the places he visited and what he thought and felt about them. It is written for the most part in baby language and was an outlet for all his natural warmth and gentleness. From it we can guess that there was a very real affection between them, but they never married. The position was a peculiar one. She was many years younger than he was and their friendship had begun as between pupil and teacher. It remained, on his side, a strange mixture of husband-and-brother love and on hers an unswerving devotion amounting almost to worship. Stella died in 1728.

In 1726 *Gulliver's Travels* was published and Swift received £200, the only money he ever earned by his pen. The next year, worn out by quarrels and intrigue, he left England for ever and thereafter devoted his life to charity and to his friends. One-third of his stipend was set apart for the poor, one-third was saved towards the foundation of St. Patrick's Hospital for imbeciles: he lived on the remainder.

Swift was by now a sick man. His malady—a kind of epilepsy —that had burdened him all his life, became worse and for the last few years of his life he was insane. He died in 1745, and was buried beside Stella in St. Patrick's, Dublin.

"An immense genius" according to Thackeray, who added, apropos of his melancholy end, "Thinking of him is like thinking of an empire falling"; but Pope reveals a worthier and more practical character:

Behold the hand that wrought a nation's cure,
Stretched to relieve the idiot and the poor;
Proud vice to brand, or injured worth adorn,
And stretch the rays to ages yet unborn.

PART I

A VOYAGE TO LILLIPUT

CHAPTER I

THE AUTHOR GIVES SOME ACCOUNT OF HIMSELF AND FAMILY—
HIS FIRST INDUCEMENTS TO TRAVEL—HE IS SHIPWRECKED
AND SWIMS FOR HIS LIFE—GETS SAFE ON SHORE IN THE COUNTRY
OF LILLIPUT—IS MADE A PRISONER AND CARRIED UP THE
COUNTRY

MY FATHER had a small estate in Nottinghamshire: I was the
third of five sons. He sent me to Emmanuel College in Cambridge,
at fourteen years old, where I resided three years, and applied
myself close to my studies; but the charge of maintaining me,
although I had a very scanty allowance, being too great for a
narrow fortune, I was bound apprentice to Mr. James Bates, an
eminent surgeon in London, with whom I continued four years;
and my father now and then sending me small sums of money, I
laid them out in learning navigation, and other parts of the
mathematics, useful to those who intend to travel, as I always
believed it would be, some time or other, my fortune to do. When
I left Mr. Bates, I went down to my father; where, by the assistance of him and my uncle John, and some other relations, I
got forty pounds, and a promise of thirty pounds a year to
maintain me at Leyden; there I studied physic two years and
seven months, knowing it would be useful in long voyages.

Soon after my return from Leyden, I was recommended by
my good master, Mr. Bates, to be surgeon to the *Swallow*, Captain
Abraham Pannell, commander, with whom I continued three
years and a half, making a voyage or two into the Levant, and
some other parts. When I came back I resolved to settle in

London; to which Mr. Bates, my master, encouraged me, and by him I was recommended to several patients. I took part of a small house in the Old Jewry; and being advised to alter my condition, I married Mrs. Mary Burton, second daughter to Mr. Edmund Burton, hosier, in Newgate Street, with whom I received four hundred pounds for a portion.

But my good master Bates dying in two years after, and I having few friends, my business began to fail; for my conscience would not suffer me to imitate the bad practice of too many among my brethren. Having therefore consulted with my wife, and some of my acquaintance, I determined to go again to sea. I was surgeon successively in two ships, and made several voyages, for six years, to the East and West Indies, by which I got some addition to my fortune. My hours of leisure I spent in reading the best authors, ancient and modern, being always provided with a good number of books; and when I was ashore, in observing the manners and dispositions of the people, as well as learning their language; wherein I had a great facility, by the strength of my memory.

The last of these voyages not proving very fortunate, I grew weary of the sea, and intended to stay at home with my wife and family. I removed from the Old Jewry to Fetter Lane, and from thence to Wapping, hoping to get business among the sailors, but it would not turn to account. After three years' expectation that things would mend, I accepted an advantageous offer from Captain William Pritchard, master of the *Antelope*, who was making a voyage to the South Seas. We set sail from Bristol, May 4, 1699, and our voyage at first was very prosperous.

It would not be proper, for some reasons, to trouble the reader with the particulars of our adventures in those seas; let it suffice to inform him, that in our passage from thence to the East Indies, we were driven by a violent storm to the north-west of Van Dieman's Land. By an observation, we found ourselves in the latitude of 30 degrees 2 minutes south. Twelve of our crew were dead by immoderate labour and ill food; the rest were in a very weak condition. On the 5th November, which was the beginning of summer in those parts, the weather being very hazy, the seaman spied a rock within half a cable's length of the ship; but the wind was so strong, that we were driven directly upon it, and split. Six of the crew, of whom I was one, having let down the boat into the sea, made a shift to get clear of the ship and the rock. We rowed, by my computation, about three leagues, till we were able to work no longer, being already spent with labour while we were in the ship. We therefore trusted ourselves to the mercy of the waves, and in about half an hour the boat was overset by a sudden flurry from the north. What became of my companions in the boat, as well as those who escaped on the rock or were left in the vessel, I cannot tell; but conclude they were all lost. For my own part, I swam as fortune directed me, and was pushed forward by the wind and tide. I often let my legs drop, and could feel no bottom; but when I was almost gone, and able to struggle no longer, I found myself within my depth; and by this time the storm was so much abated. The declivity was so small, that I walked near a mile before I got to the shore, which I conjectured was about eight o'clock in the evening. I then advanced forward near half a mile, but could not discover any sign of houses or inhabitants; at least, I was in so weak a condition that I did not observe them. I was extremely tired, and with that, and the heat of the weather, and about half a pint of brandy that I drank as I left the ship, I found myself much inclined to sleep. I lay down on the grass, which was very short and soft, where I slept sounder than ever I remember to have done in my life, and, as I reckoned, about nine hours; for when I awaked it was just day-light. I attempted to rise, but was not able to stir for as I happened to lie on my back, I found my arms and legs were strongly fastened on each side to the ground; and my hair, which was long and thick, tied down in the same manner. I likewise felt several slender ligatures across my body, from my arm-pits to my thighs. I could only look upwards; the sun began to grow hot, and the light offended my eyes. I heard a confused noise about me; but in the posture I lay could see nothing except the sky. In a little time I felt something alive moving on my left leg, which advancing gently forward over my breast, came almost up to my chin; when bending my eyes downward as much as I could, I perceived it to be a human creature not six inches high, with a bow and arrow in his hands, and a quiver at his back. In the meantime, I felt at least forty more of the same kind (as I conjectured) following the first. I was in the utmost astonishment,

and roared so loud, that they all ran back in a fright; and some
of them, as I was afterwards told, were hurt with the falls they
got by leaping from my sides upon the ground. However, they
soon returned, and one of them, who ventured so far as to get a
full sight of my face, lifting up his hands and eyes by way of
admiration, cried out in a shrill but distinct voice, *Hekinah degul;*
the others repeated the same words several times, but I then knew
not what they meant. I lay all this while, as the reader may
believe, in great uneasiness; at length, struggling to get loose, I
had the fortune to break the strings, and wrench out the pegs
that fastened my left arm to the ground; for by lifting it to my
face, I discovered the methods they had taken to bind me; at
the same time, with a violent pull, which gave me excessive pain,
I a little loosened the strings that tied down my hair on the left
side, so that I was just able to turn my head about two inches.
But the creatures ran off a second time, before I could seize them;
whereupon there was a great shout in a very shrill accent, and
after it ceased I heard one of them cry aloud, *Tolgo phonac;* when
in an instant I felt above a hundred arrows discharged on my
left hand, which pricked me like so many needles; and besides,
they shot another flight into the air, as we do bombs in Europe,
whereof many, I suppose, fell on my body (thought I felt them
not), and some on my face, which I immediately covered with
my left hand. When this shower of arrows was over, I fell
a-groaning with grief and pain, and then striving again to get
loose, they discharged another volley larger than the first, and
some of them attempted with spears to stick me in the sides; but
by good luck I had on me a buff jerkin, which they could not
pierce. I thought it the most prudent method to lie still, and my
design was to continue so till night, when, my left hand being
already loose, I could easily free myself; and as for the inhabitants,
I had reason to believe I might be a match for the greatest army
they could bring against me, if they were all of the same size
with him that I saw. But fortune disposed otherwise of me.
When the people observed I was quiet, they discharged no more
arrows; but, by the noise I heard, I knew their numbers increased;
and about four yards from me, over against my right ear, I heard
a knocking for above an hour, like that of people at work; when
turning my head that way, as well as the pegs and strings would

permit me, I saw a stage erected about a foot and a half from the ground, capable of holding four of the inhabitants, with two or three ladders to mount it; from whence one of them, who seemed to be a person of quality, made me a long speech, whereof I understood not one syllable. But I should have mentioned, that before the principle person began his oration, he cried out three times, *Langro dehul san* (these words and the former were afterwards repeated and explained to me). Whereupon, immediately about fifty of the inhabitants came and cut the strings that fastened the left side of my head, which gave me the liberty of turning it to the right, and of observing the person and gesture of him that was to speak. He appeared to be of a middle age, and taller than any of the other three who attended him, whereof one was a page that held up his train, and seemed to be somewhat longer than my middle finger; the other two stood one on each side to support him. He acted every part of an orator, and I could observe many periods of threatenings, and others of promise, pity, and kindness. I answered in a few words, but in the most submissive manner, lifting up my left hand and both my eyes to the sun, as calling him for a witness; and being famished with hunger, having not eaten a morsel for some hours before I left the ship, I found the demands of nature so strong upon me that I could not forbear showing my impatience (perhaps against the strict rules of decency) by putting my finger frequently to my mouth to signify that I wanted food. The *hurgo* (for so they call a great lord, as I afterwards learnt) understood me very well. He descended from the stage, and commanded that several ladders should be applied to my sides, on which above a hundred of the inhabitants mounted, and walked towards my mouth, laden with baskets full of meat, which had been provided and sent thither by the king's orders, upon the first intelligence he received of me. I observed there was the flesh of several animals, but I could not distinguish them by the taste. There were shoulders, legs and loins, shaped like those of mutton, and very well dressed, but smaller than the wings of a lark. I ate them by two or three at a mouthful, and took three loaves at a time, about the bigness of musket bullets. They supplied me as fast as they could, showing a thousand marks of wonder and astonishment at my bulk and appetite. I then made another sign, that I wanted drink. They found by my eating that a small quantity would not suffice me; and being a most ingenious people, they slung up, with great dexterity, one of their largest hogsheads, then rolled it towards my hand, and beat out the top; I drank it off at a draught, which I might well do, for it did not hold half a pint, and tasted like a small wine of Burgundy, but much more delicious. They brought me a second hogshead, which I drank in the same manner, and made signs for more, but they had none to give me. When I had performed these wonders, they shouted for joy, and danced upon my breast, repeating several times, as they did at first, *Hekinah degul*. They made me a sign that I should throw down the two hogsheads, but first warning the people below to stand out the way, crying aloud, *Borach mevolah;* and when they saw the vessels in the air, there was a universal shout of *Hekinah degul*. I confess I was often tempted, while they were passing backwards and forwards on my body, to seize forty or fifty of the first that came in my reach, and dash them against the ground. But the remembrance of what I had felt, which probably might not be the worst they could do, and the promise of honour I made them, for so I interpreted my submissive behaviour, soon drove out these imaginations. Besides, I now considered myself as bound by the laws of hospitality to a people who had treated me with so much expense and magnificence. However, in my thoughts I could not sufficiently wonder at the intrepidity of these diminutive mortals, who durst venture to mount and walk upon my body, while one of my hands was at liberty, without trembling at the very sight of so prodigious a creature as I must appear to them. After some time, when they observed that I made no more demands for meat, there appeared before me a person of high rank from his imperial majesty. His excellency having mounted on the small of my right leg, advanced forwards up to my face, with about a dozen of his retinue; and producing his credentials under the signet royal, which he applied close to my eyes, spoke about ten minutes without any signs of anger, but with a kind of determinate resolution; often pointing forwards, which, as I afterwards found, was towards the capital city, about half a mile distant; whither it was agreed by his majesty, in council, that I must be conveyed. I answered in few words, but to no purpose, and made a sign with my hand that was loose, putting it to the other (but over his excellency's head, for fear of hurting him or his train), and then to my own head and body to signify that I desired my liberty. It appeared that he understood me well enough, for he shook his head by way of disapprobation, and held his hand in a posture to show that I must be carried as a prisoner. However, he made other signs to let me understand that I should have meat and drink enough, and very good treatment. Whereupon I once more thought of attempting to break my bonds; but again, when I felt the smart of their arrows upon my face and hands, which were all in blisters, and many of the darts still sticking in them, and observing likewise that the number of my enemies increased, I gave tokens to let them know that they might do with me what .they pleased. Upon this the *hurgo* and his train withdrew, with much civility and cheerful countenances. Soon after I heard a general shout with frequent repetitions of the words, *Peplom selan;* and I felt great numbers of people on my left side relaxing the cords to such a degree that I was able to turn upon my right side. But before this, they had daubed my face and both my hands with a sort of ointment, very pleasant to the smell, which, in a few minutes, removed all the smart of their arrows. These circumstances, added to the refreshment I had received by their victuals and drink, which were very nourishing, disposed me to sleep. I slept about eight hours, as I was afterwards assured; and it was no wonder, for the physicians, by the emperor's order, had mingled a sleepy potion in the hogshead of wine.

It seems that upon the first moment I was discovered sleeping on the ground, after my landing, the emperor had early notice of it by an express; and determined, in council, that I should be tied in the manner I have related (which was done in the night while I slept); that plenty of meat and drink should be sent me, and a machine prepared to carry me to the capital city.

This resolution, perhaps, may appear very bold and dangerous, and I am confident would not be imitated by any prince in Europe on the like occasion. However, in my opinion, it was extremely prudent, as well as generous: for, supposing these people had endeavoured to kill me with their spears and arrows, while I was asleep, I should certainly have awaked with the first sense of smart, which might so far have roused my rage and

strength as to have enabled me to break the strings wherewith I
was tied; after which, as they were not able to make resistance, so
they could expect no mercy.

These people are most excellent mathematicians, and arrived
to a great perfection in mechanics by the countenance and
encouragement of the emperor, who is a renowned patron of
learning. This prince has several machines fixed on wheels, for
the carriage of trees and other great weights. He often builds
his largest men-of-war, whereof some are nine feet long, in the
woods where the timber grows, and has them carried on these
engines three of four hundred yards to the sea. Five hundred
carpenters and engineers were immediately set at work to prepare
the greatest engine they had. It was a frame of wood, raised
three inches from the ground, about seven feet long, and four
wide, moving upon twenty-two wheels. The shout I heard was
upon the arrival of this engine, which it seems set out in four
hours after my landing. It was brought parallel to me as I lay.
But the principal difficulty was to raise and place me in this
vehicle. Eighty poles, each of one foot high, were erected for this
purpose, and very strong cords, of the bigness of packthread, were
fastened by hooks to many bandages, which the workmen had
girt round my neck, my hands, my body, and my legs. Nine
hundred of the strongest men were employed to draw up these
cords, by many pulleys fastened on the poles; and thus, in less
than three hours, I was raised and slung into the engine, and there
tied fast. All this I was told; for, while the operation was performing, I lay in a profound sleep, by the force of that soporiferous
medicine infused into my liquor. Fifteen hundred of the emperor's largest horses, each about four and a half inches high,
were employed to draw me towards the metropolis, which, as I
said, was half a mile distant.

About four hours after we began our journey, I awaked by a
very ridiculous accident; for the carriage being stopped awhile,
to adjust something that was out of order, two or three of the
young natives had the curiosity to see how I looked when I was
asleep: they climbed up into the engine, and advancing very
softly to my face, one of them, an officer in the guards, put the
sharp end of his half-pike a good way up into my left nostril,
which tickled my nose like a straw, and made me sneeze violently;

whereupon they stole off unperceived, and it was three weeks before I knew the cause of my waking so suddenly. We made a long march the remaining part of the day, and rested at night, with five hundred guards on each side me, half with torches, and half with bows and arrows, ready to shoot me if I should offer to stir. The next morning, at sunrise, we continued our march, and arrived within two hundred yards of the city gates about noon. The emperor and all his court came out to meet us; but his great officers would by no means suffer his majesty to endanger his person by mounting on my body.

At the place where the carriage stopped there stood an ancient temple, esteemed to be the largest in the whole kingdom; which, having been polluted some years before by unnatural murder, was, according to the zeal of those people, looked upon as profane, and therefore had been applied to common use, and all the ornaments and furniture carried away. In this edifice it was determined I should lodge. The great gate fronting to the north was about four feet high and almost two feet wide, through which I could easily creep. On each side of the grate was a small window, not above six inches from the ground; into that on the left side, the king's smith conveyed four-score and eleven chains, like those that hang to a lady's watch in Europe, and almost as large, which were locked to my left leg with six-and-thirty padlocks. Over against this temple, on the other side of the great highway, at twenty feet distance, there was a turret, at least five feet high. Here the emperor ascended, with many principal lords of his court, to have an opportunity of viewing me, as I was told, for I could not see them. It was reckoned that above a hundred thousand inhabitants came out of the town upon the same errand; and, in spite of my guards, I believe there could not be fewer than ten thousand, at several times, who mounted my body, by the help of ladders. But a proclamation was soon issued to forbid, upon pain of death. When the workmen found it was impossible for me to break loose, they cut all the strings that bound me; whereupon I rose up, with as melancholy a disposition as ever I had in my life. But the noise and astonishment of the people, at seeing me rise and walk, are not to be expressed. The chain that held my left leg was about two yards long, and gave me not only the liberty of walking backwards and forwards in a semi-circle, but, being fixed within four inches of the gate, allowed me to creep in, and lie at my full length in the temple.

CHAPTER II

THE EMPEROR OF LILLIPUT, ATTENDED BY SEVERAL OF THE NOBILITY, COMES TO SEE THE AUTHOR IN HIS CONFINEMENT—THE EMPEROR'S PERSON AND HABIT DESCRIBED—LEARNED MEN APPOINTED TO TEACH THE AUTHOR THEIR LANGUAGE—HE GAINS FAVOUR BY HIS MILD DISPOSITION—HIS POCKETS ARE SEARCHED, AND HIS SWORD AND PISTOLS TAKEN FROM HIM

WHEN I found myself on my feet, I looked about me, and must confess I never beheld a more entertaining prospect. The country around appeared like a continued garden, and the enclosed fields, which were generally forty feet square, resembled so many beds of flowers. These field were intermingled with woods of half a *stang*, and the tallest trees, as I could judge, appeared to be seven feet high. I viewed the town on my left hand, which looked like the painted scenes of a city in a theatre.

I soon came out of my house, having occasion for fresh air. The emperor was already descended from the tower, and advancing on horseback, towards me, which had like to have cost him dear; for the beast, though very well trained, yet wholly unused to such a sight, which appeared as if a mountain moved before him, reared up on his hinder feet; but that prince, who is an excellent horseman, kept his seat till his attendants ran in, and held the bridle, while his majesty had time to dismount. When he alighted, he surveyed me round with great admiration; but kept beyond the length of my chain. He ordered his cooks and butlers, who were already prepared to give me victuals and drink, which they pushed forward in a sort of vehicle upon wheels, till I could reach them. I took these vehicles and soon emptied them all; twenty of them were filled with meat, and ten with liquor; each of the former afforded me two or three good mouthfuls; and I emptied the liquor of ten vessels, which was contained in earthen vials, into one vehicle, drinking it off at a draught; and so I did with the rest. The empress, and young princes of the blood of both sexes, attended by many ladies, sat at some distance in their chairs; but upon the accident that happened to the emperor's horse they alighted, and came near his person, which I am now going to describe. He is taller, by almost the breadth of my nail, than any of his court; which alone is enough to strike an awe into the beholders. His features are strong and masculine, with an Austrian lip and arched nose, his complexion olive, his countenance erect, his body and limbs well proportioned, all his motions graceful and his deportment majestic. He was then past his prime, being twenty-eight years and threequarters old, of which he had reigned about seven in great felicity, and generally victorious. For the better convenience of beholding him, I lay on my side, so that my face was parallel to his, and he stood but three yards off: however, I have had him since many times in my hand and therefore cannot be deceived in the description. His dress was very plain and simple, and the fashion of it between the Asiatic and the European: but he had on his head a light helmet of gold, adorned with jewels, and a plume on the crest. He held his sword drawn in his hand to defend himself, if I should happen to break loose; it was almost three inches long; the hilt and scabbard were gold, enriched with diamonds. His voice was shrill, but very clear and articulate; and I could distinctly hear it when I stood up. The ladies and courtiers were all most magnificently clad; so that the spot they stood upon seemed to resemble a petticoat spread on the ground, embroidered with figures of gold and silver. His imperial majesty spoke often to me, and I returned answers; but neither of us could understand a syllable. There were several of his priests and lawyers present (as I conjectured by their habits), who were commanded to address themselves to me; and I spoke to them in as many languages as I had the least smattering of, which were High and Low Dutch, Latin, French, Spanish, Italian, and Lingua Franca, but all to no purpose. After about two hours the court retired, and I was left with a strong guard, to prevent the impertinence and probably the malice, of the rabble, who were very impatient to crowd about me as near as they durst; and some of them had the impudence to shoot their arrows at me, as I sat on the ground by the door of my house, whereof one very narrowly missed my left eye. But the colonel ordered six of the ringleaders to be seized, and thought no punishment so proper as to deliver them bound into my hands; which some of his soldiers accordingly did, pushing them forward with the butt-ends of their pikes into my reach. I took them all in my right hand, put five of them into my coat-pocket, and as to the sixth, I made a countenance as if I would eat him alive. The poor man squalled terribly, and the colonel and his officers were in much pain, especially when they saw me take out my penknife; but I soon put them out of fear; for, looking mildly, and immediately cutting the strings he was bound with, I sat him gently on the ground, and away he ran. I treated the rest in the same manner, taking them one by one out of my pocket; and I observed both the soldiers and the people were highly delighted at this mark of my clemency, which was represented very much to my advantage at court.

Towards night I got with some difficulty into my house, where I lay on the ground, and continued to do so about a fortnight; during which time the emperor gave orders to have a bed prepared for me. Six hundred beds of the common measure were brought in carriages, and worked up in my house; a hundred and fifty of their beds, sewn together, made up the breadth and length; and these were four double; which, however, kept me but very indifferently from the hardness of the floor, that was of smooth stone. By the same computation, they provided me with sheets, blankets, and coverlets, tolerable enough for one who had been so long inured to hardships.

As the news of my arrival spread through the kingdom, it brought prodigious numbers—rich, idle, and curious people—to see me; so that the villages were almost emptied; and great neglect of tillage and household affairs must have ensued, if his imperial majesty had not provided, by several proclamations and orders of state, against this inconveniency. He directed that those who had already beheld me should return home, and not presume to come within fifty yards of my house, without licence from the court; whereby the secretary of state got considerable fees.

In the meantime the emperor held frequent councils, to debate what course should be taken with me; and I was afterwards assured, by a particular friend, a person of great quality, who was as much in the secret as any, that the court was under many difficulties concerning me. They apprehended my breaking loose; that my diet would be very expensive, and might cause a famine. Sometimes they determined to starve me, or at least to shoot me in the face and hands with poisonous arrows, which would soon dispatch me; but again they considered that the stench of so large a carcass might produce a plague in the metropolis, and probably spread through the whole kingdom. In the midst of these consultations, several officers of the army went to the door of the great council chamber, and two of them being admitted, gave an account of my behaviour to the six criminals above-mentioned; which made so favourable an impression in the breast of his majesty, and the whole board, in my behalf, that an imperial commission was issued out, obliging all the villagers nine hundred yards round the city, to deliver in every morning, six beeves, forty sheep, and other victuals, for my sustenance; together with a proportionable quantity of bread and wine and other liquors; for the due payment of which his majesty gave assignments upon his treasury: for this prince lives chiefly upon his own demesnes; seldom, except upon great occasions, raising any subsidies upon his subjects, who are bound to attend him in his wars at their own expense. An establishment was also made of six hundred persons to be my domestics, who had board-wages allowed for their maintenance, and tents built for them very conveniently, on each side of my door. It was likewise ordered, that three hundred tailors should make me a suit of clothes, after the fashion of the country; that six of his majesty's greatest scholars should be employed to instruct me in their language; and lastly, that the emperor's horses, and those of the nobility and troops of guards, should be frequently exercised in my sight, to accustom themselves to me. All these orders were duly put in execution; and in about three weeks I made a great progress in learning their language; during which time the emperor frequently honoured me with his visits, and was pleased to assist my masters in teaching me. We began already to converse together in some sort; and the first words I learnt were to express my desire "that he would be pleased to give me my liberty"; which I every day repeated on my knees. His answer, as I could apprehend it, was "that this must be a work of time,

B

not to be thought on without the advice of his council, and that first I must *lumos kelmin pesso desmar lon emposa";* that is, swear a peace with him and his kingdom. However, that I should be used with all kindness. And he advised me to "acquire by my patience and discreet behaviour the good opinion of himself and his subjects." He desired, "I would not take it ill if he gave orders to certain proper officers to search me; for probably I might carry about me several weapons, which must needs be dangerous things, if they answered the bulk of so prodigious a person." I said, "His Majesty should be satisfied; for I was ready to strip myself, and turn out my pockets before him." This I delivered, part in words and part in signs. He replied, "that by the laws of the kingdom, I must be searched by two of his officers; that he knew this could not be done without my consent and assistance; and he had so good an opinion of my generosity and justice, as to trust their persons in my hands; that whatever they took from me should be returned when I left the country, or paid for, at the rate which I would set upon them." I took up the two officers in my hands, put them first into my coat-pockets, and then into every other pocket about me, except my two fobs, and another secret pocket, which I had no mind should be searched, wherein I had some little necessaries that were of no consequence to any but myself. In one of my fobs there was a silver watch, and in the other a small quantity of gold in a purse. These gentlemen, having pens, ink, and paper about them, made an exact inventory of everything they saw; and when they had done, desired I would set them down, that they might deliver it to the emperor. This inventory I afterwards translated into English, and is word for word as follows:—

Imprimis, In the right coat-pocket of the great man-mountain (for so I interpret the words *quinbus flestrin*), after the strictest search, we found only one great piece of coarse cloth, large enough to be a foot cloth for your majesty's chief room of state. In the left pocket we saw a huge silver chest, with a cover of the same metal, which we, the searchers, were not able to lift. We desired it should be opened, and one of us stepping into it, found himself up to the mid-leg in a sort of dust, some part whereof flying up to our faces, set us both a-sneezing for several times together. In his right waistcoat-pocket we found a prodigious bundle of white thin substance, folded over one another, about the bigness of three men, tied with a strong cable, and marked with black figures;

which we humbly conceive to be writings, every letter almost half as large as the palm of our hands. In the left there was a sort of engine, from the back of which were extended twenty long poles, resembling the palisadoes before your majesty's court: wherewith we conjecture the man-mountain combs his head; for we did not always trouble him with questions, because we found it a great difficulty to make him understand us. In the large pocket, on the right side of his middle cover (so I translate the word *ranfu-lo*, by which they meant my breeches), we saw a hollow pillar of iron, about the length of a man, fastened to a strong piece of timber larger than the pillar; and upon one side of the pillar were huge pieces of iron sticking out, cut into strange figures, which we knew not what to make of. In the left pocket, another engine of the same kind. In the smaller pocket on the right side, were several round flat pieces of white and red metal, of different bulk; some of the white, which seemed to be silver, were so large and heavy that my comrade and I could hardly lift them. In the left pocket were two black pillars irregularly shaped: we could not, without difficulty, reach the top of them, as we stood at the bottom of his pocket. One of them was covered, and seemed all of a piece: but at the upper end of the other there appeared a white round substance, about twice the bigness of our heads. Within each of these was enclosed a prodigious plate of steel; which, by our orders, we obliged him to show us, because we apprehended they might be dangerous engines. He took them out of their cases, and told us, that in his own country his practice was to shave his beard with one of these, and cut his meat with the other. There were two pockets which we could not enter: these he called his fobs; they were two large slits cut into the tops of his middle cover, but squeezed close by the pressure of his body. Out of the right fob hung a great silver chain, with a wonderful kind of engine at the bottom. We directed him to draw out whatever was at the end of that chain; which appeared to be a globe, half silver, and half of some transparent metal; for, on the transparent side, we saw certain strange figures circularly drawn, and thought we could touch them, till we found our fingers stopped by that lucid substance. He put this engine to our ears, which made an incessant noise, like that of a water-mill; and we conjecture it is either some unknown animal, or the god that he worships; but we are more inclined to the latter opinion, because he assured us (if we understand him right, for he expressed himself very imperfectly), that he seldom did anything without consulting it. He called it his oracle, and said it pointed out the time for every action of his life. From the left fob he took out a net almost large enough for a fisherman, but contrived to open and shut like a purse, and served him for the same use: we found therein several massy pieces of yellow metal, which, if they be real gold, must be of immense value.

Having thus, in obedience to your majesty's commands, diligently searched all his pockets, we observed a girdle about his waist made of the hide of some prodigious animal, from which, on the left side, hung a sword of the length of five men; and on the right, a bag or pouch divided into two cells, each cell capable of holding three of your majesty's subjects. In one of these cells were several globes, or balls, of a most ponderous metal, about the bigness of our heads, and required a strong hand to lift them: the other cell contained a heap of certain black grains, but of no great bulk or weight, for we could hold above fifty of them in the palms of our hands.

This is an exact inventory of what we found about the body of the man-mountain, who used us with great civility, and due respect to your majesty's commission. Signed and sealed on the fourth day of the eighty-ninth moon of your majesty's auspicious reign.

CLEFRIN FRELOCK.
MARSI FRELOCK.

When this inventory was read over to the emperor, he directed me, although in very gentle terms, to deliver up the several particulars. He first called for my scimitar, which I took out, scabbard and all. In the meantime, he ordered three thousand of the choicest troops (who then attended him) to surround me at a distance, with their bows and arrows just ready to discharge; but I did not observe it, for mine eyes were wholly fixed on his majesty. He then desired me to draw my scimitar, which, although it had got some rust by the sea-water, was in most parts exceedingly bright. I did so, and immediately all the troops gave a shout between terror and surprise; for the sun shone clear, and the reflection dazzled their eyes, as I waved the scimitar to and fro in my hand. His majesty, who is a most magnanimous prince, was less daunted than I could expect; he ordered me to return it into the scabbard, and cast it on the ground as gently as I could, about six feet from the end of my chain. The next thing he demanded was one of the hollow iron pillars; by which he meant my pocket pistols. I drew it out, and at his desire, as well as I could, expressed to him the use of it; and charging it only with powder, which, by the closeness of my pouch, happened to escape wetting in the sea (an inconvenience against which all prudent mariners take special care to provide), I first cautioned the emperor not to be afraid, and then I let it off in the air. The astonishment here was greater than at the sight of the scimitar. Hundreds fell down as if they had been struck dead; and even the emperor, although he stood his ground, could not recover himself for some time. I delivered up both my pistols in the same manner as I had done my scimitar, and then my pouch of powder

and bullets; begging him that the former might be kept from
fire, for it would kindle with the smallest spark, and blow up his
imperial palace into the air. I likewise delivered up my watch,
which the emperor was very curious to see, and commanded
two of his tallest yeomen of the guards to bear it on a pole upon
their shoulders, as draymen in England do a barrel of ale. He
was amazed at the continual noise it made, and the motion of
the minute-hand, which he could easily discern; for their sight
is much more acute than ours. He asked the opinions of his
learned men about it, which were various and remote, as the
reader may well imagine without my repeating; although,
indeed, I could not very perfectly understand them. I then gave
up my silver and copper money, my purse, with nine large pieces
of gold, and some smaller ones; my knife and razor, my comb and
silver snuff-box, my handkerchief and journal-book. My
scimitar, pistols, and pouch were conveyed in carriages to his
majesty's stores; but the rest of my goods were returned me.

I had, as I before observed, one private pocket, which escaped
their search, wherein there was a pair of spectacles (which I
sometimes use for the weakness of mine eyes), a pocket perspective
and some other little conveniences; which, being of no consequence to the emperor, I did not think myself bound in honour to
discover, and I apprehended they might be lost or spoiled, if I
ventured them out of my possession.

CHAPTER III

THE AUTHOR DIVERTS THE EMPEROR, AND HIS NOBILITY OF BOTH
SEXES, IN A VERY UNCOMMON MANNER—THE DIVERSIONS OF
THE COURT OF LILLIPUT DESCRIBED—THE AUTHOR HAS HIS
LIBERTY GRANTED HIM UPON CERTAIN CONDITIONS

MY GENTLENESS and good behaviour had gained so far on the
emperor and his court, and indeed upon the army and people
in general, that I began to conceive hopes of getting my liberty
in a short time. I took all possible methods to cultivate this

favourable disposition. The natives came, by degrees, to be less apprehensive of any danger from me; I would sometimes lie down, and let five or six of them dance on my head; and at last the boys and girls would venture to come and play at hide and seek in my hair. I had now made a good progress in understanding and speaking their language. The emperor had a mind one day to entertain me with several of the country shows, wherein they exceeded all nations I have known, both for dexterity and magnificence. I was diverted with none so much as that of the rope-dancers, performed upon a slender white thread extended about two feet, and twelve inches from the ground; upon which I shall desire liberty, with the reader's patience, to enlarge a little.

This diversion is only practised by those persons who are candidates for great employments, and high favour at court. They are trained in this art from their youth, and are not always of noble birth, or liberal education. When a great office is vacant, either by death or disgrace (which often happens), five or six of those candidates petition the emperor to entertain his majesty and the court with a dance on the rope; and whoever jumps the highest, without falling, succeeds in the office. Very often the chief ministers themselves are commanded to show their skill, and to convince the emperor that they have not lost their faculty. Flimnap, the treasurer, is allowed to cut a caper on the straight rope, at least an inch higher than any other lord in the whole empire. I have seen him do the somerset several times together, upon a trencher fixed on a rope which is no thicker than a common pack-thread in England. My friend Reldresal, principal secretary for private affairs, is, in my opinion, if I am not partial, the second after the treasurer; the rest of the great officers are much upon a par.

These diversions are often attended with fatal accidents, whereof great numbers are on record. I myself have seen two or three candidates break a limb. But the danger is much greater when the ministers themselves are commanded to show their dexterity; for, by contending to excel themselves and their fellows, they strain so far that there is hardly one of them who has not received a fall, and some of them two or three. I was assured that, a year or two before my arrival, Flimnap would infallibly

have broken his neck, if one of the king's cushions, that accidentally lay on the ground, had not weakened the force of his fall.

There is likewise another diversion, which is only shown before
the emperor and empress, and first minister, upon particular
occasions. The emperor lays on the table three fine silken
threads of six inches long; one is blue, the other red, and the
third green. These threads are proposed as prizes for those
persons whom the emperor has a mind to distinguish by a peculiar
mark of his favour. The ceremony is performed in his majesty's
great chamber of state, where the candidates are to undergo a
trial of dexterity, very different from the former, and such as I
have not observed the least resemblance of in any other country
of the New or Old World. The emperor holds a stick in his
hands, both ends parallel to the horizon, while the candidates
advancing, one by one, sometimes leap over the stick, sometimes
creep under it, backward and forward, several times, according
as the stick is advanced or depressed. Sometimes the emperor
holds one end of the stick, and his first minister the other; sometimes the minister has it entirely to himself. Whoever performs
his part with most agility, and holds out the longest in leaping
and creeping, is rewarded with the blue-coloured silk; the red is
given to the next, and the green to the third, which they all
wear girt twice round about the middle; and you see few great
persons about this court who are not adorned with one of these
girdles.

The horses of the army, and those of the royal stables, having
been daily led before me, were no longer shy, but would come
up to my very feet without starting. The riders would leap them
over my hand, as I held it on the ground; and one of the emperor's
huntsmen, upon a large courser, took my foot, shoe and all;
which was indeed a prodigious leap. I had the good fortune to
divert the emperor one day after a very extraordinary manner. I
desired he would order several sticks of two feet high, and the
thickness of an ordinary cane, to be brought me; whereupon his
majesty commanded the master of his woods to give directions
accordingly; and the next morning six woodmen arrived with as
many carriages drawn by eight horses to each. I took nine of these
sticks, and fixing them firmly in the ground in a quadrangular
figure, two feet and a half square, I took four other sticks, and

tied them parallel at each corner about two feet from the ground;
then I fastened my handkerchief to the nine sticks that stood erect,
and extended it on all sides, till it was tight as the top of a drum;
and the four parallel sticks, rising about five inches higher than
the handkerchief, served as ledges on each side. When I had
finished my work I desired the emperor to let a troop of his best
horses, twenty-four in number, come and exercise upon this plain.
His majesty approved of the proposal, and I took them up, one
by one, in my hands, ready mounted and armed with the proper
officers to exercise them. As soon as they got into order, they
divided into two parties, performed mock skirmishes, discharged
blunt arrows, drew their swords, fled and pursued, attacked and
retired, and, in short, discovered the best military discipline I ever
beheld. The parallel sticks secured them and their horses from
falling over the stage; and the emperor was so much delighted
that he ordered this entertainment to be repeated several days,
and once was pleased to be lifted up, and give the word of command; and, with great difficulty, persuaded even the empress
herself to let me hold her in her close chair within two yards of
the stage, when she was able to take a full view of the whole
performance. It was my good fortune that no ill accident
happened in these entertainments; only once, a fiery horse that
belonged to one of the captains, pawing with his hoof, struck a
hole in my handkerchief, and his foot slipping, he overthrew his
rider and himself; but I immediately relieved them both, and
covering the hole with one hand I set down the troop with the
other, in the same manner as I took them up. The horse that fell
was strained in the left shoulder, but the rider got no hurt; and
I repaired my handkerchief as well as I could: however, I would
not trust the strength of it any more, in such dangerous enterprises.

About two or three days before I was set at liberty, as I was
entertaining the court with this kind of feats, there arrived an
express to inform his majesty that some of his subjects, riding near
the place where I was first taken up, had seen a great black
substance lying on the ground, very oddly shaped, extending its
edges round, as wide as his majesty's bedchamber, and rising up
in the middle as high as a man; that it was no living creature, as
they at first apprehended, for it lay on the grass without motion;
and some of them had walked round it several times; that, by

mounting upon each other's shoulders, they had got to the top, which was flat and even, and stamping upon it, they found that it was hollow within; that they humbly conceived it might be something belonging to the man-mountain; and if his majesty pleased, they would undertake to bring it with only five horses. I presently knew what they meant, and was glad at heart to receive this intelligence. It seems, upon my reaching the shore after our shipwreck, I was in such confusion, that before I came to the place where I went to sleep, my hat, which I had fastened with a string to my head while I was rowing, and had stuck on all the time I was swimming, fell off after I came to land; the string, as I conjecture, breaking by some accident, which I never observed, but thought my hat had been lost at sea. I entreated his imperial majesty to give orders it might be brought to me as soon as possible, describing to him the use and nature of it: and the next day the wagoners arrived with it, but not in a very good condition; they had bored two holes in the brim, within an inch and a half of the edge, and fastened two hooks in the holes; these hooks were tied by a long cord to the harness, and thus my hat was dragged along for above half an English mile; but, the ground in that country being extremely smooth and level, it received less damage than I expected.

Two days after this adventure, the emperor, having ordered that part of his army, which quarters in and about his metropolis to be in readiness, took a fancy of diverting himself in a very singular manner. He desired I would stand like a Colossus, with my legs as far asunder as I conveniently could. He then commanded his general (who was an old experienced leader and a great patron of mine), to draw up the troops in close order, and march them under me; the foot by twenty-four abreast, and the horse by sixteen, with drums beating, colours flying, and pikes advanced. This body consisted of three thousand foot, and a thousand horse. His majesty gave orders, upon pain of death, that every soldier in his march should observe the strictest propriety.

I had sent so many memorials and petitions for my liberty, that his majesty at length mentioned the matter, first in the cabinet, and then in a full council; where it was opposed by none, except Skyresh Bolgolam, who was pleased, without any provocation, to be my mortal enemy. But it was carried against him by the whole board, and confirmed by the emperor. That minister was *galbet*, or admiral of the realm, very much in his master's confidence and a person well versed in affairs, but of a morose and sour complexion. However, he was at length persuaded to comply; but prevailed that the articles and conditions upon which I should be set free, and to which I must swear, should be drawn up by himself. These articles were brought to me by Skyresh Bolgolam in person, attended by two under-secretaries, and several persons of distinction. After they were read, I was demanded to swear to the performance of them: first in the manner of my own country, and afterwards in the method prescribed by their laws; which was, to hold my right foot in my left hand, and to place the middle finger of my right hand on the crown of my head, and my thumb on the tip of my right ear. But because the reader may be curious to have some idea of the style and manner of expression peculiar to that people, as well as to know the articles upon which I recovered my liberty, I have made a translation of the whole instrument, word for word, as near as I was able, which I here offer to the public:—

GOLBASTO MOMAREM EVLAME GURDILO SHEFIN MULLY ULLY GUE, most mighty Emperor of Lilliput, delight and terror of the universe, whose dominions extend five thousand *blustrugs* (about twelve miles in circumference) to the extremities of the globe; monarch of all monarchs, taller than the sons of men; whose feet press down to the centre, and whose head strikes against the sun; at whose nod the princes of the earth shake their knees; pleasant as the spring, comfortable as the summer, fruitful as autumn, dreadful as the winter. His most sublime majesty proposes to the man-mountain, lately arrived at our celestial dominions, the following articles, which, by a solemn oath, he shall be obliged to perform.

I. The man-mountain shall not depart from our dominions, without our licence under our great seal.

II. He shall not presume to come into our metropolis, without our express order; at which time the inhabitants shall have two hours' warning to keep within doors.

III. The said man-mountain shall confine his walks to our principal high-roads, and not offer to walk, or lie down, in a meadow or field of corn.

IV. As he walks the said roads he shall take the utmost care not to trample upon the bodies of any of our loving subjects, their horses or carriages, nor take any of our subjects into his hands, without our own consent.

V. If an express requires extraordinary despatch, the man-mountain shall be obliged to carry, in his pocket, the messenger and horse a six days' journey, once in every moon, and return the said messenger back (if so required) safe to our imperial presence.

VI. He shall be our ally against our enemies in the island of Blefuscu, and to do his utmost to destroy their fleet, which is now preparing to invade us.

VII. That the said man-mountain shall, at his time of leisure, be aiding and assisting to our workmen, in helping to raise certain great stones, towards covering the wall of the principal park, and other our royal buildings.

VIII. That the said man-mountain shall, in two moons' time, deliver in an exact survey of the circumference of our dominions, by a computation of his own paces round the coast.

Lastly, That, upon his solemn oath to observe all the above articles, the said man-mountain shall have a daily allowance of meat and drink sufficient for the support of 1,728 of our subjects, with free access to our royal person, and other marks of our favour. Given at our palace at Belfaborac, the twelfth day of the ninety-first moon of our reign.

I swore and subscribed to these articles with great cheerfulness and content, although some of them were not so honourable as I could have wished; which proceeded wholly from the malice of Skyresh Bolgolam, the high-admiral; whereupon my chains were immediately unlocked, and I was at full liberty. The emperor himself, in person, did me the honour to be by at the whole ceremony. I made my acknowledgements by prostrating myself at his majesty's feet; but he commanded me to rise; and after many gracious expressions, which, to avoid the censure of vanity, I shall not repeat, he added, "that he hoped I should prove a useful servant, and well deserve all the favours he had already conferred upon me, or might do for the future."

The reader may please to observe that, in the last article of the recovery of my liberty, the emperor stipulates to allow me a quantity of meat and drink sufficient for the support of 1,728 Lilliputians. Some time after, asking a friend at court how they came to fix on that determinate number, he told me that his majesty's mathematicians, having taken the height of my body by the help of a quadrant, and finding it to exceed theirs in proportion of twelve to one, they concluded, from the similarity of their bodies, that mine must contain at least 1,728 of theirs, and consequently would require as much food as was necessary to support that number of Lilliputians. By which the reader may conceive an idea of the ingenuity of this people, as well as the prudent and exact economy of so great a prince.

CHAPTER IV

MILDENDO, THE METROPOLIS OF LILLIPUT, DESCRIBED, TOGETHER WITH THE EMPEROR'S PALACE—A CONVERSATION BETWEEN THE AUTHOR AND THE PRINCIPAL SECRETARY CONCERNING THE AFFAIRS OF THAT EMPIRE—THE AUTHOR OFFERS TO SERVE THE EMPEROR IN HIS WARS

THE FIRST request I made, after I had obtained my liberty, was, that I might have licence to see Mildendo, the metropolis; which the emperor easily granted me, but with a special charge to do no hurt either to the inhabitants or their houses. The people had notice, by proclamation, of my design to visit the town. The wall which encompassed it is two feet and a half high, and at least eleven inches broad, so that a coach and horses may be driven very safely round it; and it is flanked with strong towers at ten feet distance. I stepped over the great western gate, and passed very gently and sideling through the two principal streets only in my short waistcoat, for fear of damaging the roofs and eaves of the houses with the skirts of my coat. I walked with the utmost circumspection, to avoid treading on any stragglers who might remain in the streets; although the orders were very strict, that all people should keep in their houses, at their own peril. The garret windows and tops of houses were so crowded with spectators that I thought in all my travels I had not seen a more populous place. The city is an exact square, each side of the wall being five hundred feet long. The two great streets, which run across and divide it into four quarters, are five feet wide. The lanes and alleys, which I could not enter, but only viewed them as I passed, are from twelve to eighteen inches. The town is capable of holding five hundred thousand souls: the houses are from three to five stories; the shops and markets well provided.

The emperor's palace is in the centre of the city, where the two great streets meet. It is enclosed by a wall of two feet high, and twenty feet distant from the building. I had his majesty's permission to step over this wall; and the space being so wide between that and the palace, I could easily view it on every side. The outward court is a square of forty feet, and includes two other courts: in the inmost are the royal apartments, which I was very desirous to see, but found it extremely difficult; for the great gates, from one square into another, were but eighteen inches high, and seven inches wide. Now the buildings of the outer court were at least five feet high, and it was impossible for me to stride over them without infinite damage to the pile, though the walls were strongly built of hewn stone, and four inches thick. At the same time, the emperor had a great desire that I should see the magnificence of his palace; but this I was not able to do till three days after, which I spent in cutting down, with my knife, some of the largest trees in the royal park, about a hundred yards' distance from the city. Of these trees I made two stools, each about three feet high, and strong enough to bear my weight. The people having received notice a second time, I went again through the city to the palace, with my two stools in my hands. When I came to the side of the outer court I stood upon one stool, and took the other in my hand; this I lifted over the roof, and gently set it down on the space between the first and second court, which was eight feet wide. I then stepped over the building very conveniently from one stool to the other, and drew up the first after me with a hooked stick. By this contrivance I got into the inner court; and lying down upon my side, I applied my face to the windows of the middle stories, which were left open on purpose, and discovered the most splendid apartments that could be imagined. There I saw the empress and the young princes, in their several lodgings, with their chief attendants about them. Her imperial majesty was pleased to smile very graciously upon me, and gave me out of the window her hand to kiss.

But I shall not anticipate the reader with further descriptions of this kind, because I reserve them for a greater work, which is now almost ready for the press; containing a general description of this empire, from its first erection, through a long series of princes; with a particular account of their wars and politics, laws, learning and religion; their plants and animals; their peculiar manners and customs, with other matters very curious and useful: my chief design at present being only to relate such events and transactions as happened to the public or to myself during a residence of about nine months in that empire.

One morning, about a fortnight after I had obtained my liberty, Reldresal, principal secretary (as they style him) for private affairs, came to my house, attended only by one servant. He ordered his coach to wait at a distance, and desired I would give him an hour's audience; which I readily consented to, on account of his quality and personal merits, as well as of the many good offices he had done me during my solicitations at court. I offered to lie down, that he might more conveniently reach my ear; but he chose rather to let me hold him in my hand during our conversation. He began with compliments on my liberty, said "he might pretend to some merit in it"; but, however, added, "that if it had not been for the present situation of things at court, perhaps I might not have obtained it so soon. For," said he, "as flourishing a condition as we may appear to be in to foreigners, we labour under two mighty evils—a violent faction at home, and the danger of an invasion by a most potent enemy from abroad. As to the first, you are to understand, that for above seventy moons past there has been two struggling parties in this empire, under the names *Tramecksan* and *Slamecksan*, from the high and low heels of their shoes, by which they distinguish themselves. It is alleged, indeed, that the high heels are most agreeable to our ancient constitution; but, however this be, his majesty has determined to make use only of low heels in the administration of the government, and all offices in the gift of the crown, as you cannot but observe; and particularly that his majesty's imperial heels are lower by at least a *drurr* than any of his court (*drurr* is a measure about the fourteenth part of an inch). The animosities between these two parties run so high that they will neither eat, nor drink, nor talk with each other. We compute the *Tramecksan*, or high heels, to exceed us in number; but the power is wholly on our side. We apprehend his imperial highness, the heir to the crown, to have some tendency towards the high heels; at least we can plainly discover that one of his high heels is higher than the other, which gives him a hobble in his gait. Now, in the midst of these intestine disquiets, we are threatened with an invasion from the island of Blefuscu, which is the other great empire of the universe, almost as large and powerful as this of his majesty. For as to what we have heard you affirm, that there are other kingdoms and states in the world inhabited by human creatures as large as yourself, our philosophers are in much doubt, and would rather conjecture that you dropped from the moon, or one of the stars; because it is certain that a hundred mortals of your bulk would in a short time destroy all the fruits and cattle of his majesty's dominions: besides, our histories of six thousand moons make no mention of any other regions than the two great empires of Lilliput and Blefuscu, which two mighty powers have, as I was going to tell you, been engaged in a most obstinate war for six-and-thirty moons past. It began upon the following occasion: it is allowed on all hands that the primitive mode of breaking eggs, before we eat them, was upon the larger end; but his majesty's grandfather, while he was a boy, going to eat an egg, and breaking it according to the ancient practice, happened to cut one of his fingers; whereupon the emperor, his father, published an edict, commanding all his subjects, upon great penalties, to break the smaller ends of their eggs. The people so highly resented this law, that our histories tell us, there have been six rebellions raised on that account; wherein one emperor lost his life, and another his crown. These civil commotions were constantly fomented by the monarchs of Blefuscu; and when they were quelled, the exiles always fled for refuge to that empire. It is computed that eleven thousand persons have at several times suffered death rather than submit to break their eggs at the smaller end. Many hundred large volumes have been published upon this controversy: but the books of the Big Endians have been long forbidden, and the whole party rendered incapable by law of holding employments. During the course of these troubles, the emperors of Blefuscu did frequently expostulate by their ambassadors, accusing us of making a schism in religion, by offending against a fundamental doctrine of our great prophet Lustrog, in the fifty-fourth chapter of the Blundecral, which is their Alcoran. This, however, is thought to be a mere strain upon the text; for the words are these: that all true believers break their eggs at the convenient end; and which is the convenient end seems, in my humble opinion, to be left to every man's conscience, or at least in the power of the chief magistrate to determine. Now, the Big Endian exiles have found so much credit in the Emperor of Blefuscu's court, and so much private assistance and encouragement from their private party here at home, that a bloody war has been carried on between the two empires for six-and-thirty moons, with varied success; during which time we have lost forty capital ships, and a much greater number of smaller vessels, together with thirty thousand of our best seamen and soldiers; and the damage received by the enemy is reckoned to be somewhat greater than ours. However, they have now equipped a numerous fleet, and are just preparing to make a descent upon us; and his imperial majesty, placing great confidence in your valour and strength, has commanded me to lay this account of his affairs before you."

I desired the secretary to present my humble duty to the emperor; and to let him know, "that I thought it would not become me, who was a foreigner, to interfere with parties; but I was ready, with the hazard of my life, to defend his person and state against all invaders."

CHAPTER V

THE AUTHOR, BY AN EXTRAORDINARY STRATAGEM, PREVENTS AN INVASION—A HIGH TITLE OF HONOUR IS CONFERRED UPON HIM—AMBASSADORS ARRIVE FROM THE EMPEROR OF BLEFUSCU AND SUE FOR PEACE

THE EMPIRE of Blefuscu is an island situated to the north-east of Lilliput, from which it is parted only by a channel of eight hundred yards wide. I had not yet seen it, and upon this notice of an intended invasion I avoided appearing on that side of the coast, for fear of being discovered by some of the enemy's ships, who had received no intelligence of me; all intercourse between the two empires having been strictly forbidden during the war, upon pain of death, and an embargo laid by our emperor upon all vessels whatsoever. I communicated to his majesty a project I had formed of seizing the enemy's whole fleet; which, as our scouts assured us, lay at anchor in the harbour, ready to sail with the first fair wind. I consulted the most experienced seamen upon the depth of the channel, which they had often plumbed; who told me, that in the middle at high water it was seventy *glumgluffs* deep, which is about six feet of European measure; and the rest of it fifty *glumgluffs* at most. I walked towards the north-east coast, over against Blefuscu; where, lying down behind a hillock, I took out my small perspective glass, and viewed the enemy's fleet at anchor, consisting of about fifty men-of-war, and a great number of transports; I then came back to my house, and gave orders (for which I had a warrant) for a great quantity of the strongest cable and bars of iron. The cable was about as thick as packthread, and the bars of the length and size of a knitting-needle. I trebled the cable to make it stronger, and for the same reason I twisted three of the iron bars together, bending the extremities into a hook. Having thus fixed fifty hooks to as many cables, I went back to the north-east coast, and putting off my coat, shoes, and stockings, walked into the sea, in my leathern jerkin, about half an hour before high water. I waded with what haste I could, and swam in the middle about thirty yards, till I felt ground. I arrived at the fleet in less than half an hour. The enemy were so frightened when they saw me, that they leaped out of their ships and swam to shore, where there could not be fewer than thirty thousand souls; I then took my tackling, and fastening a hook to the hole at the prow of each, I tied all the cords together at the end. While I was thus employed, the enemy discharged several thousand arrows, many of which stuck in my hands and face; and, besides the excessive smart, gave me much disturbance in my work. My greatest apprehension was for mine eyes, which I should have infallibly lost, if I had not suddenly thought of an expedient. I kept among other little necessaries, a pair of spectacles in a private pocket which, as I observed before, had escaped the emperor's searchers. These I took out, and fastened as strongly as I could upon my nose, and thus armed, went on boldly with my work, in spite of the enemy's arrows, many of which struck against the glasses of my spectacles, but without any other effect than a little to discompose them. I had now fastened all the hooks, and taking the knot in my hand, began to pull: but not a ship would stir, for they were all too fast held by their anchors; so that the boldest part of my enterprise remained. I therefore let go the cord, and leaving the hooks fixed to the ships, I resolutely cut with my knife the cables that fastened the anchors, receiving about two hundred shots in my face and hands; then I took up the knotted end of the cables, to which my hooks were tied, and with the greatest ease drew fifty of the enemy's largest men-of-war after me.

The Blefuscudians, who had not the least imagination of what I intended, were at first confounded with astonishment. They had seen me cut the cables, and thought my design was only to let the ships run adrift, or fall foul of each other; but when they perceived the whole fleet moving in order, and saw me pulling at the end, they set up such a scream of grief and despair as it is almost impossible to describe or conceive. When I had got out of danger, I stopped awhile to pick out the arrows that stuck in my hands and face; and rubbed on some of the same ointment that was given me on my first arrival, as I have formerly mentioned. I then took off my spectacles, and waiting about an hour, till the tide was a little fallen, I waded through the middle with my cargo, and arrived safe at the royal port of Lilliput.

The emperor and his whole court stood on the shore, expecting the issue of this great adventure. They saw the ships move forward in a large half-moon, but could not discern me, who was up to my breast in water. When I advanced to the middle of the channel, they were yet in pain, because I was under water to my neck. The emperor concluded me to be drowned and that the enemy's fleet was approaching in a hostile manner; but he was soon eased of his fears; for the channel growing shallower every step I made, I came in a short time within hearing, and holding up the end of the cable, by which the fleet was fastened, I cried in a loud voice, "Long live the most puissant King of Lilliput!" This great prince received me at my landing with all possible encomiums, and created me a *nardac* upon the spot, which is the highest title of honour among them.

His majesty desired I would take some other opportunity of bringing all the rest of his enemy's ships into his ports. And so immeasurable is the ambition of princes, that he seemed to think of nothing less than reducing the whole empire of Blefuscu into a province, and governing it by a Viceroy; of destroying the Big Endian exiles, and compelling that people to break the smaller end of their eggs, by which he would remain the sole monarch of the whole world. But I endeavoured to divert him from this design, by many arguments drawn from the topics of policy as well as justice; and I plainly protested, "that I would never be an instrument of bringing a free and brave people into slavery"; and, when the matter was debated in council, the wisest part of the Ministry were of my opinion.

This open, bold declaration of mine was so opposite to the schemes and politics of his imperial majesty, that he could never forgive me. He mentioned it in a very artful manner at council, where I was told that some of the wisest appeared, at least by their silence, to be of my opinion; but others, who were my enemies, could not forbear some expressions which by a side wind reflected on me; and from this time began an intrigue between his majesty and a junto of ministers, maliciously bent against me, which broke out in less than two months, and had like to have ended in my utter destruction. Of so little weight are the greatest services to princes, when put into the balance with a refusal to gratify their passions.

About three weeks after this exploit, there arrived a solemn embassy from Blefuscu, with humble offers of a peace; which was soon concluded upon conditions very advantageous to our emperor, wherewith I shall not trouble the reader. There were six ambassadors, with a train of about five hundred persons: and their entry was very magnificent, suitable to the grandeur of their master, and the importance of their business. When their treaty was finished, wherein I did them several good offices by the credit I now had, or at least appeared to have, at court, their excellencies, who were privately told how much I had been their friend, made me a visit in form. They began with many compliments upon my valour and generosity, invited me to that kingdom, in the emperor their master's name, and desired me to show them some proofs of my prodigious strength, of which they had heard so many wonders; wherein I readily obliged them, but shall not trouble the reader with the particulars.

When I had for some time entertained their excellencies, to their infinite satisfaction and surprise, I desired they would do me the honour to present my most humble respects to the emperor their master, the renown of whose virtues had so justly filled the whole world with admiration, and whose royal person I resolved to attend, before I returned to my own country. Accordingly, the next time I had the honour to see the emperor, I desired his general licence to wait on the Blefuscudian monarch, which he was pleased to grant me, as I could perceive, in a very cold manner; but could not guess the reason, till I had a whisper from a certain person, "that Flimnap and Bolgolam had represented my intercourse with those ambassadors as a mark of disaffection"; from which I am sure my heart was wholly free. And this was the first time I began to conceive some imperfect idea of courts and ministers.

It is to be observed that these ambassadors spoke to me by an interpreter, the languages of both empires differing as much from each other as any two in Europe, and each nation priding itself upon the antiquity, beauty, and energy of their own tongue, with an avowed contempt of that of their neighbour: yet our emperor, standing upon the advantage he had got by the seizure of their fleet, obliged them to deliver their credentials, and make their speech, in the Lilliputian tongue. And it must be confessed, that from the great intercourse of trade and commerce between both realms; from the continual reception of exiles, which is mutual among them; and from the custom, in each empire, to send their young nobility and richer gentry to the other, in order to polish themselves by seeing the world, and understanding men and manners; there are few persons of distinction, or merchants, or seamen, who dwell in the maritime parts, but what can hold conversation in both tongues; as I found some weeks after, when I went to pay my respects to the emperor of Blefuscu, which in the midst of great misfortunes through the malice of my enemies, proved a very happy adventure to me, as I shall relate in its proper place.

CHAPTER VI

OF THE INHABITANTS OF LILLIPUT; THEIR LEARNING, LAWS, AND
CUSTOMS; THE MANNER OF EDUCATING THEIR CHILDREN—THE
AUTHOR'S WAY OF LIVING IN THAT COUNTRY—HIS VINDICATION
OF A GREAT LADY

ALTHOUGH I intend to leave the description of this empire to a
particular treatise, yet, in the meantime, I am content to gratify
the curious reader with some general ideas. As the common size
of the natives is somewhat under six inches high, so there is an
exact proportion in all other animals, as well as plants and trees;
for instance, the tallest horses and oxen are between four and five
inches in height, the sheep an inch and a half, more or less; their
geese about the bigness of a sparrow; and so the several gradations
downwards, till you come to the smallest, which, to my sight,
were almost invisible; but Nature has adapted the eyes of the
Lilliputians to all objects proper for their view; they see with
great exactness, but at no great distance. And to show the
sharpness of their sight towards objects that are near, I have been
much pleased with observing a cook pulling a lark which was not
as large as the common fly; and a young girl threading an
invisible needle with invisible silk. Their tallest trees are about
seven feet high; I mean some of those in the great royal park, the
tops whereof I could but just reach with my fist clenched. The
other vegetables are in the same proportion; but this I leave to
the reader's imagination.

I shall say but little at present of their learning, which, for
many ages, has flourished in all its branches among them; but
their manner of writing is very peculiar, being neither from the
left to the right, like the Europeans; nor from the right to the left,
like the Arabians; nor from up to down, like the Chinese; but
aslant, from one corner of the paper to the other, like ladies in
England.

There are some laws and customs in this empire very peculiar;
and if they were not so directly contrary to those of my own dear

country, I should be tempted to say a little in their justification. It is only to be wished they were as well executed. The first I shall mention relates to informers. All crimes against the state are punished here with the utmost severity; but, if the person accused make his innocence plainly to appear upon his trial, the accuser is immediately put to an ignominious death: and out of his goods or lands the innocent person is quadruply recompensed for the loss of his time, for the danger he underwent, for the hardship of his imprisonment, and all for the charges he has been at in making his defence; or, if that fund be insufficient, it is largely supplied by the crown. The emperor also confers on him some public mark of his favour, and proclamation of his innocence is made throughout the whole city.

They look upon fraud as a greater crime than theft, and therefore seldom fail to punish it with death; for they allege that care and vigilance, with a very common understanding, may preserve a man's goods from thieves; but honesty has no fence against superior cunning; and since it is necessary that there should be a perpetual intercourse of buying and selling, and dealing upon credit, where fraud is permitted and connived at, or has no law to punish it, the honest dealer is always undone, and the knave gets the advantage. I remember, when I was once interceding with the king for a criminal who had wronged his master of a great sum of money, which he had received by order, and ran away with; and happened to tell his majesty, by way of extenuation, that it was only a breach of trust, the emperor thought it monstrous in me to offer as a defence the greatest aggravation of the crime; and truly I had little to say in return, further than the common answer, that different nations had different customs; for, I confess, I was heartily ashamed.

Although we usually call reward and punishment the two hinges upon which all government turns, yet I could never observe this maxim to be put in practice by any nation, except that of Lilliput. Whoever can there bring sufficient proof that he has strictly observed the laws of his country for seventy-three moons, has a claim to certain privileges, according to his quality or condition in life, with a proportionate sum of money out of a fund appropriated for that use: he likewise acquires the title of *snilpall*, or legal, which is added to his name, but does not descend to his posterity. And these people thought it a prodigious defect of policy among us, when I told them that our laws were enforced only by penalties, without any mention of reward. It is upon this account that the image of Justice, in their courts of judicature, is formed with six eyes, two before, as many behind, and on each side one, to signify circumspection; with a bag of gold open in her right hand, and a sword sheathed in her left, to show she is more disposed to reward than to punish.

In choosing persons for all employments, they have more regard to good morals than to great abilities; for since government is necessary to mankind, they believe that the common size of human understanding is fitted to some station or other; and that Providence never intended to make the management of public affairs a mystery to be comprehended only by a few persons of sublime genius, of which there are seldom three born in an age; but they suppose truth, justice, temperance, and the like, to be in every man's power; the practice of which virtues, assisted by experience and a good intention, would qualify any man for the service of his country, except where a course of study is required. But they thought the want of moral virtues was so far from being supplied by superior endowments of the mind, that employments could never be put into such dangerous hands as those of persons so qualified; and at least, that the mistakes committed by ignorance, in a virtuous disposition, would never be of such fatal consequence to the public weal, as the practices of a man whose inclinations led him to be corrupt, and who had great abilities to manage, to multiply, and defend his corruptions.

In like manner, the disbelief of a Divine Providence renders a man incapable of holding any public station; for, since kings avow themselves to be the deputies of Providence, the Lilliputians think nothing can be more absurd than for a prince to employ such men as disown the authority under which he acts.

In relating these and the following laws, I would only be understood to mean the original institutions, and not the most scandalous corruptions into which these people are fallen by the degenerate nature of man.

For, as to that infamous practice of acquiring great employments by dancing on the ropes, or badges of favour and distinction by leaping over sticks and creeping under them, the reader is to observe, that they were first introduced by the grandfather of the emperor now reigning, and grew to the present height by the gradual increase of party and faction.

Ingratitude is among them a capital crime, as we read it to have been in some other countries; for they reason thus: that whoever makes ill return to his benefactor must needs be a common enemy to the rest of mankind, from whom he has received no obligation; and therefore such a man is not fit to live.

Their notions relating to the duties of parents and children differ extremely from ours. They think that the tenderness of parents towards their young proceeds from natural principle: for which reason, they will never allow that a child is under any obligation to his father or his mother for bringing him into the world: which, considering the miseries of human life, was neither a benefit in itself, nor intended so by his parents. Upon these, and the like reasonings, their opinion is that parents are the last of all others to be trusted with the education of their own children; and therefore they have in every town public nurseries, where all parents, except cottagers and labourers, are obliged to send their infants of both sexes to be reared and educated, when they come to the age of twenty moons, at which time they are supposed to have some rudiments of docility. These schools are of several kinds, suited to different qualities, and both sexes. They have certain professors, well skilled in preparing children for such a condition of life as befits the rank of their parents, and their own caprices as well as inclinations.

I shall first say something of the male nurseries, and then of the female.

The nurseries for males of noble or eminent birth are provided with grave and learned professors and their several deputies. The clothes and food of the children are plain and simple. They are bred up in the principles of honour, justice, courage, modesty, clemency, religion, and love of their country; they are always employed in some business, except in the times of eating and sleeping, which are very short, and two hours for diversions, consisting of bodily exercises. They are dressed by men till four years of age, and then are obliged to dress themselves, although their quality be ever so great; and the women attendants, who are aged proportionately to ours at fifty, perform only the most menial offices. They are never suffered to converse with servants, but go together in smaller or greater numbers to take their diversions, and always in the presence of a professor, or one of his deputies; whereby they avoid those early bad impressions of folly and vice to which our children are subject. Their parents are suffered to see them only twice a year; the visit is to last but an hour; they are allowed to kiss the child at meeting and parting; but a professor, who always stands by on those occasions, will not suffer them to whisper, or use any fondling expressions, or bring any presents of toys, sweetmeats, and the like.

The pension from each family for the education and entertainment of a child, upon failure of due payment, is levied by the emperor's officers.

The nurseries for children of ordinary gentlemen, merchants, traders, and handicrafts, are managed proportionably after the same manner; only those designed for trades are put out apprentices at eleven years old: whereas, those of persons of quality continue in their exercises till fifteen, which answers to twenty-one with us; but the confinement is gradually lessened for the last three years.

In the female nurseries, the young girls of quality are educated much like the males, only they are dressed by orderly servants of their own sex; but always in the presence of a professor or deputy, till they come to dress themselves, which is at five years old. And if it be found that these nurses ever presume to entertain the girls with frightful or foolish stories, or the common follies practised by chambermaids among us, they are publicly whipped thrice about the city, imprisoned for a year, and banished for life to the most desolate part of the country. Thus, the young ladies there are as much ashamed of being cowards and fools as the men; and despise all personal ornaments, beyond decency and cleanliness: neither did I perceive any difference in their education made by their difference of sex, only that the exercises of the females were not altogether so robust: and that some rules were given them relating to domestic life, and a smaller compass of learning was enjoined them: for their maxim is, that among people of quality, a wife should always be a reasonable and agreeable companion, because she cannot always be young. When the girls are twelve years old, which among them is the marriageable age, their parents or guardians take them home, with great expressions of gratitude to the professors, and seldom without the tears of the young lady and her companions.

In the nurseries of females of the meaner sort, the children are instructed in all kinds of work proper for their sex, and their several degrees; those intended for apprentices are dismissed at seven years old; the rest are kept to eleven.

The meaner families who have children at these nurseries are obliged, beside their annual pension, which is as low as possible, to return to the steward of the nursery a small monthly share of their gettings, to be a portion for the child; and therefore all parents are limited in their expenses by the law. For the Lilliputians think nothing can be more unjust than for people, in subservience to their own appetites, to bring children into the world, and leave the burden of supporting them on the public. As to persons of quality, they give security to appropriate a certain sum for each child, suitable to their condition: and these funds are always managed with good husbandry and the most exact justice.

The cottagers and labourers keep their children at home, their business being only to till and cultivate the earth, and therefore their education is of little consequence to the public: but the old and diseased among them are supported by hospitals; for begging is a trade unknown in this empire.

And here it may, perhaps, divert the curious reader to give some account of my domestics, and my manner of living in this country, during a residence of nine months and thirteen days. Having a head mechanically turned, and being likewise forced by necessity, I had made for myself a table and chair convenient enough, out of the largest trees in the royal park. Two hundred sempstresses were employed to make me shirts, and linen for my bed and table, all of the strongest and coarsest kind they could get; which, however, they were forced to quilt together in several folds, for the thickest was some degrees finer than lawn. Their linen is usually three inches wide, and three feet make a piece. The sempstresses took my measure as I lay on the ground, one standing at my neck, and another at my middle, with a strong cord extended, that each held by the end, while a third measured the length of the cord with the rule of an inch long. Then they measured my right thumb, and desired no more; for by a mathematical computation, that twice round the thumb is once round the wrist, and so on to the neck and waist, and by the help of my old shirt, which I displayed on the ground before them for a pattern, they fitted me exactly. Three hundred tailors were employed in the same manner to make me clothes; but they had another contrivance for taking my measure. I kneeled down, and they raised a ladder from the ground to my neck; upon this ladder one of them mounted and let fall a plumbline from my collar to the floor, which just answered the length of my coat; but my waist and arms I measured myself. When my clothes were finished, which was done in my house (for the largest of theirs would not have been able to hold them), they looked like the patchwork made by ladies in England, only that mine were all of a colour.

I had three hundred cooks to dress my victuals, in little convenient huts, built about my house, where they and their families lived, and prepared two dishes a-piece. I took up twenty waiters in my hand, and placed them on the table: a hundred more attended below on the ground, some with dishes of meat, and some with barrels of wine and liquors slung on their shoulders: all which the waiters above drew up, as I wanted, in a very ingenious manner, by certain cords, as we drew the bucket up a well in Europe. A dish of their meat was a good mouthful, and a barrel of their liquor a reasonable draught. Their mutton yields to ours, but their beef is excellent. I have had a sirloin so large that I have been forced to make three bites of it; but this is rare. My servants were astonished to see me eat it, bones and all, as in our country we do the leg of a lark. Their geese and turkeys I usually ate at a mouthful, and I confess they far exceed ours. Of their smaller fowl I could take up twenty or thirty at the end of my knife.

One day his imperial majesty, being informed of my way of living, desired "that himself and his royal consort, with the young princes of the blood of both sexes, might have the happiness," as he was pleased to call it, "of dining with me." They came accordingly, and I placed them in chairs of state, upon my table, just over against me, with their guards about them. Flimnap, the lord high treasurer, attended there likewise with his white staff;

and I observed he often looked on me with a sour countenance, which I would not seem to regard, but ate more than usual, in honour to my dear country, as well as to fill the court with admiration. I have some private reasons to believe that this visit from his majesty gave Flimnap an opportunity of doing me ill offices to his master. That minister had always been my secret enemy, though he outwardly caressed me more than was usual to the moroseness of his nature. He represented to the emperor "the low condition of his treasury; that he was forced to take up money at a great discount; that exchequer bills would not circulate under nine per cent. below par; that I had cost his majesty above a million and a half of *sprugs* (their greatest gold coin, about the bigness of a spangle); and, upon the whole, that it would be advisable in the emperor to take the first fair occasion of dismissing me."

I am here obliged to vindicate the reputation of an excellent lady, who was an innocent sufferer upon my account. The treasurer took a fancy to be jealous of his wife, from the malice of some evil tongues, who informed him that her grace had taken a violent affection for my person; and the court scandal ran for some time, that she once came privately to my lodgings. This I solemnly declare to be a most infamous falsehood, without any grounds, further than that her grace was pleased to treat me with all innocent marks of freedom and friendship. I own she came often to my house, but always publicly, nor ever without three more in the coach, who were usually her sister and young daughter, and some particular acquaintance: but this was common to many other ladies of the court; and I will appeal to my servants around whether they at any time saw a coach at my door without their knowing what persons were in it. On those occasions, when a servant had given me notice, my custom was to go immediately to the door; and, after paying my respects, to take up the coach and two horses very carefully in my hands (for, if there were six horses, the postillion always unharnessed four), and place them on a table, where I had fixed a movable rim, quite round, of five inches high, to prevent accidents; and I have often had four coaches and horses at once on my table, full of company, while I sat in my chair leaning my face towards them; and while I was engaged with one set, the coachmen would gently drive the others round my table. I have passed many an afternoon very agreeably in these conversations. But I defy the treasurer, or his two informers (I will name them, and let them make the best of it), Clustril and Drunlo, to prove that any person ever came to me *incognito*, except the secretary Reldresal, who was sent by express command of his imperial majesty, as I have before related. I should not have dwelt so long upon this particular, if it had not been a point wherein the reputation of a great lady is so nearly concerned, to say nothing of my own; though I then had the honour to be a *nardac*, which the treasurer himself is not; for all the world knows, that he is only a *glumglum*, a title inferior by one degree, as that of a marquis is to a duke in England; yet I allow he preceded me in right of his post. These false informations, which I afterwards came to the knowledge of by an accident not proper to mention, made the treasurer show his lady for some time an ill countenance, and me a worse; and although he was at last undeceived and reconciled to her, yet I lost all credit with him, and found my interest decline very fast with the emperor himself, who was, indeed, too much governed by that favourite.

CHAPTER VII

THE AUTHOR, BEING INFORMED OF A DESIGN TO ACCUSE HIM OF HIGH TREASON, MAKES HIS ESCAPE TO BLEFUSCU—HIS RECEPTION THERE

BEFORE I proceed to give an account of my leaving this kingdom, it may be proper to inform the reader of a private intrigue, which had been for two months forming against me.

I had been hitherto, all my life, a stranger to courts, for which I was unqualified by the meanness of my condition. I had, indeed, heard and read enough of the dispositions of great princes and ministers; but never expected to have found such terrible effects of them in so remote a country, governed, as I thought, by very different maxims from those in Europe.

While I was just preparing to pay my attendance on the

emperor of Blefuscu, a considerable person at court (to whom I had been very serviceable, at a time when he lay under the highest displeasure of his imperial majesty) came to my house very privately at night, in a close chair, and, without sending in his name, desired admittance. The chairmen were dismissed; I put the chair, with his lordship in it, into my coat-pocket; and, giving orders to a trusty servant to say I was indisposed and gone to sleep, I fastened the door of my house, placed the chair on the table, according to my usual custom, and sat down by it. After the common salutations were over, observing his lordship's countenance full of concern, and inquiring into the reason, he desired I would hear him with patience, in a matter that highly concerned my honour and my life. His speech was to the following effect, for I took notes of it as soon as he left me:—

"You are to know," said he, "that several committees of council have lately been called in the most private manner, on your account; and it is but two days since his majesty came to a full resolution.

"You are very sensible that Skyresh Bolgolam (*galbet* or high-admiral) has been your mortal enemy, almost ever since your arrival. His original reasons I know not; but his hatred is increased since your great success against Blefuscu, by which his glory as admiral is much obscured.

"This lord, in conjunction with Flimnap, the high-treasurer, whose enmity against you is notorious, on account of his lady; Limtoc, the general; Lalcon, the chamberlain; and Balmuff, the grand justiciary, have prepared articles of impeachment against you for treason and other capital crimes."

The preface made me so impatient, being conscious of my own merits and innocence, that I was going to interrupt him; when he entreated me to be silent, and thus proceeded:—

"Out of gratitude for the favours you have done me, I procured information of the whole proceedings, and a copy of the articles; wherein I ventured my head for your service."

ARTICLES OF IMPEACHMENT AGAINST QUINBUS FLESTRIN, THE MAN-MOUNTAIN

ARTICLE I.—That the said Quinbus Flestrin, having brought the imperial fleet of Blefuscu into the royal port, and being afterwards commanded by his imperial majesty to seize all the other ships of the said empire of Blefuscu, and reduce that empire to a province, to be governed by a viceroy from hence, and to destroy and to put to death, not only all the Big Endian exiles, but likewise all the people of that empire who would not immediately forsake the Big Endian heresy; he, the said Flestrin, like a false traitor against his most auspicious, serene, imperial majesty, did petition to be excused from the said service, upon pretence of unwillingness to force the consciences or destroy the liberties and lives of an innocent people.

ARTICLE II.—That, whereas certain ambassadors arrived from the court of Blefuscu, to sue for peace in his majesty's court; he, the said Flestrin, did, like a false traitor, aid, abet, comfort, and divert the said ambassadors, although he knew them to be servants to a prince who was lately an open enemy to his imperial majesty, and in an open war against his said majesty.

ARTICLE III.—That the said Quinbus Flestrin, contrary to the duty of a faithful subject, is now preparing to make a voyage to the court and empire of Blefuscu, for which he has received only verbal licence from his imperial majesty; and, under colour of the said licence, does falsely and traitoriously intend to take the said voyage, and thereby to aid, comfort, and abet the emperor of Blefuscu, so lately an enemy and in open war with his imperial majesty aforesaid.

"There are some other articles; but these are the most important, of which I have read you an abstract.

"In the several debates upon this impeachment, it must be confessed that his majesty gave many marks of his great lenity; often urging the services you had done him, and endeavouring to extenuate your crimes. The treasurer and admiral insisted that you should be put to the most painful and ignominious death, by setting fire to your house at night; and the general was to attend with twenty thousand men, armed with poisoned arrows, to shoot you on the face and hands. Some of your servants were to have private orders to strew a poisonous juice on your shirts and sheets, which would soon make you tear your own flesh, and die in the utmost torture. The general came into the same opinion; so that, for a long time, there was a majority against you; but his majesty resolving, if possible, to spare your life, at last bought off the chamberlain.

"Upon this incident, Reldresal, principal secretary for private affairs, who always approved himself your true friend, was commanded by the emperor to deliver his opinion, which he accordingly did; and therein justified the good thoughts you have of him. He allowed your crimes to be great, but that there was still room for mercy, the most commendable virtue in a prince, and for which his majesty was so justly celebrated. He said, the friendship between you and him was so well known to the world, that perhaps the most honourable board might think him partial; however, in obedience to the command he had received, he would freely offer his sentiments. That if his majesty, in consideration of your services, and pursuant to his own merciful disposition, would please to spare your life, and only give orders to put out both your eyes, he humbly conceived that by this expedient justice might in some measure be satisfied, and all the world would applaud the lenity of the emperor, as well as the fair and generous proceedings of those who have the honour to be his counsellors. That the loss of your eyes would be no impediment to your bodily strength, by which you might still be useful to his majesty; that blindness is an addition to courage, by concealing dangers from us; that the fear you had for your eyes was the greatest difficulty in bringing over the enemy's fleet; and it would be sufficient for you to see by the eyes of the ministers, since the greatest princes do no more.

"This proposal was received with the utmost disapprobation by the whole board. Bolgolam, the admiral, could not preserve his temper; but rising up in a fury, said, he wondered how the secretary durst presume to give his opinion for preserving the life of a traitor; that the services you had performed were, by all true reasons of state, the great aggravation of your crimes; the same strength which enabled you to bring over the enemy's fleet might serve, upon the first discontent, to carry it back; that he had good reasons to think that you were a Big Endian in your heart; and, as treason begins in the heart before it appears in overt acts, so he accused you as a traitor on that account, and therefore insisted you should be put to death.

"The treasurer was of the same opinion; he showed to what straits his majesty's revenue was reduced, by the charge of maintaining you, which would soon grow insupportable; that the secretary's expedient of putting out your eyes was so far from being a remedy against this evil that it would probably increase it, as is manifest from the common practice of blinding some kind of fowls, after which they fed the faster, and grew sooner fat; that his sacred majesty and the council, who are your judges, were, in their own consciences, fully convinced of your guilt, which was a sufficient argument to condemn you to death, without the formal proofs required by the strict letter of the law.

"But his imperial majesty, fully determined against capital punishment, was graciously pleased to say, that since the council thought the loss of your eyes too easy a censure, some other way may be inflicted hereafter. And your friend the secretary, humbly desiring to be heard again, in answer to what the treasurer had objected, concerning the great charge his majesty was at in maintaining you, said, that his excellency, who had the sole disposal of the emperor's revenue, might easily provide against that evil, by gradually lessening your establishment; by which, for want of sufficient food, you will grow weak and faint, and lose your appetite, and consume in a few months; neither would the stench of your carcass be then so dangerous, when it should become more than half diminished; and immediately upon your death five or six thousand of his majesty's subjects might, in two or three days, cut your flesh from your bones, take it away by cart loads, and bury it in distant parts to prevent infection, leaving the skeleton as a monument of admiration to posterity.

"Thus, upon the great friendship of the secretary, the whole affair was compromised. It was strictly enjoined that the project of starving you by degrees should be kept a secret; but the sentence of putting out your eyes was entered on the books; none dissenting except Bolgolam, the admiral, who, being a creature of the empress, was perpetually instigated by her majesty to insist upon your death.

"In three days, your friend, the secretary, will be directed to come to your house, and read before you the articles of impeachment; and then to signify the great lenity and favour of his majesty and council, whereby you are only condemned to the loss of your eyes, which his majesty does not question you will gratefully and humbly submit to; and twenty of his majesty's surgeons will attend, in order to see the operation well performed, by discharging very sharp-pointed arrows into the balls of your eyes, as you lie on the ground.

c

"I leave to your prudence what measures you will take; and to avoid suspicion, I must immediately return in as private a manner as I came."

His lordship did so; and I remained alone, under many doubts and perplexities of mind.

It was a custom introduced by this prince and his ministry (very different, as I have been assured, from the practice of former times), that after the court had decreed any cruel execution, either to gratify the monarch's resentment, or the malice of a favourite, the emperor always made a speech to his whole council, expressing his great lenity and tenderness, as qualities known and confessed by all the world. This speech was immediately published throughout the kingdom; nor did anything terrify the people so much as those encomiums on his majesty's mercy; because it was observed that the more these praises were enlarged and insisted on, the more inhuman was the punishment, and the more innocent the sufferer. Yet as to myself, I must confess, having never been designed for a courtier, either by my birth or education, I was so ill a judge of things, that I could not discover the lenity and favour of this sentence, but conceived it (perhaps erroneously) to be rather rigorous than gentle. I sometimes thought of standing my trial; for although I could not deny the facts alleged in the several articles, yet I hoped they would admit of some extenuation. But having in my life perused many state trials, which I ever observed to terminate as the judges thought fit to direct, I durst not rely on so dangerous a decision, in so critical a juncture, and against such powerful enemies.

Once I was strongly bent upon resistance: for while I had liberty, the whole strength of that empire could hardly subdue me, and I might easily with stones pelt the metropolis to pieces; but I soon rejected that project with horror, by remembering the oath I had made to the emperor, the favours I received from him, and the high title of *nardac* he conferred upon me. Neither had I so soon learned the gratitude of courtiers, to persuade myself that his majesty's present severities acquitted me of all past obligations.

At last, I fixed upon a resolution, for which it is probable I may incur some censure, and not unjustly; for I confess I owe the preserving of mine eyes, and consequently my liberty, to my own great rashness and want of experience; because, if I had then known the nature of princes and ministers, which I have since observed in many other courts, and their methods of treating criminals less obnoxious than myself, I should, with great alacrity and readiness, have submitted to so easy a punishment. But hurried on by the precipitancy of youth, and having his imperial majesty's licence to pay my attendance upon the Emperor of Blefuscu, I took this opportunity, before the three days were elapsed, to send a letter to my friend the secretary, signifying my resolution of setting out that morning for Blefuscu, pursuant to the leave I had got; and, without waiting for an answer, I went to that side of the island where our fleet lay. I seized a large man-of-war, and tied the cable to the prow; and, lifting up the anchors, I stripped myself, put my clothes (together with my coverlet, which I carried under my arm) into the vessel, and drawing it after me, between wading and swimming arrived at the royal port of Blefuscu, where the people had long expected me. They lent me two guides to direct me to the capital city, which is of the same name: I held them in my hands, till I came within two hundred yards of the gate, and desired them "to signify my arrival to one of the secretaries, and let him know I there waited his majesty's commands." I had an answer in about an hour, "that his majesty, attended by the royal family and great officers of the court, was coming out to receive me." I advanced a hundred yards. The emperor and his train alighted from their horses, the empress and ladies from their coaches, and I did not perceive they were in any fright or concern. I lay on the ground to kiss his majesty and the empress's hands. I told his majesty, that I was come according to my promise, and with the licence of the emperor, my master, to have the honour of seeing so mighty a monarch, and to offer him any service in my power, consistent with my duty to my own prince; not mentioning a word of my disgrace, because I had hitherto no regular information of it, and might suppose myself wholly ignorant of any such design; neither could I reasonably conceive that the emperor would discover the secret while I was out of his power; wherein, however, it soon appeared I was deceived.

I shall not trouble the reader with the particular account of my reception at this court, which was suitable to the generosity of so great a prince; nor of the difficulties I was in for want of a house and bed, being forced to lie on the ground wrapped up in my coverlet.

CHAPTER VIII

THE AUTHOR, BY A LUCKY ACCIDENT, FINDS MEANS TO LEAVE BLEFUSCU; AND, AFTER SOME DIFFICULTIES, RETURNS SAFE TO HIS NATIVE COUNTRY

THREE days after my arrival, walking, out of curiosity, to the north-east coast of the island, I observed, about half a league off in the sea, somewhat that looked like a boat overturned. I pulled off my shoes and stockings, and, wading two or three hundred yards, I found the object to approach nearer by force of the tide; and then plainly saw it to be a real boat, which I supposed might by some tempest have been driven from a ship:—whereupon I returned immediately towards the city, and desired his imperial majesty to lend me twenty of the tallest vessels he had left, after the loss of his fleet, and three thousand seamen, under the command of his vice-admiral. This fleet sailed round while I went back the shortest way to the coast, where I first discovered the boat. I found the tide had driven it still nearer. The seamen were all provided with cordage, which I had beforehand twisted to a sufficient strength. When the ships came up, I stripped myself, and waded till I came within a hundred yards of the boat, after which I was forced to swim till I got up to it. The seamen threw me the end of the cord, which I fastened to a hole in the forepart of the boat, and the other end to a man-of-war; but I found all my labour to little purpose; for, being out of my depth, I was not able to work. In this necessity I was forced to swim behind and push the boat forward, as often as I could, with one of my hands; and the tide favouring me, I advanced so far that I could just hold up my chin and feel the ground. I rested two or three minutes, and then gave the boat another shove, and so on, till the sea was no higher than my armpits; and now the most laborious part being over I took out my other cables, which were stowed in one of the ships, and fastened them first to the boat, and then to nine of the vessels which attended me; the wind being favourable, the seamen towed, and I shoved, until we arrived within forty yards of the shore, and waiting till the tide was out, I got dry to the boat; and by the assistance of two thousand men, with ropes and engines, made a shift to turn it on its bottom, and found it was but little damaged.

I shall not trouble the reader with the difficulties I was under, by the help of certain paddles, which cost me ten days making, to get my boat into the royal port of Blefuscu, where a mighty concourse of people appeared upon my arrival, full of wonder at the sight of so prodigious a vessel. I told the emperor "that my good fortune had thrown this boat in my way, to carry me to some place whence I might return to my native country; and begged his majesty's orders for getting materials to fit it up, together with his licence to depart"; which, after some kind expostulations, he was pleased to grant.

I did very much wonder, in all this time, not to have heard of any express relating to me from our emperor to the court of Blefuscu. But I was afterwards given privately to understand, that his imperial majesty, never imagining I had the least notice of his designs, believed I was only gone to Blefuscu in performance of my promise, according to the licence he had given me, which was well known at our court, and would return in a few days, when the ceremony was ended. But he was at last in pain at my long absence; and, after consulting with the treasurer and the rest of that cabal, a person of quality was dispatched with the copy of the articles against me. This envoy had instructions to represent to the monarch of Blefuscu "the great lenity of his master, who was content to punish me no further than the loss of mine eyes; that I had fled from justice; and, if I did not return in two hours, I should be deprived of my title of *nardac*, and declared a traitor." The envoy further added, "that, in order to maintain the peace and amity between both empires, his master expected that his brother of Blefuscu would give orders to have me sent back to Lilliput, bound hand and foot, to be punished as a traitor."

The emperor of Blefuscu, having taken three days to consult, returned an answer consisting of many civilities and excuses. He said, "that as for sending me bound, his brother knew it was impossible; that although I had deprived him of his fleet, yet he owed great obligations to me for many good offices I had done him in making the peace. That, however, both their majesties would soon be made easy; for I had found a prodigious vessel on the shore, able to carry me on the sea, which he had given orders to fit up, with my own assistance and direction; and he hoped in a few weeks both empires would be freed from so insupportable an incumbrance."

With this answer the envoy returned to Lilliput, and the monarch of Blefuscu related to me all that had passed, offering me at the same time (but under the strictest confidence) his gracious protection, if I would continue in his service; wherein, although I believed him sincere, yet I resolved never more to put any confidence in princes or ministers where I could possibly avoid it; and therefore, with all due acknowledgement of his favourable intentions, I humbly begged to be excused. I told him, "that since fortune, whether good or evil, had thrown a vessel in my way, I was resolved to venture myself on the ocean, rather than be an occasion of difference between two such mighty monarchs." Neither did I find the emperor at all displeased; and I discovered, by a certain accident, that he was very glad of my resolution, and so were most of his ministers.

These considerations moved me to hasten my departure somewhat sooner than I intended; to which the court, impatient to have me gone, very readily contributed. Five hundred workmen were employed to make two sails to my boat according to my directions, by quilting thirteen folds of their strongest linen together. I was at the pains of making ropes and cables, by twisting ten, twenty, or thirty of the thickest and strongest of theirs. A great stone that I happened to find, after a long search, by the sea-shore, served me for an anchor. I had the tallow of three hundred cows for greasing my boat and other uses. I was at incredible pains in cutting down some of the largest timber-trees for oars and masts, wherein I was, however, much assisted by his majesty's ship-carpenters, who helped me in smoothing them after I had done the rough work.

In about a month, when all was prepared, I sent to receive his majesty's commands, and to take my leave. The emperor and royal family came out of the palace; I lay down on my face to kiss his hand, which he very graciously gave me; so did the empress and the young princes of the blood. His majesty presented me with fifty purses of two hundred *sprugs* a-piece, together with his picture at full length, which I put immediately into one of my gloves to keep it from being hurt. The ceremonies at my departure were too many to trouble the reader with at this time.

I stored the boat with the carcasses of a hundred oxen and three hundred sheep, with bread and drink proportionable, and as much meat ready dressed as four hundred cooks could provide. I took with me six cows and two bulls alive, with as many ewes and rams, intending to carry them into my own country, and propagate the breed; and to feed them on board, I had a good bundle of hay, and a bag of corn. I would gladly have taken a dozen of the natives, but this was a thing the emperor would by no means permit; and, besides a diligent search into my pockets, his majesty engaged my honour "not to carry away any of his subjects, although with their own consent and desire."

Having thus prepared all things as well as I was able, I set sail on the 24th day of September, 1701, at six in the morning; and when I had gone about four leagues to the northward, the wind being at the south-east, at six in the evening I descried a small island, about half a league to the north-west. I advanced forward, and cast anchor on the lee-side of the island, which seemed to be uninhabited. I then took some refreshment, and went to my rest. I slept well, as I conjecture at least six hours, for I found the day broke in two hours after I awoke. It was a clear night. I ate my breakfast before the sun was up; and heaving anchor, the wind being favourable, I steered the same course that I had done the day before, wherein I was directed by my pocket-compass. My intention was to reach, if possible, one of those islands which I had reason to believe lay to the north-east of Van Diemen's Land. I discovered nothing all that day; but upon the next, about three in the afternoon, when I had by my computation made twenty-four leagues from Blefuscu, I descried a sail steering to the south-east; my course was due east, I hailed her, but could get no answer; yet I found that I gained upon her, for the wind slackened. I made all the sail I could, and in half an hour she spied me, then hung out her ancient, and discharged a gun. It is not easy to express the joy I was in, upon the unexpected hope of once more seeing my beloved country and the dear pledges I left in it. The ship slackened her sails, and I came up with her between five and six in the evening, September 26th; but my heart leaped within me to see her English colours. I put my cows and sheep into my coat pocket, and got on board with all my little cargo of provisions. The vessel was an English merchantman, returning from Japan by the North and South Seas; the captain, Mr. John Biddle, of Deptford, a very civil man, and an excellent sailor. We were now in the latitude 30 degrees south; there were about fifty men in the ship; and here I met an old comrade of mine, one Peter Williams, who gave me a good character to the captain. This gentleman treated me with kindness, and desired I would let him know what place I came from last, and whither I was bound, which I did in a few words, but he thought I was raving, and that the dangers I had undergone had disturbed my head; whereupon I took my black cattle and sheep out of my pocket, which, after great astonishment, clearly convinced him of my veracity. I then showed him the gold given me by the emperor of Blefuscu, together with his majesty's picture at full length, and some other rarities of that country. I gave him two purses of two hundred *sprugs* each, and promised, when we arrived in England, to make him a present of a cow and a sheep.

I shall not trouble the reader with a particular account of this voyage, which was very prosperous for the most part. We arrived in the Downs on the 13th of April, 1702. I had only one misfortune, that the rats on board carried away one of my sheep; I found her bones in a hole, picked clean from the flesh. The rest of my cattle I got safe ashore, and set them a-grazing in a bowling-green at Greenwich, where the fineness of the grass made them feed very heartily, though I had always feared the contrary; neither could I possibly have preserved them in so long a voyage, if the captain had not allowed me some of his best biscuit, which, rubbed to powder and mingled with water, was their constant food. The short time I continued in England, I made a considerable profit by showing my cattle to many persons of quality and others; and before I began my second voyage I sold them for six hundred pounds. Since my last return I find the breed is considerably increased, especially the sheep, which I hope will prove much to the advantage of the woollen manufacture, by the fineness of their fleeces.

I stayed but two months with my wife and family, for my insatiable desire of seeing foreign countries would suffer me to continue no longer. I left fifteen hundred pounds with my wife, and fixed her in a good house at Redriff. My remaining stock I carried with me, part in money and part in goods, in hopes to improve my fortunes. My eldest uncle, John, had left me an estate in land, near Epping, of about thirty pounds a year; and I had a long lease of the "Black Bull" in Fetter Lane, which yielded me as much more; so that I was not in any danger of leaving my family upon the parish. My son Johnny, named so after his uncle, was at the grammar-school, and a towardly child. My daughter Betty (who is now well married, and has children) was then at her needle-work. I took leave of my wife, and boy and girl, with tears on both sides, and went on board the *Adventure*, a merchant-ship of three hundred tons, bound for Surat; Captain John Nicholas, of Liverpool, commander. But my account of this voyage must be referred to the second part of my travels.

PART II

A VOYAGE TO BROBDINGNAG

CHAPTER I

A GREAT STORM DESCRIBED—THE LONG-BOAT SENT TO FETCH
WATER—THE AUTHOR GOES WITH IT TO DISCOVER THE
COUNTRY—HE IS LEFT ON SHORE, IS SEIZED BY ONE OF THE
NATIVES AND CARRIED TO A FARMER'S HOUSE—HIS RECEPTION
THERE, WITH SEVERAL ACCIDENTS THAT HAPPENED THERE—
A DESCRIPTION OF THE INHABITANTS

HAVING been condemned, by nature and fortune, to an active
and restless life, in two months after my return, I again left my
native country, and took shipping in the Downs, on the 20th
day of June, 1702, in the *Adventure*—Captain John Nicholas, a
Cornishman, commander—bound for Surat. We had a prosperous gale, till we arrived at the Cape of Good Hope, where we
landed for fresh water; but discovering a leak, we unshipped our
goods, and wintered there; for the captain falling sick of an ague,
we could not leave the Cape till the end of March. We then set
sail, and had a good voyage till we passed the Straits of Madagascar; but having got northward of that island, and to about
five degrees south latitude, the winds, which in those seas are
observed to blow a constant equal gale between the north and
west, from the beginning of December to the beginning of
May, on the 19th of April began to blow with much greater
violence, and more westerly than usual, continuing so for twenty
days together; during which time, we were driven a little to the
east of the Molucca Islands, and about three degrees northward of the line, as our captain found by an observation he took
the 2nd of May, at which time the wind ceased, and it was a

70

perfect calm, whereat I was not a little rejoiced. But he, being a man well experienced in the navigation of those seas, bid us all prepare against a storm, which accordingly happened the day following; for the southern wind, called the southern monsoon, began to set in.

Finding it was likely to over-blow, we took in our sprit-sail, and stood by to hand the fore-sail; but, making foul weather, we looked the guns were all fast, and handed the mizen. The ship lay very broad off, so we thought it better spooning before the sea, than trying or hulling. We reefed the fore-sail, and set him, and hauled aft the fore-sheet; the helm was hard a-weather. The ship wore bravely. We belayed the fore down-haul; but the sail was split, and we hauled down the yard, and got the sail into the ship, and unbound all the things clear of it. It was a very fierce storm; the sea broke strange and dangerous. We hauled off upon the lanyards of the whip-staff, and helped the man at the helm. We would not get down our topmast, but let all stand, because she scudded before the sea very well, and we knew that the topmast being aloft, the ship was the wholesomer, and made better way through the sea, seeing we had sea-room. When the storm was over, we set fore-sail and main-sail, and brought the ship to. Then we set the mizen, main-top-sail, and the fore-top-sail. Our course was east-north-east, the wind was at south-west. We got the starboard tacks aboard; we cast off the weather-bowlings, weather-braces and lifts; we set in the lee-braces, and hauled them tight, and belayed them; and hauled over the mizen and hauled forward by tack to windward, and kept her full and by as near as she would lie.

During this storm, which was followed by a strong wind west-south-west, we were carried, by my computation, about five hundred leagues to the east, so that the oldest sailor on board could not tell in what part of the world we were. Our provisions held out well; our ship was staunch, and our crew all in good health; but we lay in the utmost distress for water. We thought it best to hold on the same course, rather than turn more northerly, which might have brought us to the north-west part of Great Tartary, and into the Frozen Sea.

On the 16th day of June, 1703, a boy on the topmast discovered land. On the 17th we came in full view of a great island or continent (for we knew not whether); on the south side whereof was a small neck of land jutting out into the sea, and a creek too shallow to hold a ship of above one hundred tons. We cast anchor within a league of this creek, and our captain sent a dozen of his men well armed in the long-boat, with vessels for water, if any could be found. I desired his leave to go with them, that I might see the country, and make what discoveries I could. When we came to land, we saw no river or spring, nor any sign of inhabitants. Our men therefore wandered on the shore to find out some fresh water near the sea, and I walked alone about a mile on the other side, when I observed the country all barren and rocky. I now began to be weary, and seeing nothing to entertain my curiosity, I returned gently down towards the creek; and the sea being full in my view, I saw our men already got into the boat, and rowing for life to the ship. I was going to holloa after them, although it had been to little purpose, when I observed a huge creature walking after them in the sea, as fast as he could; he waded not much deeper than his knees, and took prodigious strides; but our men had the start of him half a league, and the sea thereabouts being full of sharp-pointed rocks, the monster was not able to overtake the boat. This I was afterwards told, for I durst not stay to see the issue of the adventure; but ran as fast as I could the way I first went, and then climbed up a steep hill, which gave me some prospect of the country. I found it fully cultivated; but that which first surprised me was the length of the grass, which, in those grounds that seemed to be kept for hay, was about twenty feet high.

I fell into a high road, for so I took it to be, though it served to the inhabitants only as a foot-path through a field of barley. Here I walked on for some time, but could see little on either side, it being now near harvest, and the corn rising at least forty feet. I was an hour walking to the end of this field, which was fenced in with a hedge of at least one hundred and twenty feet high, and the trees so lofty that I could make no computation of their altitude. There was a stile to pass from this field into the next. It had four steps, and a stone to cross over when you came to the uppermost. It was impossible for me to climb this stile, because every step was six feet high, and the upper stone about twenty. I was endeavouring to find some gap in the hedge, when I discovered one of the inhabitants in the next field, advancing towards the stile, of the same size with him whom I saw in the sea pursuing our boat. He appeared as tall as an ordinary spire steeple, and took about ten yards at every stride, as near as I could guess. I was struck with the utmost fear and astonishment, and ran to hide myself in the corn, whence I saw him at the top of the stile looking back into the next field on the right hand, and heard him call in a voice many degrees louder than a speaking-trumpet; but the noise was so high in the air that at first I certainly thought it was thunder. Whereupon seven monsters, like himself, came towards him with reaping-hooks in their hands, each hook about the largeness of six scythes. These people were not so well clad as the first, whose servants or labourers they seemed to be; for, upon some words he spoke, they went to reap the corn in the field where I lay. I kept from them at as great a distance as I could, but was forced to move with extreme difficulty, for the stalks of the corn were sometimes not above a foot distant, so that I could hardly squeeze my body betwixt them. However, I made a shift to go forward, till I came to a part of the field where the corn had been laid by the rain and wind. Here it was impossible for me to advance a step; for the stalks were so interwoven that I could not creep through, and the beards of the fallen ears so strong and pointed, that they pierced through my clothes into my flesh. At the same time I heard the reapers not above a hundred yards behind me. Being quite dispirited with toil, and wholly overcome by grief and despair, I lay down between two ridges, and heartily wished I might there end my days. I bemoaned my desolate widow and fatherless children. I lamented my own folly and wilfulness, in attempting a second voyage, against the advice of all my friends and relations. In this terrible agitation of mind, I could not forbear thinking of Lilliput, whose inhabitants looked upon me as the greatest prodigy that ever appeared in the world; where I was able to draw an imperial fleet in my hand, and perform those other actions which will be recorded for ever in the chronicles of that empire; while posterity shall hardly believe them, although attested by millions. I reflected what a mortification it must prove to me to appear as inconsiderable in this nation as one single Lilliputian would be among us. But this I conceived

was to be the least of my misfortunes; for, as human creatures
are observed to be more savage and cruel in proportion to their
bulk, what could I expect but to be a morsel in the mouth cf the
first among these enormous barbarians who should happen to
seize me? Undoubtedly philosophers are in the right, when they
tell us nothing is great or little otherwise than by comparison. It
might have pleased Fortune to have let the Lilliputians find
some nation where the people were as diminutive with respect
to them as they were to me. And who knows but that even this
prodigious race of mortals might be equally overmatched in
some distant part of the world, whereof we have yet no discovery?

Scared and confounded as I was, I could not forbear going
on with these reflections, when one of the reapers approaching
within ten yards of the ridge where I lay, made me apprehend
that with the next step I should be squashed to death under his
foot, or cut in two with his reaping-hook. And therefore, when
he was again about to move, I screamed as loud as fear could
make me; whereupon the huge creature trod short, and looking
round about under him for some time, at last espied me as I lay
on the ground. He considered awhile, with the caution of one
who endeavours to lay hold on a small, dangerous animal, in
such a manner that it shall not be able either to scratch or bite
him, as I myself had sometimes done with a weasel in England.
At length he ventured to take me behind, by the middle, between
his forefinger and thumb, and brought me within three yards of
his eyes, that he might behold my shape more perfectly. I guessed
his meaning, and my good fortune gave me so much presence of
mind, that I resolved not to struggle in the least as he held me
in the air, above sixty feet from the ground, although he grievously
pinched my sides, for fear I should slip through his fingers. All
I ventured was to raise mine eyes towards the sun, and place
my hands together in a supplicating posture, and to speak
some words in a humble, melancholy tone, suitable to the
condition I then was in: for I apprehended every moment that
he would dash me against the ground, as we usually do any little
hateful animal which we have a mind to destroy. But my good
star would have it, that he appeared pleased with my voice and
gestures, and began to look upon me as a curiosity, much
wondering to hear me pronounce articulate words, although

he could not understand them. In the meantime I was not able to forbear groaning and shedding tears, and turning my head towards my sides; letting him know, as well as I could, how cruelly I was hurt by the pressure of his thumb and finger. He seemed to apprehend my meaning; for, lifting up the lappet of his coat, he put me gently into it, and immediately ran along with me to his master, who was a substantial farmer, and the same person I had first seen in the field.

The farmer having (as I supposed by their talk) received such an account of me as his servant could give him, took a piece of small straw, about the size of a walking-staff, and therewith lifted up the lappets of my coat; which it seems he thought to be some kind of covering that nature had given me. He blew my hair aside, to take a better view of my face. He called his hinds about him, and asked them, as I afterwards learned, whether they had ever seen in the fields any little creature that resembled me. He then placed me softly on the ground upon all fours, but I got immediately up, and walked slowly backward and forward, to let those people see I had no intent to run away. They all sat down in a circle about me, the better to observe my motions. I pulled off my hat, and made a low bow towards the farmer. I fell on my knees, and lifted up my hands and eyes, and spoke several words as loud as I could; I took a purse of gold out of my pocket, and humbly presented it to him. He received it on the palm of his hand, then applied it close to his eye to see what it was, and afterward turned it several times with the point of a pin (which he took out of his sleeve), but could make nothing of it. Whereupon I made a sign that he should place his hand on the ground. I then took the purse, and opening it, poured all the gold into his palm. There were six Spanish pieces of four pistoles each, beside twenty or thirty smaller coins. I saw him wet the tip of his little finger upon his tongue, and take up one of my largest pieces, and then another; but he seemed to be wholly ignorant what they were. He made me a sign to put them again into my purse, and the purse again into my pocket, which, after offering it to him several times, I thought it best to do.

The farmer, by this time, was convinced I must be a rational creature. He spoke often to me; but the sound of his voice

pierced my ears like that of a water-mill, yet his words were
articulate enough. I answered as loud as I could in several
languages, and he often laid his ear within two yards of me:
but all in vain, for we were wholly unintelligible to each other.
He then sent his servants to their work, and taking his handkerchief out of his pocket, he doubled and spread it on his left
hand, which he placed flat on the ground with the palm upward,
making me a sign to step into it, as I could easily do, for it was
not above a foot in thickness. I thought it my part to obey, and,
for fear of falling, laid myself at full length upon the handkerchief, with the remainder of which he wrapped me up to the head
for further security; and in this manner carried me home to his
house. There he called his wife and showed me to her; but she
screamed and ran back, as women in England do at the sight of a
toad or a spider. However, when she had awhile seen my
behaviour, and how well I observed the signs her husband made,
she was soon reconciled, and by degrees grew extremely tender
of me.

It was about twelve at noon, and a servant brought in dinner.
It was only one substantial dish of meat (fit for the plain condition
of a husbandman), in a dish of about four-and-twenty feet
diameter. The company were, the farmer and his wife, three
children, and an old grandmother. When they were set down, the
farmer placed me at some distance from him on the table, which
was thirty feet high from the floor. I was in a terrible fright, and
kept as far as I could from the edge, for fear of falling. The wife
minced a bit of meat, then crumbled some bread on a trencher,
and placed it before me. I made her a low bow, took out my
knife and fork, and fell to eating, which gave them exceeding
delight. The mistress sent her maid for a small dram cup, which
held about two gallons, and filled it with drink; I took up the
vessel with much difficulty in both hands, and in a most respectful
manner drank to her ladyship's health, expressing the words as
loud as I could in English, which made the company laugh so
heartily, that I was almost deafened with the noise. This liquor
tasted like a small cider, and was not unpleasant. Then the master
made me a sign to come to his trencher side; but as I walked on the
table, being in great surprise all the time, as the indulgent reader
will easily conceive and excuse, I happened to stumble against a

crust, and fell flat on my face, but received no hurt. I got up immediately, and observing the good people to be in much concern, I took my hat (which I held under my arm out of good manners), and waving it over my head, made three huzzas, to show I had got no mischief by my fall. But advancing forward towards my master (as I shall henceforth call him), his youngest son, who sat next to him, an arch boy of about ten years old, took me up by the legs, and held me so high in the air, that I trembled every limb: but his father snatched me from him, and at the same time gave him such a box on the left ear, as would have felled a European troop of horse to the earth, ordering him to be taken from the table. But being afraid this boy might owe me a spite, and well remembering how mischievous all children among us naturally are to sparrows, rabbits, young kittens, and puppy dogs, I fell on my knees, and pointing to the boy, made my master to understand as well as I could, that I desired his son might be pardoned. The father complied, and the lad took his seat again, whereupon I went to him and kissed his hand, which my master took, and made him stroke me gently with it.

In the midst of dinner, my mistress's favourite cat leaped into her lap. I heard a noise behind me like that of a dozen stocking-weavers at work; and turning my head, I found it proceeded from the purring of that animal, who seemed to be three times larger than an ox, as I computed by the view of her head and one of her paws, while her mistress was feeding and stroking her. The fierceness of this creature's countenance altogether discomposed me; though I stood at the further end of the table, above fifty feet off; and though my mistress held her fast, for fear she might give a spring, and seize me in her talons. But it happened there was no danger, for the cat took not the least notice of me, when my master placed me within three yards of her. And as I have been always told, and found true by experience in my travels, that flying or discovering fear before a fierce animal, is a certain way to make it pursue or attack you, so I resolved, in this dangerous juncture, to show no manner of concern. I walked with intrepidity five or six times before the very head of the cat, and came within half a yard of her; whereupon she drew herself back, as if she were more afraid of me. I had less apprehension concerning the dogs, whereof three or

four came into the room, as it is usual in farmers' houses; one
of which was a mastiff, equal in bulk to four elephants, and a
greyhound, somewhat taller than the mastiff, but not so large.

When dinner was almost done, the nurse came in with a
child of a year old in her arms, who immediately spied me, and
began a squall that you might have heard from London Bridge
to Chelsea, after the usual oratory of infants, to get me for a
plaything. The mother, out of pure indulgence, took me up,
and put me towards the child, who presently seized me by the
middle, and got my head into his mouth, where I roared so
loud that the urchin was frightened, and let me drop; and I
should infallibly have broke my neck, if the mother had not held
her apron under me. The nurse, to quiet her babe, made use
of a rattle, which was a kind of hollow vessel filled with great
stones, and fastened by a cable to the child's waist: but all in
vain; so that she was forced to apply the last remedy by giving
it drink.

The strange appearance of the spots, pimples, and freckles on
this woman's skin made me reflect upon the fair skins of our
English ladies, who appear so beautiful to us, only because they
are of our own size, and their defects not to be seen but through
a magnifying glass; where we find by experiment that the
smoothest and whitest skins look rough, and coarse, and ill-
coloured.

I remember, when I was at Lilliput, the complexions of those
diminutive people appeared to me the fairest in the world; and
talking upon this subject with a person of learning there, who
was an intimate friend of mine, he said that my face appeared
much fairer and smoother when he looked on me from the ground,
than it did upon a nearer view, when I took him up in my hand,
and brought him close, which he confessed was at first a very
shocking sight. He said he could discover great holes in my skin;
that the stumps of my beard were ten times stronger than the
bristles of a boar, and my complexion made up of several colours
altogether disagreeable: although I must beg leave to say for
myself, that I am as fair as most of my sex and country, and very
little sunburnt by all my travels. On the other side, discoursing
of the ladies in that emperor's court, he used to tell me, "one
had freckles, another too large a mouth, a third too large a

nose!'' nothing of which I was able to distinguish. I confess, this reflection was obvious enough; which, however, I could not forbear, lest the reader might think these vast creatures were actually deformed: for I must do them the justice to say, they are a comely race of people, and particularly the features of my master's countenance, although he was but a farmer, when I beheld him from the height of sixty feet, appeared very well proportioned.

When dinner was done, my master went out to his labourers, and, as I could discover by his voice and gesture, gave his wife a strict charge to take care of me. I was very much tired, and disposed to sleep, which my mistress perceiving, she put me on her own bed, and covered me with a clean white handkerchief, but larger and coarser than the mainsail of a man-of-war.

I slept about two hours, and dreamt I was at home with my wife and children, which aggravated my sorrows when I awaked, and found myself alone in a vast room, between two and three hundred feet wide, and about two hundred high, lying in a bed twenty yards wide. My mistress was gone about her household affairs, and had locked me in. The bed was eight yards from the floor. Although wishing to get down, I durst not presume to call; and if I had, it would have been in vain, with such a voice as mine, at so great a distance as from the room where I lay to the kitchen where the family *kept*. While I was under these circumstances, two rats crept up the curtains, and ran smelling backwards and forwards on my bed. One of them came up almost to my face, whereupon I rose in a fright, and drew out my hanger to defend myself. These horrible animals had the boldness to attack me on both sides, and one of them held his fore-feet at my collar; but I had the good fortune to rip up his belly before he could do me any mischief. He fell down at my feet; and the other, seeing the fate of his comrade, made his escape, but not without one good wound on the back, which I gave him as he fled, and made the blood run trickling from him. After this exploit, I walked gently to and fro on the bed, to recover my breath and loss of spirits. These creatures were of the size of a large mastiff, but infinitely more nimble and fierce; so that if I had taken off my belt before I went to sleep, I must have infallibly been torn to pieces and devoured. I measured the tail of the dead rat, and found it to be two yards long, wanting an inch; but it went against my stomach to draw the carcass off the bed, where it lay still bleeding; I observed it had yet some life, but with a strong slash across the neck, I thoroughly dispatched it.

Soon after my mistress came into the room, who seeing me all bloody, ran and took me up in her hand. I pointed to the dead rat, smiling, and making other signs to show I was not hurt; whereat she was extremely rejoiced, calling the maid to take up the dead rat with a pair of tongs, and throw it out of the window. Then she set me on a table, where I showed her my hanger all bloody, and, wiping it on the lappet of my coat, returned it to the scabbard. I was anxious to wash and dress myself, and therefore endeavoured to make my mistress understand that I desired to be set down on the floor; which after she had done, my bashfulness would not suffer me to express myself further than by pointing at the door, and bowing several times. The good woman, with much difficulty, at last perceived what I would be at, and left me to myself for a short time.

I hope the gentle reader will excuse me for dwelling on these and the like particulars, which, however insignificant they may appear to grovelling, vulgar minds, yet will certainly help a philosopher to enlarge his thoughts and imagination, and apply them to the benefit of public as well as private life, which was my sole design in presenting this and other accounts of my travels to the world; wherein I have been chiefly studious of truth, without affecting any ornaments of learning or of style. But the whole scene of this voyage made so strong an impression on my mind, and is so deeply fixed in memory, that in committing it to paper I did not omit one material circumstance; however, upon a strict review I blotted out several passages of less moment, which were in my first copy, for fear of being censured as tedious and trifling, whereof travellers are often, perhaps not without justice, accused.

CHAPTER II

A DESCRIPTION OF THE FARMER'S DAUGHTER—THE AUTHOR
CARRIED TO A MARKET TOWN, AND THEN TO THE METROPOLIS
—THE PARTICULARS OF HIS JOURNEY

MY MISTRESS had a daughter of nine years old, a child of towardly
parts for her age, very dextrous at her needle, and skilful in
dressing her baby. Her mother and she contrived to fit up the
baby's cradle for me against night: the cradle was put into a
small drawer of a cabinet, and the drawer placed upon a hanging
shelf, for fear of the rats. This was my bed all the time I stayed
with those people, though made more convenient by degrees, as
I began to learn their language, and make my wants known.
This young girl was so handy, that after I had once or twice
pulled off my clothes before her, she was able to dress or undress
me, though I never gave her that trouble when she would let me
do either myself. She made me seven shirts, and some other
linen, of as fine cloth as could be got, which indeed was coarser
than sackcloth; and these she constantly washed for me with her
own hands. She was likewise my school-mistress, to teach me
the language: when I pointed to anything, she told me the name
of it in her own tongue, so that in a few days I was able to call
for whatever I had a mind to. She was very good-natured, and
not above forty feet high, being little of her age. She gave me
the name of *grildrig*, which the family took up, and afterwards
the whole kingdom. The word imports what the Latins call
homunculus; the Italians, *homunceletion*; and the English, *manikin*.
To her I chiefly owe my preservation in that country; we never
parted while I was there; I called her my *glumdalclitch*, or little
nurse; and should be guilty of great ingratitude if I omitted
this honourable mention of her care and affection towards
me, which I heartily wish it lay in my power to requite as she
deserves, instead of being the innocent but unhappy instrument
of her disgrace, as I have too much reason to fear.

It now began to be known and talked of in the neighbourhood,

that my master had found a strange animal in the field, about
the bigness of a *splacnuck*, but exactly shaped in every part like
a human creature; which it likewise imitated in all its actions;
seemed to speak in a little language of its own, had already learnt
several words of theirs, went erect upon two legs, was tame and
gentle, would come when it was called, do whatever it was bid,
had the finest limbs in the world, and a complexion fairer than
a nobleman's daughter of three years old. Another farmer, who
lived hard by, and was a particular friend of my master, came
on a visit on purpose to inquire into the truth of this story. I
was immediately produced and placed upon a table, where I
walked as I was commanded, drew my hanger, put it up again,
made my reverence to my master's guest, asked him in his own
language how he did, and told him he was welcome, just as my
little nurse had instructed me. This man, who was old and
dim-sighted, put on his spectacles to behold me better; at which
I could not forbear laughing very heartily, for his eyes appeared
like the full moon shining into a chamber at two windows.
Our people, who discovered the cause of my mirth, bore me
company in laughing, at which the old fellow was fool enough
to be angry and out of countenance. He had the character of a
great miser: and, to my misfortune, he well deserved it, by the
bad advice he gave my master, to show me as a sight upon a
market-day in the next town, which was half an hour's riding,
about two-and-twenty miles from our house. I guessed there
was some mischief abroad contriving, when I observed my
master and his friend whispering long together, sometimes
pointing at me; and my fears made me fancy that I overheard
and understood some of their words. But the next morning
Glumdalclitch, my little nurse, told me the whole matter,
which she had cunningly picked out from her mother. The poor
girl laid me on her bosom, and fell weeping with shame and grief.
She apprehended some mischief would happen to me from rude,
vulgar folks, who might squeeze me to death, or break one of
my limbs by taking me in their hands. She had also observed
how modest I was in my nature, how nicely I regarded my
honour, and what an indignity I should conceive it to be exposed
for money, as a public spectacle, to the meanest of the people.
She said her papa and mamma had promised that Grildrig

should be hers; but now she found they meant to serve her as they did last year, when they pretended to give her a lamb, and yet, as soon as it was fat, sold it to a butcher. For my own part, I may truly affirm, that I was less concerned than my nurse. I had a strong hope, which never left me, that I should one day recover my liberty: and as to the ignominy of being carried about for a monster, I considered myself to be a perfect stranger in the country, and that such a misfortune could never be charged upon me as a reproach, if ever I should return to England; since the king of Great Britain himself, in my condition, must have undergone the same distress.

My master, pursuant to the advice of his friend, carried me in a box, the next market-day, to the neighbouring town and took along with him his little daughter, my nurse, upon a pillion behind him. The box was close on every side, with a little door for me to go in and out, and a few gimlet holes to let in air. The girl had been so careful as to put the quilt of her baby's bed into it, for me to lie down on. However, I was terribly shaken and discomposed in this journey, though it were but of half an hour; for the horse went about forty feet at every step, and trotted so high, that the agitation was equal to the rising and falling of a ship in a great storm, but much more frequent. Our journey was somewhat farther than from London to St. Alban's. My master alighted at an inn which he used to frequent; and after consulting awhile with the innkeeper, and making some necessary preparations, he hired the *grultred*, or crier, to give notice through the town of a strange creature to be seen at the sign of the Green Eagle, not so big as a *splacnuck* (an animal in that country very finely shaped), about six feet long, and in every part of the body resembling a human creature, which could speak several words, and perform a hundred diverting tricks.

I was placed upon a table in the largest room of the inn, which might be near three hundred feet square. My little nurse stood on a low stool close to the table, to take care of me, and direct what I should do. My master, to avoid a crowd, would suffer only thirty people at a time to see me. I walked about on the table as the girl commanded: she asked me questions, as far as she knew my understanding of the language reached, and I answered them as loud as I could. I turned about several times to the company, paid my humble respects, said they were welcome, and used some other speeches I had been taught. I took up a thimble filled with liquor, which Glumdalclitch had given me for a cup, and drank their health. I drew out my hanger, and flourished with it after the manner of fencers in England. My nurse gave me a part of a straw, which I exercised as a pike, having learnt the art in my youth. I was that day shown to twelve sets of company, and as often forced to act over again the same fopperies, till I was half dead with weariness and vexation; for those who had seen me made such wonderful reports, that the people were ready to break down the doors to come in. My master, for his own interest, would not suffer any one to touch me except my nurse; and to prevent danger, benches were set round the table at such a distance as put me out of everybody's reach. However, an unlucky schoolboy aimed a hazel-nut at my head, which very narrowly missed me; otherwise it came with so much violence, that it would have infallibly knocked out my brains, for it was almost as large as a small pumpkin; but I had the satisfaction to see the young rogue well beaten, and turned out of the room.

My master gave public notice that he would show me again the next market-day; and in the meantime he prepared a more convenient vehicle for me, which he had reason enough to do; for I was so tired with my first journey, and with entertaining company for eight hours together, that I could hardly stand upon my legs or speak a word. It was at least three days before I recovered my strength; and that I might have no rest at home, all the neighbouring gentlemen from a hundred miles around hearing of my fame, came to see me at my master's own house. There could not be fewer than thirty persons, with their wives and children (for the country is very populous); and my master demanded the rate of a full room whenever he showed me at home, although it were only to a single family; so that for some time I had but little ease every day of the week (except Wednesday, which is their Sabbath), although I were not carried to the town.

My master, finding how profitable I was likely to be, resolved to carry me to the most considerable cities in the kingdom. Having therefore provided himself with all things necessary for a long journey, and settled his affairs at home, he took leave of his wife, and on the 17th of August, 1703, about two months after my arrival, we set out for the metropolis, situate near the middle of that empire, and about three thousand miles' distance from our house. My master made his daughter, Glumdalclitch, ride behind him. She carried me on her lap, in a box tied about her waist. The girl had lined it on all sides with the softest cloth she could get, well quilted underneath, furnished it with her baby's bed, provided me with linen and other necessaries, and made everything as convenient as she could. We had no other company but a boy of the house, who rode after us with the luggage.

My master's design was to show me in all the towns by the way; and to step out of the road, for fifty or a hundred miles, to any village or person of quality's house, where he might expect custom. We made easy journeys, of not above seven or eight score miles a day: for Glumdalclitch, on purpose to spare me, complained she was tired with the trotting of the horse. She often took me out of my box at my desire, to give me air, and show me the country, but always held me fast by a leading string. We passed over five or six rivers, many degrees broader and deeper than the Ganges: and there was hardly a rivulet so small as the Thames at London Bridge. We were ten weeks in our journey, and I was shown in eighteen large towns, besides many villages and private families.

On the 26th day of October, we arrived at the metropolis, called in their language *Lorbrulgrud*, or Pride of the Universe. My master took a lodging in the principal street of the city, not far from the royal palace, and put out bills in the usual form, containing an exact description of my person and parts. He hired a large room, between three and four hundred feet wide. He provided a table sixty feet in diameter, upon which I was to act my part, and palisadoed it round three feet from the edge, and as many high, to prevent my falling over. I was shown ten times a day, to the wonder and satisfaction of all people. I could now speak the language tolerably well, and perfectly understood every word that was spoken to me. Besides, I had learnt their alphabet, and could make a shift to explain a sentence, here and there: for Glumdalclitch had been my instructor while we were at home, and at leisure hours during our journey. She carried a

little book in her pocket, not much larger than Sanson's Atlas;
it was a common treatise for the use of young girls, giving a short
account of their religion: out of this she taught me my letters, and
interpreted the words.

CHAPTER III

THE AUTHOR SENT FOR TO COURT—THE QUEEN BUYS HIM OF HIS
MASTER, THE FARMER, AND PRESENTS HIM TO THE KING—
HE DISPUTES WITH HIS MAJESTY'S GREAT SCHOLARS—AN
APARTMENT AT COURT PROVIDED FOR THE AUTHOR—HE IS
IN HIGH FAVOUR WITH THE QUEEN—HE STANDS UP FOR THE
HONOUR OF HIS OWN COUNTRY—HIS QUARRELS WITH THE
QUEEN'S DWARF

THE FREQUENT labours I underwent every day made, in a few
weeks, a very considerable change in my health; the more my
master got by me, the more insatiable he grew; I had quite lost
my stomach, and was almost reduced to a skeleton. The farmer
observing it, and concluding I must soon die, resolved to make as
good a hand of me as he could. While he was thus reasoning and
resolving with himself, a *sardral*, or a gentleman-usher, came from
court, commanding my master to carry me immediately thither,
for the diversion of the queen and her ladies. Some of the latter
had already been to see me, and reported strange things of my
beauty, behaviour, and good sense. Her majesty, and those who
attended her, were beyond measure delighted with my de-
meanour. I fell on my knees, and begged the honour of kissing
her imperial foot; but this gracious princess held out her little
finger towards me, after I was set on the table, which I embraced
in both my arms, and put the tip of it with the utmost respect to
my lip. She asked me some general questions about my country
and my travels, which I answered as distinctly and in as few
words as I could. She asked whether I could be content to live
at court. I bowed down to the board of the table, and humbly
answered, that I was my master's slave; but if I were at my own
disposal, I should be proud to devote my life to her majesty's

service. She then asked my master, whether he was willing to sell me at a good price. He, who apprehended that I could not live a month, was ready enough to part with me, and demanded a thousand pieces of gold, which were ordered him on the spot, each piece being about the bigness of eight hundred moidores; but allowing for the proportion of all things between that country and Europe, and the high price of gold among them, this was hardly so great a sum as a thousand guineas would be in England. I then said to the queen, since I was now her majesty's most humble creature and vassal, I must beg the favour that Glumdalclitch, who had always tended me with so much care and kindness, and knew how to do it so well, might be admitted into the service, and continue to be my nurse and instructor.

Her majesty agreed to my petition, and easily got the farmer's consent, who was glad enough to have his daughter preferred at court, and the poor girl herself was not able to hide her joy. My late master withdrew, bidding me farewell, and saying he had left me in a good service: to which I replied not a word, only making him a slight bow.

The queen observed my coldness; and when the farmer was gone out of the apartment, asked me the reason. I made bold to tell her majesty, that I owed no other obligation to my late master, than his not dashing out the brains of a poor harmless creature, found by chance in his fields; which obligation was amply recompensed by the gain he had made in showing me through half the kingdom, and the price he had now sold me for. That the life I had since led was laborious enough to kill an animal of ten times my strength. That my health was much impaired, by the continual drudgery of entertaining the rabble every hour of the day; and that, if my master had not thought my life in danger, her majesty would not have got so cheap a bargain. But as I was out of all fear of being ill-treated under the protection of so great and good an empress, the ornament of Nature, the darling of the world, the delight of her subjects, the phœnix of the creation; so, I hoped my late master's apprehensions would appear to be groundless; for I had already found my spirits revive by the influence of her most august presence.

This was the sum of my speech, delivered with great improprieties and hesitation. The latter part was altogether framed

in the style peculiar to that people, whereof I learned some
phrases from Glumdalclitch, while she was carrying me to court.

The queen, giving great allowance for my defectiveness in
speaking, was, however, surprised at so much wit and good sense
in so diminutive an animal. She took me in her own hand, and
carried me to the king, who was then retired to his cabinet. His
majesty, a prince of much gravity and austere countenance, not
well observing my shape at first view, asked the queen, after a
cold manner, how long it was since she grew fond of a *splacnuck*?
For such, it seems, he took me to be, as I lay upon my breast in
her majesty's right hand. But this princess, who has an infinite
deal of wit and humour, set me gently on my feet upon the
scrutoire, and commanded me to give his majesty an account of
myself, which I did in a very few words: and Glumdalclitch, who
attended at the cabinet door, and could not endure I should be
out of her sight, being admitted, confirmed all that had passed
from my arrival at her father's house.

The king, although he is as learned a person as any in his
dominions, having been educated in the study of philosophy,
and particularly mathematics, yet when he observed my shape
exactly, and saw me walk erect, before I began to speak, conceived I might be a piece of clockwork (which has in that country
arrived to a very great perfection), contrived by some ingenious
artist. But when he heard my voice, and found what I delivered
to be regular and rational, he could not conceal his astonishment.
He was by no means satisfied with the relation I gave him of the
manner I came into his kingdom, but thought it a story concerted
between Glumdalclitch and her father, who had taught me a set
of words, to make me sell at a better price. Upon this imagination he put several other questions to me, and still received
rational answers: no otherwise defective than by a foreign accent
and an imperfect knowledge of the language, with some rustic
phrases which I had learned at the farmer's house, and did not
suit the polite style of a court.

His majesty sent for three great scholars, who were then in the
weekly waiting, according to the custom in that country. These
gentlemen, after they had examined my shape with much nicety,
were of different opinions concerning me. They all agreed that
I could not be produced according to the regular laws of Nature,

because I was not framed with a capacity of preserving my life, either by swiftness, or climbing of trees, or digging holes in the earth. They observed by my teeth, which they viewed with great exactness, that I was a carnivorous animal; yet most quadrupeds being an over-match for me, and field mice, with some others, too nimble, they could not imagine how I should be able to support myself, unless I fed upon snails and other insects, which they offered, by many learned arguments, to evince that I could not possibly do. One of these virtuosi seemed to think that I might be an embryo or abortive birth. But this opinion was rejected by the other two, who observed my limbs to be perfect and finished; and that I had lived several years, as it was manifest from my beard, the stumps whereof they plainly discovered through a magnifying-glass. They would not allow me to be a dwarf, because my littleness was beyond all degrees of comparison; for the queen's favourite dwarf, the smallest ever known in the kingdom, was nearly thirty feet high. After much debate, they concluded unanimously that I was only *relplum scalcath*, which is, interpreted literally, *lusus naturæ*; a determination exactly agreeable to the modern philosophy of Europe, whose professors, disdaining the old evasion of occult causes, whereby the followers of Aristotle endeavoured in vain to disguise their ignorance, have invented this wonderful solution of all difficulties, to the unspeakable advancement of human knowledge.

After this decisive conclusion, I entreated to be heard a word or two. I applied myself to the king, and assured his majesty that I came from a country which abounded with several millions of both sexes, and of my own stature; where the animals, trees, and houses were all in proportion, and where, by consequence, I might be as able to defend myself, and to find sustenance, as any of his majesty's subjects could do here; which I took for a full answer to those gentlemen's arguments. To this they only replied by a smile of contempt, saying that the farmer had instructed me very well in my lesson. The king, who had a much better understanding, dismissing his learned men, sent for the farmer, who, by good fortune, was not yet gone out of the town. Having therefore first examined him privately, and then confronted him with me and the young girl, his majesty began to think that what

we told him might possibly be true. He desired the queen to
order that a particular care should be taken of me; and was of
opinion that Glumdalclitch should still continue in her office of
tending me, because he observed we had great affection for each
other. A convenient apartment was provided for her at court;
she had a sort of governess appointed to take care of her education, a maid to dress her, and two other servants for menial
offices; but the care of me was wholly appropriated to herself.
The queen commanded her own cabinet-maker to contrive a box,
that might serve me for a bed-chamber, after the model that
Glumdalclitch and I should agree upon. This man was a most
ingenious artist; and according to my direction, in three weeks
finished for me a wooden chamber of sixteen feet square, and
twelve high, with sash-windows, a door, and two closets, like a
London bed-chamber. The board, that made the ceiling, was
to be lifted up and down by two hinges, to put in a bed ready
furnished by her majesty's upholsterer, which Glumdalclitch took
out every day to air, made it with her own hands, and letting it
down at night, locked up the roof over me. A nice workman, who
was famous for little curiosities, undertook to make me two chairs,
with backs and frames, of a substance not unlike ivory, and two
tables, with a cabinet to put my things in. The room was quilted
on all sides, as well as the floor and the ceiling, to prevent any
accident from the carelessness of those who carried me, and to
break the force of a jolt, when I went in a coach. I desired a lock
for my door, to prevent rats and mice from coming in. The smith,
after several attempts, made the smallest that ever was seen among
them, for I have known a larger at the gate of a gentleman's
house in England. I made a shift to keep the key in a pocket of
my own, fearing Glumdalclitch might lose it. The queen likewise ordered the thinnest silks that could be gotten, to make me
clothes, not much thicker than an English blanket, very cum-
brous till I was accustomed to them. They were after the fashion
of the kingdom, partly resembling the Persian, and partly the
Chinese, and are a very grave and decent habit.

The queen became so fond of my company, that she could not
dine without me. I had a table placed upon the same at which
her majesty ate, just at her elbow, and a chair to sit on. Glumdalclitch stood on a stool on the floor, near my table, to assist and

take care of me. I had an entire set of silver dishes and plates, and other necessaries, which, in proportion to those of the queen, were not much bigger than what I have seen in a London toy-shop, for the furniture of a baby-house: these my little nurse kept in her pocket in a silver box, and gave me at meals as I wanted them, always cleaning them herself. No person dined with the queen but the two princesses royal, the eldest sixteen years old, and the younger at that time thirteen and a month. Her majesty used to put a bit of meat upon one of my dishes, out of which I carved for myself, and her diversion was to see me eat in minia-ture; for the queen (who had indeed but a weak stomach) took up, at one mouthful, as much as a dozen English farmers could eat at a meal, which to me was for some time a very nauseous sight. She would craunch the wing of a lark, bones and all, between her teeth, although it were nine times as large as that of a full-grown turkey; and put a bit of bread in her mouth, as big as two twelve-penny loaves. She drank, out of a golden cup, above a hogshead at a draught. Her knives were twice as long as a scythe, set straight upon the handle. The spoons, forks, and other instruments were all in the same proportion. I remember, when Glumdalclitch carried me, out of curiosity, to see some of the tables at court, where ten or a dozen of those enormous knives and forks were lifted up together, I thought I had never till then beheld so terrible a sight.

It is the custom, that every Wednesday (which, as I have observed, is their Sabbath) the king and queen, with the royal issue of both sexes, dine together in the apartment of his majesty, to whom I was now become a great favourite; and at these times, my little chair and table were placed at his left hand, before one of the salt-cellars. This prince took a pleasure in conversing with me, inquiring into the manners, religion, laws, government, and learning of Europe; wherein I gave him the best account I was able. His apprehension was so clear, and his judgment so exact, that he made very wise reflections and observations upon all I said. But I confess, that after I had been a little too copious in talking of my own beloved country, of our trade and wars by sea and land, of our schisms in religion and parties in the state, the prejudices of his education prevailed so far, that he could not forbear taking me up in his right hand, and, stroking me gently with the other, after a hearty fit of laughing, asked me whether I was a Whig or a Tory? Then turning to his first minister, who waited behind him with a white staff nearly as tall as the main-mast of the *Royal Sovereign*, he observed how contemptible a thing was human grandeur, which could be mimicked by such diminutive insects as I: "and yet," says he, "I dare engage these creatures have their titles and distinctions of honour; they contrive little nests, and burrows, that they call houses and cities; they make a figure and dress in equipage; they love, they fight, they dispute, they cheat, they betray." And thus he continued, while my colour came and went several times, with indignation, to hear our noble country—the mistress of arts and arms; the scourge of France; the arbitress of Europe; the seat of virtue, piety, honour, and truth; the pride and envy of the world—so contemptuously treated.

But as I was not in a condition to resent injuries, so upon mature thoughts I began to doubt whether I was injured or no. For, after having been accustomed several months to the sight and converse of this people, and observed every object upon which I cast mine eyes to be of proportionable magnitude, the horror I had at first conceived from their bulk and aspect was so far worn off, that if I had then beheld a company of English lords and ladies in their finery and birthday clothes, acting their several parts in the most courtly manner of strutting, and bowing, and prating, to say the truth, I should have been strongly tempted to laugh as much at them as the king and his grandees did at me. Neither, indeed, could I forbear smiling at myself, when the queen used to place me upon her hand towards a looking-glass, by which both our persons appeared before me in full view together; and there could be nothing more ridiculous than the comparison; so that I really began to imagine myself dwindled many degrees below my usual size.

Nothing angered and mortified me so much as the queen's dwarf; who, being of the lowest stature that was ever in that country (for I verily think he was not full thirty feet high), became so insolent at seeing a creature so much beneath him, that he would always affect to swagger and look big as he passed by me in the queen's ante-chamber, while I was standing on some table talking with the lords or ladies of the court, and he seldom failed of a smart word or two upon my littleness; against which I could only revenge myself by calling him "brother," challenging him to wrestle, and such repartees as are usually in the mouths of court pages. One day at dinner, this malicious little cub was so nettled with something I had said to him, that, raising himself upon the frame of her majesty's chair, he took me up by the middle, as I was sitting down, not thinking any harm, and let me drop into a large silver bowl of cream, and then ran away as fast as he could. I fell over head and ears, and, if I had not been a good swimmer, it might have gone very hard with me; for Glumdalclitch at that instant happened to be at the other end of the room, and the queen was in such a fright, that she wanted presence of mind to assist me. But my little nurse ran to my relief, and took me out, after I had swallowed about a quart of cream. I was put to bed; however, I received no other damage than the loss of a suit of clothes, which were utterly spoiled. The dwarf was soundly whipped, and, as a further punishment, forced to drink up the bowl of cream into which he had thrown me, neither was he ever restored to favour; for soon after the queen bestowed him on a lady of high quality, so that I saw him no more, to my very great satisfaction: for I could not tell to what extremity such a malicious urchin might have carried his resentment.

He had before served me a scurvy trick, which set the queen a-laughing, although at the same time she was heartily vexed, and would have immediately cashiered him, if I had not been so generous as to intercede. Her majesty had taken a marrow-bone upon her plate, and, after knocking out the marrow, placed the bone again on the dish erect, as it stood before; the dwarf, watching his opportunity when Glumdalclitch was gone to the sideboard, mounted the stool that she stood on to take care of me at meals, took me up in both hands, and squeezing my legs together, wedged them into the marrow-bone above my waist, where I stuck for some time, and made a very ridiculous figure. I believe it was near a minute before any one knew what was become of me; for I thought it below me to cry out. But, as princes seldom get their meat hot, my legs were not scalded, only my stockings and breeches were in a sad condition. The dwarf, at my entreaty, had no other punishment than a sound whipping.

D

I was frequently rallied by the queen upon account of my fearfulness; and she used to ask me whether the people of my country were as great cowards as myself. The occasion was this: the kingdom is much pestered with flies in summer; and these odious insects, each of them as big as a Dunstable lark, hardly gave me any rest while I sat at dinner, with their continual humming and buzzing about mine ears. They would sometimes alight upon my victuals, and they would fix upon my nose or forehead, where they stung me to the quick, smelling very offensively; and I could easily trace that viscous matter which, our naturalists tell us, enables those creatures to walk with their feet upwards upon a ceiling. I had much ado to defend myself against these detestable animals, and could not forbear starting when they came on my face. It was the common practice of the dwarf to catch a number of these insects in his hand, as schoolboys do among us, and let them out suddenly under my nose, on purpose to frighten me, and divert the queen. My remedy was to cut them in pieces with my knife, as they flew in the air, wherein my dexterity was much admired.

I remember, one morning, when Glumdalclitch had set me in a box upon a window, as she usually did in fair days, to give me air (for I durst not venture to let the box be hung on a nail out of the window, as we do with cages in England), after I had lifted up one of my sashes, and sat down at my table to eat a piece of sweet cake for my breakfast, above twenty wasps, allured by the smell, came flying into the room, humming louder than the drones of as many bagpipes. Some of them seized my cake, and carried it piecemeal away: others flew about my head and face, confounding me with their noise, and putting me in the utmost terror of their stings. However, I had the courage to rise and draw my hanger, and attack them in the air. I dispatched four of them, but the rest got away, and I presently shut my window. These insects are as large as partridges: I took out their stings, and found them an inch and a half long, and as sharp as needles. I carefully preserved them all; and having since shown them, with other curiosities, in several parts of Europe, upon my return to England I gave three to Gresham College, and kept the fourth for myself.

CHAPTER IV

THE COUNTRY DESCRIBED—A PROPOSAL FOR CORRECTING MODERN
MAPS—THE KING'S PALACE, AND SOME ACCOUNT OF THE
METROPOLIS—THE AUTHOR'S WAY OF TRAVELLING—THE
CHIEF TEMPLE DESCRIBED

I NOW intend to give the reader a short description of this country,
as far as I travelled in it which was not above two thousand miles
round Lorbrulgrud, the metropolis. For the queen, whom I
always attended, never went farther when she accompanied the
king in his progresses, and there stayed till his majesty returned
from viewing his frontiers. The whole extent of this prince's
dominions reaches about six thousand miles in length, and from
three to five in breadth: whence I cannot but conclude that our
geographers of Europe are in a great error, by supposing nothing
but sea between Japan and California; for it was ever my opinion
that there must be a balance of earth to counterpoise the great
continent of Tartary; and therefore they ought to correct their
maps and charts, by joining this vast tract of land to the north-
west parts of America, wherein I shall be ready to lend them my
assistance.

The kingdom is a peninsula, terminating to the north-east of
a ridge of mountains thirty miles high, which are altogether im-
passable, by reason of the volcanoes upon the tops: neither do the
most learned know what sort of mortals inhabit beyond those
mountains, or whether they be inhabited at all. On the three
other sides, it is bounded by the ocean. There is not one sea-port
in the whole kingdom; and those parts of the coast into which
the rivers issue are so full of pointed rocks, and the sea generally
so rough, that there is no venturing with the smallest of their
boats; so that these people are wholly excluded from any commerce with the rest of the world. But the large rivers are full of
vessels, and abound with excellent fish: for they seldom get any
from the sea, because the sea-fish are of the same size with those
in Europe, and consequently not worth catching; whereby it is

manifest that Nature, in the production of plants and animals of
so extraordinary a bulk, is wholly confined to this continent, of
which I leave the reasons to be determined by philosophers.
However, now and then they take a whale that happens to be
dashed against the rocks, which the common people feed on
heartily. These whales I have known so large, that a man could
hardly carry one upon his shoulders; and sometimes, for curiosity,
they are brought in hampers to Lorbrulgrud: I saw one of them
in a dish at the king's table, which passed for a rarity, but I did
not observe he was fond of it; for, I think indeed, the bigness
disgusted him, although I have seen one somewhat larger in
Greenland.

The country is well inhabited, for it contains fifty-one cities,
near a hundred walled towns, and a great number of villages.
To satisfy my curious reader, it may be sufficient to describe
Lorbrulgrud. The city stands upon almost two equal parts, on
each side the river that passes through. It contains about eighty
thousand houses, and about six hundred thousand inhabitants.
It is in length three *glomglungs* (which make about fifty-four
English miles), and two and a half in breadth; as I measured it
myself in the royal map made by the king's order, which was
laid on the ground on purpose for me, and extended a hundred
feet: I paced the diameter and circumference several times bare-
foot, and computing by the scale, measured it pretty exactly.

The king's palace is no regular edifice, but a heap of buildings,
about seven miles round: the chief rooms are generally two
hundred and forty feet high, and broad and long in proportion.
A coach was allowed to Glumdalclitch and me, wherein her
governess frequently took her out to see the town, or go among
the shops; and I was always of the party, carried in my box;
although the girl, at my own desire, would often take me out,
and hold me in her hand, that I might more conveniently view
the houses and the people, as we passed along the streets. I
reckoned our coach to be about the square of Westminster Hall,
but not altogether so high: however, I cannot be very exact.
One day the governess ordered the coachman to stop at several
shops, where the beggars, watching their opportunity, crowded
to the sides of the coach, and gave me the most horrible spectacle
that ever a European eye beheld. There was a fellow with a wen

in his neck, larger than five woolpacks; and another with a couple of wooden legs, each about twenty feet high. But the most hateful sight of all was the insects crawling on their clothes.

Besides the large box in which I was usually carried, the queen ordered a smaller one to be made for me, of about twelve feet square, and ten high, for the convenience of travelling; because the other was somewhat too large for Glumdalclitch's lap, and cumbersome in the coach; it was made by the same artist, whom I directed in the whole contrivance. This travelling closet was an exact square, with a window in the middle of three of the squares, and each window was latticed with iron wire on the outside, to prevent accidents in long journeys. On the fourth side, which had no window, two strong staples were fixed, through which the person who carried me, when I had a mind to be on horseback, put a leathern belt, and buckled it about his waist. This was always the office of some grave and trusty servant, in whom I could confide, whether I attended the king and queen in their progresses, or were disposed to see the gardens, or pay a visit to some great lady or minister of state in the court, when Glumdalclitch happened to be out of order; for I soon began to be known and esteemed among the greatest officers, I suppose more upon account of their majesties' favour than any merit of my own. In journeys, when I was weary of the coach, a servant on horseback would buckle on my box, and place it upon a cushion before him; and there I had a full prospect of the country on three sides, from my three windows. I had, in this closet, a field-bed and a hammock hung from the ceiling, two chairs and a table, neatly screwed to the floor, to prevent being tossed about by the agitation of the horse or the coach. And having been long used to sea voyages, these motions, although sometimes very violent, did not much discompose me.

Whenever I had a mind to see the town, it was always in my travelling closet; which Glumdalclitch held in her lap in a kind of open sedan, after the fashion of the country, borne by four men, and attended by two others in the queen's livery. The people, who had often heard of me, were very curious to crowd about the sedan; and the girl was complaisant enough to make the bearers stop, and to take me in her hand, that I might be more conveniently seen.

I was very desirous to see the chief temple, and particularly the tower belonging to it, which is reckoned the highest in the kingdom. Accordingly, one day my nurse carried me thither, but I may truly say I came back disappointed for the height is not above three thousand feet, reckoning from the ground to the highest pinnacle top; which, allowing for the difference between the size of those people and us in Europe, is no great matter for admiration, nor at all equal in proportion (if I rightly remember) to Salisbury steeple. But, not to detract from a nation to which, during my life, I shall acknowledge myself extremely obliged, it must be allowed, that whatever this famous tower wants in height is amply made up in beauty and strength; for the walls are near a hundred feet thick, built of hewn stone, whereof each is about forty feet square, and adorned on all sides with statues of gods and emperors, cut in marble, larger than life, placed in their several niches. I measured a little finger which had fallen down from one of these statues, and lay unperceived among some rubbish, and found it exactly four feet and an inch in length. Glumdalclitch wrapped it up in her handkerchief; and carried it home in her pocket, to keep among other trinkets of which the girl was very fond, as children at her age usually are.

The king's kitchen is indeed a noble building, vaulted at top, and about six hundred feet high. The great oven is not so wide, by ten paces, as the cupola at St. Paul's: for I measured the latter on purpose, after my return. But if I should describe the kitchen grate, the prodigious pots and kettles, the joints of meat turned on the spits, with many other particulars, perhaps I should be hardly believed: at least, a severe critic would be apt to think I enlarged a little, as travellers are often suspected to do. To avoid which censure, I fear I have run too much into the other extreme; and that if this treatise should happen to be translated into the language of Brobdingnag (which is the general name of that kingdom), and transmitted thither, the king and his people would have reason to complain that I had done them an injury, by a false and diminutive representation.

His majesty seldom keeps above six hundred horses in his stables: they are generally from fifty-four to sixty feet high. But when he goes abroad on solemn days, he is attended, for state, by a militia guard of five hundred horse, which, indeed, I thought

was the most splendid sight that could be ever beheld, till I saw
part of his army in battalia, whereof I shall find another occasion
to speak.

CHAPTER V

SEVERAL ADVENTURES THAT HAPPENED TO THE AUTHOR—THE
   EXECUTION OF A CRIMINAL—THE AUTHOR SHOWS HIS SKILL
   IN NAVIGATION

I SHOULD have lived happy enough in that country, if my littleness had not exposed me to several ridiculous and troublesome
accidents: some of which I shall venture to relate. Glumdalclitch
often carried me into the gardens of the court in my smaller box,
and would sometimes take me out of it, and hold me in her hand,
or set me down to walk. I remember, before the dwarf left the
queen, he followed us one day into those gardens, and my nurse
having set me down, he and I being close together, near some
dwarf apple-trees, I must needs show my wit, by a silly allusion
between him and the trees, which happens to hold in their
language as it does in ours. Whereupon, the malicious rogue,
watching his opportunity, when I was walking under one of
them, shook it directly over my head, by which a dozen apples,
each of them near as large as a Bristol barrel, came tumbling
about my ears; one of them hit me on the back as I chanced to
stoop, and knocked me down flat on my face; but I received no
other hurt, and the dwarf was pardoned at my desire, because I
had given the provocation.

Another day, Glumdalclitch left me on a smooth grass-plot to
divert myself, while she walked at some distance with her governess. In the meantime there suddenly fell such a violent shower
of hail, that I was immediately, by the force of it, struck to the
ground: and when I was down, the hailstones gave me such cruel
bangs all over the body, as if I had been pelted with tennis-balls;
however, I made a shift to creep on all fours, and shelter myself,
by lying flat on my face, on the lee-side of a border of lemon-
thyme; but so bruised from head to foot, that I could not go

abroad for ten days. Neither is this at all to be wondered at, because Nature, in that country, observing the same proportion through all her operations, a hailstone is near eighteen hundred times as large as one in Europe; which I can assert upon experience, having been so curious as to weigh and measure them.

But a more dangerous accident happened to me in the same garden, where my little nurse, believing she had put me in a secure place (which I often entreated her to do, that I might enjoy my own thoughts), and having left the box at home, to avoid the trouble of carrying it, went to another part of the garden with her governess and some ladies of her acquaintance. While she was absent, and out of hearing, a small spaniel that belonged to one of the chief gardeners, having got by accident into the garden, happened to range near the place where I lay; the dog, following the scent, came directly up, and taking me in his mouth, ran straight to his master wagging his tail, and set me gently on the ground. By good fortune he had been so well taught, that I was carried between his teeth without the least hurt, or even tearing my clothes. But the poor gardener, who knew me well, and had a great kindness for me, was in a terrible fright: he gently took me up in both his hands, and asked me how I did; but I was so amazed and out of breath, that I could not speak a word. In a few minutes I came to myself, and he carried me safe to my little nurse, who, by this time, had returned to the place where she left me, and was in cruel agonies when I did not appear, nor answer when she called. She severely reprimanded the gardener on account of his dog. But the thing was hushed up, and never known at court, for the girl was afraid of the queen's anger; and truly, as to myself, I thought it would not be for my reputation that such a story should go about.

This accident determined Glumdalclitch never to trust me abroad, for the future, out of her sight. I had been long afraid of this resolution, and therefore concealed from her some little unlucky adventures that happened in those times when I was left by myself. Once a kite, hovering over the garden, made a swoop at me, and if I had not resolutely drawn my hanger, and run under a thick espalier, he would have certainly carried me away in his talons. Another time, walking to the top of a fresh mole-hill, I fell to my neck in the hole through which that animal had cast up the earth; and coined a reason, not worth remembering, to excuse myself for spoiling my clothes. I likewise broke my right shin against the shell of a snail, which I happened to stumble over, as I was walking along and thinking on poor England.

I cannot tell whether I was more pleased or mortified to observe, in these solitary walks, that the smaller birds did not appear to be at all afraid of me, but would hop about within a yard's distance, looking for worms and other food, with as much indifference and security as if no creature at all were near them. I remember, a thrush had the confidence to snatch out of my hand, with his bill, a piece of cake, that Glumdalclitch had just given me for my breakfast. When I attempted to catch any of these birds, they would boldly turn against me, endeavouring to peck my fingers, which I durst not venture within their reach; and then they would hop back unconcerned, to hunt for worms or snails, as they did before. But one day I took a thick cudgel, and threw it with all my strength, so luckily, at a linnet, that I knocked him down, and seizing him by the neck with both my hands, ran with him in triumph to my nurse. However, the bird, who had been only stunned, recovering himself, gave me so many boxes with his wings, on both sides of my head and body, though I held him at arm's length, and was out of the reach of his claws, that I was twenty times thinking to let him go. But I was soon relieved by one of our servants, who wrung off the bird's neck, and I had him next day for dinner, by the queen's command. This linnet, as near as I can remember, seemed to be somewhat larger than an English swan.

The maids of honour often invited Glumdalclitch to their apartments, and desired she would bring me along with her, on purpose to have the pleasure of seeing and touching me. To me their endearments were very disgusting, which I do not mention or intend to the disadvantage of those excellent ladies, for whom I have all manner of respect; but I conceive that my sense was more acute in proportion to my littleness, and that those illustrious persons were no more disagreeable to their lovers, or to each other, than people of the same quality are with us in England. And after all, I found the natural odour of their skin was much more supportable, than when they used perfumes, under which I immediately swooned away. I cannot forget that

an intimate friend of mine in Lilliput took the freedom, in a warm
day, when I had used a good deal of exercise, to complain of a
strong smell about me, although I am as little faulty that way as
most of my sex; but I suppose his faculty of smelling was as nice
with regard to me, as mine was to that of this people. Upon this
point, I cannot forbear doing justice to the queen, my mistress,
and Glumdalclitch, my nurse, whose persons were as sweet as
those of any lady in England.

One day, a young gentleman, who was nephew to my nurse's
governess, came and pressed them both to see an execution. It
was of a man, who had murdered one of that gentleman's intimate acquaintance. Glumdalclitch was prevailed on to be of the
company, very much against her inclination, for she was naturally tender-hearted: and as for myself, although I abhorred such
kind of spectacles, yet my curiosity tempted me to see something
that I thought must be extraordinary. The malefactor was fixed
in a chair upon a scaffold erected for that purpose, and his head
cut off at one blow, with a sword of forty feet long. The veins
and arteries spouted up such a prodigious quantity of blood,
and so high in the air, that the great *jet d'eau* at Versailles was not
equal, for the time it lasted; and the head, when it fell upon the
scaffold floor, gave such a bounce as made me start, although I
was at least half an English mile distant.

The queen, who often used to hear me talk of sea-voyages, and
took all occasions to divert me when I was melancholy, asked me
whether I understood how to handle a sail or an oar, and whether
a little exercise of rowing might not be convenient for my health.
I answered that I understood both very well; for although my
proper employment had been to be surgeon or doctor to the ship,
yet often, upon a pinch, I was forced to work like a common
mariner. But I could not see how this could be done in their
country, where the smallest wherry was equal to a first-rate man
of war among us; and such a boat as I could manage would never
live in any of their rivers. Her majesty said, if I would contrive a
boat, her own joiner should make it, and she would provide a place
for me to sail in. The fellow was an ingenious workman, and by
my instructions, in ten days, finished a pleasure-boat, with all
its tackling, able conveniently to hold eight Europeans. When
it was finished, the queen was so delighted, that she ran with it

in her lap to the king, who ordered it to be put in a cistern full of water, with me in it, by the way of trial; where I could not manage my two sculls, or little oars, for want of room. But the queen had before contrived another project. She ordered the joiner to make a wooden trough of three hundred feet long, fifty broad, and eight deep; which being well pitched, to prevent leaking, was placed on the floor along the wall, in an outer room of the palace. It had a tap near the bottom, to let out the water, when it began to grow stale; and two servants could easily fill it in half an hour. Here I often used to row for my own diversion, as well as that of the queen and her ladies, who thought themselves well entertained with my skill and agility. Sometimes I would put up my sail, and then my business was only to steer, while the ladies gave me a gale with their fans; and when they were weary, some of their pages would blow my sail forward with their breath, while I showed my art by steering starboard or larboard as I pleased. When I had done, Glumdalclitch always carried back my boat into her closet, and hung it on a nail to dry.

In this exercise I once met with an accident, which had like to have cost me my life; for one of the pages having put my boat into the trough, the governess who attended Glumdalclitch very officiously lifted me up, to place me in the boat; but I happened to slip through her fingers, and should infallibly have fallen down forty feet, upon the floor, if, by the luckiest chance in the world I had not been stopped by a corking-pin that stuck in the good gentlewoman's stomacher; the head of the pin passed between my shirt and the waistband of my breeches, and thus I was held by the middle in the air, till Glumdalclitch ran to my relief.

Another time, one of the servants, whose office it was to fill my trough every third day with fresh water, was so careless as to let a huge frog (not perceiving it) slip out of his pail. The frog lay concealed till I was put into my boat, but then, seeing a resting-place, climbed up, and made it lean so much on one side, that I was forced to balance it with all my weight on the other, to prevent overturning. When the frog was got in, it hopped at once half the length of the boat, and then over my head, backward and forward, daubing my face and clothes with its odious slime. The largeness of its features made it appear the most deformed animal that can be conceived. However, I desired

Glumdalclitch to let me deal with it alone. I banged it a good while with one of my sculls, and at last forced it to leap out of the boat.

But the greatest danger I ever underwent in that kingdom was from a monkey, who belonged to one of the clerks of the kitchen. Glumdalclitch had locked me up in her closet, while she went somewhere upon business, or a visit. The weather being very warm, the closet window was left open, as well as the windows and the door of my bigger box, in which I usually lived, because of its largeness and conveniency. As I sat quietly meditating at my table, I heard something bounce in at the closet window, and skip about from one side to the other: whereat, although I was much alarmed, yet I ventured to look out, but not stirring from my seat; and then I saw this frolicsome animal frisking and leaping up and down, till at last he came to my box, which he seemed to view with great pleasure and curiosity, peeping in at the door and every window. I retreated to the farther corner of my room, or box; but the monkey, looking in at every side, put me into such a fright, that I wanted presence of mind to conceal myself under the bed, as I might easily have done. After some time spent in peeping, grinning, and chattering, he at last espied me; and reaching one of his paws in at the door, as a cat does when she plays with a mouse, although I often shifted place to avoid him, he at length seized the lappet of my coat (which, being made of that country silk, was very thick and strong), and dragged me out. He took me up in his right forefoot and held me as a nurse does a child she is going to suckle, just as I have seen the same sort of creature do with a kitten in Europe: and when I offered to struggle, he squeezed me so hard, that I thought it more prudent to submit. I have good reason to believe that he took me for a young one of his own species, by his often stroking my face very gently with his other paw. In these diversions he was interrupted by a noise at the closet-door, as if somebody was opening it: whereupon he suddenly leaped up to the window, at which he had come in, and thence upon the leads and gutters, walking upon three legs, and holding me in the fourth, till he clambered up a roof next to ours. I heard Glumdalclitch give a shriek at the moment he was carrying me out. The poor girl was almost distracted: that quarter of the palace was all in an uproar; the servants ran for ladders: the monkey was seen by hundreds in the court, sitting upon the ridge of a building, holding me like a baby in one of his forepaws, and feeding me with the other, by cramming into my mouth some victuals he had squeezed out of the bag on one side of his chaps, and patting me when I would not eat; whereat many of the rabble below could not forbear laughing; neither do I think they justly ought to be blamed, for without question, the sight was ridiculous enough to everybody but myself. Some of the people threw up stones, hoping to drive the monkey down: but this was strictly forbidden, or else, very probably, my brains had been dashed out.

The ladders were now applied, and mounted by several men; which the monkey observing, and finding himself almost encompassed, not being able to make speed enough with his three legs, let me drop on a ridge tile, and made his escape. Here I sat for some time, five hundred yards from the ground, expecting every moment to be blown down by the wind, or to fall by my own giddiness, and come tumbling over and over from the ridge to the eaves: but an honest lad, one of my nurse's footmen, climbed up, and putting me into his breeches pocket, brought me down safe.

I was almost choked with the filthy stuff the monkey crammed down my throat: but my dear little nurse picked it out of my mouth with a small needle, and then I fell a-vomiting, which gave me great relief. Yet I was so weak and bruised in the sides with the squeezes given me by this odious animal, that I was forced to keep my bed a fortnight. The king, queen, and all the court sent every day to inquire after my health; and her majesty made me several visits during my sickness. The monkey was killed, and an order made that no such animal should be kept about the palace.

When I attended the king after my recovery, to return him thanks for his favours, he was pleased to rally me a good deal upon this adventure. He asked me what my thoughts and speculations were, while I lay in the monkey's paw; how I liked the victuals he gave me; his manner of feeding; and whether the fresh air on the roof had sharpened my stomach. He desired to know what I would have done upon such an occasion in my own country. I told his majesty that in Europe we had no monkeys, except such as were brought as curiosities from other places, and so small that I could deal with a dozen of them together, if they presumed to attack me. And as for that monstrous animal with whom I was so lately engaged (it was, indeed, as large as an elephant), if my fears had suffered me to think so far as to make use of my hanger (looking fiercely, and clapping my hand upon the hilt as I spoke), when he poked his paw into my chamber, perhaps I should have given him such a wound as would have made him glad to withdraw it with more haste than he put it in. This I delivered in a firm tone, like a person who was jealous lest his courage should be called in question. However, my speech produced nothing else besides a loud laughter, which all the respect due to his majesty from those about him could not make them contain. This made me reflect how vain an attempt it is for a man to endeavour to do himself honour among those who are out of all degrees of equality or comparison with him. And yet I have seen the moral of my own behaviour very frequent in England since my return; where a little contemptible varlet, without the least title to birth, person, wit, or common sense, shall presume to look with importance, and put himself upon a footing with the greatest person of the kingdom.

I was every day furnishing the court with some ridiculous story, and Glumdalclitch, although she loved me to excess, yet was arch enough to inform the queen whenever I committed any folly that she thought would be diverting to her majesty. The girl, who had been out of order, was carried by her governess to take the air about an hour's distance, or thirty miles from town. They alighted out of the coach near a small footpath in a field, and Glumdalclitch setting down my travelling box, I went out of it to walk. There was a small heap of dirt in the path, and I must needs try my activity by attempting to leap over it. I took a run, but unfortunately jumped short, and found myself just in the middle, up to my knees. I waded through with some difficulty, and one of the footmen wiped me as clean as he could with his handkerchief, for I was filthily bemired; and my nurse confined me to my box till we returned home, when the queen was soon informed of what had passed, and the footman spread it about the court; so that all the mirth for some days was at my expense.

CHAPTER VI

SEVERAL CONTRIVANCES OF THE AUTHOR TO PLEASE THE KING
AND QUEEN—HE SHOWS HIS SKILL IN MUSIC—THE KING
INQUIRES INTO THE STATE OF ENGLAND, WHICH THE AUTHOR
RELATES TO HIM—THE KING'S OBSERVATIONS THEREON

I USED to attend the king's levee once or twice a week, and had
often seen him under the barber's hand, which indeed was at
first very terrible to behold: for the razor was almost twice as
long as an ordinary scythe.

His majesty, according to the custom of the country, was only
shaved twice a week. I once prevailed on the barber to give me
some of the suds or lather, out of which I picked forty or fifty of
the strongest stumps of hair. I then took a piece of fine wood,
and cut it like the back of a comb, making several holes in it at
equal distances with as small a needle as I could get from Glumdalclitch. I fixed in the stumps so artifically, scraping and sloping
them with my knife towards the points, that I made a very tolerable comb; which was a seasonable supply, my own being so
much broken in the teeth that it was almost useless: neither did
I know any artist in that country so nice and exact as would
undertake to make me another.

And this puts me in mind of an amusement wherein I spent
many of my leisure hours. I desired the queen's woman to save
for me the combings of her majesty's hair, whereof in time I got
a good quantity; and consulting with my friend the cabinet-
maker, who had received general orders to do little jobs for me,
I directed him to make two chair-frames, no larger than those I
had in my box, and to bore little holes with a fine awl round
those parts where I designed the backs and seats; through these
holes I wove the strongest hairs I could pick out, just after the
manner of the cane-chairs in England. When they were finished,
I made a present of them to her majesty, who kept them in her
cabinet, and used to show them for curiosities, as, indeed, they
were the wonder of every one that beheld them. The queen

would have had me sit upon one of these chairs, but I absolutely
refused to obey her, protesting I would rather die a thousand
deaths than sit contemptuously upon those precious hairs that
once adorned her majesty's head. Of these hairs (as I had always
a mechanical genius) I likewise made a neat little purse, about
five feet long, with her majesty's name deciphered in gold letters,
which I gave to Glumdalclitch by the queen's consent. To say
the truth, it was more for show than use, being not of strength to
bear the weight of the larger coins, and therefore she kept nothing
in it but some little toys that girls are fond of.

The king, who delighted in music, had frequent concerts at
court, to which I was sometimes carried, and set in my box on
the table to hear them; but the noise was so great that I could
hardly distinguish the tunes. I am confident that all the drums
and trumpets of the royal army, beating and sounding together
just at your ears, could not equal it. My practice was to have my
box removed from the place where the performers sat, as far as I
could; then to shut the doors and windows of it, and draw the
window curtains; after which I found their music not disagreeable.

I had learned in my youth to play a little upon the spinet.
Glumdalclitch kept one in her chamber, and a master attended
twice a week to teach her: I called it a spinet, because it somewhat resembled that instrument, and was played upon in the
same manner. A fancy came into my head that I would entertain
the king and queen with an English tune upon this instrument.
But this appeared extremely difficult; for the spinet was near
sixty feet long, each key being almost a foot wide, so that with my
arms extended I could not reach to above five keys; and to press
them down required a good smart stroke with my fist, which
would be too great a labour, and to no purpose. The method
I contrived was this: I prepared two round sticks, about the
bigness of common cudgels; they were thicker at one end than
the other, and I covered the thicker ends with pieces of a mouse's
skin, that by rapping on them I might neither damage the tops
of the keys nor interrupt the sound. Before the spinet a bench was
placed, about four feet below the keys, and I was put upon the
bench. I ran sideling upon it, that way and this, as fast as I
could, banging the proper keys with my two sticks, and made a

shift to play a jig, to the great satisfaction of both their majesties; but it was the most violent exercise that I ever underwent; and yet I could not strike above sixteen keys, nor consequently play the bass and treble together, as other artists do; which was a great disadvantage to my performance.

The king, who, as I before observed, was a prince of excellent understanding, would frequently order that I should be brought in my box, and set upon the table in his closet; he would then command me to bring one of my chairs out of my box, and sit down within three yards' distance upon the top of the cabinet, which brought me almost to a level with his face. In this manner I had several conversations with him. I one day took the freedom to tell his majesty that the contempt he discovered towards Europe and the rest of the world did not seem answerable to those excellent qualities of mind that he was master of; that reason did not extend itself with the bulk of the body; on the contrary, we observed in our country that the tallest persons were usually the least provided with it: that among other animals, bees and ants had the reputation of more industry, art, and sagacity than many of the larger kinds; and that, as inconsiderable as he took me to be, I hoped I might live to do his majesty some signal service. The king heard me with attention, and began to conceive a much better opinion of me than he had ever before. He desired I would give him as exact an account of the government of England as I possibly could; because, as fond as princes commonly are of their own customs (for so he conjectured of other monarchs by my former discourses), he should be glad to hear of anything that might deserve imitation.

Imagine with thyself, courteous reader, how often I then wished for the tongue of Demosthenes or Cicero, that might have enabled me to celebrate the praise of my own dear native country, in a style equal to its merits and felicity.

I began my discourse by informing his majesty that our dominions consisted of two islands, which composed three mighty kingdoms, under one sovereign, besides our plantations in America. I dwelt long upon the fertility of our soil and the temperature of our climate. I then spoke at large upon the constitution of an English Parliament; partly made up of an illustrious body, called the House of Peers—persons of the noblest blood, and of the most ancient and ample patrimonies. I described that extraordinary care was always taken of their education in arts and arms, to qualify them for being counsellors both to the king and kingdom; to have a share in the legislature; to be members of the highest court of judicature, whence there can be no appeal; and to be champions always ready for the defence of their prince and country, by their valour, conduct, and fidelity. That these were the ornament and bulwark of the kingdom, worthy followers of their most renowned ancestors, whose honour had been the reward of their virtue, from which their posterity were never once known to degenerate. To these were joined several holy persons, as part of that assembly, under the title of bishops, whose peculiar business is to take care of religion and of those who instruct the people therein. These were searched and sought out through the whole nation, by the prince and his wisest counsellors, among such of the priesthood as were most deservedly distinguished by the sanctity of their life and the depth of their erudition; who were, indeed, the spiritual fathers of the clergy and the people.

That the other part of the Parliament consisted of an assembly called the House of Commons, who were all principal gentlemen, freely picked and culled out by the people themselves, by their great abilities and love of their country, to represent the wisdom of the whole nation. And that these two bodies made up the most august assembly in Europe, to whom, in conjunction with the prince, the whole legislature is committed.

I then descended to the courts of justice; over which the judges, those venerable sages and interpreters of the law, presided, for determining the disputed rights and properties of men, as well as for the punishment of vice and protection of innocence. I mentioned the prudent management of our treasury; the valour and achievements of our forces, by sea and land. I computed the number of our people, by reckoning how many millions there might be of each religious sect or political party among us. I did not omit even our sports and pastimes, or any other particular which I thought might redound to the honour of my country. And I finished all with a brief historical account of affairs and events in England for about a hundred years past.

This conversation was not ended under five audiences, each of several hours; and the king heard the whole with great attention, frequently taking notes of what I spoke, as well as memorandums of what questions he intended to ask me.

When I had put an end to these long discourses, his majesty, in a sixth audience, consulted his notes, proposed many doubts, queries, and objections upon every article. He asked what methods were used to cultivate the minds and bodies of our young nobility, and in what kind of business they commonly spent the first and most teachable part of their lives; what course was taken to supply that assembly, when any noble family became extinct; what qualifications were necessary in those who are to be created new lords—whether the humour of the prince, a sum of money to a court lady, or a design of strengthening a party opposite to the public interest, ever happened to be the motive in those advancements; what share of knowledge these lords had in the laws of their country, and how they come by it, so as to enable them to decide the properties of their fellow-subjects, in the last resort; whether they were always so free from avarice, partialities, or want, that a bribe, or some other sinister view, could have no place among them; whether those holy lords I spoke of were always promoted to that rank on account of their knowledge in religious matters, and the sanctity of their lives— had never been compliers with the times, while they were common priests, or slavish, prostitute chaplains to some nobleman, whose opinions they continued servilely to follow, after they were admitted into that assembly.

He then desired to know what arts were practised in electing those whom I called commoners—whether a stranger, with a strong purse, might not influence the vulgar voters to choose him before their own landlord, or the most considerable gentleman in the neighbourhood; how it came to pass that people were so violently bent upon getting into this assembly, which I allowed to be a great trouble and expense, often to the ruin of their families, without any salary or pension—because this appeared such an exalted strain of virtue and public spirit, that his majesty seemed to doubt it might possibly not be always sincere. And he desired to know whether such zealous gentlemen could have any views of re-funding themselves for the charges and trouble they were at, by sacrificing the public good to the designs of a weak and vicious prince, in conjunction with a corrupted ministry. He multiplied his questions, and sifted me thoroughly upon every part of this head, proposing numberless inquiries and objections, which I think it not prudent or convenient to repeat.

Upon what I said in relation to our courts of justice, his majesty desired to be satisfied in several points: and this I was the better able to do, having been formerly almost ruined by a long suit in Chancery, which was decreed for me with costs. He asked what time was usually spent in determining between right and wrong, and what degree of expense; whether advocates and orators had liberty to plead in causes manifestly known to be unjust, vexatious, or oppressive; whether party, in religion or politics, was observed to be of any weight in the scale of justice; whether those pleading orators were persons educated in the general knowledge of equity, or only in provincial, national, and other local customs; whether they or their judges had any part in penning those laws, which they assumed the liberty of interpreting, and glossing upon at their pleasure; whether they had ever, at different times, pleaded for and against the same cause, and cited precedents to prove contrary opinions; whether they were a rich or a poor corporation; whether they received any pecuniary reward for pleading or delivering their opinions; and particularly, whether they were ever admitted as members in the lower senate.

He fell next upon the management of our treasury; and said he thought my memory failed me, because I computed our taxes at about five or six millions a year, and when I came to mention the issues, he found they sometimes amounted to more than double; for the notes he had taken were very particular in this point, because he hoped, as he told me, that the knowledge of our conduct might be useful to him, and he could not be deceived in his calculations. But, if what I told him were true, he was still at a loss how a kingdom could run out of its estate, like a private person. He asked me who were our creditors, and where we found money to pay them. He wondered to hear me talk of such chargeable and expensive wars; that certainly we must be a quarrelsome people, or live among very bad neighbours, and that our generals must needs be richer than our kings. He asked what business we had out of our own islands, unless upon the score of trade, or treaty, or to defend the coast with our fleets.

Above all, he was amazed to hear me talk of a mercenary standing army, in the midst of peace and among a free people. He said, if we were governed by our own consent, in the persons of our representatives, he could not imagine of whom we were afraid, or against whom we were to fight; and would hear my opinion, whether a private man's house might not be better defended by himself, his children, and family, than by half-a-dozen rascals, picked up at a venture in the streets for small wages, who might get a hundred times more by cutting their throats.

He laughed at my odd kind of arithmetic, as he was pleased to call it, in reckoning the numbers of our people by a computation drawn from the several sects among us in religion and politics. He said, he knew no reason why those who entertain opinions prejudicial to the public should be obliged to change, or should not be obliged to conceal them. And as it was tyranny in any government to require the first, so it was weakness not to enforce the second: for a man may be allowed to keep poisons in his closet, but not to vend them for cordials.

He observed, that among the diversions of our nobility and gentry, I had mentioned gaming: he desired to know at what age this entertainment was usually taken up, and when it was laid down; how much of their time it employed; whether it ever went so high as to affect their fortunes; whether mean, vicious people, by their dexterity in that art, might not arrive at great riches, and sometimes keep our very nobles in dependence, as well as habituate them to vile companions; wholly take them from the improvement of their mind, and force them, by the losses they received, to learn and practise that infamous dexterity upon others.

He was perfectly astonished with the historical account I gave him of our affairs during the last century; protesting it was only a heap of conspiracies, rebellions, murders, massacres, revolutions, banishments; the very worst effects that avarice, faction, hypocrisy, perfidiousness, cruelty, rage, madness, hatred, envy, lust, malice, and ambition could produce.

His majesty, in another audience, was at the pains to recapitulate the sum of all I had spoken; compared the questions he made with the answers I had given; then, taking me into his hands, and stroking me gently, delivering himself in these words, which

I shall never forget, nor the manner he spoke them in: "My little friend Grildrig, you have made a most admirable panegyric upon your country; you have clearly proved that ignorance, idleness, and vice are the proper ingredients for qualifying a legislator; that laws are best explained, interpreted, and applied by those whose interest and abilities lie in perverting, confounding, and eluding them. I observe among you some lines of an institution, which in its original might have been tolerable, but these half erased, and the rest wholly blurred and blotted by corruption. It does not appear, from all you have said, how any one perfection is required towards the procurement of any one station among you; much less, that men are ennobled on account of their virtue; that priests are advanced for their piety or learning; soldiers, for their conduct or valour; judges, for their integrity, senators, for the love of their country; or counsellors for their wisdom.

"As for yourself," continued the king, "who have spent the greatest part of your life in travelling, I am well disposed to hope you may hitherto have escaped many vices of your country. But by what I have gathered from your own relation, and the answers I have with much pains wringed and extorted from you, I cannot but conclude the bulk of your natives to be the most pernicious race of little odious vermin that Nature ever suffered to crawl upon the surface of the earth."

CHAPTER VII

THE AUTHOR'S LOVE OF HIS COUNTRY—HE MAKES A PROPOSAL OF
MUCH ADVANTAGE TO THE KING, WHICH IS REJECTED—
THE KING'S GREAT IGNORANCE IN POLITICS—THE LEARNING
OF THAT COUNTRY VERY IMPERFECT AND CONFINED—THE
LAWS, MILITARY AFFAIRS, AND PARTIES IN THE STATE

NOTHING but an extreme love of truth could have hindered me from concealing this part of my story. It was in vain to discover my resentments, which were always turned into ridicule;

and I was forced to rest with patience, while my noble and beloved country was so injuriously treated. I am as heartily sorry as any of my readers can possibly be, that such an occasion was given: but this prince happened to be so curious and inquisitive upon every particular, that it could not consist either with gratitude or good manners to refuse giving him what satisfaction I was able. Yet thus much I may be allowed to say in my own vindication, that I artfully eluded many of his questions, and gave to every point a more favourable turn, by many degrees, than the strictness of truth would allow. For I have always borne that laudable partiality to my own country which Dionysius Halicarnassensis, with so much justice, recommends to an historian: I would hide the frailties and deformities of my political mother, and place her virtues and beauties in the most advantageous light. This was my sincere endeavour in those many discourses I had with that monarch, although it unfortunately failed of success.

But great allowance should be given to a king who lives wholly secluded from the rest of the world, and must therefore be altogether unacquainted with the manners and customs that most prevail in other nations; the want of which knowledge will ever produce many prejudices, and a certain narrowness of thinking, from which we, and the politer countries of Europe, are wholly exempted. And it would be hard indeed, if so remote a prince's notions of virtue and vice were to be offered as a standard for all mankind.

To confirm what I have now said, and further to show the miserable effects of a confined education, I shall here insert a passage, which will hardly obtain belief. In hopes to ingratiate myself further into his majesty's favour, I told him of an invention discovered between three and four hundred years ago, to make certain powder, into a heap of which the smallest spark of fire falling, would kindle the whole in a moment, although it were as big as a mountain, and make it all fly up in the air together, with a noise and agitation greater than thunder. That a proper quantity of this powder rammed into a hollow tube of brass or iron, according to its bigness, would drive a ball of iron or lead with such violence and speed, as nothing was able to sustain its force. That the largest balls thus discharged would not only destroy whole ranks of an army at once, but batter the strongest walls to the ground; sink down ships, with a thousand men in each, to the bottom of the sea; and when linked together by a chain, would cut through masts and rigging, divide hundreds of bodies in the middle, and lay all waste before them. That we often put this powder into large hollow balls of iron, and discharged them by an engine into some city we were besieging, which would rip up the pavements, tear the houses to pieces, burst and throw splinters on every side, dashing out the brains of all who came near. That I knew the ingredients very well, which were cheap and common; I understood the manner of compounding them, and could direct his workmen how to make those tubes of a size proportionable to all other things in his majesty's kingdom, and the largest need not be above a hundred feet long; twenty or thirty of which tubes, charged with the proper quantity of powder and balls, would batter down the walls of the strongest town in his dominions in a few hours, or destroy the whole metropolis, if ever it should pretend to dispute his absolute commands. This I humbly offered to his majesty, as a small tribute of acknowledgement, in turn for so many marks that I had received of his royal favour and protection.

The king was struck with horror at the description I had given of those terrible engines, and the proposal I had made. He was amazed how so impotent and grovelling an insect as I (these were his expressions) could entertain such inhuman ideas, and in so familiar a manner, as to appear wholly unmoved at all the scenes of blood and desolation which I had painted, as the common effects of those destructive machines; "whereof," he said, "some evil genius, enemy to mankind, must have been the first contriver." As for himself, he protested that, although few things delighted him so much as new discoveries in art or nature, yet he would rather lose half his kingdom than be privy to such a secret; which he commanded me, as I valued my life, never to mention any more.

A strange effect of narrow principles and views! that a prince possessed of every quality which procures veneration, love, and esteem; of strong parts, great wisdom, and profound learning, endowed with admirable talents, and almost adored by his subjects, should, from a nice, unnecessary scruple, whereof in Europe we can have no conception, let slip an opportunity put into his hands that would have made him absolute master of the lives, the liberties, and the fortunes of his people. Neither do I say this with the least intention to detract from the many virtues of that excellent king, whose character, I am sensible, will, on this account, be very much lessened in the opinion of an English reader: but I take this defect among them to have arisen from their ignorance, by not having hitherto reduced politics into a science, as the more acute wits of Europe have done. For, I remember very well, in a discourse one day with the king, when I happened to say there were several thousand books among us written upon the art of government, it gave him (directly contrary to my intention) a very mean opinion of our understandings. He professed both to abominate and despise all mystery, refinement, and intrigue, either in a prince or a minister. He could not tell what I meant by secrets of state, where an enemy, or some rival nation, were not in the case. He confined the knowledge of governing within very narrow bounds—to common sense and reason, to justice and lenity, to the speedy determination of civil and criminal causes; with some other obvious topics, which are not worth considering. And he gave it for his opinion, that whoever would make two ears of corn, or two blades of grass, to grow upon a spot of ground where only one grew before, would deserve better of mankind, and do more essential service to his country, than the whole race of politicians put together.

The learning of this people is very defective, consisting only of morality, history, poetry, and mathematics, wherein they must be allowed to excel. But the last of these is wholly applied to what may be useful in life, to the improvement of agriculture, and all mechanical arts; so that among us it would be little esteemed. And as to ideas, entities, abstractions, and transcendentals, I could never drive the least conception into their heads.

No law of that country must exceed in words the number of letters in their alphabet, which consists only of two-and-twenty. But, indeed, few of them extend even to that length. They are expressed in the most plain and simple terms, wherein those

people are not mercurial enough to discover above one inter-
pretation: and to write a comment upon any law is a capital
crime. As to the decision of civil causes, or proceedings against
criminals, their precedents are so few, that they have little reason
to boast of any extraordinary skill in either.

They have had the art of printing, as well as the Chinese,
time out of mind; but their libraries are not very large; for
that of the king, which is reckoned the largest, does not amount
to above a thousand volumes, placed in a gallery of twelve
hundred feet long, whence I had liberty to borrow what books I
pleased. The queen's joiner had contrived in one of Glumdalclitch's rooms a kind of wooden machine, five-and-twenty
feet high, formed like a standing ladder; the steps were each
fifty feet long; it was, indeed, a movable pair of stairs, the lowest
end placed at ten feet distance from the wall of the chamber.
The book I had a mind to read was put up leaning against the
wall: I first mounted to the upper step of the ladder, and turning
my face towards the book, began at the top of the page, and so
walking to the right and left about eight or ten paces, according
to the length of the lines, till I had gotten a little below the
level of mine eyes, and then descending gradually till I came to
the bottom: after which I mounted again, and began the other
page in the same manner, and so turned over the leaf, which I
could easily do with both my hands, for it was as thick and
stiff as pasteboard, and in the largest folios not above eighteen
or twenty feet long.

Their style is clear, masculine, and smooth, but not florid;
for they avoid nothing more than multiplying unnecessary
words, or using various expressions. I have perused many of
their books, especially those on history and morality. Among
the rest, I was very much diverted with a little old treatise, which
always lay in Glumdalclitch's bed-chamber, and belonged to
her governess, a grave elderly gentlewoman, who dealt in morality
and devotion. The book treats of the weakness of human kind,
and is in little esteem, except among the women and the vulgar.
However, I was curious to see what an author of that country
could say upon such a subject. This writer went through all
the usual topics of European moralists, showing how diminutive,
contemptible, and helpless an animal was man in his own

nature; how unable to defend himself from the inclemencies of the air, or the fury of wild beasts; how much he was excelled by one creature in strength, by another in speed, by a third in fore-sight, by a fourth in industry. He added, that Nature was degenerated in these latter declining ages of the world and could now produce only small abortive births, in comparison of those in ancient times. He said it was very reasonable to think, not only that the species of men were originally much larger, but also that there must have been giants in former ages: which, as it is asserted by history and tradition, so it has been confirmed by huge bones and skulls, casually dug up in several parts of the kingdom, far exceeding the common dwindled race of men in our days. He argued that the very laws of Nature absolutely required we should have been made, in the beginning, of a size more large and robust; not so liable to destruction from every little accident, of a tile falling from a house, or a stone cast from the hand of a boy, or being drowned in a little brook. From this way of reasoning, the author drew several moral applications, useful in the conduct of life, but needless here to repeat. For my own part, I could not avoid reflecting how universally this talent was spread of drawing lectures in morality or indeed rather matter of discontent and repining, from the quarrels we raise with Nature. And I believe, upon a strict inquiry, those quarrels might be shown as ill-grounded among us as they are among that people.

As to their military affairs, they boast that the king's army consists of a hundred and seventy-six thousand foot, and thirty-two thousand horse; if that may be called an army, which is made up of tradesmen in the several cities, and farmers in the country whose commanders are only the nobility or gentry, without pay or reward. They are indeed perfect enough in their exercises, and under very good discipline, wherein I saw no great merit; for how should it be otherwise, where every farmer is under the command of his own landlord and every citizen under that of the principal men in his own city, chosen, after the manner of Venice, by ballot?

I have often seen the militia of Lorbrulgrud drawn out to exercise, in a great field near the city, of twenty miles square. They were in all not above twenty-five thousand foot, and six thousand horse; but it was impossible for me to compute their number, considering the space of ground they took up. A cavalier mounted on a large steed, might be about ninety feet high. I have seen this whole body of horse, upon the word of command, draw their swords at once, and brandish them in the air. Imagination can picture nothing so grand, so surprising, and so astonishing; it looked as if ten thousand flashes of lightning were darting at the same time from every quarter of the sky.

I was curious to know how this prince, to whose dominions there is no access from any other country, came to think of armies, or to teach his people the practice of military discipline. But I was soon informed, both by conversation and reading their histories; for in the course of many ages, they have been troubled with the same disease to which the whole race of mankind is subject; the nobility often contending for power, the people for liberty, and the king for absolute dominion: all which, however happily tempered by the laws of that kingdom, have been sometimes violated by each of the three parties, and have more than once occasioned civil wars; the last whereof was happily put an end to by this prince's grandfather, in a general composition; and the militia, then settled with common consent, has been ever since kept in the strictest duty.

CHAPTER VIII

THE KING AND QUEEN MAKE A PROGRESS TO THE FRONTIERS—
THE AUTHOR ATTENDS THEM—THE MANNER IN WHICH HE
LEAVES THE COUNTRY VERY PARTICULARLY RELATED—HE
RETURNS TO ENGLAND

I HAD always a strong impulse that I should some time recover my liberty, though it was impossible to conjecture by what means, or to form any project with the least hope of succeeding. The ship in which I sailed was the first ever known to be driven within sight of that coast, and the king had given strict orders, that if at any time another appeared, it should be taken ashore, and with all its crew and passengers brought in a tumbril to Lorbrulgrud. I was indeed treated with much kindness: I was the favourite of a great king and queen, and the delight of the whole court; but it was upon such a footing as ill became the dignity of human kind. I could never forget those domestic pledges I had left behind me. I wanted to be among people with whom I could converse upon even terms, and walk about the streets and fields without being afraid of being trod to death like a frog or a young puppy. But my deliverance came sooner than I expected, and in a manner not very common; the whole story and circumstances of which I shall faithfully relate.

I had now been two years in this country: and about the beginning of the third, Glumdalclitch and I attended the king and queen, in a progress to the south coast of the kingdom. I was carried as usual, in my travelling-box, which, as I have already described, was a very convenient closet, of twelve feet wide; and I had ordered a hammock to be fixed, by silken ropes, from the four corners at the top, to break the jolts, when a servant carried me before him on horseback, as I sometimes desired; and would often sleep in my hammock, while we were upon the road. On the roof of my closet, not directly over the middle of the hammock, I ordered the joiner to cut out a hole of a foot square, to give me air in hot weather, as I slept; which hole I shut at pleasure with a board that drew backward and forward through a groove.

When we came to our journey's end, the king thought proper to pass a few days at a palace he has near Flanflasnic, a city within eighteen English miles of the sea side. Glumdalclitch and I were much fatigued. I had gotten a small cold, but the poor girl was so ill as to be confined to her chamber. I longed to see the ocean, which must be the only scene of my escape, if ever it should happen. I pretended to be worse than I really was, and desired to take the fresh air of the sea, with a page whom I was very fond of, and who had sometimes been trusted with me. I shall never forget with what unwillingness Glumdalclitch consented, nor the strict charge she gave the page to be careful of me, bursting at the same time into a flood of tears, as if she had some foreboding of what was to happen. The boy took me out in my box, about half an hour's walk from the palace, towards the rocks on the sea-shore. I ordered him to set me down. and lifting up one of my sashes, cast many a wistful, melancholy look towards the sea. I found myself not very well, and told the page that I had a mind to take a nap in my hammock, which I hoped would do me good. I got in, and the boy shut the window close down, to keep out the cold. I soon fell asleep, and all I conjecture is, while I slept, the page, thinking no danger could happen, went among the rocks to look for birds' eggs, having before observed him from my window searching about, and picking up one or two in the clefts. Be that as it will, I found myself suddenly awaked with a violent pull upon the ring which was fastened at the top of my box, for the convenience of carriage. I felt my box raised very high in the air, and then borne forward with prodigious speed. The first jolt had like to have shaken me out of my hammock, but afterwards the motion was easy enough. I called out several times as loud as I could raise my voice, but all to no purpose. I looked towards my windows, and could see nothing but the clouds and sky. I heard a noise just over my head, like the clapping of wings, and then began to perceive the woeful condition I was in; that some eagle had got the ring of my box in his beak, with an intent to let it fall on a rock, like a tortoise in a shell, and then pick out my body and devour it: for the sagacity and smell of this bird enables him to discover his quarry at a great distance, though better concealed than I could be within a two-inch board.

In a little time, I observed the noise and flutter of wings to increase very fast, and my box tossed up and down like a sign on a windy day. I heard several bangs or buffets, as I thought, given to the eagle (for such I am certain it must have been that held the ring of my box in his beak), and then, all on a sudden, felt myself falling perpendicularly down, for above a minute, but with such incredible swiftness that I almost lost my breath. My fall was stopped by a terrible squash, that sounded louder to my ears than the cataract of Niagara; after which, I was quite in the dark for another minute, and then my box began to rise so high, that I could see light from the tops of the windows. I now perceived I was fallen into the sea. My box, by the weight of my body, the goods that were in, and the broad plate of iron fixed for strength at the four corners of the top and bottom, floated about five feet deep in water. I did then, and do now suppose, that the eagle which flew away with my box was pursued by two or three others, and forced to let me drop, while he defended himself against the rest, who hoped to share in the prey. The plates of iron fastened at the bottom of the box (for those were the strongest) preserved the balance while it fell, and hindered it from being broken on the surface of the water. Every joint of it was well grooved; and the door did not move on hinges, but up and down like a sash, which kept my closet so tight that very little water came in. I got with much difficulty out of my hammock, having first ventured to draw back the slip-board on the roof already mentioned, contrived on purpose to let in air, for want of which I found myself almost stifled.

How often did I then wish myself with my dear Glumdalclitch, from whom one single hour had so far divided me! And I may say with truth, that in the midst of my own misfortunes I could not forbear lamenting my poor nurse, the grief she would suffer for my loss, the displeasure of the queen, and the ruin of her fortune. Perhaps many travellers have not been under greater difficulties and distress than I was at this juncture, expecting every moment to see my box dashed to pieces, or at least overset by the first violent blast or rising wave. A breach in one pane of glass would have been immediate death: nor could anything have preserved the windows, but the strong lattice wires on the outside, against accidents in travelling. I saw the water ooze in at several crannies, although the leaks were not considerable, and I endeavoured to stop them as well as I could. I was not able to lift up the roof of my closet, which otherwise I certainly should have done, and sat on the top of it, where I might at least preserve myself some hours longer than by being shut up (as I may call it) in the hold. Or if I escaped these dangers for a day or two, what could I expect but a miserable death of cold and hunger? I was four hours under these circumstances, expecting, and indeed wishing, every moment to be my last.

I have already told the reader that there were two strong staples fixed upon that side of my box which had no window, and into which the servant who used to carry me on horseback would put a leathern belt, and buckle it about his waist. Being in this disconsolate state, I heard, or at least thought I heard, some kind of grating noise on that side of my box where the staples were fixed; and soon after I began to fancy that the box was pulled or towed along the sea; for I now and then felt a sort of tugging, which made the waves rise near the tops of my windows, leaving me almost in the dark. This gave me some faint hopes of relief, although I was not able to imagine how it could be brought about. I ventured to unscrew one of my chairs, which were always fastened to the floor; and having made a hard shift to screw it down again, directly under the slipping-board that I had lately opened, I mounted on the chair, and putting my mouth as near as I could to the hole, I called for help in a loud voice, and in all the languages I understood. I then fastened my handkerchief to a stick I usually carried, and thrusting it up the hole, waved it several times in the air, that if any boat or ship were near, the seamen might conjecture some unhappy mortal to be shut up in the box.

I found no effect from all I could do, but plainly perceived my closet to be moved along; and in the space of an hour, or better, that side of the box where the staples were, and had no windows, struck against something that was hard. I apprehended it to be a rock, and found myself tossed more than ever. I plainly heard a noise upon the cover of my closet, like that of a cable, and the grating of it as it passed through the ring. I then found myself hoisted up, by degrees, at least three feet higher than I was before. Whereupon I again thrust up my stick and hand-kerchief, calling for help till I was almost hoarse. In return to which, I heard a great shout repeated three times, giving me such transports of joy as are not to be conceived but by those who feel them. I now heard a trampling over my head and somebody calling through the hole with a loud voice, in the English tongue, "If there be anybody below, let them speak." I answered, I was an Englishman drawn by ill fortune into the greatest calamity that ever any creature underwent, and begged by all that was moving, to be delivered out of the dungeon I was in. The voice replied I was safe, for my box was fastened to their ship; and the carpenter should immediately come and saw a hole in the cover, large enough to pull me out. I answered that was needless, and would take up too much time; for there was no more to be done, but to let one of the crew put his finger into the ring, and take the box out of the sea into the ship, and so into the captain's cabin. Some of them, upon hearing me talk so wildly, thought I was mad; others laughed; for indeed it never came into my head that I was now got among people of my own stature and strength. The carpenter came, and in a few minutes sawed a passage of about four feet square, then let down a small ladder, upon which I mounted, and thence was taken into the ship in a very weak condition.

The sailors were all in amazement, and asked me a thousand questions which I had no inclination to answer. I was equally confounded at the sight of so many pigmies, for such I took them to be, after having so long accustomed mine eyes to the monstrous objects I had left. But the captain, Mr. Thomas Wilcocks, an honest worthy Shropshire man, observing I was ready to faint, took me into his cabin, gave me a cordial to comfort me, and made me turn in upon his own bed, advising me to take a little rest, of which I had great need. Before I went to sleep, I gave him to understand that I had some valuable furniture in my box, too good to be lost: a fine hammock, a handsome field-bed, two chairs, a table, and a cabinet; that my closet was hung on all sides, or rather quilted, with silk and cotton; that if he would let one of the crew bring my closet into his cabin, I would open it there before him, and show him my goods. The captain, hearing me utter these absurdities, concluded I was raving; however (I suppose to pacify me) he promised to give orders as I desired, and going upon deck, sent some of his men down into my closet, whence (as I afterwards found) they drew up all my goods and stripped off the quilting; but the chairs, cabinet and bedstead, being screwed to the floor, were much damaged by the ignorance of the seamen, who tore them up by force. Then they knocked off some of the boards for the use of the ship, and when they had got all they had a mind for, let the hull drop into the sea, which, by reason of many breaches made in the bottom and sides, sunk outright. And, indeed, I was glad not to have been a spectator of the havoc they made; because I am confident it would have sensibly touched me, by bringing former passages into my mind which I would rather have forgot.

I slept some hours, but perpetually disturbed with dreams of the place I had left, and the dangers I had escaped. However,

E

upon waking, I found myself much recovered. It was now about eight o'clock at night, and the captain ordered supper immediately, thinking I had already fasted too long. He entertained me with great kindness, observing me not to look wildly, or talk inconsistently; and, when we were left alone, desired I would give him a relation of my travels, and by what accident I came to be set adrift, in that monstrous wooden chest. He said, that about twelve o'clock at noon, as he was looking through his glass, he espied it at a distance, and thought it was a sail, which he had a mind to make, being not much out of his course, in hopes of buying some biscuits, his own beginning to fall short. That upon coming nearer, and finding his error, he sent out his long-boat, to discover what it was; that his men came back in a fright saying they had seen a swimming house. That he laughed at their folly, and went himself in the boat, ordering his men to take a strong cable along with them. That the weather being calm, he rowed round me several times, observing my windows and wire lattices that defended them. That he discovered two staples upon one side, which was all of boards, without any passage for light. He then commanded his men to row up to that side, and fastening a cable to one of the staples, ordered them to tow my chest, as they called it, towards the ship. When it was there, he gave directions to fasten another cable to the ring fixed in the cover, and to raise up my chest with pulleys, which all the sailors were not able to do above two or three feet. He said they saw my stick and handkerchief thrust out of the hole, and concluded that some unhappy man must be shut up in the cavity. I asked whether he or the crew had seen any prodigious birds in the air, about the time he first discovered me. To which he answered, that discoursing this matter with the sailors while I was asleep, one of them said he had observed three eagles flying towards the north, but remarked nothing of their being larger than the usual size; which I suppose must be imputed to the great height they were at; and he could not guess the reason of my question. I then asked the captain how far he reckoned we might be from land. He said, by the best computation he could make, we were at least a hundred leagues. I assured him he must be mistaken by almost half, for I had not left the country whence I came above two hours before I dropped into the sea. Whereupon he began to think that my brain was disturbed, of which he gave me a hint, and advised me to go to bed in a cabin he had provided. I assured him I was well refreshed with his good entertainment and company, and as much in my senses as ever I was in my life. He then grew serious, and desired to ask me freely whether I were not troubled in my mind by the consciousness of some enormous crime, for which I was punished, at the command of some prince, by exposing me in that chest; as great criminals, in other countries, have been forced to sea in a leaky vessel, without provisions: for although he should be sorry to have taken so ill a man into his ship, yet he would engage his word to set me safe ashore, in the first port where we arrived. He added, that his suspicions were much increased by some very absurd speeches I had delivered at first to his sailors and afterwards to himself, in relation to my closet or chest, as well as by my odd looks and behaviour while I was at supper.

I begged his patience to hear me tell my story, which I faithfully did, from the last time I left England to the moment he first discovered me. And as truth always forces its way into rational minds, so this honest, worthy gentleman, who had some tincture of learning, and very good sense, was immediately convinced of my candour and veracity. But, further to confirm all I had said, I entreated him to give order that my cabinet should be brought, of which I had the key in my pocket, for he had already informed me how the seamen disposed of my closet. I opened it in his own presence, and showed him the small collection of rarities I made in the country from which I had been so strangely delivered. There was the comb I had contrived out of the stumps of the king's beard, and another of the same materials, but fixed into a paring of her majesty's thumb nail, which served for the back. There was a collection of needles and pins, from a foot to half-a-yard long: four wasp stings, like joiners' tacks; some combings of the queen's hair; a gold ring, which one day she made me a present of in the most obliging manner, taking it from her little finger, and throwing it over my head like a collar. I desired the captain would please to accept this ring in return for his civilities; which he absolutely refused. I showed him a corn that I had cut off with my own hand from a maid of honour's toe; it was about the bigness of a Kentish pippin, and grown so hard, that when I returned to England, I got it hollowed into a cup, and set in silver. Lastly, I desired him to see the breeches I had then on, which were made of a mouse's skin.

I could force nothing on him but a footman's tooth, which I observed him to examine with great curiosity, and found he had a fancy for it. He received it with abundance of thanks, more than such a trifle could deserve. It was drawn by an unskilful surgeon, in a mistake, from one of Glumdalclitch's men, who was afflicted with the toothache, but it was as sound as any in his head. I got it cleaned, and put it into my cabinet. It was about a foot long, and four inches in diameter.

The captain was very well satisfied with this plain relation I had given him, and said, he hoped when we returned to England, I would oblige the world by putting it on paper, and making it public. My answer was, that I thought we were overstocked with books of travels: that nothing could now pass which was not extraordinary; wherein I doubted some authors less consulted truth than their own vanity, or interest, or the diversion of ignorant readers; that my story could contain little beside common events, without those ornamental descriptions of strange plants, trees, birds, and other animals; or of the barbarous customs and idolatry of savage people with which most writers abound. However, I thanked him for his good opinion, and promised to take the matter into my thoughts.

He said he wondered at one thing very much, which was to hear me speak so loud; asking me whether the king or queen of that country were thick of hearing. I told him it was what I had been used to for above two years past, and that I admired as much at the voices of him and his men, who seemed to me only to whisper, and yet I could hear them well enough. But when I spoke in that country, it was like a man talking in the streets to another looking out from the top of a steeple, unless when I was placed on a table, or held in any person's hand. I told him I had likewise observed another thing—that when I first got into the ship, and the sailors stood all about me, I thought they were the most contemptible little creatures I had ever beheld. For, indeed, while I was in the prince's country, I could never endure to look in a glass, after mine eyes had been accustomed to such prodigious objects, because the comparisons gave me so despicable a conceit of myself. The captain said that while we were at supper he observed me to look at everything with a sort of wonder, and that I often seemed hardly able to contain my laughter, which he knew not well how to take, but imputed it to some disorder in my brain. I answered, it was very true, and I wondered how I could forbear, when I saw his dishes of the size of a silver threepence, a leg of pork hardly a mouthful, a cup not so big as a nutshell; and so I went on, describing the rest of his household-stuff and provisions after the same manner. For, although the queen had ordered a little equipage of all things necessary for me, while I was in her service, yet my ideas were wholly taken up with what I saw on every side of me, and I winked at my own littleness, as people do at their own faults.

The captain understood my raillery very well, and merrily replied with an old English proverb, that he doubted mine eyes were bigger than my belly, for he did not observe my stomach so good, although I had fasted all day: and continuing in his mirth, protested he would have gladly given a hundred pounds to have seen my chest in the eagle's bill, and afterwards in its fall from so great a height into the sea; which would certainly have been a most astonishing object, worthy to have the description of it transmitted to future ages: and the comparison of Phaëton was so obvious, that he could not forbear applying it, although I did not much admire the conceit.

The captain having been at Tonquin, was, in his return to England, driven north-eastward to the latitude of 44 degrees, and longitude of 143. But meeting a trade wind two days after I came on board him, we sailed southward a long time, and coasting New Holland, kept our course west-south-west, and then south-south-west, till we doubled the Cape of Good Hope. Our voyage was very prosperous, but I shall not trouble the reader with a journal of it. The captain called in at one or two ports, and sent in his longboat for provisions and fresh water; but I never went out of the ship till we came into the Downs, which was on the 3rd day of June, 1706, about nine months after my escape. I offered to leave my goods in security for the payment of my freight, but the captain protested he would not receive

one farthing. We took a kind leave of each other, and I made
him promise he would come to see me at my house in Redriff.
I hired a horse and guide for five shillings, which I borrowed of the
captain.

As I was on the road, observing the littleness of the houses,
the trees, the cattle, and the people, I began to think myself in
Lilliput. I was afraid of trampling on every traveller I met, and
often called aloud to have them stand out of the way, so that I
had like to have gotten one or two broken heads for my impertinence.

When I came to my own house, for which I was forced to
inquire, one of the servants opening the door, I bent down to
go in (like a goose under a gate), for fear of striking my head.
My wife ran out to embrace me, but I stooped lower than her
knees, thinking she could otherwise never be able to reach my
mouth. My daughter kneeled to ask my blessing, but I could not
see her till she arose, having been so long used to stand with my
head and eyes erect to above sixty feet; and then I went to take her
up with one hand by the waist. I looked down upon the servants
and one or two friends who were in the house, as if they had been
pigmies, and I a giant. I told my wife she had been too thrifty,
for I found she had starved herself and her daughter to nothing.
In short, I behaved myself so unaccountably, that they were all
of the captain's opinion when he first saw me, and concluded
I had lost my wits. This I mention as an instance of the great
power of habit and prejudice.

In a little time, I and my family and friends came to a right
understanding; but my wife protested I should never go to sea
any more; although my evil destiny so ordered, that she had not
power to hinder me, as the reader may know hereafter. In the
meantime, I here conclude the second part of my unfortunate
voyages.

PART III

A VOYAGE TO LAPUTA, BALNIBARBI, LUGG-
NAGG, GLUBBDUBDRIB, AND JAPAN

CHAPTER I

THE AUTHOR SETS OUT ON HIS THIRD VOYAGE—IS TAKEN BY
PIRATES—THE MALICE OF A DUTCHMAN—HIS ARRIVAL AT
AN ISLAND—HE IS RECEIVED INTO LAPUTA

I HAD not been at home above ten days when Captain William
Robinson, a Cornishman, commander of the *Hopewell*, a stout
ship of three hundred tons, came to my house. I had formerly
been surgeon of another ship, where he was master, and a
fourth part owner, in a voyage to the Levant. He had
always treated me more like a brother than an inferior officer;
and hearing of my arrival, made me a visit, as I apprehended
only out of friendship, for nothing passed more than what is
usual after long absences. But repeating his visits often, expressing his joy to find me in good health, asking whether I were now
settled for life, adding that he intended a voyage to the East
Indies in two months; at last he plainly invited me, though with
some apologies, to be surgeon of the ship: that I should have
another surgeon under me, besides our two mates; that my
salary should be double to the usual pay; and that having
experienced my knowledge in sea affairs to be at least equal to
his, he would enter into any engagement to follow my advice,
as much as if I had shared in the command.

He said so many other obliging things, and I knew him to
be so honest a man, that I could not reject his proposal; the
thirst I had for seeing the world, notwithstanding my past misfortunes, continuing as violent as ever. The only difficulty that

remained was to persuade my wife, whose consent, however, I
at last obtained, by the prospect of advantage she proposed to
her children.

We set out the 5th day of August, 1706, and arrived at Fort
St. George the 11th of April, 1707. We stayed there three weeks
to refresh our crew, many of whom were sick. From thence we
went to Tonquin, where the captain resolved to continue some
time, because many of the goods he intended to buy were not
ready, nor could he expect to be dispatched in several months.
Therefore, in hopes to defray some of the charges he must be
at, he bought a sloop, loaded it with several sorts of goods, wherewith the Tonquinese usually trade to the neighbouring islands,
and putting fourteen men on board, whereof three were of the
country, he appointed me master of the sloop, and gave me
power to traffic, while he transacted his affairs at Tonquin.

We had not sailed above three days, when a great storm
arising, we were driven five days to the north-north-east, and
then to the east: after which we had fair weather, but still with
a pretty strong gale from the west. Upon the tenth day we were
chased by two pirates, who soon overtook us; for my sloop was
so deeply laden, that she sailed very slow, neither were we in a
condition to defend ourselves.

We were boarded about the same time by both the pirates,
who entered furiously at the head of their men; but finding us
all prostrate upon our faces (for so I gave order), they pinioned
us with strong ropes, and setting a guard upon us, went to search
the sloop.

I observed among them a Dutchman, who seemed to be of
some authority, though he was not commander of either ship.
He knew us by our countenances to be Englishmen, and jabber-
ing to us in our own language, swore we should be tied back to
back and thrown into the sea. I spoke Dutch tolerably well;
I told him who we were, and begged him, in consideration of
our being Christians and Protestants, of neighbouring countries
in strict alliance, that he would move the captains to take some
pity on us. This inflamed his rage; he repeated the threatenings,
and turning to his companions, spoke with great vehemence in
the Japanese language, as I suppose, often using the word
Christianos.

The largest of the two pirate ships was commanded by a Japanese captain, who spoke a little Dutch, but very imperfectly. He came up to me, and after several questions, which I answered in great humility, he said we should not die. I made the captain a very low bow, and then, turning to the Dutchman, said I was sorry to find more mercy in a heathen than in a brother Christian. But I had soon reason to repent those foolish words: for that malicious reprobate, having often endeavoured in vain to persuade both the captains that I might be thrown into the sea (which they would not yield to, after the promise made me that I should not die), however, prevailed so far as to have a punishment inflicted on me worse, in all human appearance, than death itself. My men were sent by an equal division into both the pirate ships, and my sloop new manned. As to myself, it was determined that I should be set adrift in a small canoe, with paddles and a sail, and four days' provisions; which last the Japanese captain was so kind as to double out of his own stores, and would permit no man to search me. I got down into the canoe, while the Dutchman, standing upon the deck, loaded me with all the curses and injurious terms his language could afford.

About an hour before we saw the pirates I had taken an observation, and found we were in the latitude of 46 N. and longitude of 183. When I was at some distance from the pirates, I discovered by my pocket-glass several islands to the southeast. I set up my sail, the wind being fair, with a design to reach the nearest of those islands, which I made a shift to do in about three hours. It was all rocky: however, I got many birds' eggs; and striking fire, I kindled some heath and dry sea-weed, by which I roasted my eggs. I ate no other supper, being resolved to spare my provisions as much as I could. I passed the night under the shelter of a rock, strewing some heath under me, and slept pretty well.

The next day I sailed to another island, and thence to a third and fourth, sometimes using my sail, sometimes my paddles. But, not to trouble the reader with a particular account of my distresses, let it suffice that on the fifth day I arrived at the last island in my sight which lay south-south-east to the former.

This island was at a greater distance than I expected, and I did not reach it in less than five hours. I encompassed it almost round before I could find a convenient place to land in; which was a small creek, about three times the wideness of my canoe. I found the island to be all rocky, only a little intermingled with tufts of grass, and sweet-smelling herbs. I took out my small provisions, and after having refreshed myself, I secured the remainder in a cave, whereof there were great numbers; I gathered plenty of eggs upon the rocks, and got a quantity of dry sea-weed and parched grass, which I designed to kindle the next day, and roast my eggs as well as I could, for I had about me my flint, steel, watch, and burning-glass. I lay all night in the cave where I had lodged my provisions. My bed was the same dry grass and sea-weed which I intended for fuel. I slept very little, for the disquiet of my mind prevailed over my weariness, and kept me awake. I considered how impossible it was to preserve my life in so desolate a place, and how miserable my end must be: yet found myself so listless and desponding, that I had not the heart to rise; and before I could get spirits enough to creep out of my cave, the day was far advanced. I walked awhile among the rocks; the sky was perfectly clear, and the sun so hot, that I was forced to turn my face from it: when all on a sudden it became obscure, as I thought, in a manner very different from what happens by the interposition of a cloud. I turned back, and perceived a vast opaque body between me and the sun, moving forward towards the island; it seemed to be about two miles high, and hid the sun six or seven minutes; but I did not observe the air to be much colder, or the sky more darkened, than if I had stood under the shade of a mountain. As it approached nearer over the place where I was, it appeared to be a firm substance, the bottom flat, smooth, and shining very bright, from the reflection of the sea below. I stood upon a height of about two hundred yards from the shore, and saw this vast body descending almost to a parallel with me, at less than an English mile distance. I took out my pocket perspective, and could plainly discover numbers of people moving up and down the sides of it, which appeared to be sloping; but what those people were doing, I was not able to distinguish.

The natural love of life gave me some inward motion of joy, and I was ready to entertain a hope that this adventure might, some way or other, help to deliver me from the desolate place and condition I was in. But at the same time the reader can hardly conceive my astonishment to behold an island in the air, inhabited by men, who were able (as it should seem) to raise or sink, or put it into progressive motion, as they pleased. But not being at that time in a disposition to philosophise upon this phenomenon, I rather chose to observe what course the island would take, because it seemed for a while to stand still. Yet soon after it advanced nearer, and I could see the sides of it encompassed with several gradations of galleries and stairs, at certain intervals, to descend from one to the other. In the lowest gallery I beheld some people fishing with long angling-rods, and others looking on. I waved my cap (for my hat was long since worn out) and my handkerchief towards the island; and upon its nearer approach I called and shouted with the utmost strength of my voice; and then looking, circumspectly, I beheld a crowd gathered to that side which was most in my view. I found by their pointing towards me and to each other, that they plainly discovered me, although they made no return to my shouting. But I could see four or five men running in great haste up the stairs, to the top of the island, who then disappeared. I happened rightly to conjecture that these were sent for orders, to some person in authority, upon this occasion.

The number of people increased, and in less than half an hour the island was moved and raised in such a manner that the lowest gallery appeared in a parallel of less than a hundred yards' distance from the height where I stood. I then put myself in the most supplicating posture, and spoke in the humblest accent, but received no answer. Those who stood nearest over against me seemed to be persons of distinction, as I supposed by their habits. They conferred earnestly with each other, looking often upon me. At length one of them called out in a clear, polite, smooth dialect, not unlike in sound to the Italian; and therefore I returned an answer in that language, hoping at least that the cadence might be more agreeable to his ears. Although neither of us understood the other, yet my meaning was easily known, for the people saw the distress I was in.

They made signs for me to come down from the rock, and go towards the shore, which I accordingly did; and the flying island being raised to a convenient height, the verge directly over me, a chain was let down from the lowest gallery, with a seat fastened to the bottom, to which I fixed myself, and was drawn up by pulleys.

CHAPTER II

THE HUMOURS AND DISPOSITION OF THE LAPUTIANS DESCRIBED— AN ACCOUNT OF THEIR LEARNING—OF THE KING AND HIS COURT—THE AUTHOR'S RECEPTION THERE—THE INHABITANTS SUBJECT TO FEAR AND DISQUIETUDES—AN ACCOUNT OF THE WOMEN

AT MY alighting, I was surrounded by a crowd of people, but those who stood nearest seemed to be of better quality. They beheld me with all the marks and circumstances of wonder: neither, indeed, was I much in their debt; having never till then seen a race of mortals so singular in their shapes, habits, and countenances. Their heads were all reclined, either to the right or the left; one of their eyes turned inward, and the other directly up to the zenith. Their outward garments were adorned with the figures of suns, moons, and stars; interwoven with those of fiddles, flutes, harps, trumpets, guitars, harpsichords, and many other instruments of music, unknown to us in Europe. I observed, here and there, many in the habit of servants, with blown bladders, fastened like a flail to the end of a stick, which they carried in their hands. In each bladder was a small quantity of dried peas, or little pebbles, as I was afterwards informed. With these bladders they now and then flapped the mouth and ears of those who stood near them, of which practice I could not then conceive the meaning. It seems the minds of these people are so taken up with intense speculations, that they can neither speak, nor attend to the discourses of others, without being roused by some external action upon the organs of speech and hearing; for which reason, those persons who are able to afford it always keep a flapper (the original is *climenole*) in their family as one of their domestics; nor ever walk abroad or make visits without him. And the business of this officer is, when, two, three, or more persons are in company, gently to strike with his bladder the mouth of him who is to speak, and the right ear of him or them to whom the speaker addresses himself. This flapper is likewise employed diligently to attend his master in his walks, and upon occasion to give him a soft flap on his eyes; because he is always so wrapped up in cogitation, that he is in manifest danger of falling down every precipice, and bouncing his head against every post; and in the streets of jostling others, or being jostled himself into the kennel.

It is necessary to give the reader this information, without which he would be at the same loss with me to understand the proceedings of these people as they conducted me up the stairs, to the top of the island, and from thence to the royal palace. While we were ascending, they forgot several times what they were about, and left me to myself, till their memories were again roused by their flappers: for they appeared altogether unmoved by the sight of my foreign habit and countenance, and by the shouts of the vulgar, whose thoughts and minds were more disengaged.

At last we entered the palace, and proceeded to the chamber of presence, where I saw the king seated on his throne, attended on each side by persons of prime quality. Before the throne was a large table filled with globes and spheres and mathematical instruments of all kinds. His majesty took not the least notice of us, although our entrance was not without sufficient noise, by the concourse of all persons belonging to the court. But he was then deep in a problem; and we attended at least an hour, before he could solve it. There stood by him, on each side, a young page with flaps in their hands, and when they saw he was at leisure, one of them gently struck his mouth, and the other his right ear; at which he started like one awakened on a sudden, and looking towards me and the company I was in, recollected the occasion of our coming, whereof he had been informed before. He spoke some words; whereupon, immediately a young man with a flap came up to my side, and flapped me gently on the right ear; but I made signs, as well as I could, that I had no occasion for such an instrument; which, as I afterward found, gave his majesty and the whole court a very mean opinion of my understanding. The king, as far as I could conjecture, asked me several questions, and I addressed myself to him in all the languages I had. When it was found I could neither understand nor be understood, I was conducted by his order to an apartment in his palace (this prince being distinguished above all his predecessors for his hospitality to strangers), where two servants were appointed to attend me. My dinner was brought, and four persons of quality, whom I remembered to have seen very near the king's person, did me the honour to dine with me. We had two courses, of three dishes each. In the first course there was a shoulder of mutton cut into an equilateral triangle, a piece of beef into a rhomboid, and a pudding into a cycloid. The second course was two ducks trussed up in the form of fiddles, sausages and puddings resembling flutes and hautboys, and a breast of veal in the shape of a harp. The servants cut our bread into cones, cylinders, parallelograms, and other mathematical figures.

While we were at dinner, I made bold to ask the names of several things in their language, and those noble persons, by the assistance of their flappers, delighted to give me answers, hoping to raise my admiration of their great abilities, if I could be brought to converse with them. I was soon able to call for bread and drink, or whatever else I wanted.

After dinner my company withdrew, and a person was sent by the king's orders, attended by a flapper. He brought with him pens, ink, and paper, and three or four books, giving me to understand, by signs, that he was sent to teach me the language. We sat together four hours, in which time I wrote down a great number of words in columns, with the translations over against them: I likewise made a shift to learn several short sentences; for my tutor would order some of my servants to fetch something, to turn about, to make a bow, to sit, or to stand or walk, and the like. Then I took down the sentence in writing. He showed me also, in one of the books, the figures of the sun, moon, and stars, the zodiac, the tropics, and polar circles, together with the denominations of many planes and solids. He gave me the names and descriptions of all their musical instruments, and the general terms of art in playing on each of them.

After he had left me, I placed all my words with their interpretations, in alphabetical order. And thus, in a few days, by the help of a very faithful memory, I got some insight into their language.

The word, which I interpret the flying or floating island is in the original *Laputa*, whereof I could never learn the true etymology. *Lap*, in the old obsolete language, signifies high; and *untuh*, a governor; from which they say, by corruption, was derived *Laputa*, from *Lapuntah*. But I do not approve of this derivation, which seems to be a little strained. I ventured to offer to the learned men among them a conjecture of my own, that Laputa was *quasi lap outed*: *lap*, signifying properly, the dancing of the sun-beams in the sea; and *outed*, a wing; which, however, I shall not obtrude, but submit to the judicious reader.

Those to whom the king had entrusted me, observing how ill I was clad, ordered a tailor to come next morning, and take my measure for a suit of clothes. This operator did his office after a different manner from those of his trade in Europe. He first took my altitude by a quadrant, and then, with rule and compasses, described the dimensions and outlines of my whole body, all which he entered upon paper; and in six days brought my clothes very ill-made, and quite out of shape, by happening to make a mistake of a figure in the calculation. But my comfort was, that I observed such accidents very frequent, and little regarded.

During my confinement for want of clothes, and by an indisposition that held me some days longer, I much enlarged my dictionary; and when I next went to court, was able to understand many things the king spoke, and to return him some kind of answers. His majesty had given orders that the island should move north-east and by east, to the vertical point over Lagado, the metropolis of the whole kingdom below, upon the firm earth. It was about ninety leagues distant, and our voyage lasted four days and a half. I was not in the least sensible of the progressive motion made in the air by the island. On the second morning, about eleven o'clock, the king himself in person, attended by his nobility, courtiers, and officers, having prepared all their musical instruments, played on them for three hours, without intermission, so that I was quite stunned with the noise; neither could I possibly guess the meaning, till my tutor informed me. He said that the people of their island had their ears adapted to hear the music of the spheres, which always played at certain periods, and the court was now prepared to bear their part, in whatever instruments they most excelled.

In our journey towards Lagado, the capital city, his majesty ordered that the island should stop over certain towns and villages, from whence he might receive the petitions of his subjects. And to this purpose, several packthreads were let down, with small weights at the bottom. On these packthreads the people strung their petitions, which mounted up directly, like the scraps of paper fastened by schoolboys at the end of the string that holds the kite. Sometimes we received wine and victuals from below, which were drawn up by pulleys.

The knowledge I had in mathematics gave me great assistance in acquiring their phraseology, which depended much upon that science, and music; and in the latter I was not unskilled. Their ideas are perpetually conversant in lines and figures. If they would, for example, praise the beauty of a woman, or any other animal, they describe it by rhombs, circles, parallelograms, ellipses, and other geometrical terms, or by words of art drawn from music, needless here to repeat. I observed in the king's kitchen all sorts of mathematical and musical instruments, after the figures of which they cut up the joints that were served at his majesty's table.

Their houses are very ill built, the walls bevel, without one right angle in any apartment; and this defect arises from the contempt they bear to practical geometry, which they despise as vulgar and mechanical: those instructions they give being too refined for the intellects of their workmen, which occasion perpetual mistakes. And although they are dexterous enough upon a piece of paper, in the management of the rule, the pencil and the divider, yet in the common actions and behaviour of life I have not seen a more clumsy, awkward, and unhandy people, nor so slow and perplexed in their conceptions upon all other subjects except those of mathematics and music. They are very bad reasoners, and vehemently given to opposition, unless when they happen to be of the right opinion, which is seldom their case. Imagination, fancy, and invention they are wholly

strangers to, nor have any words in their language by which
those ideas can be expressed: the whole compass of their thoughts
and mind being shut up within the two fore-mentioned sciences.

Most of them, and especially those who deal in the astronomical part, have great faith in judicial astrology, although
they are ashamed to own it publicly. But what I chiefly admired,
and thought altogether unaccountable, was the strong disposition
I observed in them towards news and politics, perpetually inquiring into public affairs, giving their judgments in matters of
state, and passionately disputing every inch of a party opinion.
I have, indeed, observed the same disposition among most of
the mathematicians I have known in Europe, although I could
never discover the least analogy between the two sciences; unless
those people suppose, that because the smallest circle has as
many degrees as the largest, therefore the regulation and management of the world require no more abilities than the handling
and turning of a globe: but I rather take this quality to spring
from a very common infirmity of human nature, inclining us
to be most curious and conceited in matters where we have
least concern, and for which we are least adapted by study
or nature.

These people are under continual disquietudes, never enjoy-
ing a minute's peace of mind: and their disturbances proceed from
causes which very little affect the rest of mortals. Their apprehensions arise from several changes they dread in the celestial
bodies: for instance, that the earth, by the continual approaches
of the sun towards it, must, in course of time, be absorbed, or
swallowed up; that the face of the sun, will, by degrees, be
encrusted with its own effluvia, and give no more light to the
world; that the earth very narrowly escaped a brush from the
tail of the last comet, which would have infallibly reduced it
to ashes; and that the next, which they have calculated for one-
and-thirty years hence, will probably destroy us. For if, in its
perihelion, it should approach within a certain degree of the
sun (as by their calculations they have reason to dread), it will
receive a degree of heat ten thousand times more intense than
that of red-hot, glowing iron; and, in its absence from the sun,
carrying a blazing tail ten hundred thousand and fourteen miles
long; through which, if the earth should pass at the distance of

one hundred thousand miles from the nucleus, or main body of the comet, it must in its passage be set on fire, and reduced to ashes: that the sun, daily spending its rays without any nutriment to supply them, will at last be wholly consumed and annihilated, which must be attended with the destruction of this earth, and of all the planets that receive their light from it.

They are so perpetually alarmed with the apprehension of these and the like impending dangers, that they can neither sleep quietly in their beds nor have any relish for the common pleasures and amusements of life. When they meet an acquaintance in the morning, the first question is about the sun's health, how he looked at his setting and rising, and what hopes they have to avoid the stroke of the approaching comet. This conversation they are apt to run into with the same temper that boys discover in delighting to hear terrible stories of spirits and hobgoblins, which they greedily listen to, and dare not go to bed for fear.

The women of the island have abundance of vivacity: they contemn their husbands, and are exceedingly fond of strangers, whereof there is always a considerable number from the continent below, attending at court, either upon affairs of the several towns and corporations or their own particular occasions, but are much despised, because they want the same endowments. Among these the ladies choose their gallants; for the husband is always so wrapt in speculation, that the mistress and lover may proceed to the greatest familiarities before his face, if he be but provided with paper and implements, and without his flapper at his side.

The wives and daughters lament their confinement to the island, although I think it the most delicious spot of ground in the world: and although they live here in the greatest plenty and magnificence, and are allowed to do whatever they please, they long to see the world, and take the diversions of the metropolis; which they are not allowed to do without a particular licence from the king; and this is not easy to be obtained, because the people of quality have found, by frequent experience, how hard it is to persuade their women to return from below. I was told that a great court lady, who had several children—is married to the

prime minister, the richest subject in the kingdom, a very graceful person, extremely fond of her, and lives in the finest palace
of the island—went down to Lagado on the pretence of health,
there hid herself for several months, till the king sent a warrant
to search for her; and she was found in an obscure eating-house
all in rags, having pawned her clothes to maintain an old deformed footman, who beat her every day, and in whose company
she was taken, much against her will. And although her husband
received her with all possible kindness, and without the least
reproach, she soon after contrived to steal down again, with all
her jewels, to the same gallant, and has not been heard of since.

This may, perhaps, pass with the reader rather for a European
or English story, than for one of a country so remote. But he
may please to consider, that the caprices of womankind are not
limited by any climate or nation, and that they are much more
uniform than can be easily imagined.

In about a month's time, I had made a tolerable proficiency
in their language, and was able to answer most of the king's
questions, when I had the honour to attend him. His majesty
discovered not the least curiosity to inquire into the laws, government, history, religion, or manners of the countries where I had
been; but confined his questions to the state of mathematics, and
received the account I gave him with great contempt and indifference, though often roused by his flapper on each side.

CHAPTER III

A PHENOMENON SOLVED BY MODERN PHILOSOPHY AND ASTRONOMY
—THE LAPUTIANS' GREAT IMPROVEMENTS IN THE LATTER—
THE KING'S METHOD OF SUPPRESSING INSURRECTIONS

I DESIRED leave of this prince to see the curiosities of the island,
which he was graciously pleased to grant, and ordered my tutor
to attend me. I chiefly wanted to know to what cause in art or
nature it owed its several motions, whereof I will now give a
philosophical account to the reader.

The flying or floating island is exactly circular, its diameter 7,837 yards, or about four miles and a half, and consequently contains ten thousand acres. It is three hundred yards thick. The bottom, or under surface, which appears to those who view it below, is one of even regular plate of adamant, shooting up to the height of about two hundred yards. Above it lie the several minerals in their usual order, and over all is a coat of rich mould, ten or twelve feet deep. The declivity of the upper surface, from the circumference to the centre, is the natural cause why all the dews and rains which fall upon the island are conveyed in small rivulets towards the middle, where they are emptied into four large basins, each of about half a mile in circuit, and two hundred yards' distance from the centre. From these basins the water is continually exhaled by the sun in the daytime, which effectually prevents their overflowing. Besides, as it is in the power of the monarch to raise the island above the region of clouds and vapours, he can prevent the falling of dews and rain whenever he pleases. For the highest clouds cannot rise above two miles, as naturalists agree; at least, they were never known to do so in that country.

At the centre of the island there is a chasm about fifty yards in diameter, whence the astronomers descend into a large dome, which is therefore called *flandona gagnole*, or the astronomers' cave, situated at the depth of a hundred yards beneath the upper surface of the adamant. In this cave are twenty lamps continually burning, which, from the reflection of the adamant, cast a strong light into every part. The place is stored with a great variety of sextants, quadrants, telescopes, astrolabes, and other astronomical instruments. But the greatest curiosity, upon which the fate of the island depends, is a loadstone of prodigious size, in shape resembling a weaver's shuttle. It is in length six yards, and in the thickest part at least three yards over. This magnet is sustained by a very strong axle of adamant passing through its middle, upon which it plays, and is poised so exactly that the weakest hand can turn it. It is hooped round with a hollow cylinder of adamant four feet deep, as many thick, and twelve yards in diameter, placed horizontally, and supported by eight adamantine feet, each six yards high. In the middle of the concave side there is a groove twelve inches deep, in which the extremities of the axle are lodged, and turned round as there is occasion.

The stone cannot be removed from its place by any force, because the hoop and its feet are one continued piece with that body of adamant which constitutes the bottom of the island.

By means of this loadstone, the island is made to rise and fall, and move from one place to another. For, with respect to that

part of the earth over which the monarch presides, the stone is endued at one of its sides with an attractive power, and at the other with a repulsive. Upon placing the magnet erect, with its attractive end towards the earth, the island descends; but when the repelling extremity points downwards, the island mounts directly upward. When the position of the stone is oblique, the motion of this island is so too: for in this magnet, the forces always act in lines parallel to its direction.

By this oblique motion, the island is conveyed to different parts of the monarch's dominions. To explain the manner of its progress let AB represent a line drawn across the dominions of Balnibarbi; let the line *c d* represent the loadstone, of which let *d* be the repelling end, and *c* the attracting end, the island being over C: let the stone be placed in position *c d*, with its repelling end downward; then the island will be driven upwards obliquely towards D. When it is arrived at D, let the stone be turned upon its axle, till its attracting end points towards E, and then the island will be carried obliquely towards E; where, if the stone be again turned up on its axle till it stands in the position E F, with its repelling point downwards, the island will rise obliquely towards F, where, by directing the attracting end towards G, the island may be carried to G, and from G to H, by turning the stone so as to make its repelling extremity point directly downward. And thus, by changing the situation of the stone as often as there is occasion, the island is made to rise and fall by turns in an oblique direction, and by those alternate risings and fallings (the obliquity being not considerable) is conveyed from one part of the dominions to the other.

But it must be observed that this island cannot move beyond the extent of the dominions below, nor can it rise above the height of four miles; for which the astronomers (who have written large systems concerning the stone) assign the following reason: that the magnetic virtue does not extend beyond the distance of four miles, and that the mineral, which acts upon the stone in the bowels of the earth, and in the sea about six leagues distant from the shore, is not diffused through the whole globe, but terminates with the limits of the king's dominions; and it was easy, from the great advantage of such a superior situation, for a prince to bring under his obedience whatever country lay within the attraction of that magnet.

When the stone is put parallel to the plane of the horizon, the island stands still; for in that case the extremities of it, being at equal distances from the earth, act with equal force, the one in drawing downwards, and the other in pushing upwards, and consequently no motion can ensue.

This loadstone is under the care of certain astronomers, who, from time to time, give it such positions as the monarch directs.

They spend the greatest part of their lives in observing the celestial bodies, which they do by the assistance of glasses, far exceeding ours in goodness. For, although their largest telescopes do not exceed three feet, they magnify much more than those of a hundred with us, and show the stars with greater clearness. This advantage has enabled them to extend their discoveries much farther than our astronomers in Europe; for they have made a catalogue of ten thousand fixed stars, whereas the largest of ours does not contain above one-third part of that number. They have likewise discovered two lesser stars, or satellites, which revolve about Mars; whereof the innermost is distant from the centre of the primary planet exactly three of his diameters, and the outermost five; the former revolves in the space of ten hours, and the latter in twenty-one and a half; so that the squares of their periodical times are very nearly in the same proportion with the cubes of their distance, from the centre of Mars; which evidently shows them to be governed by the same law of gravitation that influences the other heavenly bodies.

They have observed ninety-three different comets, and settled their periods with great exactness. If this be true (and they affirm it with great confidence), it is much to be wished that their observations were made public, whereby the theory of comets, which at present is very lame and defective, might be brought to the same perfection as other parts of astronomy.

The king would be the most absolute prince in the universe, if he could but prevail on his ministry to join with him; but these having their estates below on the continent, and considering that the office of a favourite has a very uncertain tenure, would never consent to the enslaving of their country.

If any town should engage in rebellion or mutiny, fall into violent factions, or refuse to pay the usual tribute, the king has two methods of reducing them to obedience. The first and the mildest course is by keeping the island hovering over such a town and the lands about it, whereby he can deprive them of the benefit of the sun and the rain, and consequently afflict the inhabitants with dearth and diseases: and if the crime deserve it, they are at the same time pelted from above with great stones, against which they have no defence but by creeping into cellars or caves, while the roofs of their houses are beaten to pieces.

But if they still continue obstinate, or offer to raise insurrections, he proceeds to the last remedy, by letting the island drop directly upon their heads, which makes a universal destruction both of houses and men. However, this is an extremity to which the prince is seldom driven; neither, indeed, is he willing to put it into execution; nor dare his ministers advise him to an action which, as it would render them odious to the people, so it would be a great damage to their own estates, which lie all below; for the island is the king's demesne.

But there is still, indeed, a more weighty reason why the kings of this country have been always averse from executing so terrible an action, unless upon the utmost necessity. For, if the town intended to be destroyed should have in it any tall rocks, as it generally falls out in the larger cities—a situation probably chosen at first with a view to prevent such a catastrophe—or if it abound in high spires or pillars of stone, a sudden fall might endanger the bottom or under surface of the island, which, although it consists, as I have said, of one entire adamant, two hundred yards thick, might happen to crack by too great a shock, or burst by approaching too near the fires from the houses below, as the backs, both of iron and stone, will often do in our chimneys. Of all this the people are well appraised, and understand how far to carry their obstinacy, where their liberty or property is concerned. And the king, when he is highly provoked, and most determined to press a city to rubbish, orders the island to descend with great gentleness, out of a pretence of tenderness to his people, but, indeed, for fear of breaking the adamantine bottom; in which case, it is the opinion of all their philosophers that the loadstone could no longer hold it up, and the whole mass would fall to the ground.

By a fundamental law of this realm, neither the king nor either of his two eldest sons are permitted to leave the island; nor the queen, till she has attained a certain age.

CHAPTER IV

THE AUTHOR LEAVES LAPUTA—IS CONVEYED TO BALNIBARBI—
    ARRIVES AT THE METROPOLIS—A DESCRIPTION OF THE
    METROPOLIS AND THE COUNTRY ADJOINING—THE AUTHOR
    HOSPITABLY RECEIVED BY A GREAT LORD—HIS CONVERSA-
    TION WITH THAT LORD

ALTHOUGH I cannot say I that was ill treated in this island, yet
I must confess I thought myself too much neglected, not without
some degree of contempt; for neither prince nor people appeared
to be curious in any part of knowledge, except mathematics and
music, wherein I was far their inferior, and upon that account
very little regarded.

On the other side, after having seen all the curiosities of the
island, I was very desirous to leave it, being heartily weary of
those people. They were indeed excellent in two sciences for
which I have great esteem, and wherein I am not unversed; but,
at the same time, so abstracted and involved in speculation, that
I never met with such disagreeable companions. I conversed
only with women, tradesmen, flappers, and court pages, during
two months of my abode there, by which, at last, I rendered
myself extremely contemptible; yet these were the only people
from whom I could ever receive a reasonable answer.

I had obtained, by hard study, a good degree of knowledge in
their language: I was weary of being confined to an island,
where I received so little countenance, and resolved to leave it
with the first opportunity.

There was a great lord at court, nearly related to the king,
and for that reason alone treated with respect. He was universally reckoned the most ignorant and stupid person among them.
He had performed many eminent services for the crown, had
great natural and acquired parts, adorned with integrity and
honour, but so ill an ear for music, that his detractors reported
"he had often been known to beat time in the wrong place";
neither could his tutors, without extreme difficulty, teach him to

demonstrate the most easy proposition in the mathematics. He
was pleased to show me many marks of favour; often did me
the honour of a visit; desired to be informed in the affairs of
Europe, the laws and customs, the manner and learning of the
several countries where I had travelled. He listened to me with
great attention, and made very wise observations on all I spoke.
He had two flappers attending him for state, but never made
use of them, except at court and in visits of ceremony, and
would always command them to withdraw when we were alone
together.

I entreated with this illustrious person to intercede in my
behalf with his majesty for leave to depart; which he accordingly
did, as he was pleased to tell me, with regret: for, indeed, he had
made me several offers, very advantageous, which, however, I
refused with expressions of the highest acknowledgement.

On the 16th of February I took leave of his majesty and the
court. The king made me a present, to the value of about two
hundred pounds English; and my protector, his kinsman, as
much more, together with a letter of recommendation to a friend
of his in Lagado, the metropolis. The island being then hovering
over a mountain about two miles from it, I was let down from
the lowest gallery, in the same manner as I had been taken up.

The continent, as far as it is subject to the monarch of the
flying island, passes under the general name of *Balnibarbi*; and the
metropolis, as I said before, is called *Lagado*. I felt some little
satisfaction in finding myself on firm ground. I walked to the
city without any concern, being clad like one of the natives, and
sufficiently instructed to converse with them. I soon found out
the person's house to whom I was recommended, presented my
letter from his friend, the grandee, in the island, and was received
with much kindness. This great lord, whose name was Munodi,
ordered me an apartment in his own house, where I continued
during my stay, and was entertained in a most hospitable manner.

The next morning after my arrival, he took me in his chariot to
see the town, which is about half the bigness of London; but the
houses were strangely built, and most of them out of repair. The
people in the streets walked fast, looked wild, their eyes fixed,
and were generally in rags. We passed through one of the town
gates, and went about three miles into the country, where I saw

many labourers working with several sorts of tools in the ground, but was not able to conjecture what they were about; neither did I observe any expectation either of corn or grass, although the soil appeared to be excellent. I could not forbear admiring at these odd appearances, both in town and country; and I made bold to desire my conductor that he would be pleased to explain to me what could be meant by so many busy heads, hands, and faces, both in the streets and in the fields, because I did not discover any good effect they produced; but, on the contrary, I never knew a soil so unhappily cultivated, houses so ill-contrived and so ruinous, or a people whose countenances and habits expressed so much misery and want.

This Lord Munodi was a person of the first rank, and had been some years governor of Lagado, but, by a cabal of ministers, was discharged for inefficiency. However, the king treated him with tenderness as a well-meaning man, but of low, contemptible understanding.

When I gave that free censure of the country and its inhabitants, he made no further answer than by telling me that I had not been long enough among them to form a judgment, and that the different nations of the world had different customs, with other common topics to the same purpose. But, when we returned to his palace, he asked me how I liked the building, what absurdities I observed, and what quarrel I had with the dress or looks of his domestics. This he might safely do; because everything about him was magnificent, regular, and polite. I answered that his excellency's prudence, quality, and fortune had exempted him from those defects which folly and beggary had produced in others. He said, if I would go with him to his country house, about twenty miles distant, where his estate lay, there would be more leisure for this kind of conversation. I told his excellency that I was entirely at his disposal, and accordingly we set out next morning.

During our journey he made me observe the several methods used by farmers in managing their lands, which to me were wholly unaccountable; for, except in some very few places, I could not discover one ear of corn or blade of grass. But, in three hours' travelling, the scene was wholly altered; we came into a most beautiful country—farmers' houses, at small distances, neatly built; the fields enclosed, containing vineyards, corn-grounds, and meadows. Neither do I remember to have seen a more delightful prospect. His excellency observed my countenance to clear up; he told me, with a sigh, that there his estate began, and would continue the same till we should come to his house; that his countrymen ridiculed and despised him for managing his affairs no better, and for setting so ill an example to the kingdom; which, however, was followed by very few, such as were old, and wilful, and weak, like himself.

We came, at length, to the house, which was indeed a noble structure, built according to the best rules of architecture. The fountains, gardens, walks, avenues, and groves were all disposed with exact judgment and taste. I gave due praise to everything I saw, whereof his excellency took not the least notice till after supper, when, there being no third companion, he told me, with a very melancholy air, that he doubted he must throw down his houses in town and country, to rebuild them after the present mode; destroy all his plantations, and cast others into such a form as modern usage required, and give the same directions to all his tenants, unless he would submit to incur the censure of pride, singularity, affectation, ignorance, caprice, and perhaps increase his majesty's displeasure; that the admiration I appeared to be under would cease or diminish when he had informed me of some particulars which, probably, I never heard of at court; the people there being too much taken up in their own speculations to have regard to what passed here below.

The sum of his discourse was to this effect: that about forty years ago, certain persons went up to Laputa, either upon business or diversion, and, after five months' continuance, came back with a very little smattering in mathematics, but full of volatile spirits, acquired in that airy region; that these persons, upon their return, began to dislike the management of everything below, and fell into schemes of putting all arts, sciences, languages, and mechanics upon a new footing. To this end, they procured a royal patent for erecting an academy of projectors in Lagado; and the humour prevailed so strongly among the people, that there is not a town of any consequence in the kingdom without such an academy. In these colleges the professors contrive new rules and methods of agriculture and

building, and new instruments and tools for all trades and manufactures; whereby, as they undertake one man shall do the work
of ten, a palace may be built in a week, of materials so durable
as to last for ever without repair. All the fruits of the earth shall
come to maturity at whatever season they think fit to choose,
and increase a hundred-fold more than they do at present, with
innumerable other happy proposals. The only inconvenience
is that none of these projects are yet brought to perfection, and,
in the meantime, the whole country lies miserably waste, the
houses in ruins, and the people without food or clothes. By all
which, instead of being discouraged, they are fifty times more
violently bent upon prosecuting their schemes, driven equally
on by hope and despair: that, as for himself, being not of an
enterprising spirit, he was content to go on in the old forms,
to live in the house his ancestors had built, and act as they did,
in every part of life, without innovation; that some few other
persons of quality and gentry had done the same, but were looked
on with an eye of contempt and ill-will, as enemies to art,
ignorant, and ill commonwealth's men, preferring their own ease
and sloth before the general improvement of their country.

His lordship added that he would not, by any further particulars, prevent the pleasure I should certainly take in viewing
the grand academy, whither he was resolved I should go. He
only desired me to observe a ruined building, upon the side of
a mountain about three miles distant, of which he gave me this
account: that he had a very convenient mill within half a mile
of his house, turned by a current from a large river, and sufficient
for his own family, as well as a great number of his tenants:
that, about seven years ago, a club of those projectors came to
him with proposals to destroy this mill, and build another
on the side of that mountain, on the long ridge whereof a long
canal must be cut, for a repository of water, to be conveyed up
by pipes and engines to supply the mill; because the wind and
air upon a height agitated the water, and thereby made it
fitter for motion; and because the water, descending down a
declivity, would turn the mill with half the current of a river,
whose course is more upon a level. He said that, being then not
very well with the court, and pressed by many of his friends, he
complied with the proposal, and after employing a hundred men

for two years, the work miscarried, the projectors went off, laying the blame entirely upon him, railing at him ever since, and putting others upon the same experiment, with equal assurance of success, as well as equal disappointment.

In a few days we came back to town; and his excellency, considering the bad character he had in the academy, would not go with me himself, but recommended me to a friend of his to bear me company thither. My lord was pleased to represent me as a great admirer of projects, and a person of much curiosity and easy belief—which, indeed, was not without truth, for I had myself been a sort of projector in my younger days.

CHAPTER V

THE AUTHOR PERMITTED TO SEE THE GRAND ACADEMY OF LAGADO —THE ACADEMY LARGELY DESCRIBED—THE ARTS WHEREIN THE PROFESSORS EMPLOY THEMSELVES

THIS ACADEMY is not an entire single building, but a continuation of several houses on both sides of a street, which growing waste, was purchased and applied to that use.

I was received very kindly by the warden, and went for many days in the academy. Every room has in it one or more projectors; and I believe I could not be in fewer than five hundred rooms.

The first man I saw was of a very meagre aspect, with sooty hands and face, his hair and beard long, ragged, and singed in several places. His clothes, shirt, and skin were all of the same colour. He had been eight years upon a project for extracting sunbeams out of cucumbers, which were to be put in phials hermetically sealed, and let out to warm the air in raw, inclement summers. He told me he did not doubt that in eight years more he should be able to supply the governor's gardens with sunshine at a reasonable rate; but he complained that his stock was low, and entreated me to give him something as an encouragement to ingenuity, especially since this had been a very dear year for cucumbers. I made him a small present, for my lord had furnished me with money on purpose, because he knew their practice of begging from all who go to see them.

I saw another at work to calcine ice into gunpowder; who likewise showed me a treatise he had written concerning the malleability of fire, which he intended to publish.

There was a most ingenious architect, who had contrived a new method for building houses, by beginning at the roof and working downwards to the foundation, which he justified to me by the like practice of those two prudent insects, the bee and the spider.

There was a man born blind, who had several apprentices in his own condition. Their employment was to mix colours for painters, which their master taught them to distinguish by feeling and smelling. It was indeed my misfortune to find them at that time not very perfect in their lessons, and the professor himself happened to be generally mistaken. This artist is much encouraged and esteemed by the whole fraternity.

In another apartment I was highly pleased with a projector who had found a device of ploughing the ground with hogs, to save the charges of ploughs, cattle, and labour. The method is this: in an acre of ground you bury, at six inches' distance and eight deep, a quantity of acorns, dates, chestnuts, and other mast or vegetables whereof these animals are fondest; then you drive six hundred of them into the field, where, in a few days, they will root up the whole ground in search of their feed, and make it fit for sowing, at the same time manuring it with their dung. It is true, upon experiment, they found the charge and trouble very great, and they had little or no crop. However, it is not doubted that his invention may be capable of great improvement.

I went into another room, where the walls and ceiling were all hung round with cobwebs, except a narrow passage for the artist to go in and out. At my entrance, he called aloud to me not to disturb his webs. He lamented the fatal mistake the world had been so long in of using silkworms while we had such plenty of domestic insects who infinitely excelled the former, because they understood how to weave as well as spin. And he proposed further that, by employing spiders, the charge of dyeing silks should be wholly saved, whereof I was fully convinced when he showed me a vast number of flies most beautifully coloured, wherewith he fed his spiders, assuring us that the webs would take a tincture from them; and as he had them of all hues, he hoped to fit everybody's fancy, as soon as he could find proper food for the flies, of certain gums, oils, and other glutinous matter, to give a strength and consistence to the threads.

There was an astronomer who had undertaken to place a sun-dial upon the great weathercock on the town-house, by adjusting the annual and diurnal motions of the earth and sun, so as to answer and coincide with all accidental turnings of the wind.

I visited many other apartments, but shall not trouble my reader with all the curiosities I observed, being studious of brevity.

I had hitherto seen only one side of the academy, the other being appropriated to the advancers of speculative learning, of of whom I shall say something, when I have mentioned one illustrious person more, who is called among them the "Universal Artist." He told us he had been thirty years employing his thoughts for the improvement of human life. He had two large rooms full of wonderful curiosities, and fifty men at work. Some were condensing air into a dry, tangible substance, by extracting the nitre and letting the aqueous or fluid particles percolate; others softening marble for pillows and pincushions; others petrifying the hoofs of a living horse, to preserve them from foundering. The artist himself was at that time busy upon two great designs: the first, to sow land with chaff, wherein he affirmed the true seminal virtue to be contained, as he demonstrated by several experiments, which I was not skilful enough to comprehend. The other was, by a certain composition of gums, minerals, and vegetables, outwardly applied, to prevent the growth of wool upon two young lambs; and he hoped, in a reasonable time, to propagate the breed of naked sheep all over the kingdom.

We crossed a walk to the other part of the academy, where, as I have already said, the projectors in speculative learning resided.

The first professor I saw was in a very large room, with forty pupils about him. After salutation, observing me to look earnestly upon a frame, which took up the greatest part of both the length and breadth of the room, he said, perhaps I might wonder to see him employed in a project for improving speculative knowledge, by practical and mechanical operations. But the world would soon be sensible of its usefulness; and he flattered himself that a more noble, exalted thought never sprang in any other man's head. Everyone knew how laborious the usual method is of attaining to arts and sciences; whereas, by his contrivance, the most ignorant person, at a reasonable charge and with little bodily labour, might write books in philosophy, poetry, politics, laws, mathematics, and theology, without the least assistance from genius or study. He then led me to the frame, about the sides whereof all his pupils stood in ranks. It was twenty feet square, placed in the middle of the room. The superficies was composed of several bits of wood, about the bigness of a die, but some larger than others. They were all linked together by slender wires. These bits of wood were covered, on every square, with paper pasted on them; and on these papers were written all the words of their language, in their several moods, tenses, and declensions, but without any order. The professor then desired me to observe, for he was going to set his engine at work. The pupils at his command, took each of them hold of an iron handle, whereof there were forty fixed round the edges of the frame; and giving them a sudden turn, the whole disposition of the words was entirely changed. He then commanded six-and-thirty of the lads to read the several lines softly, as they appeared upon the frame; and where they found three or four words together that might make part of a sentence, they dictated to the four remaining boys, who were scribes. This work was repeated three or four times; and at every turn, the engine was so contrived, that the words shifted into new places, as the square bits of wood moved upside down.

Six hours a day the young students were employed in this labour; and the professor showed me several volumes in large folio already collected of broken sentences, which he intended to piece together, and out of those rich materials to give the world a complete body of all arts and sciences; which, however, might be still improved and much expedited, if the public would raise a fund for making and employing five hundred such frames in Lagado, and oblige the managers to contribute in common their several collections.

He assured me that the invention had employed all his thoughts from his youth; that he had emptied the whole vocabu-

lary into his frame, and made the strictest computation of the general proportion there is in books between the number of particles, nouns, and verbs, and other parts of speech.

I made my humblest acknowledgment to this illustrious person for his great communicativeness; and promised, if ever I had the good fortune to return to my native country, that I would do him justice, as the sole inventor of this wonderful machine; the form and contrivance of which I desired leave to delineate on paper. I told him, although it was the custom of our learned in Europe to steal inventions from each other, who had thereby at least this advantage, that it became a controversy which was the right owner, yet I would take such caution, that he should have the honour entire, without a rival.

We next went to the school of languages, where three professors sat in consultation upon improving that of their own country.

The first project was, to shorten discourse, by cutting polysyllables into one, and leaving out verbs and participles; because in reality all things imaginable are but nouns.

The other project was a scheme for entirely abolishing all words whatsoever; and this was urged as a great advantage in point of health, as well as brevity. For it is plain that every word we speak is, in some degree, a diminution of our lungs by corrosion, and consequently contributes to the shortening of our lives. An expedient was therefore offered, that since words are only names for things, it would be more convenient for all men to carry about with them such things as were necessary to express a particular business they are to discourse on. And this invention would certainly have taken place, to the great ease as well as health of the subject, if the women, in conjunction with the vulgar and illiterate, had not threatened to raise a rebellion unless they might be allowed the liberty to speak with their tongues, after the manner of their forefathers; such constant, irreconcilable enemies to science are the common people. However, many of the most learned and wise adhere to the new scheme of expressing themselves by things; which has only this inconvenience attending it, that if a man's business be very great, and of various kinds, he must be obliged, in proportion, to carry a greater bundle of things upon his back, unless he can afford one or two strong servants to attend him. I have often beheld two of these sages almost sinking under the weight of their packs, like pedlars among us; who, when they met in the street, would lay down their loads, open their packs, and hold conversation for an hour together; and then put up their implements, help each other to resume their burdens, and take their leave.

But for short conversations, a man may carry implements in his pockets, and under his arms, enough to supply him; and in his house he cannot be at a loss. Therefore the room where company meet who practise this art is full of all things, ready at hand, requisite to furnish matter for this kind of artificial converse.

Another great advantage proposed by this invention was that it would serve as a universal language, to be understood in all civilised nations, whose goods and utensils are generally of the same kind, or nearly resembling, so that their uses might easily be comprehended. And thus ambassadors would be qualified to treat with foreign princes, or ministers of state, to whose tongues they were utter strangers.

I was at the mathematical school, where the master taught his pupils after a method scarcely imaginable to us in Europe. The proposition and demonstration were fairly written on a thin wafer, with ink composed of a cephalic tincture. This the student was to swallow upon a fasting stomach, and for three days following eat nothing but bread and water. As the wafer digested, the tincture mounted to his brain, bearing the proposition along with it. But the success has not hitherto been answerable, partly by some error in the quantum or composition, and partly by the perverseness of the lads, to whom this bolus is so nauseous that they generally steal aside, and discharge it upwards before it can operate; neither have they been yet persuaded to use so long an abstinence as the prescription requires.

CHAPTER VI

A FURTHER ACCOUNT OF THE ACADEMY—THE AUTHOR PROPOSES SOME IMPROVEMENTS, WHICH ARE HONOURABLY RECEIVED

IN THE school of political projectors I was but ill entertained, the professors appearing, in my judgment, wholly out of their senses, which is a scene that never fails to make me melancholy. These unhappy people were proposing schemes for persuading monarchs to choose favourites upon the score of their wisdom, capacity, and virtue; of teaching ministers to consult the public good; of rewarding merit, great abilities, and eminent services; of instructing princes to know their true interest, by placing it on the same foundation with that of their people; of choosing for employments persons qualified to exercise them; with many other wild, impossible chimeras, that never entered before into the heart of a man to conceive; and confirmed in me the old observation, that "there is nothing so extravagant and irrational which some philosophers have not affirmed for truth."

But, however, I shall so far do justice to this part of the academy as to acknowledge that all of them were not so visionary. There was a most ingenious doctor, who seemed to be perfectly versed in the whole nature and system of government. This illustrious person had very usefully employed his studies in finding out effectual remedies for all diseases and corruptions to which the several kinds of public administration are subject, by the vices and infirmities of those who govern, as well as by the licentiousness of those who are to obey. For instance:—— Whereas all writers and reasoners have agreed that there is a strict universal resemblance between the natural and political body, can there be anything more evident than that the health of both must be preserved, and the diseases cured, by the same prescriptions? It is allowed that senates and great councils are often troubled with redundant, ebullient, and other peccant humours; with many diseases of the head, and more of the heart; with strong convulsions, with grievous contraction of the nerves and sinews in both hands, but especially the right; with spleen, flatus, vertigoes, and deliriums, with scrofulous tumours, full of fœtid purulent matter; with canine appetites, and crudeness of digestion, beside many others, needless to mention. This doctor therefore proposed, that upon the meeting of the senate, certain physicians should attend at the three first days of their sitting, and at the close of each day's debate feel the pulses of every senator; after which, having maturely considered and consulted upon the nature of the several maladies, and the methods of cure, they should, on the fourth day, return to the senate-house, attended by their apothecaries stored with proper medicines, and before the members sat, administer to each of them lenitives, aperients, abstersives, corrosives, restringents, palliatives, laxatives, cephalalgics, icterics, aphphlegmatics, acoustics, as the several cases required; and, according as these medicines should operate, repeat, alter, or omit them at the next meeting.

This project could not be of any great expense to the public, and might, in my poor opinion, be of much use for the dispatch of business in those countries where senates have any share in the legislative power; beget unanimity, shorten debates, open a few mouths which are now closed, and close many more which are now open; curb the petulancy of the young, and correct the positiveness of the old; rouse the stupid, and damp the pert.

Again: because it is a general complaint that the favourites of princes are troubled with short and weak memories, the same doctor proposed, that whoever attended a first minister, after having told his business, with the utmost brevity and in the plainest words, should, at his departure, give the said minister a tweak by the nose, or tread on his corns, or lug him thrice by both ears, or pinch his arm black and blue, to prevent forgetfulness; and at every levee day repeat the same operation, till the business were done or absolutely refused.

He likewise directed that every senator in the great council of a nation, after he had delivered his opinion and argued in the defence of it, should be obliged to give his vote directly contrary; because, if that were done, the result would infallibly terminate in the good of the public.

When parties in a state are violent, he offered a wonderful contrivance to reconcile them. The method is this:—You take a hundred leaders of each party; you dispose them into couples of such whose heads are nearest of a size; then let two nice operators saw off the occiput of each couple at the same time, in such a manner that the brains may be equally divided. Let the occiputs thus cut off be interchanged, applying each to the head of his opposite party-man. It seems, indeed, to be a work that requires some exactness, but the professor assured us that if it were dextrously performed, the cure would be infallible. For he argued thus: that the two half brains being left to debate the matter between themselves within the space of one skull, would soon come to a good understanding, and produce that moderation, as well as regularity of thinking, so much to be wished for in the heads of those who imagine they come into the world only to watch and govern its motions: and as to the difference of brains, in quantity or quality, among those who are directors in faction, the doctor assured us, from his own knowledge, that it was a perfect trifle.

I heard a very warm debate between two professors about the most commodious and effectual ways and means of raising money without grieving the subject. The first affirmed the justest method would be, to lay a certain tax upon vice and folly; and the sum fixed upon every man to be rated, after the fairest manner, by a jury of his neighbours. The second was of an opinion directly contrary—to tax those qualities of body and mind for which men chiefly value themselves; the rate to be more or less, according to the degrees of excelling; the decision whereof should be left entirely to their own breasts. Wit, valour, and politeness were likewise proposed to be largely taxed and collected in the same manner, by every person's giving his own word for the quantum of what he possessed. But as to honour, justice, wisdom, and learning, they shall not be taxed at all; because they are qualifications of so singular a kind, that no man will either allow them in his neighbour or value them in himself.

The women were proposed to be taxed according to their beauty and skill in dressing, wherein they had the same privilege with the men, to be determined by their own judgment.

To keep senators in the interest of the crown, it was proposed that the members shall raffle for employments; every man first taking an oath, and giving security, that he would vote for the court, whether he won or not; after which, the losers had, in their turn, the liberty of raffling upon the next vacancy. Thus, hope and expectation would be kept alive; none would complain of broken promises, but impute their disappointments wholly to fortune, whose shoulders are broader and stronger than those of a ministry.

Another professor showed me a large paper of instructions for discovering plots and conspiracies against the government. The whole discourse was written with great acuteness, containing many observations, both curious and useful for politicians; but, as I conceived, not altogether complete. This I ventured to tell the author, and offered, if he pleased, to supply him with some additions. He received my proposition with more compliance than is usual among writers, especially those of the projecting species, professing he would be glad to receive further information.

I told him that in the kingdom Tribnia, by the natives called Langden, where I sojourned some time in my travels, "the bulk of the people consist in a manner wholly of discoverers, witnesses, informers, accusers, prosecutors, evidences, swearers, together with their several subservient and subaltern instruments, all under the colours, the conduct, and the pay of ministers of state, and their deputies. The plots in that kingdom are usually the workmanship of those persons who desire to raise their own characters of profound politicians; to restore new vigour to a crazy administration; to stifle or divert general discontents; to fill their coffers with forfeitures; and raise or sink the opinions of public credit, as either shall best answer their private advantage. It is first agreed and settled among them what suspected persons should be accused of a plot, then effectual care is taken to secure all their letters and papers, and put the owners in chains. These papers are delivered to a set of artists, very dextrous in finding out the mysterious meanings of words, syllables, and letters; for instance, they can discover a flock of geese to signify a senate; a lame dog, an invader; the plague, a standing army; a buzzard, a prime minister; the gout, a high priest; a gibbet, a secretary of state; a sieve, a court lady; a broom, a revolution; a mouse-trap, an employment; a sink, a court; a cap and bells, a favourite; a broken reed, a court of justice; an empty tun, a general; a running sore, the administration.

"When this method fails, they have two others more effectual, which the learned among them call acrostics and anagrams. First, they can decipher all initial letters into political meanings. Thus, *N* shall signify a plot; *B*, a regiment of horse; *L*, a fleet at sea: or secondly, by transposing the letter of the alphabet in any suspected paper, they can lay open the deepest designs of a discontented party. And this is the anagrammatic method."

The professor made me great acknowledgments for communicating these observations, and promised to make honourable mention of me in his treatise.

I saw nothing in this country that could invite me to a longer continuance, and began to think of returning home to England.

CHAPTER VII

THE AUTHOR LEAVES LAGADO; ARRIVES AT MALDONADA—NO SHIP
   READY—HE TAKES A SHORT VOYAGE TO GLUBBDUBDRIB—
   HIS RECEPTION BY THE GOVERNOR

THE CONTINENT, of which this kingdom is a part, extends itself,
as I have reason to believe, eastward, to that unknown tract of
America westward of California; and north, to the Pacific
Ocean, which is not above a hundred and fifty miles from
Lagado; where there is a good port, and much commerce from
the great island of Luggnagg, situated to the north-west about
29 degrees north latitude and 140 longitude. This island of
Luggnagg stands south-eastward of Japan, about a hundred
leagues distant. There is a strict alliance between the Japanese
emperor and the king of Luggnagg, which affords frequent
opportunities of sailing from one island to the other. I determined
therefore to direct my course this way, in order to my return
to Europe. I hired two mules, with a guide to show me the way,
and carry my small baggage. I took leave of my noble protector
who had shown me much favour, and made me a generous
present at my departure.

My journey was without any accident or adventure worth
relating. When I arrived at the port of Maldonada (for so it is
called), there was no ship in the harbour bound for Luggnagg,
nor likely to be for some time. The town is about as large as
Portsmouth. I soon fell into some acquaintance, and was very
hospitably received. A gentleman of distinction said to me, that
since the ships bound for Luggnagg could not be ready in less
than a month, it might be no disagreeable amusement for me to
take a trip to the little island of Glubbdubdrib, about five leagues
off to the south-west. He offered himself and a friend to accompany me, and that I should be provided with a small convenient
barque for the voyage.

Glubbdubdrib, as near as I can interpret the word, signifies
the island of sorcerers or magicians. It is about one-third as

large as the Isle of Wight, and extremely fruitful: it is governed
by the head of a certain tribe, who are all magicians. This tribe
marries only among each other, and the eldest in succession is
a prince or governor. He has a noble palace, and a park of three
thousand acres, surrounded by a wall of hewn stone twenty
feet high. In this park are several small enclosures for cattle, corn,
and gardening.

The governor and his family are served and attended by
domestics of a kind somewhat unusual. By his skill in necromancy, he has a power of calling whom he pleases from the dead,
and commanding their service for twenty-four hours, but no
longer; nor can he call the same persons up again in less than
three months, except upon very extraordinary occasion.

When we arrived at this island, which was about eleven in
the morning, one of the gentlemen who accompanied me went
to the governor, and desired admittance for a stranger, who
came on purpose to have the honour of attending on his highness.
This was immediately granted, and we all three entered the gate
of the palace between two rows of guards, armed and dressed
after a very antique manner, and something in their countenances
that made my flesh creep with horror I cannot express. We
passed through several apartments, between servants of the
same sort, ranked on each side as before, till we came to the
chamber of presence; where, after three profound obeisances,
and a few general questions, we were permitted to sit on three
stools, near the lowest step of his highness's throne. He understood the language of Balnibarbi, although it was different from
that of this island. He desired me to give him some account
of my travels; and to let me see that I should be treated without
ceremony, he dismissed all his attendants with a turn of his
finger; at which, to my great astonishment, they vanished in
an instant, like visions in a dream when we awake on a sudden.
I could not recover myself in some time, till the governor assured
me that I should receive no hurt; and observing my two companions to be under no concern, who had been often entertained
in the same manner, I began to take courage, and related to
his highness a short history of my several adventures, yet not
without some hesitation, and frequently looking behind me to
the place where I had seen those domestic spectres. I had the

honour to dine with the governor, where a new set of ghosts served up the meat and waited at table. I now observed myself to be less terrified than I had been in the morning. I stayed till sunset, but humbly desired his highness to excuse me for not accepting his invitation of lodging in the palace. My two friends and I lay at a private house in the town adjoining, which is the capital of this little island; and the next morning we returned to pay our duty to the governor, as he was pleased to command us.

After this manner we continued in the island for ten days, most part of every day with the governor, and at night in our lodging. I soon grew so familiarised to the sight of spirits, that after the third or fourth time they gave me no emotion at all; or if I had any apprehensions left, my curiosity prevailed over them. For his highness the governor ordered me to call up whatever persons I might choose to name, and in whatever numbers, among all the dead from the beginning of the world to the present time, and commanded them to answer any questions I should think fit to ask; with this condition, that my question be confined within the compass of the times they lived in. And one thing I might depend upon, that they would certainly tell me the truth, for lying was a talent of no use in the lower world.

I made my humble acknowledgments to his highness for so great a favour. We were in a chamber from whence there was a fair prospect into the park. And because my first inclination was to be entertained with scenes of pomp and magnificence, I desired to see Alexander the Great at the head of his army, just after the battle of Arbela, which, upon a motion of the governor's finger, immediately appeared in a large field, under the window where we stood. Alexander was called up into the room; it was with great difficulty I understood his Greek, and had but little of my own. He assured me upon his honour that he was not poisoned, but died of a bad fever by excessive drinking.

Next, I saw Hannibal passing the Alps, who told me he had not a drop of vinegar in his camp.

I saw Caesar and Pompey at the head of their troops, just ready to engage. I saw the former in the last great triumph. I desired that the senate of Rome might appear before me, in one large chamber, and a modern representative in counterview, in another.

The first seemed to be an assembly of heroes and demi-gods; the other, a knot of pedlars, pickpockets, highwaymen, and bullies.

The governor, at my request, gave the sign for Caesar and Brutus to advance towards us. I was struck with a profound veneration at the sight of Brutus, and could easily discover the most consummate virtue, the greatest intrepidity and firmness of mind, the truest love of his country, and general benevolence of mankind, in every lineament of his countenance. I observed, with much pleasure, that these two persons were in good intelligence with each other; and Caesar freely confessed to me that the greatest actions of his own life were not equal, by many degrees, to the glory of taking it away. I had the honour to have much conversation with Brutus, and was told that his ancestors, Junius, Socrates, Epaminondas, Cato the younger, Sir Thomas More, and himself, were perpetually together—a sextumvirate, to which all the ages in the world cannot add a seventh.

It would be tedious to trouble the reader with relating what vast numbers of illustrious persons were called up, to gratify that insatiable desire I had to see the world in every period of antiquity placed before me. I chiefly fed mine eyes with beholding the destroyers of tyrants and usurpers, and the restorers of liberty to oppressed and injured nations. But it is impossible to express the satisfaction I received in my own mind, after such a manner as to make it a suitable entertainment to the reader.

CHAPTER VIII

A FURTHER ACCOUNT OF GLUBBDUBDRIB—ANCIENT AND MODERN HISTORY CORRECTED

HAVING a desire to see those ancients who were most renowned for wit and learning, I set apart one day on purpose. I proposed that Homer and Aristotle might appear at the head of all their commentators; but these were so numerous, that some hundreds were forced to attend in the court and outward rooms of the palace. I knew and could distinguish those two heroes, at first sight, and not only from the crowd, but from each other. Homer was the comelier of the two, walked very erect for one of his age, and his eyes were the most quick and piercing I ever beheld. Aristotle stooped much, and made use of a staff. His visage was meagre, his hair lank and thin, and his voice hollow. I soon discovered that both of them were perfect strangers to the rest of the company, and had never seen or heard of them before; and I had a whisper from a ghost who shall be nameless, that these commentators always kept in the most distant quarters from their principals in the lower world, through a consciousness of shame and guilt, because they had so horribly misrepresented the meaning of those authors to posterity. I introduced Didymus and Eustathius to Homer, and prevailed on him to treat them better than perhaps they deserved, for he soon found they wanted a genius to enter into the spirit of a poet. But Aristotle was out of all patience with the account I gave him of Scotus and Ramus, as I presented them to him; and he asked them whether the rest of the tribe were as great dunces as themselves.

I then desired the governor to call up Descartes and Gassendi, with whom I prevailed to explain their systems to Aristotle. The great philosopher freely acknowledged his own mistakes in natural philosophy, because he proceeded in many things upon conjecture, as all men must do; and he found that Gassendi, who had made the doctrine of Epicurus as palatable as he could, and the vortices of Descartes, were equally to be exploded. He predicted the same fate to attraction, whereof the present learned are such zealous assertors. He said that new systems of nature were but new fashions, which would vary in every age; and even those who pretend to demonstrate them from mathematical principles would flourish but a short period of time, and be out of vogue when that was determined.

I spent five days in conversing with many others of the ancient learned. I saw most of the Roman emperors. I prevailed on the governor to call up Heliogabalus's cooks to dress us a dinner, but they could not show us much of their skill, for want of materials. A helot of Agesilaus made us a dish of Spartan broth, but I was not able to get down a second spoonful.

The two gentlemen who conducted me to the island were pressed by their private affairs to return in three days, which I employed in seeing some of the modern dead, who had made the greatest figure for two or three hundred years past, in our own and other countries of Europe; and having been always a great admirer of old illustrious families, I desired the governor would call up a dozen or two of kings, with their ancestors, in order, for eight or nine generations. But my disappointment was grievous and unexpected. For, instead of a long train with royal diadems, I saw in one family two fiddlers, three spruce courtiers, and an Italian prelate; in another, a barber, an abbot, and two cardinals. I have too great a veneration for crowned heads to dwell any longer on so nice a subject. But as to counts, marquises, dukes, earls, and the like, I was not so scrupulous. And I confess it was not without some pleasure that I found myself able to trace the particular features by which certain families are distinguished up to their originals. I could plainly discover whence one family derives a long chin; why a second has abounded with knaves for two generations, and fools for two more; why a third happened to be crack-brained, and a fourth to be sharpers: when it came, what Polydore Virgil says of a certain great house, *Nec vir fortis, nec fæmina casta*; how cruelty, falsehood, and cowardice grew to be characteristics by which certain families are distinguished as much as by their coats of arms. Neither could I wonder at all this, when I saw such an interruption of lineages, by pages, lackeys, valets, coachmen, gamesters, fiddlers, players, captains and pickpockets.

I was chiefly disgusted with modern history. For having strictly examined all the persons of greatest name in the courts of princes, for a hundred years past, I found how the world had been misled by writers, to ascribe the greatest exploits in war to cowards; the wisest counsel to fools; sincerity to flatterers; Roman virtue to betrayers of their country; piety to atheists; truth to informers: how many innocent and excellent persons had been condemned to death or banishment, by the practising of great ministers upon the corruption of judges, and the malice of factions: how many villains had been exalted to the highest places of trust, power, dignity, and profit: how great a share in the motions and events of courts, councils, and senates might be challenged by parasites and buffoons. How low an opinion I had of human wisdom and integrity, when I was truly informed of the springs and motives of great enterprises and revolutions in the world, and of the contemptible accidents to which they owed their success!

Here I discovered the roguery and ignorance of those who pretend to write anecdotes, or secret history; who send so many kings to their graves with a cup of poison; minister, where no witness was by; unlock the thoughts and cabinets of ambassadors and secretaries of state; and have the perpetual misfortune to be mistaken. Here I discovered the true causes of many great events that have surprised the world. A general confessed, in my presence, that he got a victory purely by the force of cowardice and ill conduct; and an admiral, that for want of proper intelligence, he beat the enemy to whom he intended to betray the fleet. Three kings protested to me that in their whole reigns they never did once prefer any person of merit, unless by mistake, or treachery of some minister in whom they confided: neither would they do it if they were to live again: and they showed, with great strength of reason, that the royal throne could not be supported without corruption, because that positive, confident, restive temper, which virtue infused into a man, was a perpetual clog to public business.

I had the curiosity to inquire, in a particular manner, by what methods great numbers had procured to themselves high titles of honour, and prodigious estates; and I confined my inquiry to a very modern period: however, without grating upon present times, because I would be sure to give no offence even to foreigners; for I hope the reader need not be told, that I do not in the least intend my own country, in what I say upon this occasion. A great number of persons concerned were called up; and, upon a very slight examination, discovered such a scene of infamy, that I cannot reflect upon it without some seriousness. Perjury, oppression, subornation, fraud, pandarism, and the like infirmities, were among the most excusable arts they had to mention; and for these I made, as it was reasonable, great allowance. But when some confessed they owed their greatness and wealth to debauchery; others to the betraying of their country or their prince; some, to poisoning; more, to the perverting of justice, in order to destroy the innocent; I hope I may be pardoned if these discoveries inclined me a little to abate of that profound veneration which I am naturally apt to pay to persons of high rank, who ought to be treated with the utmost respect due to their sublime dignity, by us their inferiors.

I had often read of some great services done to princes and states, and desired to see the persons by whom those services were performed. Upon inquiry I was told that their names were to be found on no record, except a few of them, whom history has represented as the vilest of rogues and traitors. As to the rest, I had never once heard of them. They all appeared with dejected looks, and in the meanest habits; most of them telling me they died in poverty and disgrace, and the rest on a scaffold or on a gibbet.

Among others, there was one person whose case appeared a little singular. He had a youth about eighteen years old standing by his side. He told me he had for many years been commander of a ship, and in the sea-fight at Actium had the good fortune to break through the enemy's great line of battle, sink three of their capital ships, and take a fourth, which was the sole cause of Antony's flight, and of the victory that ensued; that the youth standing by him, his only son, was killed in the action. He added, that upon the confidence of some merit, the war being at an end, he went to Rome, and solicited at the court of Augustus to be preferred to a greater ship, whose commander had been killed; but, without any regard to his pretensions, it was given to a boy who had never seen the sea, the son of Libertina, who waited on one of the emperor's mistresses. Returning back to his own vessel, he was charged with neglect of duty, and the ship given to a favourite page of Publicola, the vice-admiral; whereupon he retired to a poor farm at a great distance from Rome, and there ended his life. I was so curious to know the truth of this story, that I desired Agrippa might be called, who was admiral in that fight. He appeared, and confirmed the whole account; but with much more advantage to the captain, whose modesty had extenuated or concealed a great part of his merit.

I was surprised to find corruption grown so high and so quick in that empire, by the force of luxury so lately introduced; which made me less wonder at many parallel cases in other countries, where vices of all kinds have reigned so much longer, and where the whole praise, as well as pillage, has been engrossed by the chief commander, who, perhaps, had the least title to either.

As every person called up made exactly the same appearance he had done in the world, it gave me melancholy reflections to observe how much the race of human kind was degenerated among us within these hundred years past; how disease, under all its consequences and denominations, had altered every lineament of an English countenance; shortened the size of bodies, unbraced the nerves, relaxed the sinews and muscles, introduced a sallow complexion, and rendered the flesh loose and rancid.

I descended so low, as to desire some English yeomen of an old stamp might be summoned to appear; once so famous for the simplicity of their manners, diet, and dress; for justice in their dealings; for their true spirit of liberty; for their valour, and love of their country. Neither could I be wholly unmoved, after comparing the living with the dead, when I considered how all these pure native virtues were prostituted for a piece of money by their grandchildren, who, in selling their votes and managing at elections, have acquired every vice and corruption that can possibly be learned in a court.

CHAPTER IX

THE AUTHOR RETURNS TO MALDONADA—SAILS TO THE KINGDOM OF LUGGNAGG—THE AUTHOR CONFINED—HE IS SENT FOR TO COURT—THE MANNER OF HIS ADMITTANCE—THE KING'S GREAT LENITY TO HIS SUBJECTS

THE DAY of our departure being come, I took leave of his highness, the governor of Glubbdubdrib, and returned with my two companions to Maldonada, where, after a fortnight's waiting, a ship was ready to sail for Luggnagg. The two gentlemen, and some others, were so generous and kind as to furnish me with provisions, and see me on board. I was a month on this voyage. We had one violent storm, and were under a necessity of steering westward to get into the trade-wind, which holds for about sixty leagues. On the 21st of April, 1708, we sailed into the river of Clumegnig, which is a seaport town, at the south-east point of

Luggnagg. We cast anchor within a league of the town, and made a signal for a pilot. Two of them came on board in less than half an hour, by whom we were guided between certain shoals and rocks which are very dangerous in the passage, to a large basin, where a fleet may ride in safety within a cable's length of the town wall.

Some of our sailors, either out of treachery or inadvertence, had informed the pilots that I was a stranger, and a great traveller; whereof these gave notice to a custom-house officer, by whom I was examined very strictly upon my landing. This officer spoke to me in the language of Balnibarbi, which, by the force of much commerce, is generally understood in that town, especially by seamen and those employed in the customs. I gave him a short account of some particulars, and made my story as plausible and consistent as I could; but I thought it necessary to disguise my country, and call myself a Hollander: because my intentions were for Japan, and I knew the Dutch were the only Europeans permitted to enter into that kingdom. I therefore told the officer, that having been shipwrecked on the coast of Balnibarbi, and cast on a rock, I was received up into Laputa, or the flying island (of which he had often heard), and was now endeavouring to get to Japan, whence I might find a convenience of returning to my own country. The officer said I must be confined till he could receive orders from a court, for which he would write immediately, and hoped to receive an answer in a fortnight. I was carried to a convenient lodging, with a sentry placed at the door; however, I had the liberty of a large garden, and was treated with humanity enough, being maintained all the time at the king's charge. I was visited by several persons, chiefly out of curiosity, because it was reported that I came from countries very remote, of which they had never heard.

I hired a young man, who came in the same ship, to be an interpreter; he was a native of Luggnagg, but had lived some years at Maldonada, and was a perfect master of both languages. By his assistance, I was able to hold a conversation with those who came to visit me; but this consisted only of their questions and my answers.

The dispatch came from court about the time we expected. It contained a warrant for conducting me and my retinue to *Traldragdubh*, or *Trildrogdrib* (for it is pronounced both ways as near as I can remember), by a party of ten horse. All my retinue was that poor lad for an interpreter, whom I persuaded into my service, and, at my humble request, we had each of us a mule to ride on. A messenger was dispatched half a day's journey before us, to give the king notice of my approach, and to desire that his majesty would please to appoint a day and hour when it would be his gracious pleasure that I might have the honour to lick the dust before his footstool. This is the court style, and I found it to be more than matter of form: for, upon my admittance two days after my arrival, I was commanded to crawl upon my belly, and lick the floor as I advanced; but, on account of my being a stranger, care was taken to have it made so clean, that the dust was not offensive. However, this was a peculiar grace, not allowed to any but persons of the highest rank, when they desire an admittance. Nay, sometimes the floor is strewed with dust on purpose, when the person to be admitted happens to have powerful enemies at court; and I have seen a great lord with his mouth so crammed, that when he had crept to the proper distance from the throne, he was not able to speak a word. Neither is there any remedy; because it is capital for those who receive an audience to spit or wipe their mouth in his majesty's presence. There is indeed another custom, which I cannot altogether approve of: when the king has a mind to put any of his nobles to death in a gentle, indulgent manner, he commands the floor to be strewed with a certain brown powder of a deadly composition, which being licked up, infallibly kills him in twenty-four hours. But in justice to this prince's great clemency, and the care he has of his subjects' lives (wherein it were much to be wished that the monarchs of Europe would imitate him), it must be mentioned for this honour, that strict orders are given to have the infected parts of the floor well washed after every such execution, which, if his domestics neglect, they are in danger of incurring his royal displeasure. I myself heard him give directions that one of his pages should be whipped, whose turn it was to give notice about washing the floor after an execution, but maliciously had omitted it; by which neglect, a young lord of great hopes, coming to an audience, was unfortunately poisoned, although the king at that time had no design against his life. But this good prince was so gracious as to forgive the poor page his whipping, upon promise that he would do so no more, without special orders.

To return from this digression: when I had crept to within four yards of the throne, I raised myself gently upon my knees, and then striking my forehead seven times against the ground, I pronounced the following words, as they had been taught me the night before: *Inckpling gloffthrobb squw tserumm blhiop mlashnalt zwin tnodbalkuff hsthiophad kurdlubhasht.* This is the compliment, established by laws of the land, for all persons admitted to the king's presence. It may be rendered into English thus: "May your celestial majesty outlive the sun, eleven moons and a half!" To this the king returned some answer, which, although I could not understand, yet I replied as I had been directed: *Flute drin yalerick dwuldom prtasrad mirpush;* which properly signifies, "My tongue is in the mouth of my friend"; and by this expression was meant that I desired leave to bring my interpreter: whereupon the young man already mentioned was accordingly introduced, by whose intervention I answered as many questions as his majesty could put in about an hour. I spoke in the Balnibarbian tongue, and my interpreter delivered my meaning in that of Luggnagg. The king was much delighted with my company, and ordered his *bliffmarklub*, or high chamberlain, to appoint a lodging in the court for me and my interpreter, with a daily allowance for my table, and a large piece of gold for my common expenses.

I stayed three months in this country, out of perfect obedience to his majesty, who was pleased highly to favour me, and made me very honourable offers. But I thought it more consistent with prudence and justice to pass the remainder of my days with my wife and family.

CHAPTER X

THE LUGGNAGGIANS COMMENDED—A PARTICULAR DESCRIPTION OF THE STRULDBRUGS, WITH MANY CONVERSATIONS BETWEEN THE AUTHOR AND SOME EMINENT PERSONS UPON THAT SUBJECT

THE LUGGNAGGIANS are a polite and generous people, and although they are not without some share of that pride which is peculiar to all Eastern countries, yet they show themselves courteous to strangers, especially such as are countenanced by the court. I had many acquaintances, and among persons of the best fashion; and being always attended by my interpreter, the conversation we had was not disagreeable.

One day, in much good company, I was asked by a person of quality whether I had seen any of their *struldbrugs*, or immortals. I said I had not, and desired he would explain to me what he meant by such an appellation, applied to a mortal creature. He told me that sometimes, though very rarely, a child happened to be born in a family, with a red circular spot on the forehead, directly over the left eyebrow, which was an infallible mark that it would never die. The spot, as he described it, was about the compass of a silver threepence, but in the course of time grew larger, and changed its colour: for at twelve years old it became green, so continued till five-and-twenty, then turned to a deep-blue; at five-and-forty it grew coal black, and as large as an English shilling; but never admitted any further alteration. He said these births were so rare, that he did not believe there could be above eleven hundred *struldbrugs*, of both sexes, in the whole kingdom; of which he computed about fifty in the metropolis, and among the rest a young girl born about three years ago: that these productions were not peculiar to any family, but a mere effect of chance; and the children of the *struldbrugs* themselves were equally mortal with the rest of the people.

I freely own myself to have been struck with inexpressible delight, upon hearing this account: and the person who gave it me happening to understand the Balnibarbian language, which I spoke very well, I could not forbear breaking out into expressions perhaps a little too extravagant. I cried out, as in a rapture. "Happy nation, where every child has at least a chance of being immortal! Happy people, who enjoy so many living examples of ancient virtue, and have masters ready to instruct them in the wisdom of all former ages! but happiest, beyond all comparison, are those excellent *struldbrugs*, who, being born exempt from that universal calamity of human nature, have their minds free and disengaged, without the weight and depression of spirits caused by the continual apprehension of death." I discovered my admiration that I had not observed any of these illustrious persons at court; the black spot on the forehead being so remarkable a distinction, that I could not have easily overlooked it: and it was impossible that his majesty, a most judicious prince, should not provide himself with a good number of such wise and able counsellors. Yet perhaps the virtue of those reverend sages was too strict for the corrupt and libertine manners of a court: and we often find, by experience, that young men are too opinionated and volatile, to be guided by the sober dictates of their seniors. However, since the king was pleased to allow me access to his royal person, I was resolved, upon the very first occasion, to deliver my opinion to him on this matter freely and at large, by the help of my interpreter; and whether he would please to take my advice or not, yet in one thing I was determined: that his majesty, having frequently offered me an establishment in this country, I would, with great thankfulness, accept the favour, and pass my life here in the conversation of those superior beings, the *struldbrugs*, if they would please to admit me.

The gentleman to whom I addressed my discourse, because (as I have already observed) he spoke the language of Balnibarbi, said to me, with a sort of a smile, which usually arises from them to the ignorant, that he was glad of any occasion to keep me among them, and desired my permission to explain to the company what I had said. He did so, and they talked together for a long time in their own language, whereof I understood not a syllable, neither could I observe by their countenances what impression my discourse had made on them. After a short silence the same person told me that his friends and mine (so he thought fit to express himself) were very much pleased with the judicious remarks I had just made on the great happiness and advantages of immortal life, and they were desirous to know, in a particular manner, what scheme of living I should have formed to myself, if it had fallen to my lot to have been born a *struldbrug*.

I answered it was easy to be eloquent on so copious and delightful a subject, especially to me, who had been often apt to amuse myself with visions of what I should do, if I were a king, a general, or a great lord: and upon this very case, I had frequently run over the whole system how I should employ myself, and pass the time, if I were sure to live for ever.

"If it had been my good fortune to come into the world a *struldbrug*, as soon as I could discover my own happiness, by understanding the difference between life and death, I would first resolve, by all arts and methods whatsoever, to procure myself riches in pursuit of which, by thrift and management, I might reasonably expect, in about two hundred years, to be the wealthiest man in the kingdom. In the second place, I would, from my earliest youth, apply myself to the study of arts and sciences, by which I should arrive in time to excel all others in learning. Lastly, I would carefully record every action, and event of consequence that happened in the public, impartially draw the characters of the several successions of princes and great ministers of state, with my own observations on every point. I would exactly set down the several changes and customs, language, fashions of dress, diet, and diversions; by all which acquirements I should be a great treasure of knowledge and wisdom, and certainly become the oracle of the nation.

"I would never marry after threescore, but live in an hospitable manner, yet still on the saving scale. I would entertain myself in forming and directing the minds of hopeful young men, by convincing them, from my own remembrance, experience, and observation, fortified by numerous examples, of the usefulness of virtue in public and private life. But my choice and constant companions should be a set of my own immortal brotherhood, among whom I would elect a dozen, from the most ancient down to my own contemporaries. Where any of these wanted fortunes, I would provide them with convenient lodges round my own estate, and have some of them always at my table; only mingling a few of the most valuable among you mortals, whom length of time would harden me to lose with little or no reluctance, and treat your posterity after the same manner; just as a man diverts himself with the annual succession of pinks and tulips in his garden, without regretting the loss of those which withered the preceding year.

"What wonderful discoveries should we make in astronomy, by outliving and confirming our own predictions; by observing the progress and returns of comets, with the changes of motion in the sun, moon, and stars!"

I enlarged upon many other topics, which the natural desire

of endless life, and sublunary happiness, could easily furnish me
with. When I had ended, and the sum of my discourse had been
interpreted, as before, to the rest of the company, there was a
good deal of talk among them in the language of the country, not
without some laughter at my expense. At last, the same gentleman who had been my interpreter, said, "He was desired by the
rest to set me right in a few mistakes, which I had fallen into
through the common imbecility of human nature, and upon that
allowance was less answerable for them. That this breed of
struldbrugs was peculiar to their country, for there were no such
people either in Balnibarbi or Japan, where he had the honour
to be ambassador from his majesty, and found the natives in both
these kingdoms very hard to believe that the fact was possible:
and it appeared from my astonishment when he first mentioned
the matter to me, that I received it as a thing wholly new, and
scarcely to be credited. That in the two kingdoms above-
mentioned, where during his residence he had conversed very
much, he observed long life to be the universal desire and wish of
mankind. That whoever had one foot in the grave was sure to
hold back the other as strongly as he could. That the oldest had
still hopes of living one day longer, and looked on death as the
greatest evil, from which nature always prompted him to retreat.
Only in this island of Luggnagg the appetite for living was not so
eager, from the continual example of the *struldbrugs* before their
eyes.

"That the system of living contrived by me was unreasonable
and unjust; because it supposed a perpetuity of youth, health,
and vigour, which no man could be so foolish to hope, however
extravagant he may be in his wishes. That the question therefore
was not whether a man would choose to be always in the prime
of youth, attended with prosperity and health; but how he would
pass a perpetual life, under all the usual disadvantages which old
age brings along with it; for although few men will avow their
desires of being immortal, upon such hard conditions, yet in the
two kingdoms before mentioned, of Balnibarbi and Japan, he
observed that every man desired to put off death some time
longer, let it approach ever so late: and he rarely heard of any man
who died willingly, except he were incited by the extremity of
grief or torture. And he appealed to me, whether in those

countries I had travelled, as well as my own, I had not observed the same general disposition."

After this preface, he gave me a particular account of the *struldbrugs* among them. He said they commonly acted like mortals till about thirty years old; after which, by degrees, they grew melancholy and dejected, increasing in both till they came to fourscore. This he learned from their own confession; for otherwise, there not being above two or three of that species born in an age, they were too few to form a general observation by. When they came to fourscore years, which is reckoned the extremity of living in this country, they had not only all the follies and infirmities of other old men, but many more which arose from the dreadful prospect of never dying. They were not only opinionated, peevish, covetous, morose, vain, talkative; but incapable of friendship, and dead to all natural affection, which never descended below their grandchildren. "Envy and impotent desires are their prevailing passions. But those objects against which their envy seems principally directed are the vices of the younger sort, and the deaths of the old. By reflecting on the former, they find themselves cut off from all possibility of pleasure; and whenever they see a funeral, they lament and repine that others are gone to a harbour of rest, to which they themselves never can hope to arrive. They have no remembrance of anything but what they learned and observed in their youth and middle-age, and even that is very imperfect; and for the truth or particulars of any fact, it is safer to depend on common tradition than upon their best recollections. The least miserable among them appear to be those who turn to dotage, and entirely lose their memories; these meet with more pity and assistance, because they want many bad qualities which abound in others.

"If a *struldbrug* happens to marry one of his own kind, the marriage is dissolved, of course, by the courtesy of the kingdom, as soon as the younger of the two comes to the fourscore; for the law thinks it a reasonable indulgence, that those who are condemned, without any fault of their own, to a perpetual continuance in the world, should not have their miseries doubled by the load of a wife.

"As soon as they have completed the term of eighty years, they are looked on as dead in law; their heirs immediately succeed to their estates; only a small pittance is reserved for their support; and the poor ones are maintained at the public charge. After that period, they are held incapable of any employment of trust or profit; they cannot purchase lands, or take leases; neither are they allowed to be witnesses in any cause, either civil or criminal, not even for the decision of meers and bounds.

"At ninety, they lose their teeth and hair; they have at that age no distinction of taste, but eat and drink whatever they can get, without relish or appetite. The diseases they were subject to still continue, without increasing or diminishing. In talking, they forget the common appellation of things, and the names of persons, even of those who are their nearest friends and relations. For the same reason, they never can amuse themselves with reading, because their memory will not serve to carry them from the beginning of a sentence to the end; and by this defect they are deprived of the only entertainment whereof they might otherwise be capable.

"The language of this country being always upon the flux, the *struldbrugs* of one age do not understand those of another; neither are they able after two hundred years to hold any conversation (further than by a few general words) with their neighbours, the mortals; and thus they lie under the disadvantage of living like foreigners in their own country."

This was the account given me of the *struldbrugs*, as near as I can remember. I afterwards saw five or six different ages, the youngest not above two hundred years old, who were brought to me at several times by some of my friends; but although they were told that I was a great traveller, and had seen all the world, they had not the least curiosity to ask me a question; only desired I would give them *slumskudash*, or a token of remembrance, which is a modest way of begging, to avoid the law, that strictly forbids it, because they are provided for by the public, although indeed with a very scanty allowance.

They are despised and hated by all sorts of people. When one of them is born, it is reckoned ominous and their birth is recorded very particularly: so that you may know their age by consulting the register, which, however, has not been kept above a thousand years past, or at least has been destroyed by time or public disturbances. But the usual way of computing how old they are is by asking them what kings or great persons they can remember, and then consulting history; for infallibly the last prince in their mind did not begin his reign after they were fourscore years old.

They were the most mortifying sight I ever beheld; and the women were more horrible than the men. Besides the usual deformities in extreme old age, they acquired an additional ghastliness, in proportion to their number of years, which is not to be described; and among half a dozen, I soon distinguished which was the eldest, although there was not above a century or two between them.

The reader will easily believe, that from what I had heard and seen, my keen appetite for perpetuity of life was much abated. I grew heartily ashamed of the pleasing visions I had formed; and thought no tyrant could invent a death into which I would not run with pleasure, from such a life. The king heard of all that had passed between me and my friends upon this occasion, and rallied me very pleasantly; wishing I could send a couple of *struldbrugs* to my own country to arm our people against the fear of death; but this, it seems, is forbidden by the fundamental laws of the kingdom, or else I should have been well content with the trouble and expense of transporting them.

I could not but agree that the laws of this kingdom relative to the *struldbrugs* were founded upon the strongest reasons, and such as any other country would be under the necessity of enacting, in the like circumstances. Otherwise, as avarice is the necessary consequent of old age, those immortals would in time become proprietors of the whole nation, and engross the civil power, which, for want of abilities to manage, must end in the ruin of the public.

CHAPTER XI

THE AUTHOR LEAVES LUGGNAGG, AND SAILS TO JAPAN—FROM THENCE HE RETURNS IN A DUTCH SHIP TO AMSTERDAM, AND FROM AMSTERDAM TO ENGLAND

I THOUGHT this account of the *struldbrugs* might be some entertainment to the reader, because it seems to be a little out of the common way; at least I do not remember to have met the like in any book of travels that has come to my hands: and if I am deceived, my excuse must be, that it is necessary for travellers who describe the same country, very often to agree in dwelling on the same particulars, without deserving the censure of having borrowed or transcribed from those who wrote before them.

There is indeed a perpetual commerce between this kingdom and the great empire of Japan; and it is very probable that the Japanese authors may have given some account of the *struldbrugs*; but my stay in Japan was so short, and I was so entirely a stranger to the language, that I was not qualified to make any inquiries. But I hope the Dutch, upon this notice, will be curious and able enough to supply my defects.

His majesty, having often pressed me to accept some employment in his court, and finding me absolutely determined to return to my native country, was pleased to give me his licence to depart; and honoured me with a letter of recommendation, under his own hand, to the Emperor of Japan. He likewise presented me with four hundred and forty-four large pieces of gold (this nation delighted in even numbers), and a red diamond which I sold in England for eleven hundred pounds.

On the 6th of May, 1709, I took a solemn leave of his majesty, and all my friends. This prince was so gracious as to order a guard to conduct me to Glanguenstald, which is a royal port to the south-west part of the island. In six days I found a vessel ready to carry me to Japan, and spent fifteen days in the voyage. We landed at a small port-town, called Xamoschi, situated on the south-east part of Japan; the town lies on the western point, where there is a narrow strait leading northward into a long arm of the sea, upon the north-west part of which Yedo, the metropolis, stands. At landing I showed the custom-house officer my letter from the King of Luggnagg to his imperial majesty. They knew the seal perfectly well; it was as broad as the palm of my hand. The impression was, "A king lifting up a lame beggar from the earth." The magistrates of the town, hearing of my letter, received me as a public minister; they provided me with carriages and servants, and bore my charges to Yedo, where I was admitted to an audience, and delivered my letter, which was opened with great ceremony, and explained to the emperor by an interpreter;

who then gave me notice, by his majesty's order, that I should signify my request, and, whatever it were, it should be granted, for the sake of his royal brother of Luggnagg. This interpreter was a person employed to transact affairs with the Hollanders: he soon conjectured, by my countenance, that I was a European, and therefore repeated his majesty's commands in Low Dutch, which he spoke perfectly well. I answered, as I had before determined, that I was a Dutch merchant, shipwrecked in a very remote country, whence I had travelled by sea and land to Luggnagg, and then took shipping for Japan; where I knew my countrymen often traded, and with some of these I hoped to get an opportunity of returning into Europe. I therefore most humbly entreated his royal favour, to give order that I should be conducted in safety to Nangasac. To this I added another petition, that for the sake of my patron, the King of Luggnagg, his majesty would condescend to excuse my performing the ceremony imposed on my countrymen, of trampling upon the crucifix; because I had been thrown into this kingdom by my misfortunes, without any intention of trading. When this latter petition was interpreted to the emperor, he seemed a little surprised, and said he believed I was the first of my countrymen who ever made any scruple on this point, and that he began to doubt whether I was a real Hollander or not; but rather suspected I must be a Christian. However, for the reasons I had offered, but chiefly to gratify the King of Luggnagg by an uncommon mark of his favour, he would comply with the singularity of my humour; but the affair must be managed with dexterity, and his officers should be commanded to let me pass, as it were by forgetfulness; for he assured me, that if the secret should be discovered by my countrymen, the Dutch, they would cut my throat in the voyage. I returned my thanks, by the interpreter, for so unusual a favour; and some troops being at that time on the march to Nangasac, the commanding officer had orders to convey me safe thither, with particular instructions about the business of the crucifix.

On the 9th of June, 1709, I arrived at Nangasac, after a very long and troublesome journey. I soon fell into the company of some Dutch sailors belonging to the *Amboyna* of Amsterdam, a stout ship of 450 tons. I had lived long in Holland, pursuing my studies in Leyden, and I spoke Dutch well. The seamen soon knew whence I came last; they were curious to inquire into my voyages and course of life. I made up a story as short and probable as I could, but concealed the greatest part. I knew many persons in Holland; I was able to invent names for my parents, whom I pretended to be obscure people in the province of Guelderland. I would have given the captain (one Theodorus Vangrult) what he pleased to ask for my voyage to Holland; but understanding I was a surgeon, he was contented to take half the usual rate, on condition that I would serve him in the way of my calling. Before we took shipping, I was often asked by some of the crew whether I had performed the ceremony above mentioned. I evaded the question by general answers—that I had satisfied the emperor and court in all particulars. However, a malicious rogue of a skipper went to an officer, and pointing to me, told him I had not yet trampled on the crucifix; but the other, who had received instructions to let me pass, gave the rascal twenty strokes on the shoulders with a bamboo; after which I was no more troubled with such questions.

Nothing happened worth mentioning in this voyage. We sailed with a fair wind to the Cape of Good Hope, where we stayed only to take in fresh water. On the 10th of April, 1710, we arrived safe at Amsterdam, having lost only three men by sickness in the voyage, and a fourth, who fell from the foremast into the sea, not far from the coast of Guinea. From Amsterdam I soon after set sail for England, in a small vessel belonging to that city.

On the 16th of April we put in at the Downs. I landed next morning, and saw once more my native country, after an absence of five years and six months complete. I went straight to Redriff, where I arrived the same day, at two in the afternoon, and found my wife and family in good health.

PART IV

A VOYAGE TO THE COUNTRY OF THE HOUYHNHNMS

CHAPTER I

THE AUTHOR SETS OUT AS CAPTAIN OF A SHIP—HIS MEN CONSPIRE AGAINST HIM, CONFINE HIM A LONG TIME TO HIS CABIN, AND SET HIM ON SHORE IN AN UNKNOWN LAND—HE TRAVELS UP INTO THE COUNTRY—THE YAHOOS, A STRANGE SORT OF ANIMAL, DESCRIBED—THE AUTHOR MEETS TWO HOUYHNHNMS

I CONTINUED at home with my wife and children about five months in a very happy condition, if I could have learned the lesson of knowing when I was well. I left my poor wife once more, and accepted an advantageous offer made me to be captain of the *Adventure*, a stout merchantman of 350 tons: for I understood navigation well, and being grown weary of a surgeon's employment at sea, which, however, I could exercise upon occasion, I took a skilful young man of that calling, one Robert Purefoy, into my ship. We set sail from Portsmouth upon the 7th day of September, 1710; on the 14th we met with Captain Pocock, of Bristol, at Teneriffe, who was going to the Bay of Campechy to cut logwood. On the 16th, he was parted from us by a storm; I heard since my return, that his ship foundered, and none escaped but one cabin boy. He was an honest man, and a good sailor, but a little too positive in his own opinions, which was the cause of his destruction, as it has been of several others; for if he had followed my advice, he might have been safe at home with his family at this time as well as myself.

I had several men die in my ship of calentures, so that I was forced to get recruits out of Barbados and the Leeward Islands, where I touched, by the direction of the merchants who employed

me; which I had soon too much cause to repent; for I found
afterwards that most of them had been buccaneers. I had fifty
hands on board; and my orders were, that I should trade with
the Indians in the South Sea, and make what discoveries I could.
These rogues, whom I had picked up, debauched my other men,
and they all formed a conspiracy to seize the ship, and secure me;
which they did one morning, rushing into my cabin, and binding
me hand and foot, threatening to throw me overboard if I offered
to stir. I told them I was their prisoner, and would submit. This
they made me swear to do, and then they unbound me, only
fastening one of my legs with a chain, near my bed, and placed
a sentry at my door with his piece charged, who was commanded
to shoot me dead, if I attempted my liberty. They sent me down
victuals and drink, and took the government of the ship to themselves. Their design was to turn pirates, and plunder the Span-
iards, which they could not do till they got more men. But first
they resolved to sell the goods in the ship, and then go to Madagascar for recruits, several among them having died since my
confinement. They sailed many weeks, and traded with the
Indians; but I knew not what course they took, being kept a
close prisoner in my cabin, and expecting nothing less than to be
murdered, as they often threatened me.

Upon the 9th day of May, 1711, one James Welch came down
to my cabin, and said he had orders from the captain to set me
ashore. I expostulated with him, but in vain; neither would he
so much as tell me who their new captain was. They forced me
into the long-boat, letting me put on my best suit of clothes,
which were as good as new, and take a small bundle of linen, but
no arms, except my hanger; and they were so civil as not to search
my pockets, into which I conveyed what money I had, with some
other little necessaries. They rowed about a league, and then
set me down on a strand. I desired them to tell me what country
it was. They all swore they knew no more than myself; but said
that the captain (as they called him) was resolved, after they had
sold the lading, to get rid of me in the first place where they could
discover land. They pushed off immediately, advising me to
make haste, for fear of being overtaken by the tide, and so bade
me farewell.

In this desolate condition I advanced forward, and soon got

upon firm ground, where I sat down on a bank to rest myself,
and consider what I had best do. When I was a little refreshed,
I went up into the country, resolving to deliver myself to the
first savages I should meet, and purchase my life from them by
some bracelets, glass rings, and other toys, with which sailors
usually provide themselves in those voyages, and whereof I had
some. The land was divided by long rows of trees, not regularly
planted, but naturally growing; there was plenty of grass, and
several fields of oats. I walked very circumspectly, for fear of
being surprised, or suddenly shot with an arrow from behind or
on either side. I fell into a beaten road, where I saw many tracks
of human feet, and some of cows, but most of horses. At last I
beheld several animals in a field, and one or two of the same kind
sitting on trees. Their shape was very singular and deformed,
which a little discomposed me, so that I lay down behind a
thicket to observe them better. Some of them coming forward
near the place where I lay, gave me an opportunity of distinctly
marking their form. They climbed high trees as nimbly as a
squirrel, for they had strong extended claws before and behind,
terminating in sharp points, and hooked. They would often
spring, and bound, and leap with prodigious agility. The females
were not so large as the males; they had long lank hair on their
heads, but none on their faces. Upon the whole, I never beheld,
in all my travels, so disagreeable an animal, or one against which
I naturally conceived so strong an antipathy; so that thinking I
had seen enough, full of contempt and aversion, I got up, and
pursued the beaten road, hoping it might direct me to the cabin
of some Indian. I had not gone far, when I met one of these
creatures full in my way, and coming up directly to me. The
ugly monster, when he saw me, distorted several ways every
feature of his visage, and stared, as at an object he had never seen
before; then approaching nearer, lifted up his fore-paw, whether
out of curiosity or mischief I could not tell; but I drew my hanger,
and gave him a good blow with the flat side of it, for I durst not
strike with the edge, fearing the inhabitants might be provoked
against me, if they should come to know that I had killed or
maimed any of their cattle. When the beast felt the smart, he
drew back, and roared so loud, that a herd of at least forty came
flocking about me from the next field, howling and making

G

hideous faces; but I ran to the body of a tree, and leaning my back against it, kept them off by waving my hanger.

In the midst of this distress, I observed them all to run away on a sudden as fast as they could; at which I ventured to leave the tree, and pursue the road, wondering what it was that could put them into this fright. But looking on my left hand, I saw a horse walking softly in the field; which my persecutors having sooner discovered, was the cause of their flight. The horse started a little when he came near me, but soon recovering himself, looked full in my face with manifest tokens of wonder. He viewed my hands and feet, walking round me several times. I would have pursued my journey, but he placed himself directly in the way, yet looking with a very mild aspect, never offering the least violence. We stood gazing at each other for some time: at last I took the boldness to reach my hand towards his neck, with a design to stroke it, using the common style and whistle of jockeys, when they are going to handle a strange horse. But this animal seemed to receive my civilities with disdain, shook his head and bent his brows, softly raising up his right fore-foot to remove my hand. Then he neighed three or four times, but in so different a cadence, that I almost began to think he was speaking to himself, in some language of his own.

When he and I were thus employed, another horse came up, who applying himself first in a very formal manner, they gently struck each other's right hoof before, neighing several times by turns, and varying the sound, which seemed to be almost articulate. They went some paces off, as if it were to confer together, walking side by side, backward and forward, like persons deliberating upon some affair of weight, but often turning their eyes towards me, as it were to watch that I might not escape. I was amazed to see such actions and behaviour in brute beasts, and concluded with myself, that if the inhabitants of this country were endued with a proportionable degree of reason, they must needs be the wisest people upon earth. This thought gave me so much comfort, that I resolved to go forward, until I could discover some house or village, or meet with any of the natives, leaving the two horses to discourse together as they pleased. But the first, who was a dapple grey, observing me to steal off, neighed after me in so expressive a tone, that I fancied myself to understand what he meant; whereupon I turned back, and came near to him to expect his further commands; but concealing my fear as much as I could; for I began to be in some pain how this adventure might terminate; and the reader will easily believe I did not much like my present situation.

The two horses came up close to me, looking with great earnestness upon my face and hands. The grey steed rubbed my hat all round with his right fore-hoof, and discomposed it so much, that I was forced to adjust it better by taking it off, and settling it again, whereat both he and his companion (who was a brown bay) appeared to be much surprised; the latter felt the lappet of my coat, and finding it to hang loose about me, they both looked with new signs of wonder. He stroked my right hand, seeming to admire the softness and colour; but he squeezed it so hard between his hoof and his pastern, that I was forced to roar; after which they both touched me with all possible tenderness. They were under great perplexity about my shoes and stockings, which they felt very often, neighing to each other, and using various gestures, not unlike those of a philosopher, when he would attempt to solve some new and difficult phenomenon.

Upon the whole, the behaviour of these animals was so orderly and rational, so acute and judicious, that I at last concluded they must needs be magicians, who had thus metamorphosed themselves upon some design, and seeing a stranger in the way, resolved to divert themselves with him; or perhaps were really amazed at the sight of a man so very different in habit, feature, and complexion from those who might probably live in so remote a climate. Upon the strength of this reasoning, I ventured to address them in the following manner: "Gentlemen, if you be conjurers, as I have good cause to believe, you can understand any language; therefore I make bold to let your worships know that I am a poor distressed Englishman, driven by my misfortunes upon your coast; and I entreat one of you to let me ride on his back, as if he were a real horse, to some house or village where I can be relieved. In return for which favour, I will make you a present of this knife and bracelet"; taking them out of my pocket. The two creatures stood silent while I spoke, seeming to listen with great attention: and when I had ended, they neighed frequently towards each other, as if they were engaged in serious conversation. I plainly observed that their language expressed the passions very well, and the words might, with little pains, be resolved into an alphabet more easily than the Chinese.

I could frequently distinguish the word *Yahoo*, which was repeated by each of them several times; and although it was impossible for me to conjecture what it meant, yet while the two horses were busy in conversation, I endeavoured to practise this word upon my tongue; and as soon as they were silent, I boldly pronounced *Yahoo* in a loud voice, imitating at the same time, as near as I could, the neighing of a horse; at which they were both visibly surprised; and the grey repeated the same words twice, as if he meant to teach the right accent; wherein I spoke after him as well as I could, and found myself perceivably to improve every time, though very far from any degree of perfection. Then the bay tried me with a second word, much harder to be pronounced; but reducing it to the English orthography, may be spelt thus, *Houyhnhnm*. I did not succeed in this so well as in the former; but after two or three further trials, I had better fortune; and they both appeared amazed at my capacity.

After some further discourse, which I then conjectured might relate to me, the two friends took their leaves, with the same compliment of striking each other's hoof; and the grey made me signs that I should walk before him; wherein I thought it prudent to comply, till I could find a better director. When I offered to slacken my pace, he would cry *hhuun, hhuun*: I guessed his meaning, and gave him to understand, as well as I could, that I was weary, and not able to walk faster; upon which he would stand awhile, to let me rest.

CHAPTER II

THE AUTHOR CONDUCTED BY A HOUYHNHNM TO HIS HOUSE—THE HOUSE DESCRIBED—THE AUTHOR'S RECEPTION—THE FOOD OF THE HOUYHNHNMS—THE AUTHOR IN DISTRESS FOR WANT OF MEAT— IS AT LAST RELIEVED—HIS MANNER OF FEEDING IN THIS COUNTRY

HAVING travelled about three miles, we came to a long kind of building, made of timber stuck in the ground, and wattled across; the roof was low, and covered with straw. I now began to be a little comforted; and took out some toys, which travellers usually carry for presents to the savage Indians of America, and other parts, in hopes the people of the house would be thereby encouraged to receive me kindly. The horse made me a sign to go in first; it was a large room, with a smooth clay floor, and a rack and manger, extending the whole length on one side. There were three nags and two mares, not eating, but some of them sitting down upon their hams, which I very much wondered at; but wondered more to see the rest employed in domestic business: these seemed but ordinary cattle; however, this confirmed my first opinion, that a people who could so far civilise brute animals, must needs excel in wisdom all the nations of the world. The grey came in just after, and thereby prevented any ill treatment which the others might have given me. He neighed to them several times in a style of authority, and received answers.

Beyond this room there were three others, reaching the length of the house, to which you passed through three doors, opposite to each other, in the manner of a vista; we went through the second room towards the third. Here the grey walked in first, beckoning me to attend. I waited in the second room, and got ready my presents for the master and mistress of the house; they were two knives, three bracelets of false pearl, a small looking-glass, and a bead necklace. The horse neighed three or four times, and I waited to hear some answers in a human voice, but I heard no other returns than in the same dialect, only one or two a little shriller than his. I began to think that this house must belong to some person of great note among them, because there appeared so much ceremony before I could gain admittance. But, that a man of quality should be served all by horses, was beyond my comprehension; I feared my brain was disturbed by my sufferings and misfortunes: I roused myself, and looked about me in the room where I was left alone; this was furnished like the first, only after a more elegant manner. I rubbed my eyes often, but the same objects still occurred. I pinched my arms and sides to awake myself, hoping I might be in a dream. I then absolutely concluded that all these appearances could be nothing else but necromancy and magic. But I had no time to pursue these reflections; for the grey horse came to the door, and made me a sign to follow him into the third room, where I saw a very comely mare, together with a colt and foal, sitting on their haunches upon mats of straw, not unartfully made, and perfectly neat and clean.

The mare, soon after my entrance, rose from her mat, and coming up close, after having nicely observed my hands and face, gave me a most contemptuous look; and turning to the horse, I heard the word *Yahoo* often repeated betwixt them; the meaning of which word I could not then comprehend, although it was the first I had learned to pronounce; but I was soon better informed, to my everlasting mortification; for the horse, beckoning to me with his head, and repeating the *hhuun, hhuun,* as he did upon the road, which I understood was to attend him, led me out into a kind of court, where was another building at some distance from the house. Here we entered, and I saw three of those detestable creatures, which I first met after my landing, feeding upon roots and the flesh of some animals, which I afterwards found to be that of asses and dogs, and now and then a cow, dead by accident or disease. They were all tied by the neck with strong withes fastened to a beam; they held their food between the claws of their fore-feet, and tore it with their teeth.

The master horse ordered a sorrel nag, one of his servants, to untie the largest of these animals, and take him into the yard. The beast and I were brought close together and our countenance diligently compared both by master and servant, who thereupon repeated several times the word *Yahoo*. My horror and astonishment are not to be described, when I observed, in this abominable animal, a perfect human figure: the face of it indeed was flat and broad, the nose depressed, the lips large, and the mouth wide; but the differences are common to all savage nations, where the lineaments of the countenance are distorted, by the natives suffering their infants to lie grovelling on the earth, or by carrying them on their backs, nuzzling with their face against the mother's shoulders. The fore-feet of the *Yahoo* differed from my hands in nothing else but the length of the nails, the coarseness and brownness of the palms, and the hairiness on the backs. There was the same resemblance between our feet, with the same differences; which I knew very well, though the horses did not, because of my shoes and stockings: the same in every part of our bodies, except as to hairiness and colour, which I have already described.

The great difficulty that seemed to stick with the two horses was to see the rest of my body so very different from that of a *Yahoo*, for which I was obliged to my clothes, whereof they had no conception.

About noon I saw coming towards the house a kind of vehicle drawn like a sledge by four *Yahoos*. There was in it an old steed, who seemed to be of quality; he alighted with his hind feet forward, having by accident got a hurt in his left fore-foot. He came to dine with our horse, who received him with great civility. They dined in the best room, and had oats boiled with milk for the second course, which the old horse ate warm, but the rest cold. Their mangers were placed circular in the middle of the room, and divided into several partitions, round which they sat on their haunches, upon bosses of straw. In the middle was a large rack, with angles answering to every partition of the manger; so that each horse and mare ate their own hay, and their own mash of oats and milk, with much decency and regularity. The behaviour of the young colt and foal appeared very modest, and that of the master and mistress extremely cheerful and complaisant to their guest. The grey ordered me to stand by him; and much discourse passed between him and his friend concerning me, as I found by the stranger often looking on me, and the frequent repetition of the word *Yahoo*.

I happened to wear my gloves, which the master grey observing, seemed perplexed, discovering signs of wonder what I had done to my fore-feet; he put his hoof three or four times to them, as if he would signify that I should reduce them to their former shape, which I presently did, pulling off both my gloves, and putting them into my pocket.

This occasioned further talk, and I saw the company were pleased with my behaviour, whereof I soon found the good effects. I was ordered to speak the few words I understood; and while they were at dinner, the master taught me the names for oats, milk, fire, water, and some others; which I could readily pronounce after him, having from my youth a great faculty in learning languages.

When dinner was done, the master horse took me aside, and by signs and words, he made me understand the concern he was in that I had nothing to eat. Oats in their tongue are called *hlunnh.* This word I pronounced two or three times; for although I had refused them at first, yet upon second thoughts I considered that I could contrive to make of them a kind of bread, which might be sufficient, with milk, to keep me alive, till I could make my escape to some other country, and to creatures of my own species. The horse immediately ordered a white mare-servant of his family to bring me a good quantity of oats in a sort of wooden tray. These I heated before the fire, as well as I could, and rubbed them till the husks came off, which I made a shift to winnow from the grain: I ground and beat them between two stones, and then took water and made them into a paste or cake, which I toasted at the fire, and ate warm with milk. It was at first a very insipid diet, though common enough in many parts of Europe, but grew tolerable by time; and having been often reduced to hard fare in my life, this was not the first experiment I had made how easily nature is satisfied. And I cannot but observe that I never had one hour's sickness while I stayed in this island. It is true I sometimes made a shift to catch a rabbit, or bird, by springs made of *Yahoo's* hairs; and I often gathered wholesome herbs, which I boiled, and ate as salads with my bread; and now and then, for a rarity, I made a little butter, and drank the whey. I was at first at a great loss for salt, but custom soon reconciled me to the want of it; and I am confident that the frequent use of salt among us is an effect of luxury, and was first introduced only as a provocative to drink, except where it is necessary for preserving flesh in long voyages, or in places remote from great markets; for we observe no animal to be fond of it but man; and as to myself, when I left this country, it was a great while before I could endure the taste of it in anything that I ate.

This is enough to say upon this subject of my diet, wherewith other travellers fill their books, as if the readers were personally concerned whether we fare well or ill. However, it was necessary to mention this matter, lest the world should think it impossible that I could find sustenance for three years in such a country, and among such inhabitants.

When it grew towards evening, the master horse ordered a place for me to lodge in; it was but six yards from the house, and separated from the stable of the *Yahoos*. Here I got some straw, and covering myself with my own clothes, slept very sound. But

I was in a short time better accommodated, as the reader shall know hereafter, when I come to treat more particularly about my way of living.

CHAPTER III

THE AUTHOR STUDIES TO LEARN THE LANGUAGE—THE HOUYHNHNM, HIS MASTER, ASSISTS IN TEACHING HIM—THE LANGUAGE DESCRIBED—SEVERAL HOUYHNHNMS OF QUALITY COME OUT OF CURIOSITY TO SEE THE AUTHOR—HE GIVES HIS MASTER A SHORT ACCOUNT OF HIS VOYAGE

MY PRINCIPAL endeavour was to learn the language, which my master (for so I shall henceforth call him), and his children, and every servant of his house, were desirous to teach me: for they looked upon it as a prodigy that a brute animal should discover such marks of a rational creature. I pointed to everything, and inquired the name of it, which I wrote down in my journal-book when I was alone, and corrected my bad accent by desiring those of the family to pronounce it often. In this employment a sorrel nag, one of the under-servants, was very ready to assist me.

In speaking, they pronounce through the nose and throat and their language approaches nearest to the High Dutch, or German, of any I know in Europe; but it is much more graceful and significant. The Emperor Charles V made almost the same observation when he said that if he were to speak to his horse, it should be in High Dutch. The curiosity and impatience of my master were so great, that he spent many hours of his leisure to instruct me. He was convinced (as he afterwards told me) that I must be a *Yahoo*; but my teachableness, civility, and cleanliness astonished him, which were qualities altogether opposite to those animals. He was most perplexed about my clothes, reasoning sometimes with himself whether they were a part of my body; for I never pulled them off till the family were asleep, and got them on before they woke in the morning. My master was eager to learn whence I came; how I acquired those appearances of reason which I discovered in all my actions; and to know my story from my own mouth, which he hoped he should soon do by the great proficiency I made in learning and pronouncing their words and sentences. To help my memory, I formed all I learned into the English alphabet, and wrote the words down, with the translations. This last, after some time, I ventured to do in my master's presence. It cost me much trouble to explain to him what I was doing, for the inhabitants have not the least idea of books or literature.

In about ten weeks' time I was able to understand most of his questions, and in three months could give some tolerable answers. He was extremely curious to know from what part of the country I came, and how I was taught to imitate rational creatures; because the *Yahoos* (whom he saw I exactly resembled in my head, hands, and face, which were only visible), with some appearance of cunning and the strongest disposition to mischief, were observed to be the most unteachable of all brutes. I answered that I came over the sea from a far place, with many others of my own kind, in a great hollow vessel, made of the bodies of trees; that my companions forced me to land on this coast, and then left me to shift for myself. It was with some difficulty, and by the help of many signs, that I brought him to understand me. He replied that I must needs be mistaken, or that I said the thing which was not, for they have no word in their language to express lying or falsehood. He knew it was impossible that there could be a country beyond the sea, or that a parcel of brutes could move a wooden vessel whither they pleased upon water. He was sure no *Houyhnhnms* alive could make such a vessel, nor would trust *Yahoos* to manage it.

The word *Houyhnhnm*, in their tongue, signifies a horse, and, in its etymology, the perfection of nature. I told my master, that I was at a loss for expression, but would improve as fast as I could; and hoped, in a short time, I should be able to tell him wonders. He was pleased to direct his own mare, his colt, and foal, and the servants of the family, to take all opportunities of instructing me; and every day, for two or three hours, he was at the same pains himself. Several horses and mares of quality in the neighbourhood came often to our house, upon the report spread of "a wonderful *Yahoo*, that could speak like a *Houyhnhnm*, and seemed, in his words and actions, to discover some glimmerings of reason." These delighted to converse with me: they put many questions, and received such answers as I was able to return. By all these advantages I made so great a progress, that, in five months from my arrival, I understood whatever was spoken, and could express myself tolerably well.

The *Houyhnhnms*, who came to visit my master out of a design of seeing and talking with me, could hardly believe me to be a right *Yahoo*, because my body had a different covering from others of my kind. They were astonished to observe me without the usual hair or skin, except on my head, face and hands; but I discovered that secret to my master upon an accident which happened about a fortnight before.

I had hitherto concealed the secret of my dress, in order to distinguish myself, as much as possible, from that cursed race of *Yahoos*; but now I found it in vain to do so any longer. Besides, I considered that my clothes and shoes would soon wear out, which already were in a declining condition and must be supplied by some contrivance from the hides of *Yahoos*, or other brutes; whereby the whole secret would be known. I therefore told my master that, in the country whence I came, those of my kind always covered their bodies with hairs of certain animals prepared by art, as well for decency as to avoid the inclemencies of the air, both hot and cold: of which, as to my own person, I would give him immediate conviction, if he pleased to command me: whereupon I first unbuttoned my coat, and pulled it off. I did the same with my waistcoat. I drew off my shoes, stockings, and breeches. I let my shirt down to my waist, and drew up the bottom, fastening it like a girdle about my middle.

My master observed the whole performance with great signs of curiosity and admiration. He took up all my clothes in his pastern, one piece after another, and examined them diligently; he then stroked my body very gently, and looked round me several times; after which, he said, it was plain I must be a perfect *Yahoo*; but that I differed very much from the rest of my species, in the softness, whiteness, and smoothness of my skin, the shape and shortness of my claws behind and before, and my affection of walking continually on my two hinder feet. He desired to see no more; and gave me leave to put on my clothes again, for I was shuddering with cold.

I expressed my uneasiness at his giving me so often the appellation of *Yahoo*, an odious animal, for which I had so utter a
hatred and contempt. I begged he would forbear applying that
word to me, and make the same order in his family and among
his friends whom he suffered to see me. I requested likewise that
the secret of my having a false covering to my body might be
known to none but himself, at least as long as my present clothing
should last; for, as to what the sorrel nag, his valet, had observed,
his honour might command him to conceal it.

All this my master very graciously consented to, and thus the
secret was kept till my clothes began to wear out, which I was
forced to supply by several contrivances that shall hereafter be
mentioned. In the meantime he desired I would go on with my
utmost diligence to learn their language, because he was more
astonished at my capacity for speech and reason than at the
figure of my body, whether it were covered or not; adding, that
he waited with some impatience to hear the wonders which I
promised to tell him.

Thenceforward he doubled the pains he had been at to
instruct me; he brought me into all company, and made them
treat me with civility, because, as he told them privately, this
would put me into good humour and make me more diverting.

Every day, when I waited on him, besides the trouble he was
at in teaching, he would ask me several questions concerning
myself, which I answered as well as I could; and by these means
he had already received some general ideas, though very imperfect. It would be tedious to relate the several steps by which I
advanced to a more regular conversation; but the first account
I gave of myself in any order and length was to this purpose:

That I came from a very far country, as I already had attempted to tell him, with about fifty more of my own species; that we
travelled upon the seas in a great, hollow vessel, made of wood,
and larger than his honour's house. I described the ship to him
in the best terms I could, and explained, by the help of my
handkerchief displayed, how it was driven forward by the wind;
that, upon a quarrel among us, I was set on shore on this coast,
where I walked forward, without knowing whither, till he
delivered me from the persecution of those execrable *Yahoos*. He
asked me who made the ship, and how it was possible that the

Houyhnhnms of my country would leave it to the management of brutes. My answer was that I durst proceed no further in my relation, unless he would give me his word of honour that he would not be offended. He agreed; and I went on by assuring him that the ship was made by creatures like myself, who, in all the countries I had travelled, as well as in my own, were the only governing rational animals, and that upon my arrival hither I was as much astonished to see the *Houyhnhnms* act like rational creatures as he or his friends could be in finding some marks of reason in a creature he was pleased to call a *Yahoo*, to which I owned my resemblance in every part, but could not account for their degenerate and brutal nature. I said further, that if good fortune ever restored me to my native country to relate my travels hither, as I resolved to do, everybody would believe that I said the thing that was not, that I had invented the story out of my own head, and (with all possible respect to himself, his family, and friends, and under his promise of not being offended) our countrymen would hardly think it probable that a *Houyhnhnm* should be the presiding creature of a nation, and a *Yahoo* the brute.

CHAPTER IV

THE HOUYHNHNMS' NOTION OF TRUTH AND FALSEHOOD—THE AUTHOR'S DISCOURSE DISAPPROVED BY HIS MASTER—THE AUTHOR GIVES A MORE PARTICULAR ACCOUNT OF HIMSELF AND THE ACCIDENTS OF HIS VOYAGE

DURING MY relation, my master's countenance indicated great appearance of uneasiness; because doubting, or not believing, are so little known in this country that the inhabitants cannot tell how to behave themselves under such circumstances; and I remember, in frequent discourses with my master concerning the nature of manhood in other parts of the world, having occasion to talk of lying and false representation, it was with much difficulty that he comprehended what I meant, although he had otherwise a most acute judgment. For he argued thus: that the use of speech was to make us understand one another and to receive information of facts; now, if any one said the thing which was not, these ends were defeated, because I cannot properly be said to understand him, and I am so far from receiving information that he leaves me worse than in ignorance, for I am led to believe a thing black when it is white, and short when it is long. And these were all the notions he had concerning that faculty of lying, perfectly well understood and so universally practised among human creatures.

To return from this digression. When I asserted that the *Yahoos* were the only governing animals in my country, which my master said was altogether past his conception, he desired to know whether we had *Houyhnhnms* among us, and what was their employment. I told him we had great numbers; that in summer grazed in the fields, and in winter were kept in houses with hay and oats, where *Yahoo* servants were employed to rub their skins smooth, comb their manes, pick their feet, serve them with food, and make their beds. "I understand you well," said my master; "it is now very plain, from all you have spoken, that whatever share of reason the *Yahoos* pretend to, the *Houhynhnms* are your masters; I heartily wish our *Yahoos* would be so tractable." I begged his honour would please to excuse me from proceeding any further, because I was very certain that the account he expected from me would be highly displeasing. But he insisted in commanding me to let him know the best and the worst. I told him he should be obeyed. I owned that the *Houyhnhnms* among us, whom we called "horses," were the most generous and comely animals we had; that they excelled in strength and swiftness, and, when they belonged to persons of quality, were employed in travelling, racing, or drawing chariots; they were treated with much kindness and care, till they fell into diseases or became foundered in the feet; but then were sold and used to all kinds of drudgery till they died, after which their skins were stripped and sold for what they were worth, and their bodies left to be devoured by dogs and birds of prey. But the common race of horses had not so good fortune, being kept by farmers, and carriers, and other mean people, who put them to greater labour and fed them worse.

I described, as well as I could, our way of riding, the shape and use of a bridle, a saddle, a spur, and a whip, of harness and wheels. I added that we fastened plates of a certain hard substance, called iron, at the bottoms of their feet, to preserve their hoofs from being broken by the stony ways, on which we often travelled.

My master, after some expressions of great indignation, wondered how we dared to venture upon a *Houyhnhnm's* back, for he was sure that the weakest servant in his house would be able to shake off the strongest *Yahoo*; or, by lying down and rolling on his back, squeeze the brute to death. I answered that our horses were trained up, from three or four years old, to the several uses we intended them for; that if any of them proved intolerably vicious, they were employed for carriages; that they were severely beaten, while they were young, for any mischievous tricks; that they were indeed sensible of rewards and punishments: but his honour would please to consider that they had not the least tincture of reason, any more than the *Yahoos* in this country.

It put me to the pains of many circumlocutions to give my master a right idea of what I spoke; for their language does not abound in variety of words, because their wants and passions are fewer than among us. But it is impossible to express his noble resentment at our savage treatment of the *Houyhnhnm* race. He said, if it were possible there could be any country where *Yahoos* alone were endued with reason, they certainly must be the governing animal, because reason, in time, will always prevail against brutal strength. But, considering the frame of our bodies, and especially of mine, he thought no creature of equal bulk was so ill-contrived for employing that reason in the common offices of life; whereupon he desired to know whether those among whom I lived resembled me or the *Yahoos* of this country. I assured him that I was as well shaped as most of my age, but the younger and the females were much more soft and tender, and the skins of the latter generally as white as milk. He said I differed indeed from other *Yahoos*, being much more cleanly and not altogether so deformed; but, in point of real advantage, he thought I differed for the worse; that my nails were of no use either to my fore or hinder feet; as to my fore-feet, he could not properly call them by that name, for he never observed me to walk upon them; that they were too soft to bear the ground; that I generally went with them uncovered; neither was the covering I sometimes wore on them of the same shape or so strong as that on my feet behind; that I could not walk with any security, for if either of my hinder feet slipped, I must inevitably fall. He then began to find fault with other parts of my body—the flatness of my face, the prominence of my nose, my eyes placed directly in front, so that I could not look on either side without turning my head; that I was not able to feed myself without lifting one of my fore-feet to my mouth, and therefore Nature had placed those joints to answer that necessity. He knew not what could be the use of those several clefts and divisions in my feet behind; that these were too soft to bear the hardness and sharpness of stones without a covering made from the skin of some other brute; that my whole body wanted a fence against heat and cold, which I was forced to put on and off every day, with tediousness and trouble; and, lastly, that he observed every animal in this country naturally to abhor the *Yahoos*, whom the weaker avoided, and the stronger drove from them. So that, supposing us to have the gift of reason, he could not see how it were possible to cure that natural antipathy which every creature discovered against us, nor, consequently, how we could tame and render them serviceable. However, he would, as he said, debate the matter no farther, because he was more desirous to know my own story, the country where I was born, and the several actions and events of my life before I came hither.

I assured him how extremely desirous I was that he should be satisfied on every point; but I doubted much whether it would be possible for me to explain myself on several subjects, whereof his honour would have no conception, because I saw nothing in his country to which I could resemble them; that, however, I would do my best, and strive to express myself by similitudes, humbly desiring his assistance when I wanted proper words, which he was pleased to promise me.

I said, my birth was of honest parents, in an island called England, which was remote from this country as many days' journey as the strongest of his honour's servants could travel in the annual course of the sun; that I was bred a surgeon, whose trade it is to cure wounds and hurts in the body, gotten by accident or violence; that my country was governed by a female man, whom we called queen; that I left it to get riches, whereby I might maintain myself and family when I should return; that, in my last voyage, I was commander of the ship, and had about fifty *Yahoos* under me, many of which died at sea, and I was forced to supply them by others, picked out from several nations; that our ship was twice in danger of being sunk, the first time by a great storm, and the second by striking against a rock. Here my master interposed by asking me how I could persuade strangers, out of different countries, to venture with me, after the losses I had sustained and the hazards I had run. I said, they were fellows of desperate fortunes, forced to fly from the places of their birth on account of their poverty or their crimes, and therefore they were under the necessity of seeking a livelihood in other places.

During this discourse my master was pleased to interrupt me several times. I had made use of many circumlocutions in describing to him the nature of the several crimes for which most of our crew had been forced to fly their country. This labour took up several days' conversation before he was able to comprehend me. He was wholly at a loss to know what could be the use or necessity of practising those vices. To clear up which, I endeavoured to give some ideas of the desire of power and riches; of the terrible effects of lust, intemperance, malice, and envy. All this I was forced to define and describe by putting cases and making suppositions; after which, like one whose imagination was struck with something never seen or heard before, he would lift up his eyes with amazement and indignation. Power, government, war, law, punishment, and a thousand other things, had no term wherein that language could express them, which made the difficulty almost insuperable to give my master any conception of what I meant. But being of an excellent understanding, much improved by contemplation and converse, he at last arrived at a competent knowledge of what human nature, in our parts of the world, is capable to perform, and desired I would give him some particular account of that land which we call Europe, but especially of my own country.

CHAPTER V

THE AUTHOR, AT HIS MASTER'S COMMAND, INFORMS HIM OF THE
STATE OF ENGLAND—THE CAUSES OF WAR AMONG THE PRINCES
OF EUROPE—THE AUTHOR BEGINS TO EXPLAIN THE ENGLISH
CONSTITUTION

THE READER may please to observe that the following extract
of many conversations I had with my master contains a summary
of the most material points which were discoursed, at several
times, for above two years. His honour often desiring fuller
satisfaction as I farther improved in the *Houyhnhnm* tongue, I
laid before him, as well as I could, the whole state of Europe; I
discoursed of trade and manufacturers, of arts and sciences; and
the answers I gave to all the questions he made, as they arose
upon several subjects, were a fund of conversation not to be
exhausted. But I shall here only set down the substance of what
passed between us concerning my own country, reducing it in
order as well as I can, without any regard to time or other
circumstances, while I strictly adhere to truth. My only concern
is that I shall hardly be able to do justice to my master's arguments and expressions, which must needs suffer by my want of
capacity, as well as by a translation into our barbarous English.

In obedience, therefore, to his honour's commands, I related
to him the revolution under the Prince of Orange; the long war
with France, entered into by the said prince, and renewed by his
successor, the present queen, wherein the greatest powers of
Christendom were engaged, and which still continued; I computed, at his request, that about a million of *Yahoos* might have
been killed in the whole progress of it, and perhaps a hundred
or more cities taken, and five times as many ships burnt or
sunk.

He asked me what were the usual causes or motives that made
one country go to war with another. I answered, they were
innumerable, but I should only mention a few of the chief.
Sometimes the ambition of princes, who never think they have

land or people enough to govern; sometimes the corruption of ministers, who engage their master in a war in order to stifle or divert the clamour of the subjects against their evil administration. Difference in opinion has cost many millions of lives; for instance, whether flesh be bread, or bread be flesh; whether the juice of a certain berry be blood or wine; whether whistling be a vice or a virtue; whether it be better to kiss a post or throw it into the fire; what is the best colour for a coat, whether black, white, red, or grey, and whether it should be long or short, narrow or wide, dirty or clean, with many more. Neither are any wars so furious or bloody, or of so long continuance, as those occasioned by differences of opinion, especially if it be in things indifferent.

Sometimes the quarrel between two princes is to decide which of them shall dispossess a third of his dominions, where neither of them pretend to any right; sometimes one prince quarrels with another, for fear the other should quarrel with him; sometimes a war is entered upon because the enemy is too strong, and sometimes because he is too weak; sometimes our neighbours want the things which we have, or have the things which we want, and we both fight till they take ours or give us theirs. It is a very justifiable cause of a war to invade a country after the people have been wasted by famine, destroyed by pestilence, or embroiled by factions among themselves. It is justifiable to enter into war against our nearest alley when one of his towns lies convenient for us, or a territory of land that would render our dominions round and compact. If a prince sends forces into a nation where the people are poor and ignorant, he may lawfully put half of them to death, and make slaves of the rest, in order to civilise and reduce them from their barbarous way of living. It is a very kingly, honourable, and frequent practice, when one king desires the assistance of another, to secure him against an invasion, that the assistant, when he has driven out the invader, should seize on the dominions himself, and kill, imprison, or banish the prince he came to relieve. Alliance by blood or marriage is a frequent cause of war between princes; and the nearer the kindred is, the greater their disposition to quarrel: poor nations are hungry, and rich nations are proud, and pride and hunger will ever be at variance. For these reasons the trade of a soldier is held the most honourable of all others because a soldier is a *Yahoo* hired to kill, in cold blood, as many of his own species, who have never offended him, as he possibly can.

There is likewise a kind of beggarly princes in Europe, not able to make war by themselves, who hire out their troops to richer nations for so much a day to each man, of which they keep three-fourths to themselves, and it is the best part of their maintenance; such are those in many northern parts of Europe.

"What you have told me," said my master, "upon the subject of war, does indeed discover most admirably the effects of that reason you pretend to; however, it is happy that the shame is greater than the danger, and that Nature has left you utterly incapable of doing much mischief. For, your mouths lying flat with your faces, you can hardly bite each other to any purpose, unless by consent. Then as to the claws upon your feet, before and behind, they are so short and tender, that one of our *Yahoos* would drive a dozen of yours before him. And, therefore, in recounting the numbers of those who had been killed in battle, I cannot but think you have said the thing which is not."

I could not forbear shaking my head, and smiling a little at his ignorance; and, being no stranger to the art of war, I gave him a description of cannons, culverins, muskets, carabines, pistols, bullets, powder, swords, bayonets, battles, sieges, retreats, attacks, undermines, countermines, bombardments, sea-fights, ships sunk with a thousand men, twenty thousand killed on each side, dying groans, limbs flying in the air, smoke, noise, confusion, trampling to death under horses' feet, flight, pursuit, victory; fields strewed with carcases left for food to dogs and wolves, and birds of prey; plundering, stripping, burning, and destroying. And, to set forth the valour of my own dear countrymen, I assured him that I had seen them blow up a hundred enemies at once in a siege, and as many in a ship; and beheld the dead bodies drop down in pieces from the clouds, to the great diversion of the spectators.

I was going on to more particulars, when my master commanded me silence. He said, whoever understood the nature of the *Yahoos*, might easily believe it possible for so vile an animal to be capable of every action I had named, if their strength and cunning equalled their malice. But as my discourse had increased his abhorrence of the whole species, so he found it gave him a disturbance in his mind, to which he was wholly a stranger before. He thought his ears, being used to such abominable words, might, by degrees, admit them with less detestation: that although he hated the *Yahoos* of this country, yet he no more blamed them for their odious qualities that he did a *gnnayh* (a bird of prey) for its cruelty, or a sharp stone for cutting his hoof. But, when a creature pretending to reason could be capable of such enormities, he dreaded lest the corruption of that faculty might be worse than brutality itself. He seemed confident that, instead of reason, we were only possessed of some quality fitted to increase our natural vices; as the reflection from a troubled stream returns the image of an ill-shapen body, not only larger but more distorted.

He added, that he had heard too much upon the subject of war, both in this and some further discourses. There was another point, which a little perplexed him at present. I had informed him that some of our crew left their country on account of being ruined by law; that I had already explained the meaning of the word; but he was at a loss how it should come to pass that the law, which was intended for every man's preservation, should be any man's ruin. Therefore he desired to be further satisfied what I meant by law, and the dispensers thereof, according to the present practice in my own country: because he thought nature and reason were sufficient guides for a reasonable animal as we pretended to be, in showing us what we ought to do, and what to avoid.

I assured his honour that law was a science, in which I had not much conversed, further than by employing advocates in vain, upon some injustice that had been done me: however, I would give him all the satisfaction I was able.

I said there was a society of men among us, bred up from their youth in the art of proving, by words multiplied for the purpose, that white is black, and black is white, according as they are paid. To this society all the rest of the people are slaves. For example, if my neighbour has a mind to my cow, he has a lawyer to prove that he ought to have my cow from me. I must then hire another to defend my right, it being against all rules of law that any man should be allowed to speak for himself. "Now, in this case, I, who am the right owner, lie under two great disadvantages: first, my lawyer, being practised almost from his cradle in

defending falsehood, is quite out of his element when he would
be an advocate for justice, which is an unnatural office he always
attempts with great awkwardness, if not with ill-will. The second
disadvantage is, that my lawyer must proceed with great caution,
or else he will be reprimanded by the judges, and abhorred by his
brethren, as one that would lessen the practices of the law. And
therefore I have but two methods to preserve my cow. The first
is, to gain over my adversary's lawyer with a double fee, who will
then betray his client by insinuating that he has justice on his
side. The second way is for my lawyer to make my cause appear
as unjust as he can, by allowing the cow to belong to my adversary
and this, if it be skilfully done, will certainly bespeak the favour
of the bench. Now your honour is to know that these judges are
persons appointed to decide all controversies of property as well
as for the trial of criminals, and picked out from the most dexterous lawyers, who have grown old or lazy; and having been
biased all their lives against truth and equity, lie under such a
fatal necessity of favouring fraud, perjury, and oppression, that
I have known some of them refuse a large bribe from the side
where justice lay, rather than injure the faculty by doing anything unbecoming their nature or their office.

"It is a maxim among these lawyers, that whatever has been
done before may legally be done again; and therefore they take
special care to record all the decisions formerly made against
common justice and the general reason of mankind. These,
under the name of precedents, they produce as authorities to
justify the most iniquitous opinions; and the judges never fail of
directing accordingly.

"In pleading, they studiously avoid entering into the merits of
the cause; but are loud, violent, and tedious, in dwelling upon all
circumstances which are not to the purpose. For instance, in the
case already mentioned, they never desire to know what claim
or title my adversary has to my cow, but whether the said cow
were red or black; her horns long or short; whether the field I
graze her in be round or square; whether she was milked at
home or abroad; what diseases she is subject to, and the like;
after which they consult precedents, adjourn the cause from
time to time, and in ten, twenty, or thirty years come to an
issue.

"It is likewise to be observed, that this society has a peculiar cant and jargon of their own, that no other mortal can understand, and wherein all their laws are written, which they take special care to multiply; whereby they have wholly confounded the very essence of truth and falsehood, of right and wrong; so that it will take thirty years to decide whether the field left me by my ancestors for six generations belongs to me or to a stranger three hundred miles off.

"In the trial of persons accused for crimes against the state, the method is much more short and commendable: the judge first sends to sound the disposition of those in power, after which he can easily hang or save a criminal, strictly preserving all due forms of law."

Here my master interposing, said it was a pity that creatures endowed with such prodigious abilities of mind, as these lawyers by the description I gave of them must certainly be, were not rather encouraged to be instructors of others in wisdom and knowledge. In answer to which I assured his honour that in all points out of their own trade they were usually the most ignorant and stupid generation among us; the most despicable in common conversation, avowed enemies to all knowledge and learning, and equally disposed to pervert the general reason of mankind in every other subject of discourse as in that of their own profession.

CHAPTER VI

A CONTINUATION OF THE STATE OF ENGLAND UNDER QUEEN ANNE—
THE CHARACTER OF A FIRST MINISTER OF STATE IN EUROPEAN
COURTS

MY MASTER was yet wholly at a loss to understand what motives could incite this race of lawyers to perplex, disquiet, and weary themselves, and engage in a confederacy of injustice, merely for the sake of injuring their fellow-animals; neither could he comprehend what I meant in saying they did it for hire. Whereupon I was at much pains to describe to him the use of money,

the materials it was made of, and the value of the metals; that
when a *Yahoo* had got a great store of this precious substance he
was able to purchase whatever he had a mind to—the finest
clothing, the noblest houses, great tracts of land, the most costly
meats and drinks. Therefore, since money alone was able to
perform all these feats, our *Yahoos* thought they could never have
enough of it to spend or to save, as they found themselves inclined,
from their natural bent, either to profusion or avarice. That
the rich man enjoyed the fruit of the poor man's labour, and the
latter were a thousand to one in proportion to the former. That
the bulk of our people were forced to live very miserably by
labouring every day for small wages to make a few live plentifully.

I enlarged myself much on these and many other particulars
to the same purpose; but his honour did not understand, for he
went upon a supposition that all animals had a title to their
share in the productions of the earth, and especially those who
presided over the rest. Therefore he desired I would let him
know what these costly meats were, and how any of us happened
to want them. Whereupon I enumerated as many sorts as came
into my head, with the various methods of dressing them, which
could not be done without sending vessels by sea to every part of
the world, as well for liquors to drink as for sauces and innumerable other conveniences. I assured him that this whole globe of
earth must be at least three times gone round before one of our
better female *Yahoos* could get her breakfast, or a cup to put it
in. He said that must needs be a miserable country which cannot
furnish food for its own inhabitants; but what he chiefly wondered
at was, how such vast tracts of ground as I described should be
wholly without fresh water, and the people put to the necessity of
sending over the sea for drink. I replied that England, the dear
place of my nativity, was computed to produce three times the
quantity of food more than its inhabitants are able to consume,
as well as liquors extracted from grain, or pressed out of the
fruits of certain trees, which made excellent drink; and the same
proportion in every other convenience of life. But, in order
to feed the luxury and intemperance of the males and the vanity
of the females, we sent away the greatest part of our necessary
things to other countries, whence in return we brought the
materials of diseases, folly, and vice, to spend among ourselves.

That wine was not imported among us from foreign countries to supply the want of water or other drinks, but because it was a sort of liquid which made us merry, by putting us out of our senses, diverted all melancholy thoughts, begat wild extravagant imaginations in the brain, raised our hopes and banished our fears, suspended every office of reason for a time, and deprived us of the use of our limbs, till we fell into a profound sleep, although it must be confessed that we always awoke sick or dispirited, and that the use of this liquor filled us with diseases which made our lives uncomfortable and short.

But beside all this, the bulk of our people supported themselves by furnishing the necessities or convenience of life to the rich and to each other. "For instance, when I am at home, and dressed as I ought to be, I carry on my body the workmanship of a hundred tradesmen; the building and furniture of my house employ as many more, and five times the number to adorn my wife."

I was going on to tell him of another sort of people, who get their livelihood by attending the sick, having, upon some occasions, informed his honour that many of my crew had died of diseases. But here it was with the utmost difficulty that I brought him to apprehend what I meant. He could easily conceive that a *Houyhnhnm* grew weak and heavy a few days before his death, or by some accident might hurt a limb; but that Nature, who works all things to perfection, should suffer any pains to breed in our bodies, he thought impossible, and desired to know the reason of so unaccountable an evil.

I told him we fed on a thousand things which operated contrary to each other; that we ate when we were not hungry, and drank without the provocation of thirst; that we sat whole nights drinking strong liquors, without eating a bit, which disposed us to sloth, inflamed our bodies, and precipitated or prevented digestion; that it would be endless to give him a catalogue of all diseases incident to human bodies, for they would not be fewer than five or six hundred, spread over every limb and joint—in short, every part, external and intestine, having diseases appropriated to itself. To remedy which, there was a sort of people bred up among us in the profession, or pretence, of curing the sick.

But besides real diseases, we are subject to many that are only imaginary, for which the physicians have invented imaginary cures. These have their several names, and so have the drugs that are proper for them; and with these our female *Yahoos* are always infested.

"One great excellency in this tribe is their skill at prognostics, wherein they seldom fail; their predictions in real diseases, when they rise to any degree of malignity, generally portending death, which is always in their power, when recovery is not; and, therefore, upon any unexpected signs of amendment, after they pronounced their sentence, rather than be accused as false prophets, they know how to approve their sagacity to the world by a seasonable dose."

I had formerly upon occasions discoursed with my master upon the nature of government in general, and particularly of our own excellent constitution, deservedly the wonder and envy of the whole world. But having here accidentally mentioned a minister of state, he commanded me, some time after, to inform him what species of *Yahoo* I particularly meant by that appellation.

I told him that a first or chief minister of state, who was the person I intended to describe, was "a creature wholly exempt from joy and grief, love and hatred, pity and anger; at least he makes use of no other passions but a violent desire of wealth, power, and titles; that he applies his word to all uses, except to the indication of his mind; that he never tells a truth but with an intent that you should take if for a lie; nor a lie, but with a design that you should take it for a truth; that those he speaks worst of behind their backs are in the surest way of preferment; and when he begins to praise you to others or to yourself, you are from that day forlorn. The worst mark you can receive is a promise, especially when it is confirmed with an oath, after which every wise man retires and gives over all hopes.

"There are three methods by which a man may rise to be chief minister. The first is by knowing how, with prudence, to dispose of a wife, a daughter, or a sister; the second, by betraying or undermining his predecessors; and the third is by a furious zeal, in public assemblies, against the corruptions of the court. But a wise prince would rather choose to employ those who practise the last of these methods; because such zealots prove always the most obsequious and subservient to the will and passions of their master. That these ministers, having all employments at their disposal, preserve themselves in power by bribing the majority of a senate or great council; and, at last, by an expedient called an act of indemnity (whereof I described the nature to him), they secure themselves from after-reckonings, and retire from the public laden with the spoils of the nation.

"The palace of a chief minister is a seminary to breed up others in his own trade: the pages, lackeys, and porter, by imitating their master, become ministers of state in their several districts, and learn to excel in the three principal ingredients, of insolence, lying, and bribery. Accordingly, they have a subaltern court paid to them by persons of the best rank; and sometimes, by the force of dexterity and impudence, arrive through several graduations, to be successors to their lord.

"He is usually governed by a decayed wench or favourite footman, who are the channels through which all graces are conveyed, and may properly be called, in the last resort, the governors of the kingdom."

One day, in discourse, my master, having heard me mention the nobility of my country, was pleased to make me a compliment which I could not pretend to deserve: that he was sure I must have been born of some noble family, because I far exceeded in shape, colour, and cleanliness, all the *Yahoos* of his nation, although I seemed to fail in strength and agility, which must be imputed to my different way of living from those other brutes; and, besides, I was not only endowed with the faculty of speech, but likewise with some rudiments of reason, to a degree that, with all his acquaintance, I passed for a prodigy.

I made his honour the most humble acknowledgments for the good opinion he was pleased to conceive of me; but assured him, at the same time, that my birth was of the lower sort, having been born of plain honest parents, who were just able to give me a tolerable education; that nobility, amongst us, was altogether a different thing from the idea he had of it; that "our young noblemen are bred from their childhood in idleness and luxury, and when their fortunes are almost ruined, they marry some women of mean birth, disagreeable person, and unsound constitution (merely for the sake of money), whom they hate and despise.

The imperfections of the mind run parallel with those of the body, being a composition of spleen, dulness, ignorance, caprice, sensuality, and pride.

"Without the consent of this illustrious body no law can be enacted, repealed, or altered; and these nobles have likewise the decision of all our possessions, without appeal."

CHAPTER VII

THE AUTHOR'S GREAT LOVE OF HIS NATIVE COUNTRY—HIS MASTER'S OBSERVATIONS UPON THE CONSTITUTION AND ADMINISTRATION OF ENGLAND, AS DESCRIBED BY THE AUTHOR, WITH PARALLEL CASES AND COMPARISONS—HIS MASTER'S OBSERVATIONS UPON HUMAN NATURE

THE READER may be disposed to wonder how I could prevail on myself to give so free a representation of my own species among a race of mortals who were already too apt to conceive the vilest opinion of human kind from that entire congruity betwixt me and their *Yahoos*. But I must freely confess that the many virtues of those excellent quadrupeds, placed in opposite view to human corruptions, had so far opened my eyes and enlightened my understanding that I began to view the actions and passions of man in a very different light, and to think the honour of my own kind not worth managing, which, besides, it was impossible for me to do before a person of so acute a judgment as my master, who daily convinced me of a thousand faults in myself, whereof I had not the least perception before, and which among us would never be numbered even among human infirmities; I had likewise learned from his example an utter detestation of all falsehood or disguise, and truth appeared so amiable to me that I determined upon sacrificing everything to it.

Let me deal so candidly with the reader as to confess that there was yet a much stronger motive for the freedom I took in my representation of things. I had not been a year in this country before I contracted such a love and veneration for the inhabitants that I entered on a firm resolution never to return to human kind, but to pass the rest of my life among these admirable *Houyhnhnms* in the contemplation and practise of every virtue, where I could have no example or incitement to vice. But it was decreed by Fortune, my perpetual enemy, that so great a felicity should not fall to my share. However, it is now some comfort to reflect that in what I said of my countrymen I extenuated their faults as much as I dare before so strict an examiner, and upon every article gave as favourable a turn as the matter would bear. For, indeed, who is there alive that will not be swayed by his bias and partiality to the place of his birth?

I have related the substance of several conversations I had with my master during the greatest part of the time I had the honour to be in his service, but have indeed, for brevity's sake, omitted much more than is here set down.

When I had answered all his questions, and his curiosity seemed to be fully satisfied—he sent for me one morning early and commanded me to sit down at some distance (an honour which he had never before conferred upon me)—he said he had been very seriously considering my whole story, as far as it related both to myself and my country; that he looked upon us as a sort of animal, to whose share, by what accident he could not conjecture, some small pittance of reason had fallen, whereof we made no other use than by its assistance to aggravate our natural corruptions, and to acquire new ones which Nature had not given us; that we disarmed ourselves of the few abilities she had bestowed, had been very successful in multiplying our original wants, and seemed to spend our whole lives in vain endeavours to supply them by our own inventions. That as to myself, it was manifest I had neither the strength nor agility of a common *Yahoo*, that I walked infirmly on my hinder-feet, had found out a contrivance to make my claws of no use or defence, and to remove the hair from my chin, which was intended as a shelter from the sun and the weather. Lastly, that I could neither run with speed nor climb trees like my brethren (as he called them) the *Yahoos* in this country.

That our institutions of government and law were plainly owing to our gross defects in reason, and by consequence in virtue, because reason alone is sufficient to govern a rational creature, which was therefore a character we had no pretence to challenge, even from the account I had given of my own people, although he manifestly perceived that in order to favour them I had concealed many particulars, and often said the thing which was not.

He was the more confirmed in this opinion because he observed that as I agreed in every feature of my body with other *Yahoos*, except where it was to my real disadvantage in point of strength, speed, and activity, the shortness of my claws, and some other particulars where Nature had no part, so from the representation I had given him of our lives, our manners, and our actions, he found as near a resemblance in the disposition of our minds. He said the *Yahoos* were known to hate one another more than they did any different species of animals, and the reason usually assigned was the odiousness of their own shapes, which all could see in the rest, but not in themselves. He had therefore begun to think it not unwise in us to cover our bodies, and by that invention conceal many of our own deformities from each other, which would else be hardly supportable. But he now found he had been mistaken, and that the dissensions of those brutes in his country were owing to the same cause with ours, as I had described them. For if (said he) you throw among five *Yahoos* as much food as would be sufficient for fifty, they will, instead of eating peaceably, fall together by the ears, each single one impatient to have all to itself, and therefore a servant was usually employed to stand by while they were feeding abroad, and those kept at home were tied at a distance from each other; that if a cow died of age or accident, before a *Houyhnhnm* could secure it for his own *Yahoos*, those in the neighbourhood would come in herds to seize it, and then would ensue such a battle as I had described, with terrible wounds made by their claws on both sides, although they seldom were able to kill one another, for want of such convenient instruments of death as we had invented. At other times the like battles have been fought between the *Yahoos* of several neighbourhoods without any visible cause, those of one district watching all opportunities to surprise the next before they are prepared. But if they find their project has miscarried, they return home, and, for want of enemies, engage in what I call a civil war among themselves.

That in some fields of his country there are certain shining stones of several colours, whereof the *Yahoos* are violently fond;

and when part of these stones is fixed in the earth, as it sometimes happens, they will dig with their claws for whole days to get them out; then carry them away and hide them by heaps in their kennels, but still looking round with great caution, for fear their comrades should find out their treasure. My master said he could never discover the reason of this unnatural appetite, or how these stones could be of any use to a *Yahoo;* but now he believed it might proceed from the same principle of avarice which I had ascribed to mankind. That he had once, by way of experiment, privately removed a heap of these stones from the place where one of his *Yahoos* had buried it, whereupon the sordid animal, missing his treasure, by his loud lamenting brought the whole herd to the place, there miserably howled, then fell to biting and tearing the rest, began to pine away, would neither eat, nor sleep, nor work, till he ordered a servant privately to convey the stones into the same hole and hide them as before, which, when his *Yahoo* had found, he presently recovered his spirits and good humour, but took care to remove them to a better hiding-place, and hath ever since been a very serviceable brute.

My master further assured me, which I also observed myself, that in the fields where the shining stones abound the fiercest and most frequent battles are fought, occasioned by perpetual inroads of the neighbouring *Yahoos.*

He said it was common when two *Yahoos* discovered such a stone in a field, and were contending which of them should be the proprietor, a third would take the advantage and carry it away from them both, which my master would needs contend to have some kind of resemblance with our suits at law, wherein I thought it for our credit not to undeceive him, since the decision he mentioned was much more equitable than many decrees among us, because the plaintiff and defendant there lost nothing besides the stone they contended for, whereas our courts of equity would seldom have dismissed the cause while either of them had anything left.

My master, continuing his discourse, said there was nothing that rendered the *Yahoos* more odious than their undistinguishing appetite to devour everything that came in their way, whether herbs, roots, berries, the corrupted flesh of animals, or all mingled together; and it was peculiar in their temper that they were fonder of what they could get by rapine or stealth at a greater distance than much better food provided for them at home. If their prey held out they would eat till they were ready to burst, after which Nature had pointed out to them a certain root that gave them a general evacuation.

There was also another kind of root, very juicy, but somewhat rare and difficult to be found, which the *Yahoos* sought for with much eagerness, and would suck it with great delight; and it produced the same effects that wine has upon us. It would make them sometimes hug, sometimes tear one another; they would howl and grin, and chatter, and tumble, and then fall asleep in the dirt.

I did indeed observe that the *Yahoos* were the only animals in this country subject to any diseases, which, however, were much fewer than horses have among us, and contracted not by any ill-treatment they meet with, but by the nastiness and greediness of that sordid brute. Neither has their language any more than a general appellation for those maladies, which is borrowed from the name of the beast, and called "hnea-yahoo", or the *Yahoo's* evil, and the cure prescribed is a mixture of their own dung and urine forcibly put down the *Yahoo's* throat. This I have since often taken myself, and do freely recommend it to my countrymen for the public good as an admirable specific against all diseases produced by repletion.

As to learning, government, arts, manufactures, and the like, my master confessed he could find little or no resemblance between the *Yahoos* of that country and those in ours, for he only meant to observe what parity there was in our natures. He had heard, indeed, some curious *Houyhnhnms* observe that in most herds there was a sort of ruling *Yahoo* (as among us there is generally some leading or principal stag in a park), who was always more deformed in body and mischievous in disposition than any of the rest; that this leader had usually a favourite as like himself as he could get, whose employment was to lick his master's feet and posteriors, and drive the female *Yahoos* to his kennel, for which he was now and then rewarded with a piece of ass's flesh. This favourite is hated by the whole herd, and therefore, to protect himself, keeps always near the person of his leader. He usually continues in office till a worse can be found, but the very moment he is discarded his successor at the head of all the *Yahoos* in that district, young and old, male and female, come in a body and discharge their excrements upon him from head to foot. But how far this might be applicable to our Courts and favourites and Ministers of State, my master said I could best determine.

I dare make no return to this malicious insinuation, which debased human understanding below the sagacity of a common hound who has judgment enough to distinguish and follow the cry of the ablest dog in the pack without being ever mistaken.

My master told me there were some qualities remarkable in the *Yahoos* which he had not observed me to mention, or at least very slightly, in the accounts I had given him of human kind. He said those animals, like other brutes, had their females in common, but in this they differed, that the she *Yahoos* would admit the male while she was pregnant, and that the males would quarrel and fight with females as fiercely as with each other, both which practices were such degrees of brutality that no other sensitive creature ever arrived at.

Another thing he wondered at in the *Yahoos* was their strange disposition to nastiness and dirt, whereas there appears to be a natural love of cleanliness in all other animals. As to the two former accusations, I was glad to let them pass without any reply, because I had not a word to offer upon them in defence of my species, which otherwise I certainly had done from my own inclinations. But I could have easily vindicated human kind from the imputation of singularity upon article if there had been any swine in that country (as luckily for me, there were not), which, although it may be a sweeter quadruped than a *Yahoo* cannot, I humbly conceive, in justice pretend to more cleanliness; and so his honour himself must have owned if he had seen their filthy way of feeding and their custom of wallowing and sleeping in the mud.

My master likewise mentioned another quality which his servants had discovered in several *Yahoos*, and to him was wholly unaccountable. He said a fancy would sometimes take a *Yahoo* to retire into a corner, to lie down and howl, and growl, and spurn away all that came near him, although he were young and fat, wanted neither food nor water, nor could the servants imagine what could possibly ail him. And the only remedy they found was

H

to set him to hard work, after which he would infallibly come to himself. To this I was silent out of partiality to my own kind, yet here I could discover the true seeds of spleen, which only seize on the lazy, the luxurious, and the rich, who, if they were forced to undergo the same regimen, I would undertake for the cure.

His honour had further observed that a female *Yahoo* would often stand behind a bank or a bush to gaze on the young males passing by, and then appear and hide, using many antic gestures and grimaces, at which time it was observed that she had a most offensive smell; and when any of the males advanced would slowly retire, looking often back, and, with a counterfeit show of fear, run off into some convenient place where she knew the male would follow her.

At other times, if a female stranger came among them, three or four of her own sex would get about her, and stare, and chatter, and grin, and smell her all over, and then turn off with gestures that seemed to express contempt and disdain.

Perhaps my master might refine a little in these speculations, which he had drawn from what he observed himself or had been told him by others; however, I could not reflect without some amazement and much sorrow that the rudiments of lewdness, coquetry, censure, and scandal should have place by instinct in womankind.

I expected every moment that my master would accuse the *Yahoos* of those unnatural appetites in both sexes so common among us. But Nature, it seems, hath not been so expert a schoolmistress, and these politer pleasures are entirely the productions of art and reason on our side of the globe.

CHAPTER VIII

THE AUTHOR RELATES SEVERAL PARTICULARS OF THE YAHOOS—
THE GREAT VIRTUES OF THE HOUYHNHNMS—THE EDUCATION
AND EXERCISE OF THEIR YOUTH—THEIR GENERAL ASSEMBLY

As I OUGHT to have understood human nature much better than I supposed it possible for my master to do, so it was easy to apply the character he gave of the *Yahoos*, from time to time, to myself and my countrymen; and I believed I could yet make further discoveries from my own observation. I therefore often begged his honour to let me go among the herds of *Yahoos* in the neighbourhood, to which he always very graciously consented, being perfectly convinced that the hatred I bore these brutes would never suffer me to be corrupted by them; and his honour ordered one of his servants, a strong, sorrel nag, very honest and good-natured, to be my guard, without whose protection I durst not undertake such adventures. For I have already told the reader how much I was pestered by these odious animals upon my first arrival; and I afterwards failed very narrowly three or four times of falling into their clutches, when I happened to stray at any distance without my hanger. And I have reason to believe they had some imagination that I was of their own species, which I often assisted myself by stripping up my sleeves, and showing my naked arms in their sight, when my protector was with me; at which times they would approach as near as they durst, and imitate my actions after the manner of monkeys, but ever with great signs of hatred, as a tame jackdaw with cap and stockings is always persecuted by the wild ones when he happens to get among them.

They are prodigiously nimble from their infancy. However, I once caught a young male of three years old, and endeavoured, by all marks of tenderness, to make it quiet; but the little imp fell a squalling, and scratching, and biting with such violence, that I was forced to let it go; and it was high time, for a whole troop of old ones came about us at the noise, but finding the cub was safe (for away it ran), and my sorrel nag being by, they durst not venture near us.

By what I could discover, the *Yahoos* appear to be the most unteachable of all animals; their capacities never reaching higher than to draw or carry burdens. Yet I am of opinion this defect arises chiefly from a perverse, restive disposition: for they are cunning, malicious, treacherous, and revengeful; they are strong and hardy, but of a cowardly spirit, and by consequence insolent, abject, and cruel. It is observed that the red-haired of both sexes are more mischievous than the rest, whom yet they much excel in strength and activity.

The *Houyhnhnms* keep the *Yahoos* for present use in huts not far from the house; but the rest are sent abroad to certain fields, where they dig up roots, eat several kinds of herbs, and search about for carrion, or sometimes catch weasels and *luhimuhs* (a sort of wild rat), which they greedily devour. Nature has taught them to dig deep holes with their nails on the side of a rising ground, wherein they lie by themselves, only the kennels of the females are larger, sufficient to hold two or three cubs.

They swim from their infancy like frogs, and are able to continue long under water, where they often take fish, which the females carry home to their young.

Having lived three years in this country, the reader, I suppose, will expect that I should, like other travellers, give him some account of the manners and customs of its inhabitants, which it was indeed my principal study to learn.

As these noble *Houyhnhnms* are endowed by nature with a general disposition to all virtues, and have no conceptions or ideas of what is evil in a rational creature, so their grand maxim is to cultivate reason and to be wholly governed by it. Neither is reason among them in a point problematical, as with us, where men can argue with plausibility on both sides of the question, but strikes you with immediate conviction, as it must needs do where it is not mingled, obscured, or discoloured by passion and interest. I remember it was with extreme difficulty that I could bring my master to understand the meaning of the word "opinion", or how a point could be disputable; because reason taught us to affirm or deny only where we are certain; and beyond our knowledge we cannot do either. So that controversies, wranglings, disputes, and positiveness, in false or dubious propositions, are evils unknown among the *Houyhnhnms*. In the like manner, when I used to explain to him our several systems of natural philosophy, he would laugh, that a creature pretending to reason should value itself upon the knowledge of other people's conjectures, and in things where that knowledge, if it were certain, could be of no use. Wherein he agreed entirely with the sentiments of Socrates, as Plato delivers them, which I mention as the highest honour I can do that prince of philosophers. I have often since reflected what destruction such doctrine would make in the libraries of Europe, and how many paths of fame would be then shut up in the learned world.

Friendship and benevolence are the two principal virtues among the *Houyhnhnms*; and these not confined to particular objects, but universal to the whole race. For a stranger from the remotest part is equally treated with the nearest neighbour; and wherever he goes looks upon himself as at home. They preserve decency and civility in the highest degrees, but are altogether ignorant of ceremony. They have no fondness for their colts or foals, but the care they take in educating them proceeds entirely from the dictates of reason. And I observed my master to show the same affection to his neighbour's issue that he had for his own. They will have it that Nature teaches them to love the whole species, and it is reason only that makes a distinction of persons where there is a superior degree of virtue.

Courtship, love, presents, jointures, settlements, have no place in their thoughts, or terms whereby to express them in their language. The young couple meet, and are joined merely because it is the determination of their parents and friends; it is what they see done every day, and they look upon it as one of the necessary actions of a reasonable being. But the violation of marriage, or any other unchastity, was never heard of; and the married pair pass their lives with the same friendship and mutual benevolence that they bear to all others of the same species who come in their way, without jealousy, fondness, quarrelling, or discontent.

In educating the youth of both sexes, their method is admirable, and highly deserves our imitation. These are not suffered to taste a grain of oats, except upon certain days, till eighteen years old; nor milk, but very rarely; and in summer they graze two hours in the morning, and as many in the evening, which their parents likewise observe; but the servants are not allowed above half that time, and a great part of their grass is brought home, which they eat at the most convenient hours, when they can be best spared from work.

Temperance, industry, exercise, and cleanliness are the lessons equally enjoined to the young ones of both sexes; and my master thought it monstrous in us to give the females a different kind of education from the males, except in some articles of domestic management; whereby, as he truly observed, one half of our natives were good for nothing but bringing children into the

world: and to trust the care of our children to such useless
animals, he said, was yet a greater instance of brutality.

But the *Houyhnhnms* train up their youth to strength, speed,
and hardiness, by exercising them in running races up and down
steep hills, and over hard, stony grounds; and when they are all
in a sweat, they are ordered to leap over head and ears into a
pond or river. Four times a year the youth of a certain district
meet to show their proficiency and agility, where the victor is
rewarded with a song in his or her praise. On this festival, the
servants drive a herd of *Yahoos* into the field, laden with hay, and
oats, and milk, for a repast for the *Houyhnhnms*, after which these
brutes are immediately driven back again, for fear of being
noisome to the assembly.

Every fourth year, at the vernal equinox, there is a representative council of the whole nation, which meets in a plain
about twenty miles from our house, and continues about five or
six days. Here they inquire into the state and condition of the
several districts: whether they abound or be deficient in hay, or
oats, or cows, or *Yahoos*; and wherever there is any want (which
is but seldom), it is immediately supplied by unanimous consent
and contribution.

CHAPTER IX

A GRAND DEBATE AT THE GENERAL ASSEMBLY OF THE HOUY-
    HNHNMS, AND HOW IT WAS DETERMINED—THE LEARNING
    OF THE HOUYHNHNMS—THEIR BUILDINGS—THEIR MANNER
    OF BURIALS—THE DEFECTIVENESS OF THEIR LANGUAGE

ONE OF these grand assemblies was held in my time, about three
months before my departure, whither my master went as the
representative of our district. In this council was resumed their
old debate, and, indeed, the only debate that ever happened in
their country; whereof my master, after his return, gave me a
very particular account.

The question to be debated was, whether the *Yahoos* should
be exterminated from the face of the earth. One of the members

for the affirmative offered several arguments of great strength and weight, alleging "that as the *Yahoos* were the most filthy, noisome, and deformed animals which Nature ever produced, so they were the most restive and indocile, mischievous and malicious; they would ill treat and destroy the *Houyhnhnms*' cows, kill and devour their cats, trample down their oats and grass if they were not continually watched, and commit a thousand other extravagances." He took notice of a general tradition that *Yahoos* had not been always in their country, but that many ages ago, two of these brutes appeared together upon a mountain; whether produced by the heat of the sun upon corrupted mud and slime, or from the ooze and froth of the sea, was never known; that these *Yahoos* engendered, and their brood in a short time grew so numerous as to overrun and infest the whole nation; that the *Houyhnhnms*, to get rid of this evil, made a general hunting, and at last enclosed the whole herd; and, destroying the elder, every *Houyhnhnm* kept two young ones in a kennel, and brought them to such a degree of tameness as an animal so savage by nature can be capable of acquiring, using them for draught and carriage: that there seemed to be much truth in this tradition, and that those creatures could not be *ylnhniamshy* (or *aborigines* of the land), because of the violent hatred the *Houyhnhnms*, as well as all other animals, bore them, which, although their evil disposition sufficiently deserved, could never have arrived at so high a degree if they had been *aborigines*, or else they would have been long since rooted out; that the inhabitants, taking a fancy to use the service of the *Yahoos*, had very imprudently neglected to cultivate the breed of asses, which are a comely animal, easily kept, more tame and orderly, without any offensive smell; strong enough for labour, although they yield to the other in agility of body; and if their braying be no agreeable sound, it is far preferable to the horrible howlings of the *Yahoos*.

Several others declared their sentiments to the same purpose, when my master proposed an expedient to the assembly, whereof he had indeed borrowed the hint from me. He approved of the tradition mentioned by the honourable member who spoke before, and affirmed that the two *Yahoos*, said to be seen first among them, had been driven thither over the sea; that coming to land, and being forsaken by their companions, they retired to the mountains, and degenerated by degrees, became in process of much time more savage than those of their own species in the country whence these two originals came. The reason of this assertion was that he had now in his possession a certain wonderful *Yahoo* (meaning myself), which most of them had heard of and many of them had seen. He then related to them how he first found me; that my body was all covered with an artificial composure of the skins and hairs of other animals: that I spoke in a language of my own, and had thoroughly learned theirs; that I had related to him the accidents which brought me thither; that when he saw me without my covering I was an exact *Yahoo* in every part, only a whiter colour, less hairy, and with shorter claws. He added how I had endeavoured to persuade him that in my own and other countries the *Yahoos* acted as the governing rational animal, and held the *Houyhnhnms* in servitude; that he observed in me all the qualities of a *Yahoo*, only a little more civilised by some tincture of reason, which, however, was in a degree as far inferior to the *Houyhnhnm* race as the *Yahoos* of their country were to me; that among other things, I mentioned a mode we had of dealing with *Houyhnhnms* when they were young, in order to render them tame; that the operation was easy and safe; that it was no shame to learn wisdom from brutes, as industry is taught by the ant and building by the swallow (for so I translate the word *lynhannh*, although it be a much larger fowl); that this invention might be practised upon the younger *Yahoos* here, which, besides rendering them tractable and fitter for use, would in an age put an end to the whole species, without destroying life; that in the meantime the *Houyhnhnms* should be exhorted to cultivate the breed of asses, which, as they are in all respects more valuable brutes, so they have this advantage, to be fit for service at five years old, which the others are not till twelve.

This was all my master thought fit to tell me at that time of what passed in the grand council. But he was pleased to conceal one particular, which related personally to myself, whereof I soon felt the unhappy effect, as the reader will know in its proper place, and whence I date all the succeeding misfortunes of my life.

The *Houyhnhnms* have no letters, and consequently their knowledge is all traditional. But there happening few events of any moment among a people so well united, naturally disposed to every virtue, wholly governed by reason, and cut off from all commerce with other nations, the historical part is easily preserved without burdening their memories. I have already observed that they are subject to no diseases, and therefore can have no need of physicians. However, they have excellent medicines, composed of herbs, to cure accidental bruises and cuts in the pastern or frog of the foot by sharp stones, as well as other maims and hurts in the several parts of the body.

They calculate the year by the revolutions of the sun and moon, but use no subdivisions into weeks. They are well enough acquainted with the motions of those two luminaries, and understand the nature of eclipses; and this is the utmost progress of their astronomy.

In poetry they must be allowed to excel all other mortals, wherein the justness of their similes, and the minuteness as well as exactness of their descriptions, are indeed inimitable. Their verses abound very much in both of these, and usually contain either some exalted notions of friendship and benevolence or the praises of those who were victors in races and other bodily exercises. Their buildings, although very rude and simple, are not inconvenient, but well contrived to defend them from all injuries of cold and heat. They have a kind of tree which at forty years old loosens in the root and falls with the first storm; it grows very straight, and being pointed like stakes, with a sharp stone (for the *Houyhnhnms* know not the use of iron), they stick them erect in the ground, about ten inches asunder, and then weave in oat straw, or sometimes wattles between them. The roof is made after the same manner, and so are the doors.

The *Houyhnhnms* use the hollow part, between the pastern and the hoof of the fore-foot, as we do our hands, and this with greater dexterity than I could at first imagine. I have seen a white mare of our family thread a needle (which I lent her on purpose) with that joint. They milk their cows, reap their oats, and do all the work which requires hands in the same manner. They have a kind of hard flints, which, by grinding against other stones, they form into instruments that serve instead of wedges, axes, and hammers. With tools made of these flints, they likewise cut their hay and reap their oats, which there grow naturally in several fields; the *Yahoos* draw home the sheaves in carriages, and the servants tread them in certain covered huts to get out the grain, which is kept in stores. They made a rude kind of earthen and wooden vessels, and bake the former in the sun.

If they can avoid casualties, they die only of old age, and are buried in the obscurest places that can be found, their friends and relations expressing neither joy nor grief at their departure; nor does the dying person discover the least regret that he is leaving the world, any more than if he were upon returning home from a visit to one of his neighbours. I remember my master having once made an appointment with a friend and his family to come to his house upon some affair of importance. On the day fixed, the mistress and her two children came very late; she made two excuses, first for her husband, who, as she said, happened that every morning to *lhnuwnh*. The word is strongly expressive in their language, but not easily rendered into English; it signifies, "to retire to his first mother." Her excuse for not coming sooner was, that her husband dying late in the morning, she was a good while consulting her servants about a convenient place where his body should be laid; and I observed she behaved herself at our house as cheerfully as the rest; she died about three months after.

They live generally to seventy or seventy-five years, very seldom to fourscore. Some weeks before their death they feel a gradual decay, but without pain. During this time they are much visited by their friends, because they cannot go abroad with their usual ease and satisfaction. However, about ten days before their death, which they seldom fail in computing, they return the visits that have been made them by those who are nearest in the neighbourhood, being carried in a convenient sledge drawn by *Yahoos*, which vehicle they use, not only upon this occasion, but when they grow old, upon long journeys, or when they are lamed by an accident: and therefore when the dying *Houyhnhnms* return those visits, they take a solemn leave of their friends, as if they were going to some remote part of the country where they designed to pass the rest of their lives.

I know not whether it may be worth observing that the *Houyhnhnms* have no word in their language to express anything that is evil, except what they borrow from the deformities, or ill qualities of the *Yahoos*. Thus they denote the folly of a servant, an omission of a child, a stone that cuts their feet, a continuance of foul or unseasonable weather, and the like, by adding to each the epithet of *Yahoo*. For instance, *hhum Yahoo, whnaholm Yahoo, ynlhmndwiklma Yahoo*, and an ill-contrived house, *ynholmhnmrohlnw Yahoo*.

I could, with great pleasure, enlarge further upon the manners and virtues of this excellent people; but intending in a short time to publish a volume by itself, expressly upon that subject, I refer the reader thither; and, in the meantime, proceed to relate my own sad catastrophe.

CHAPTER X

THE AUTHOR'S ECONOMY AND HAPPY LIFE AMONG THE HOUYHNHNMS—HIS GREAT IMPROVEMENT IN VIRTUE BY CONVERSING WITH THEM—THEIR CONVERSATIONS—THE AUTHOR HAS NOTICE GIVEN HIM BY HIS MASTER THAT HE MUST DEPART FROM THE COUNTRY—HE FALLS INTO A SWOON FOR GRIEF, BUT SUBMITS—HE CONTRIVES AND FINISHES A CANOE BY THE HELP OF A FELLOW-SERVANT, AND PUTS TO SEA AT A VENTURE

I HAD settled my little economy to my own heart's content. My master had ordered a room to be made for me, after their manner, about six yards from the house, the sides and floors of which I plastered with clay, and covered with rush mats of my own contriving. I had beaten hemp, which there grows wild, and made of it a sort of ticking; this I filled with the feathers of several birds I had taken with springs made of *Yahoo's* hairs, and were excellent food. I had worked two chairs with my knife, the sorrel nag helping me in the grosser and more laborious part. When my clothes were worn to rags, I made myself others with the skins of rabbits, and of a certain beautiful animal, about the same size, called *nnuhnoh*, the skin of which is covered with a fine down. Of these I also made very tolerable stockings. I soled my shoes with wood, which I cut from a tree, and fitted to the upper leather; and when this was worn out I supplied it with the skins of *Yahoos* dried in the sun. I often got honey out of hollow trees, which I mingled with water or ate with my bread. No man could more verify the truth of these two maxims, that "Nature is very easily satisfied," and that "Necessity is the mother of invention". I enjoyed perfect health of body and tranquillity of mind; I did not feel the treachery or inconstancy of a friend, nor the injuries of a secret or open enemy. I had no occasion of bribing or flattering, to procure the favour of any great man or of his minion. I wanted no fence against fraud or oppression; here was neither physician to destroy my body, nor lawyer to ruin my fortune; no informer to watch my words and actions, or forge accusations against me for hire; here were no gibers, censurers, backbiters, pickpockets, highwaymen, house-breakers, attorneys, buffoons, gamesters, politicians, wits, splenetics, tedious talkers, controvertists, murderers, robbers, virtuosos; no leaders or followers of party and faction; no encouragers to vice by seducement or examples; no dungeons, taxes, gibbets, whipping-posts or pillories; no cheating shop-keepers or mechanics; no pride, vanity, or affectation; no fops, bullies or drunkards; no ranting or expensive wives; no stupid, proud pedants; no importunate, overbearing, quarrelsome, noisy, roaring, empty, conceited, swearing companions; no scoundrels raised from the dust upon the merits of their vices, or nobility thrown into it on account of their virtues; no lords, fiddlers, judges, or dancing-masters.

I had the favour of being admitted to several *Houyhnhnms* who came to visit or dine with my master, when his honour graciously suffered me to wait in the room and listen to their discourse. Both he and his company would often condescend to ask me questions and receive my answers. I had also sometimes the honour of attending my master in his visits to others. I never presumed to speak, except in answer to a question; and then I did it with inward regret, because it was a loss of so much time for improving myself; but I was infinitely delighted with the station of an humble auditor in such conversations, where nothing passed but what was useful, expressed in the fewest and most significant words; where, as I have already said, the greatest decency was observed without the least degree of ceremony;

where no person spoke without being pleased himself and pleasing his companions; where there was no interruption, tediousness, heat, or difference of sentiments. They have a notion that when people are met together, a short silence does much improve conversation. This I found to be true; for, during those little intermissions of talk, new ideas would arise in their minds, which very much enlivened the discourse. Their subjects are generally on friendship and benevolence, on order and economy; sometimes upon the visible operations of Nature, or ancient traditions; upon the bounds and limits of virtue; upon the unerring rules of reason, or upon some determination to be taken at the next great assembly, and often upon the various excellencies of poetry. I may add, without vanity, that my presence often gave them sufficient matter for discourse, because it afforded my master an occasion of letting his friends into the history of me and my country, upon which they were all pleased to descant, in a manner not very advantageous to human kind; and for that reason I shall not repeat what they said; only I may be allowed to observe that his honour, to my great admiration, appeared to understand the nature of *Yahoos* much better than myself. He went through all our vices and follies, and discovered many which I had never mentioned to him, by only supposing what qualities a *Yahoo* of their country, with a small proportion of reason, might be capable of exerting; and concluded with too much probability, "how vile as well as miserable such a creature must be."

I freely confess that all the little knowledge I had of any value was acquired by the lectures I had received from my master and from hearing the discourses of him and his friends; to which I should be prouder to listen than to dictate to the greatest and wisest assembly in Europe. I admired the strength, comeliness, and speed of the inhabitants; and such a constellation of virtues, in such amiable persons, produced in me the highest veneration. At first, indeed, I did not feel that natural awe which the *Yahoos* and all other animals bear towards them: but it grew upon me by degrees, much sooner than I imagined, and was mingled with a respectful love and gratitude, that they would condescend to distinguish me from the rest of my species.

When I thought of my family, my friends, my countrymen,

or the human race in general, I considered them, as they really were, *Yahoos* in shape and disposition, perhaps a little more civilised, and qualified with the gift of speech; but making no other use of reason than to improve and multiply those vices whereof their brethren in this country had only the share that nature allotted them. When I happened to see the reflection of my own form in a lake or fountain, I turned away my face in horror and detestation of myself, and could better endure the sight of a common *Yahoo* than of my own person. By conversing with the *Houyhnhnms*, and looking upon them with delight, I fell to imitate their gait and gesture, which is now grown into a habit, and my friends often tell me, in a blunt way, that I trot like a horse; which, however, I take for a great compliment: neither shall I disown that in speaking I am apt to fall into the voice and manners of the *Houyhnhnms*, and hear myself ridiculed on that account without the least mortification.

In the midst of all this happiness, and when I looked upon myself to be fully settled for life, my master sent for me one morning a little earlier than his usual hour. I observed by his countenance that he was in some perplexity, and at a loss how to begin what he had to speak. After a short silence, he told me he did not know how I would take what he was going to say: that in the last general assembly, when the affair of the *Yahoos* was entered upon, the representatives had taken offence at his keeping a *Yahoo* (meaning myself) in his family, more like a *Houyhnhnm* than a brute animal; that he was known frequently to converse with me, as if he could receive some advantage or pleasure in my company; that such a practice was not agreeable to reason or nature, or a thing ever heard of before among them; the assembly did therefore exhort him either to employ me like the rest of my species, or command me to swim back to the place whence I came: that the first of these expedients was utterly rejected by all the *Houyhnhnms* who had ever seen me at his house or their own: for they alleged that because I had some rudiments of reason, added to the natural gravity of those animals, it was to be feared I might be able to seduce them into the woody and mountainous parts of the country, and bring them in troops by night to destroy the *Houyhnhnms'* cattle as being naturally of the ravenous kind, and averse from labour.

My master added that he was daily pressed by the *Houyhnhnms* of the neighbourhood to have the assembly's exhortation executed which he could not put off much longer. He doubted it would be impossible for me to swim to another country; and therefore wished I would contrive some sort of vehicle resembling those I had described to him, that might carry me on the sea; in which work I should have the assistance of his own servants, as well as those of his neighbours. He concluded that for his own part, he could have been content to keep me in his service as long as I lived; because he found I had cured myself of some bad habits and dispositions, by endeavouring, as far as my inferior nature was capable, to imitate *Houyhnhnms*.

I should here observe to the reader, that a decree of the general assembly in this country is expressed by the word *hnhloayn*, which signifies an exhortation, as near as I can render it: for they have no conception how a rational creature can be compelled, but only advised or exhorted; because no person can disobey reason, without giving up his claim to be a rational creature.

I was struck with the utmost grief and despair at my master's discourse; and being unable to support the agonies I was under, I fell into a swoon at his feet. When I came to myself, he told me that he concluded I had been dead; for these people are subject to no such imbecilities of nature. I answered, in a faint voice, that death would have been too great a happiness: that although I could not blame the assembly's exhortation, or the urgency of his friends, yet, in my weak and corrupt judgment, I thought it might consist with reason to have been less rigorous: that I could not swim a league, and probably the nearest land to theirs might be distant above a hundred: that many materials necessary for making a small vessel to carry me off were wholly wanting in this country; which, however, I would attempt, in obedience and gratitude to his honour, although I concluded the thing to be impossible, and therefore looked on myself as already devoted to destruction; that the certain prospect of an unnatural death was the least of my evils; for, supposing I should escape with life by some strange adventure, how could I think with temper of passing days among *Yahoos*, and relapsing into my old corruptions, for want of examples to lead and keep me within the paths of virtue? that I knew too well upon what solid reasons all the determinations of the wise *Houyhnhnms* were founded, not to be shaken by arguments of mine, a miserable *Yahoo*; and therefore, after presenting him with my humble thanks for the offer of his servants' assistance in making a vessel, and desiring a reasonable time for so difficult a work, I told him I would endeavour to preserve a wretched being; and if ever I returned to England, was not without hopes of being useful to my own species, by celebrating the praises of the renowned *Houyhnhnms* and proposing their virtues to the imitation of mankind.

My master, in a few words, made me a very gracious reply; allowed me the space of two months to finish my boat: and ordered the sorrel nag, my fellow-servant—for so at this distance I may presume to call him—to follow my instructions; because I told my master that his help would be sufficient, and I knew he had a tenderness for me.

In his company, my first business was to go to that part of the coast where my rebellious crew had ordered me to be set on shore. I got upon a height, and looking on every side into the sea, fancied I saw a small island towards the north-east; I took out my pocket glass, and could then clearly distinguish it about five leagues off, as I computed: but it appeared to the sorrel nag to be only a blue cloud; for as he had no conception of any country beside his own, so he could not be as expert in distinguishing remote objects at sea, as we who so much converse in that element.

After I had discovered this island, I considered no further; but resolved it should, if possible, be the first place of my banishment, leaving the consequence to fortune.

I returned home, and consulting with the sorrel nag, we went into a copse at some distance, where I with my knife, and he with a sharp flint, fastened very artificially after their manner to a wooden handle, cut down several oak wattles, about the thickness of a walking-staff, and some larger pieces. But I shall not trouble the reader with a particular description of my own mechanics; let it suffice to say, that in six weeks' time, with the help of the sorrel nag, who performed the parts that required most labour, I finished a sort of Indian canoe, but much larger, covering it with the skins of *Yahoos*, well stitched together with hempen threads of my own making. My sail was likewise composed of the skins of the same animal; but I made use of the youngest I could get, the older being too rough and thick: and I likewise provided myself with four paddles. I laid in a stock of boiled flesh, of rabbits and fowls; and took with me two vessels, one filled with milk, and the other with water.

I tried my canoe in a large pond, near my master's house, and then corrected in it what was amiss; stopping all the chinks with *Yahoo's* tallow, till I found it staunch, and able to bear me and my freight; and, when it was as complete as I could possibly make it, I had it drawn on a carriage very gently by *Yahoos* to the sea-side, under the conduct of the sorrel nag and another servant.

When all was ready, and the day came for my departure, I took leave of my master and lady and the whole family, my eyes flowing with tears, and my heart quite sunk with grief. But his honour, out of curiosity, and perhaps (if I may speak it without vanity) partly out of kindness, was determined to see me in my canoe, and got several of his neighbouring friends to accompany him. I was forced to wait above an hour for the tide, and then, observing the wind very fortunately bearing towards the island to which I intended to steer my course, I took a second leave of my master; but as I was going to prostrate myself to kiss his hoof, he did me the honour to raise it gently to my mouth. I am not ignorant how much I have been censured for mentioning this last particular. Detractors are pleased to think it improbable that so illustrious a person should descend to give so great a mark of distinction to a creature so inferior as I. Neither have I forgotten how apt some travellers are to boast of extraordinary favours they have received. But if these censurers were better acquainted with the noble and courteous disposition of the *Houyhnhnms*, they would soon change their opinion.

I paid my respects to the rest of the *Houyhnhnms* in his honour's company; then getting into my canoe, I pushed off from shore.

CHAPTER XI

THE AUTHOR'S DANGEROUS VOYAGE—HE ARRIVES AT NEW
HOLLAND, HOPING TO SETTLE THERE—IS WOUNDED WITH
AN ARROW BY ONE OF THE NATIVES—IS SEIZED AND CARRIED
BY FORCE INTO A PORTUGUESE SHIP—THE GREAT CIVILITIES
OF THE CAPTAIN—THE AUTHOR ARRIVES AT ENGLAND

I BEGAN this desperate voyage on February 15th, 1714–15, at
nine o'clock in the morning. The wind was favourable; however, I made use at first only of my paddles; but considering
I should be weary, and that the wind might chop about, I
ventured to set up my little sail: and thus, with the help of the
tide, I went at the rate of a league and a half an hour, as near as
I could guess. My master and his friends continued on the shore
till I was almost out of sight; and I often heard the sorrel nag
(who always loved me) crying out, *Hnuy illa nyha, majah Yahoo*
("Take care of thyself, gentle *Yahoo*").

My design was, if possible, to discover some small island
uninhabited, yet sufficient by my labour to furnish me with
the necessaries of life, which I would have thought a greater
happiness than to be first minister in the politest court of Europe;
so horrible was the idea I conceived of returning to live in the
society and under the government of *Yahoos*. For in such a
solitude as I desired, I could at least enjoy my own thoughts,
and reflect with delight on the virtues of those inimitable
Houyhnhnms, without an opportunity of degenerating into the
vices and corruptions of my own species.

The reader may remember what I related when my crew
conspired against me, and confined me in my cabin; how I
continued there several weeks without knowing what course
we took; and when I was put ashore in the long-boat, how the
sailors told me with oaths, whether true or false, that they knew
not in what part of the world we were. However, I did then
believe us to be about ten degrees southward of the Cape of
Good Hope, or forty-five degrees southern latitude, as I
gathered from some general words I overheard among them,

being, as I supposed, to the south-east in their intended voyage to Madagascar. And although this were little better than a conjecture, yet I resolved to steer my course eastward, hoping to reach the south-west coast of New Holland, and perhaps some such island as I desired lying westward of it. The wind was full west, and by six in the evening I computed I had gone eastward at least eighteen leagues; when I spied a very small island about half a league off, which I soon reached. It was nothing but a rock, with one creek naturally arched by the force of tempests. Here I put in my canoe, and climbing a part of the rock, I could plainly discover land to the east, extending from south to north. I lay all night in my canoe; and repeating my voyage early in the morning, I arrived in seven hours to the south-east point of New Holland. This confirmed me in the opinion I have long entertained, that the maps and charts place this country at least three degrees more at the east than it really is; which thought I communicated many years ago to my worthy friend, Mr. Herman Moll, and gave him my reasons for it, although he has rather chosen to follow other authors.

I saw no inhabitants in the place where I landed, and being unarmed, I was afraid of venturing far into the country. I found some shell-fish on the shore, and ate them raw, not daring to kindle a fire, for fear of being discovered by the natives. I continued three days feeding on oysters and limpets, to save my own provision; and I fortunately found a brook of excellent water, which gave me great relief.

On the fourth day, venturing out early a little too far, I saw twenty or thirty natives upon a height not above five hundred yards from me. They consisted of men, women and children, sitting round a fire, as I could discover by the smoke. One of them spied me, and gave notice to the rest; five of them advanced towards me, leaving the women and children at the fire. I made what haste I could to the shore, and getting into my canoe, pushed off; the savages, observing me retreat, ran after me; and before I could get far enough into the sea, discharged an arrow, which wounded me deeply on the inside of my left knee: I shall carry the mark to my grave. I apprehended the arrow might be poisoned, and paddling out of the reach of their darts (being a calm day), I made a shift to suck the wound, and dress it as well as I could.

I was at a loss what to do, for I durst not return to the same
landing-place, but stood to the north, and was forced to paddle;
for the wind, though very gentle, was against me, blowing north-
west. As I was looking about for a secure landing-place, I saw a
sail to the north-north-east, which appearing every minute
more visible, I was in some doubt, whether I should wait for
them or not; but at last my detestation of the *Yahoo* race prevailed;
and turning my canoe, I sailed and paddled towards the south,
and got into the same creek whence I set out in the morning,
choosing rather to trust myself among these barbarians than
live with European *Yahoos*. I drew up my canoe as close as I
could to the shore, and hid myself behind a stone by the little
brook, which, as I have already said, was excellent water.

The ship came within half a league of this creek, and sent
her long-boat with vessels to take in fresh water (for the place,
it seems, was very well known); but I did not observe it till the
boat was almost on shore, and it was too late to seek another
hiding-place. The seamen at their landing observed my canoe,
and rummaging it all over, easily conjectured that the owner
could not be far off. Four of them, well armed, searched every
cranny and lurking-hole, till at last they found me flat on my
face behind the stone. They gazed awhile in admiration at my
strange, uncouth dress—my coat made of skins, my wooden-
soled shoes, and my furred stockings; whence, however, they
concluded I was not a native of the place, who all go naked. One
of the seamen, in Portuguese, bid me arise, and asked who I
was. I understood that language very well, and getting upon my
feet, said I was a poor *Yahoo* banished from the *Houyhnhnms*, and
desired they would please let me depart. They wondered to hear
me answer them in their own tongue, and saw by my complexion
I must be a European; but were at a loss to know what I meant
by *Yahoo* and *Houyhnhnms*; and at the same time fell a-laughing
at my strange tone in speaking, which resembled the neighing
of a horse. I trembled all the while betwixt fear and hatred. I
again desired leave to depart, and was gently moving to my
canoe; but they laid hold of me, desiring to know what country
I was of, whence I came, with many other questions. I told
them I was born in England, whence I came about five years ago,
and then their country and ours was at peace. I therefore hoped

they would not treat me as an enemy, since I meant them no harm; but was a poor *Yahoo* seeking some desolate place where to pass the remainder of his unfortunate life.

When they began to talk, I thought I never heard or saw anything more unnatural; for it appeared to me as monstrous as if a dog or a cow should speak in England, or a *Yahoo* in *Houyhnhnmland*. The honest Portuguese were equally amazed at my strange dress, and the odd manner of delivering my words, which, however, they understood very well. They spoke to me with great humanity, and said they were sure the captain would carry me free to Lisbon, whence I might return to my own country, that two of the seamen would go back to the ship, inform the captain of what they had seen, and receive his orders. In the meantime, unless I would give my solemn oath not to flee, they would secure me by force. I thought it best to comply with their proposal. They were very curious to know my story, but I gave them very little satisfaction, and they all conjectured that my misfortunes had impaired my reason. In two hours the boat, which went laden with vessels of water, returned, with the captain's command to fetch me on board. I fell on my knees to preserve my liberty, but all was in vain; and the men, having tied me with cords, lifted me into the boat, whence I was taken to the ship, and thence to the captain's cabin.

I gave the captain, Pedro de Mendez, a very short relation of my voyage, of the conspiracy against me by my own men, of the country where they set me on shore, and of my five years' residence there—all which he looked upon as if it were a dream or a vision; whereat I took great offence, for I had quite forgot the faculty of lying, so peculiar to *Yahoos*, in all countries where they reside, and, consequently, the disposition of suspecting truth in others of their own species. I asked him whether it were the custom in his country to say the thing which was not. I assured him I had almost forgot what he meant by falsehood, and if I had lived a thousand years in *Houyhnhnmland*, I should never have heard a lie from the meanest servant; that I was altogether indifferent whether he believed me or not: but, however, in return for his favours, I would give so much allowance to the corruption of his nature, as to answer any objection he might please to make, and then he might easily discover the truth.

The captain, a wise man, after many endeavours to catch me
tripping in some part of my story, at last began to have a better
opinion of my veracity. But he added, that since I professed so
inviolable an attachment to truth, I must give him my word and
honour to bear him company in this voyage, without attempting
anything against my life; or else he would continue me a prisoner
till we arrived at Lisbon. I gave him the promise he required;
but at the same time protested that I would suffer the greatest
hardships, rather than return to live among *Yahoos*.

Our voyage passed without any considerable accident. We
arrived at Lisbon, November 5, 1715. At our landing, the captain forced me to cover myself with his cloak, to prevent the
rabble from crowding about me. I was conveyed to his own house;
and at my earnest request he led me up to the highest room backward. I conjured him to conceal from all persons what I had
told him of the *Houyhnhnms*; because the least hint of such a story
would not only draw numbers of people to see me, but probably
put me in danger of being imprisoned, or burnt by the Inquisition.
The captain persuaded me to accept a suit of clothes newly
made; but I would not suffer the tailor to take my measure;
however, Don Pedro being almost of my size, they fitted me well
enough. He accoutred me with other necessaries, all new,
which I aired for twenty-four hours before I would use them.

The captain had no wife, nor above three servants, none of
which were suffered to attend at meals; and his whole deportment was so obliging, added to very good human understanding,
that I really began to tolerate his company. He gained so far
upon me, that I ventured to look out of the back window. By
degrees I was brought into another room, whence I peeped into
the street, but drew my head back in a fright. In a week's time he
seduced me down to the door. I found my terror gradually
lessened, but my hatred and contempt seemed to increase.

In ten days, Don Pedro, to whom I had given some account of
my domestic affairs, put it upon me, as a matter of honour and
conscience, that I ought to return to my native country, and live
at home with my wife and children. He told me there was an
English ship in the port just ready to sail, and he would furnish
me with all things necessary. It would be tedious to repeat his
arguments, and my contradictions. He said it was altogether

impossible to find such a solitary island as I desired to live in; but I might command in my own house, and pass my time in a manner as recluse as I pleased.

I complied at last, finding I could not do better. I left Lisbon the 24th day of November, in an English merchantman, but who was the master I never inquired. Don Pedro accompanied me to the ship, and lent me twenty pounds. He took kind leave of me, and embraced me at parting, which I bore as well as I could. During this last voyage I had no commerce with the master or any of his men; but, pretending I was sick, kept close in my cabin. On December 5th, 1715, we cast anchor in the Downs, about nine in the morning, and at three in the afternoon I got safe to my house at Redriff.

My wife and family received me with great surprise and joy, because they concluded me certainly dead; but I must freely confess the sight of them filled me only with hatred, disgust, and contempt; and the more, by reflecting on the near alliance I had to them. For although, since my unfortunate exile from the *Houyhnhnms'* country, I had compelled myself to tolerate the sight of *Yahoos*, and to converse with Don Pedro de Mendez, yet my memory and imagination were perpetually filled with the virtues and ideas of those exalted *Houyhnhnms*.

CHAPTER XII

THE AUTHOR'S VERACITY—HIS DESIGN IN PUBLISHING THIS WORK— HIS CENSURE OF THOSE TRAVELLERS WHO SWERVE FROM THE TRUTH—THE AUTHOR CLEARS HIMSELF FROM ANY SINISTER ENDS IN WRITING—AN OBJECTION ANSWERED—THE METHOD OF PLANTING COLONIES—HIS NATIVE COUNTRY COMMENDED— THE RIGHT OF THE CROWN TO THOSE COUNTRIES DESCRIBED BY THE AUTHOR IS JUSTIFIED—THE DIFFICULTY OF CON- QUERING THEM—THE AUTHOR TAKES HIS LAST LEAVE OF THE READER—PROPOSES HIS MANNER OF LIVING FOR THE FUTURE —GIVES GOOD ADVICE, AND CONCLUDES

THUS, GENTLE reader, I have given thee a faithful history of my travels for sixteen years and above seven months: wherein I have not been so studious of ornament as of truth. I could, perhaps, like others, have astonished thee with strange, improbable tales; but I rather chose to relate plain matter of fact, in the simplest manner and style; because my principal design was to inform, and not to amuse thee.

It is easy for us who travel into remote countries, which are seldom visited by Englishmen, or other Europeans, to form descriptions of wonderful animals both at sea and land; whereas a traveller's chief aim should be to make men wiser and better, and improve their minds by the bad as well as the good example of what they deliver concerning foreign places.

I could heartily wish a law was enacted, that every traveller, before he were permitted to publish his voyages, should be obliged to make oath before the Lord High Chancellor that all he intended to print was absolutely true to the best of his knowledge; for then the world would no longer be deceived, as it usually is, while some writers, to make their works pass the better upon the public, impose the grossest falsities on the unwary reader. I have perused several books of travels with great delight in my younger days; but having since gone over most parts of the globe, and been able to contradict many fabulous accounts from my own observation, it has given me a great disgust against this part of reading, and some indignation to see the credulity of mankind so impudently abused. Therefore, since my acquaintance were pleased to think my poor endeavours might not be unacceptable to my country, I imposed on myself a maxim never to be swerved from, that I would strictly adhere to truth; neither indeed can I be ever under the least temptation to vary from it, while I retain in my mind the lectures and example of my noble master, and the other illustrious *Houyhnhnms* of whom I had so long the honour to be an humble hearer.

> "Nec si miserum Fortuna Sinonem
> Finxit, vanum etiam, mendacemque improba finget."

I know very well how little reputation is to be got by writings, which require neither genius nor learning, nor indeed any other talent except a good memory, or an exact journal. I know likewise that writers of travels, like dictionary-makers, are sunk into oblivion by the weight and bulk of those who come last, and therefore lie uppermost. And it is highly probable that such travellers who shall hereafter visit the countries described in this work of mine, may, by detecting my errors (if there be any), and adding many new discoveries of their own, jostle me out of vogue, and stand in my place, making the world forget that ever I was an author. This indeed would be too great a mortification, if I wrote for fame; but as my sole intention was the public good, I cannot be altogether disappointed. For who can read of the virtues I have mentioned in the glorious *Houyhnhnms* without being ashamed of his own vices, when he considers himself as the reasoning, governing animal of his country? I shall say nothing of those remote nations where *Yahoos* preside, among which the least corrupted are the *Brobdingnagians*; whose wise maxims in morality and government it would be our happiness to observe. But I forbear descanting further, and rather leave the judicious reader to his own remarks and application.

I am not a little pleased that this work of mine can possibly meet with no censurers; for what objections can be made against a writer who relates only plain facts that happened in such distant countries, where we have not the least interest, with respect either to trade or negotiations? I have carefully avoided every fault with which common writers of travels are often too justly charged. Besides, I meddle not the least with any party, but write without passion, prejudice, or ill-will against any man or number of men whatsoever. I write for the noblest end, to inform and instruct mankind; over whom I may, without breach of modesty, pretend to some superiority, from the advantages I received by conversing so long among the most accomplished *Houyhnhnms*. I write without any view to profit or praise. I never suffer a word to pass that may look like reflection, or possibly give the least offence, even to those who are most ready to take it. So that I hope I may with justice pronounce myself an author perfectly blameless; against whom the tribes of Answerers, Considerers, Observers, Reflectors, Detectors, Remarkers, will never be able to find matter for exercising their talents.

I confess it was whispered to me that I was bound in duty, as a subject of England, to have given in a memorial to a secretary of state at my first coming over; because whatever lands are discovered by a subject belong to the Crown. But I doubt whether our conquests, in the countries I treat of, would be as easy as those of Fernando Cortez over the native Americans. The *Lilliputians*, I think, are hardly worth the charge of a fleet and army to reduce them; and I question whether it might be prudent or safe to attempt the *Brobdingnagians*; or whether an English army would be at their ease, with the Flying Island over their heads. The *Houyhnhnms* indeed appear not to be so well prepared for war, a science to which they are perfect strangers, and especially missive weapons. However, supposing myself to be a minister of state, I could never give my advice for invading them. Their prudence, unanimity, unacquaintedness with fear, and their love of their country, would amply supply all defects in the military art. Imagine twenty thousand of them breaking into the midst of a European army, confounding the ranks, overturning the carriages, battering the warriors' faces into mummy by terrible yerks from their hinder hoofs; for they would well deserve the character given to Augustus—*Recalcitrat undique tutus*. But instead of proposals for conquering that magnanimous nation, I rather wish they were in a capacity, or disposition, to send a sufficient number of their inhabitants for civilising Europe, by teaching us the first principles of honour, justice, truth, temperance, public spirit, fortitude, chastity, friendship, benevolence, and fidelity: the names of all which virtues are still retained among us in most languages, and are to be met with in modern as well as ancient authors; which I am able to assert from my own small reading.

But I had another reason, which made me less forward to enlarge his majesty's dominions by my discoveries. To say the truth, I had conceived a few scruples with relation to the distributive justice of princes upon these occasions. For instance, a crew of pirates are driven by a storm they know not whither; at last a boy discovers land from the topmast; they go on shore to rob and plunder; they see a harmless people; are entertained with kindness; they give the country a new name; they take formal possession of it for their king; they set up a rotten plank, a stone, for a memorial; they murder two or three dozen of the natives, bring away a couple more, by force, for a sample; return home and get their pardon. Here commences a new dominion acquired with a title by divine right. Ships are sent with the first opportunity; the natives driven out or destroyed; their princes tortured to discover their gold; a free licence given to all acts of inhumanity and lust, the earth reeking with the blood of its inhabitants: and this execrable crew of butchers, employed in so pious an expedition, is a modern colony, sent to convert and civilise an idolatrous and barbarous people.

But this description, I confess, does by no means affect the British nation, who may be an example to the whole world for their wisdom, care, and justice in planting colonies; their liberal endowments for the advancement of religion and learning; their choice of devout and able pastors to propagate Christianity; their caution in stocking their provinces with people of sober lives and conversations from this the mother kingdom; their strict regard to the distribution of justice, in supplying the civil administration through all their colonies with officers of the greatest abilities, utter strangers to corruption; and, to crown all, by sending the most vigilant and virtuous governors, who have no other views than the happiness of the people over whom they preside, and the honour of the king their master.

But as those countries, which I have described, do not appear to have any desire of being conquered and enslaved, murdered or driven out, by colonies, nor abound either in gold, silver, sugar, or tobacco, I did humbly conceive they were by no means proper objects of our zeal, our valour, or our interest. However, if those whom it more concerns, think fit to be of another opinion, I am ready to depose, when I shall be lawfully called, that no European did ever visit those countries before me. I mean if the inhabitants ought to be believed, unless a dispute may arise concerning the two *Yahoos* said to have been seen many years ago upon a mountain in *Houyhnhnmland*.

But as to the formality of taking possession in my sovereign's name, it never came once into my thoughts; and if it had, yet, as my affairs then stood, I should perhaps, in point of prudence and self-preservation, have put it off to a better opportunity.

Having thus answered the only objection that can ever be raised against me as a traveller, I here take a final leave of all my courteous readers, and I return to enjoy my own speculations in my little garden at Redriff; to apply those excellent lessons of virtue which I learned among the *Houyhnhnms*; to instruct the *Yahoos* of my own family, as far as I shall find them docile animals; to behold my figure often in a glass, and thus, if possible, habituate myself by time to tolerate the sight of a human creature; to lament the brutality of *Houyhnhnms* in my own country, but always treat their persons with respect, for the sake of my noble master, his family, his friends, and the whole *Houyhnhnm* race, whom these of ours have the honour to resemble in all their lineaments, however their intellectuals came to degenerate.

I began last week to permit my wife to sit at dinner with me, at the farthest end of a long table; and to answer (but with the utmost brevity) the few questions I asked her. And, although it be hard for a man late in life to remove old habits, I am not altogether out of hopes, in some time, to suffer a neighbour *Yahoo* in my company, without the apprehensions I am yet under of his teeth or his claws.

My reconcilement to the *Yahoo* kind in general might not be so difficult, if they would be content with those vices and follies only which nature has entitled them to. I am not in the least provoked at the sight of a lawyer, a pick-pocket, a colonel, a fool, a lord, a gamester, a politician, a physician, an evidence, a suborner, an attorney, a traitor, or the like; this is all according to the due course of things; but when I behold a lump of deformity and diseases, both in body and mind, smitten with pride, it immediately breaks all the measures of my patience; neither shall I be ever able to comprehend how such an animal and such a vice could tally together. The wise and virtuous *Houyhnhnms*, who abound in all the excellencies that can adorn a rational creature, have no name for this vice in their language; which has no terms to express anything that is evil, except those whereby they describe the detestable qualities of the *Yahoos*; among which they were not able to distinguish this of pride, for want of thoroughly understanding human nature, as it shows itself in other countries where that animal presides. But I, who had more experience, could plainly observe some rudiments of it among the wild *Yahoos*.

But the *Houyhnhnms*, who live under the government of reason, are no more proud of the good qualities they possess, than I should be for not wanting a leg or an arm; which no man in his wits would boast of, although he must be miserable without them. I dwell the longer upon this subject from the desire I have to make the society of an English *Yahoo* by any means not insupportable; and therefore I here entreat those who have any tincture of this absurd vice, that they will not presume to come in my sight.